# The
# Second
# Coming

# The
# Second
# Coming

DANIEL F. LAMB

authorHOUSE®

*AuthorHouse™*
*1663 Liberty Drive*
*Bloomington, IN 47403*
*www.authorhouse.com*
*Phone: 1-800-839-8640*

*Published by AuthorHouse 11/06/2014*

*ISBN: 978-1-4969-4909-7 (sc)*
*ISBN: 978-1-4969-4908-0 (hc)*
*ISBN: 978-1-4969-4907-3 (e)*

*Library of Congress Control Number: 2014919429*

# PART 1

# BOBBY MCGEE

OUR HOME WAS just down the road, three miles from Woodlake, Florida. To get there you went south on the old road, full of potholes, through town. You would come to an old worn out sand road on which you would turn east, drive about a mile past the dirt drive that went up to the Gatlin place. Then you would see our driveway heading back up into the woods.

As you left town going south, there were palmetto bushes beside the road but after you turned east tall cypress trees loaded with Spanish moss would rear their messed-up heads like the lady tramps on the streets of Tallahassee that I saw once when I went there with my Dad.

Down the sand road just before our driveway, you would pass a huge brier patch of blackberry vines all covered with big juicy black berries in summertime. They were delicious, but the vines were covered with sticky thorns and the water moccasins and rattlesnakes liked them too!

The little dirt driveway that led to our home back in the woods was humped in the middle with roots and grass. Beside it tall pine trees climbed out of the earth and were surrounded by palmetto bushes. And to add to the mystery, venerable old cypress trees with beards of Spanish moss lie beyond. Nearer to our home was a clearing where my Dad had chopped away the trees for a garden which now climbed green among the rotting stumps. And if you would walk a short distance into this greenery, you would find big tempting watermelons ready to be thumped and big red tomatoes hanging from the vine.

From the garden you could barely see our house hidden behind the tall pines and palmettos, and no one in the house could see us in the garden when we ate the red tomatoes from the vine and the raw yellow sweet corn straight off the cob. But we dared not eat the strawberries nor the watermelons nor the sweet yellow muskmelons because Mother would watch these fruit too closely. She knew exactly how many there were of these tasty things!

It was an early morning in late July. The sun was already blazing and climbing hot in the sky. I, Bobby McGee, my sister Charlotte, and my younger brothers, Eddie and Jonathan were finishing our breakfast.

"Mother", I had begged, "Jonathan is never going to finish his oatmeal! Can't we go play little car? Charlotte can come get Jonathan when he is finished eating."

"Absolutely not," said my mother firmly, "you have the whole day to play, and there is no reason why you can't wait another ten minutes on your little brother!"

About this time, Joe, who was black all over except for white toes, a white chest and a sliver of white on his neck, lost his patients and couldn't sit still any longer. He started running around the room like a living terror, sliding on the linoleum up against the wall, making all kinds of racket, his tongue was hanging out like a big smile. All the while he was looking at everyone as though he expected us to join the fun! But Mother saw nothing funny about it, yelling "Joe behave yourself" and at the same time opening the door and ordering him out of the house. His ears and tail had dropped in a sincere apology. But once the screen door closed behind him, he started protesting with the strangest noises ever to come out of the mouth of a dog!

When my Dad had brought Joe home, he had been a little black pup and we named him Little Black Joe but now that he was a muscular 45pounds we just called him Joe, and boy could he holler if he didn't get his way.

Mother ordered us kids to go out on the porch to wait for Jonathan so that we could keep Joe quiet.

But once on the porch, Joe wanted us to go down the driveway with him. He would run down the driveway then turn to see if we were following but then when we wouldn't, he would turn and come at us in a dead run and as he ran by me, he would make a flying leap in an attempt to give me a kiss in midair.

Finally Jonathan had finished his oatmeal, and we all headed down the driveway together, Joe running ahead to return with his glorious reports.

When our dad was home, he would usually find something for us to do, like hoe weeds in the garden. But today he was painting an old ladies house somewhere up near Tallahassee, so we were free, and I had decreed that we were to play "little car" down in the driveway just before the bend in the road that took it into the woods.

We built our homes in the sand, creating a village connected by roads carved out by the palms of our hands. And for me, "little car" was serious business. Everyone had a role to play, and it was I who determined what that role was. I would become totally involved and would rule like a dictator to the chagrin of my little brothers and sister. When someone would drop his or her role and become themselves again, while I was yet at the height of my fantasy, I would become furious and shout at them in helpless rage as I would try to cling to the wisp-like illusions of the spell that was now broken. It was depressing to have to return to just being me with years to go before I grew up. Even minor interruptions, such as Eddie or Jonathan having to go pee-pee over by the big cypress tree, were a major irritation to me! But if Charlotte had to go, you might as well forget it because she would go to the house and never return. If any one of us had to interrupt the game for any reason, the rest of us were required to stop what we were doing and wait in position as though the moment were frozen in time. Jonathan could never wait on Charlotte, and when he would move, I would start to shout at him, and he would start crying and the world I had created would start crumbling.

I was always the mayor of our town. I would drive a Cadillac and fly an airplane. No one else could own either of these luxuries. I would reward the citizens of my town by giving them airplane rides for good behavior. This at first caused some friction with Eddie because he wanted a Cadillac, but he finally agreed upon a Lincoln as long as he could have a dump truck as well. So he hauled the sand we used to build our houses. Charlotte drove an old cheap Ford but she was allowed to have the biggest house. She even had an upstairs in hers!

I would take long trips around the world when I was reasonably sure that everyone was happy and wouldn't quit the game while I was gone. I would fly into the woods to spots that I had designated as China or India or Arabia as well as some of the other places that intrigued me such as Russia and Norway.

Eddie spent most of his time in his dump truck hauling dirt. He only used his Lincoln to go to church. Charlotte owned the grocery store, but spent most of her time at home rearranging it and constantly hiring Eddie to add new additions to it. She would tax Eddie's building skills to the limit.

Jonathan ran a railroad station at the edge of town. But since he didn't have a train, he would mimic the sound of one as he came through town under strict orders to stay on the railroad tracks, and he usually did a pretty good job of it under my watchful eye. He lived in an old sand house with no windows in it, but he was almost never home.

Joe was our earthquake and hurricane, which was determined by the kind of damage he did. Sometimes he would come through town at a dead run doing limited damage to almost everything. In this case, he was a hurricane. At other times, he would totally destroy a home, leaving a crater in its place. We decided that this was an earthquake. No one was to inhibit Joe in anyway for he was nature.

If the game should last all day, though it seldom did, we would all rush to church in the late afternoon upon hearing the approaching hum of our father's motor in the nearby woods, for his car was considered the end of the world. As he approached, we would all jump up and stand by the side of the road to watch him pass and then turn to stare at the tire marks of eternity.

But on that June day, it was not to be. The sun had become intense as it burned in the copper sky. Each of us kids had drifted into our own little worlds of fantasy, lulled by the intense heat. We had become sticky and hot, sweat pouring down our faces as we sat there on the hot sunlit road. The air was silent, oppressive and still. Joe was lying on his back, his tongue hanging to one side as he slept fitfully in the shade of an old mulberry tree over near the garden.

I had just returned from a long airplane trip to the Holy Land which lay near a pleasant stream in the distant woods. Upon my return I had grown apprehensive when I noticed the sweat dripping from the long and discontented faces of my playmates. Behind the sweat on Charlotte's face, I saw the deepening frown in the quick glance she threw me. I knew what she wanted. She was putting the confrontation off as long as possible.

I said nothing as I sat down on the road in hot silence.

Suddenly a clap of thunder rumbled, coming out of the woods like an ominous warning from the Devil himself. But with the warning came relief because it settled everything. We were all afraid of thunderstorms, including Joe.

Joe led our beeline run for the house. About half way up the road, a terrible and brittle streak of lightning fire went down into the nearby woods. It was like the Devil's tongue leaping out to grab a bite to eat. It was followed by an earth shattering rumble. Behind us Jonathan screamed. We all stopped and turned except Joe. Jonathan had simply stopped in anger and fear because he couldn't keep up.

"Go back and get Jonathan, Bobby." It was my mother's voice that I heard faintly in the charged atmosphere. I hesitated as I looked up at the dark and evil sky and then at the porch where Joe sat panting beside her brown shoes. In my fear I turned, knowing I had no choice but to go back and get the little fellow and pull him by the hand as fast as I could make him walk.

# STUDS GATLIN

THE GATLINS LIVED on the main sand road that wound its way through the rural countryside. But there was a path through the woods that provided a shortcut between our two houses. They lived in a big white house with red trimming around the windows. We kids figured that they were rich folks since their house was so much bigger and nicer than ours.

Mrs. Gatlin and her two boys, Studs and Jack used to come most every Saturday to the church where my Dad preached. But they had stopped several months before. My Dad said that old man Gatlin had 'backslid'. He wouldn't even speak to my Dad and had ordered his wife and boys to stay away. According to Mrs. Gatlin, he had accused my Dad of being a womanizer and using preaching as an excuse for chasing other men's wives. Mr. Gatlin had even threatened once to kick his wife out of the house if he caught her associating with my Dad.

Mr. Gatlin ran the small hardware store in Woodlake. It was on the main road at Second Street. His only assistants were his boys, and they could usually be found working during the days of summer.

With her boys and husband all working in the store, Mrs. Gatlin would usually come to see us on Friday afternoon. We kids would start watching for her to come traipsing out of the woods, with furtive glances over her shoulder, into our clearing.

Once she got there, her and my parents would talk till almost dinnertime about the evil' of this world and the glories of the next until it would come out of my ears. Sometimes they would get so excited about it that they would start shouting hallelujah and praise the Lord and other loud things such as almighty this and almighty that.

We kids would usually love it when company came, and when Mrs. Gatlin first started coming, it was a nice break from the monotony of the quiet woods that surrounded us. At first we had sat and listened intently to the profound things that Mrs. Gatlin and my parents would say to each other. But finally it had started to get old, and long before dinnertime, I would start to worry about whether my Mother was going to stop talking in time to fix it. Then it got so that the excited talk about things that didn't exist anywhere that I could see began to bore me to death. I would start to get angry when my Mother would seem to forget dinner altogether!

Finally it got so that each Friday I would sit on the porch and stare at the path leading from the woods and wish with all my heart that Mrs. Gatlin would not come, and as the time approached, sometimes I would even pray: "dear God, don't let Mrs. Gatlin walk out of the woods." But then I would feel guilty because I was pretty sure that God wanted Mrs. Gatlin to walk out of the woods. So usually I would simply sit and silently wish it and pretend I didn't because I didn't want to wish for something that was against God's will.

And then one Friday in late August, just when I was just starting to breathe a sigh of relief because two thirty had come and gone and Mrs. Gatlin had not come out of the woods yet, I detected movement among the leaves that stood beside the hidden path further back in the woods. Then sure enough, it was as I feared, Mrs. Gatlin stepped into the sunlight of our clearing. But to my shock and surprise Studs and Jack Gatlin immediately stepped into the clearing behind her! They followed her with long, sullen and angry faces towards the front porch.

I sprung into action running into the house, Joe at my heels, to inform my parents of the surprise visitors. Mother met them from behind the screen door that had holes in it through which, I in my boredom would sometimes sit and watch the flies crawl through.

"So glad to see you Melba,' my mother said.

The three of them were soon standing in the living room. Jack simply stood there staring at his feet, while Studs stood looking about with a glare of anger and defiance. It was then that my Dad walked in.

"I was hoping Reverend McGee," Melba Gatlin said, "that you could give Studs and Jack, here, some Godly advice and talk some sense into their heads. They won't listen to me anymore. They don't want to go to church, and they have started running around with other bad boys from school. Their father is no help. He tells them that there is nothing wrong with what they are doing. I tell them they are following the ways of Satan but they tell me that their dad tells them there is no such thing as Satan! Brother McGee what am I going to do with them?"

I think my Dad always felt very important when someone would ask for his help because he would remain silent for such a long time that I began to think he wasn't going to answer at all. He first took long and serious looks at the two boys. They were looks that would pierce you as though they could see right through your body and soul. Jack fidgeted, his face becoming red and hot as he tried to tear his eyes away from my father's penetrating gaze. Studs stared back with a stare of defiance, but his face turned as red as a beet anyway. They both looked so guilty that it made me feel guilty just looking at them. My Dad then looked long and hard at the ceiling as though he expected it to speak. He finally motioned for Melba Gatlin to follow him into the kitchen.

The Gatlin boys then went and sat down on a couple of wiggly old stick chairs, and I noticed my Mother smiling wanly at their angry faces.

I was thirsty, so I followed my Dad and Mrs. Gatlin into the kitchen. I fumbled around looking for a glass so I could hear what they were going to say.

"Melba," my Father said in a low voice as he glanced in my direction, nearly causing me to drop and break my glass, "aren't you afraid that they will tell their father that you brought them here?"

"Maybe," she said, "but I told them that there would be no one there to cook their dinner if they did. And I promised to buy more of their favorite sodas and ice cream if they kept their mouths shut."

My dad said something that I couldn't hear, and they both turned and went back into the other room. I decided that I wasn't thirsty after all and followed.

Studs was staring at Charlotte. He looked so big and intimidating. Charlotte was sitting with her small feet in front of her on the chair.

Mother was looking at his stare and said, "Charlotte, sit like a lady."

Charlotte put her feet on the floor and smoothed out her dress. I don't think she saw Stud's staring eyes.

Studs then glowered angrily at Mother, but Mother was already listening to what my dad was about to say.

"Boys, do you know what Paul said in Ephesians 6.1-3?" Before anyone could answer he started reading it. He was really quick at finding stuff like that. "'Children obey your parents in the Lord: for that is right,'" he read. "'Honor thy father and mother; which is the first commandment with promise; that it might be well with thee…' Now, of course, it says 'in the lord'. If your parent be not in the Lord and they command evil things of you then obedience is not required but to honor them is. You do this by being humble and respectful. And do you know what Paul compares an evil child to?" And again before anyone could answer he told them, "backbiters, haters of God, inventers of evil things. Now boys do you know what happens to such people?" He then looked at the boys as though waiting for an answer.

Studs was staring at Charlotte again and acted like he hadn't even heard my dad. Jack, staring angrily at the floor, seemed to be twisting his lips as though attempting to say something that wouldn't come out.

Suddenly Studs said, "What do you kids do for fun around here?"

Jack looked up as though confused and startled.

"Be quiet Studs," Melba Gatlin said. "Reverend McGee has just asked you a question."

Studs' eyes looked angry, like they were shooting sparks at my dad, but he smiled anyway. "Sorry Reverend McGee, I was thinking about having fun with your kids. What was the question?"

"You boys don't want to die do you?" My father repeated.

"No," said Studs, his smile broadening.

"No," whispered Jack as though gasping for his last breath.

"Now let's go play," Studs said.

"Can we, Dad?" I asked

"Ok, but don't go too far from the house."

I didn't know how I was going to handle such big boys though. We all went out on the porch. I looked at Studs. He looked at me.

"What the hell do you do around this place for fun?"

It took my breath away. No one was supposed to talk that way at my house! I looked at the screen door, but I didn't see any faces looking out.

"We play Little Car most of the time," I responded.

"What the fuck is little car?"

I was stunned. The word struck fear in my heart, though I wasn't sure what it meant. I figured it was probably something far worse than hell.

"What is fuck?" Eddie asked.

I was aghast and knew we had to get away from that screen door!

"Let's go," I said, and rushed for the steps.

"Fuck is what you do to girls," Studs said with a grin and a glance at Charlotte. I stopped on the porch step, the fear hurting in my stomach as I turned to stare at the screen door, trying desperately to see if there were any faces behind it.

"Can you play fuck in little car, Bobby?" Eddie had asked.

"Can you pay fuck in witto car?" mimicked Jonathan.

I felt my face begin to burn with my ignorance as I led them hurriedly off the porch in silence.

"Sure you can," Studs said, from behind with words that bounced hot off the back of my neck. I walked faster, refusing to look back at his grinning face.

It was then that Charlotte suddenly stopped in her tracks while she threw me a fidgety glance and then turned her stare on Joe who sat and was now busy with his tongue trying to dislodge a flea. I was beginning to worry that she was going to spoil the game.

"I don't want to play little car today," she said with a voice that was hardly more than a whisper. My heart sank as I feared the worst.

"I won't play little car unless Charlotte does," was Studs' response in an angry voice.

"Come on, Charlotte," I pleaded.

"Ok," she said, "but I'm not going to marry him." She glanced shyly at Studs.

"I just want to go home," Jack said with a sullen voice. Up to this time he had been walking along quietly staring at his feet.

Studs turned a vicious glare upon him. "You play little car, asshole, or I'll beat the pulp out'n ya! Do ya understand?"

Jack hung his head again with eyes that threw a glance at me full of disgust and boredom as they dropped to follow his own feet moving slowly down the road.

Suddenly my dad appeared out of nowhere. "Studs, if I ever hear you talk that way around my kids again I won't allow you to play with them. You will just have to go home."

"Yes sir, I'm sorry. I didn't know it was so bad. My dad says 'asshole' all the time."

"I'm sorry to hear that," my father said, his voice becoming more gentle. "You must remember Studs that your father is not a Christian."

We were all looking at Studs as he spoke, and when we turned back to where my father stood, he was gone, like he had come, suddenly.

When we arrived at the destroyed sand dunes of our little car town, I looked at Jack and then at Studs, uncertain of myself. I wanted to be in control of the situation but wasn't sure how to go about it.

"I'm the mayor," I said with as much authority as I could muster. "Let's play little car."

Jack was staring at his dirty black shoes as they rested on the hot white sand. Studs was staring at Charlotte as though he thought she was a Baby Ruth candy bar. I had to get his eyes off Charlotte somehow and get him interested in the game. I could tell that Charlotte didn't like him staring at her, and if he didn't stop, she would probably stop playing and go home. If she quit, I knew that Studs and Jack would quit.

Studs broke the silence, "Sure," he said "how do we play?"

He was now staring boldly at me, his voice full of excitement. And I started getting excited too with the thought of being the mayor of my town with Studs and Jack as my subjects!

"Well," I said, "I'm the mayor and have the airplane. Charlotte has the grocery store. Jonathan has the railroad station at the edge of town. Eddie builds houses and has a big dump truck to carry the sand."

Eddie and Jonathan were standing and grinning proudly up at Studs as though their function in society made them proud. But Studs didn't notice.

"I want to work for Charlotte in the grocery store. I can be the checkout clerk."

He was grinning from ear to ear and staring at Charlotte again.

I had wanted him to be the doctor or run a hardware store. I couldn't understand why anyone would want to be a grocery clerk, but I said "Okay, Jack can be the town doctor."

"I don't want to be no doctor!" whined Jack.

"Ok, you can run the hardware store," I said hopefully.

"No," Jack growled, his voice turning angry. "Why would I want to run a play hardware store?"

"Quit being a whiny brat," Studs said loudly, "you gotta be something!"

I decided that Jack wasn't going to be any fun so I said, "Jack can be a farmer and live outside of town."

"That is an excellent idea," Studs said.

So Jack went to his designated spot and just sat there, his long legs sticking out in front of him so that we couldn't even build a road to his place. But it really didn't matter because he didn't want a car to play with anyway.

After this, things went smoothly for awhile. Eddie soon had all our houses built, except Jack's. Jack said the game was stupid, and he didn't want one. Studs was having a good time. He had his house built beside Charlotte's. He had said it was necessary because he worked for her. The idea didn't make any sense to me. I didn't see how anyone could get rich working in a grocery store. Anyway Charlotte seemed to kind of like bossing someone around.

After awhile, Studs got tired of spending all his time in the grocery store.

"Let's do something else, Charlotte," he said.

"You can make me a real flower garden," she said. And then Studs had run around looking for flower petals to stick into her flower garden.

I started to get bored and the hot sun was making me drowsy. No one was doing anything except sitting and watching Studs play. Eddie had stopped hauling dirt, and Jonathan sat and gawked with his mouth hanging open. And I didn't even want to look at Jack because I didn't want to see what he might be doing. With his legs sticking out in front of him, he looked too real for "little car"! Suddenly I noticed Father standing in the middle of the road watching us. I looked at Studs. He saw him too. He left the flower garden and went back to the grocery store, and then he sat and looked at my dad until he left.

When my dad was gone, Studs started to play again. He smiled and looked back at Charlotte.

"Let's go somewhere far away," he said, "and look for blooms to put in your garden. Bobby can fly us in his airplane."

"Good," I said, coming to life, "I'll fly you to India, that is the best place to look for flowers."

"Ok," Charlotte had said, "but I don't want to get married."

"Of course not," Studs had said smoothly, patting her on her head like my dad did sometimes.

We all got in the airplane. Charlotte held my back pocket. Studs had to lean way over to get in and put his arms around Charlotte's waist. We took off and flew to India deep in the woods beside a stream where flowers of all colors grew. India was a quiet place where not too many people lived.

When we got there, we all got out of the plane and I was going to help them pick flowers. But Studs said "no." He said it was "he and his boss' vacation," and that I should go back to the town.

"How are you going to get home with the flowers?" I asked.

"You can come back and get us in one hour." Studs replied.

"I don't want to get married!" Charlotte had repeated. She looked worried, but I didn't see why since there weren't any preachers around.

"Don't worry," Studs said, patting her on the head again.

I took off and flew back to town, and Eddie came running when he saw me.

"Jack is gone," he yelled at me. "He went home! I warned him that he could get into a lot of trouble doing something like that, but he just said, "fuck you little brat" and walked off."

"That is alright, Eddie," I said. "He was no fun anyway."

The sun had grown intense shining down on the hot sand road. Jonathan's head was nodding back and forth as he sat beside the railroad station. Joe slept in the shade beneath his favorite mulberry tree. My mother would probably be mad and not let him on the couch with his stomach all covered with mulberry juice. But Joe would just wait until she forgot about it and wasn't looking to silently slip back on it and curl up and go to sleep. Eddie was making a humming noise as he pushed his little car out into the country, sweat dripping from his nose, to check the spot where Jack had sat with his long legs and no house to live in. I decided to take most of Charlotte's flowers from her garden. I moved them to my front yard for something to do. I figured they would bring plenty of new flowers back from India anyway.

I wondered what Studs would say when he saw that Jack was gone, and I wondered if it was an hour yet. I was getting tired of waiting. Finally I went and started my airplane, but just as I was about ready to take off Charlotte came running out of the woods.

"I don't want to play with Studs no more," she said, "I don't like him, he's mean."

She squatted down to get her little Ford. Her panties were gone, and she was bleeding like somebody had cut it off.

"Where is Studs?" I asked.

"I don't know, but please don't go get him Bobby!" she pleaded.

"Ok," I said as I felt a sadness come over me and a wish that I was bigger than Studs so that I could beat him up, but I had always been littler than anyone that I knew.

"Let's end 'little car' Eddie," I said.

When Jonathan heard that it was the end, he came to life and got to his feet. We then, all three of us hand in hand, walked along the hot sand road in silence as we made our way towards the distant porch. I think we all knew that something really bad had happened to Charlotte.

# AGNES EVERBE

OUR CHURCH WAS at the end of third street. The streets going west from the highway ended at the cypress swamp. Our church sat right beside the swamp, and the mosquitoes coming out of it loved to suck the blood out of the people that went there.

Sometimes when it rained really heavy, the water would rise and come up out the swamp and cover the street. It once covered the church yard so that people had to take their shoes off and wade up to the steps of the church.

Only First, Second and Third Street went east from the highway. Most of the Black folks lived over there. The Black folks had a Pentecostal church on East Third Street. All the poor people lived on that side of the highway, including some white people. Most of these people lived in houses so old that the paint had turned black as dirt.

On the north side of First Street was the Duke farm. The driveway, with two white fences on both sides, went up to a huge green yard surrounded by more white fences. In the middle of it was a big white house that cost more money to build than I could even imagine.

Patricia Duke owned the farm and her boys helped her run it. The Dukes had more cows than I could count, and they had to milk them every night. They had a big milk truck that looked like a gas truck which they used to haul milk to Tallahassee.

We didn't know the Dukes very well. They went to the Baptist church also on Third Street but up nearer the highway. The Baptist church was where the rich folk went. They considered themselves more civilized because they didn't make as much noise in their church services as our church and the black folks church. In fact the Baptist had tried to pass a law to keep the Black folks from singing so loud on Sunday morning because they would get so loud that they couldn't hear themselves sing. But the judge said they couldn't pass it because it would violate freedom of religion. Of course our church was awfully loud too, but that was mostly because of Agnes Everbe. Besides we did our shouting on Saturday when everyone else was home.

There were no other churches in Woodlake. The poor white people didn't go to church at all. They would all get drunk on Saturday night over in a little rundown bar with a red neon light that only blinked half way, sitting at the end of First Street, not too far from the driveway up to the Duke house. And then they would lie around, lazy-like, and sleep all day Sunday. Some of them, though, would sneak quiet-like into the Black folks' church, when they heard the shouting and the singing down the street, to sit at the very back so they could watch 'em shout and to watch the preacher who would be dancing a jig behind the pulpit. I even heard once that some of them white people would get so excited by it all that they would end up getting the Black folks' holy ghost.

There were also a few rich Catholics in Woodlake, but they didn't have a church. So they had to fill their big expensive cars with gas and drive to Tallahassee every Sunday morning to hear whatever it was that their preacher said. I heard once from Reggie Smithers, who's father was a Catholic, that it was so quiet in a their church that you could hear his voice coming from both ends of the church, and I had figured that being that quiet must mean that they were really rich.

We went to church every Saturday morning about an hour before it was supposed to begin. My dad would always go back to a dark corner at the back of the church and sit silent-like and stare up at the cobwebs that hung from the ceiling with spiders sliding down them, and I would worry that one might slip, fall on him and bite him. But I had supposed that these weren't the dangerous kind.

My mother would take a seat in the front row then bow her head and move her lips in silence. Charlotte would usually sit and fidget beside her, occasionally glancing up to see if she was finished praying yet. She was supposed to sit in the pew like a lady, but we boys were usually allowed to go out and play until church began. On this Sabbath, Charlotte didn't even ask to go outside to play.

Sometimes we would all climb the mulberry tree so we would watch everyone drive up and get out of their cars to go to church. On this day, however, we decided to climb the fence over to the swamp to watch the jumping frogs. But as we went for the fence, I noticed Mrs. Barnes and

Reba Boon getting out of their cars. I knew they would probably be talking about something interesting, and I wanted to hear it. I was just a little guy, but I could hear really well, so I would stand a long ways off so they wouldn't know I was listening.

"We should pray for Jorje," Reba Boone was saying, "he's going to burn in Hell if God doesn't save his soul. It would be too bad for a man with such a handsome body to burn that way."

"Yeah," said Mrs. Barnes, "I wonder why he keeps his curtains closed all the time."

Reba had looked at her kind of funny but didn't say anything.

Only I knew their secret, and I dared not tell anybody, especially my parents. It had been several months before when I had overheard Reba Boones' exclamation and had seen her eyes bugging out at Jorje's window.

Jorje Carlyle lived alone and he lived directly across from the church. Everyone said his mother had come from Cuba and that was how he got the name Jorje. He was the only one in town who lived in a respectable neighborhood and didn't go to church. So everyone had decided that he was an atheist, and that was the reason why he wasn't friendly to us folks who went to church. On Saturdays sometimes after we had been singing hymns real loud, you could hear him yelling from across the street.

"Why don't you people cut the noise," he would yell or "I have a splittin headache!" Sometimes he would get real mean and yell, "cut out the goddamned noise or I'll sue the shit out of you!."

Reba Boone would look really righteous by closing her eyes and getting red in the face while Mrs. Barnes would sit and look at her like she understood.

One time when Jorje's shouting got really mean Agnes Everby started yelling real loud, "get thou behind me Satan," as she stared with closed eyes out towards Jorje's house. Then almost everyone in the congregation said, "Amen".

No one seemed to know much of anything about the atheist Jorje so I had started to think people were just making things up about him so that they would have something to talk about. I sometimes even wondered if what Reba Boone had said about him was true, but I still liked to listen to it, and at first I had believed every word of it because it sounded just like something an atheist would do.

"God Almighty," Reba Boone had exclaimed, on that Saturday morning several months before.

Mrs. Barnes and I had turned quickly to see what she was looking at. I was about ten feet away trying to act like I wasn't listening, but when she said that I nearly jumped in my effort to see it. But I couldn't see anything except Jorje's dark window!

"Reba," Mrs. Barnes had gasped in dismay, "what could have made you take God's name in vain like that?"

"Oh Betty," she had whispered hoarsely, making me walk a few steps closer, "it wasn't in vain! You won't believe what I just saw through that window over there!"

They both stared real hard at the dark window, and I think I stared even harder than anybody. But the harder I stared, the darker it got so I looked back at the two ladies to see if I could see what it was that they were looking at.

"For Christ's sake!" Mrs. Barnes said in frustration, "how long are you going to keep me in suspense, Reba? What did you see?"

"I swear Betty on a stack of bibles, that I just saw Jorje walk in front of that window without a stitch on!"

"You don't say," Betty Barnes had gasped leaving her almost as breathless as Reba Boone. "I always knew he was an atheist," she said, exhaling the last of the wind in her.

I again started to stare real hard as I listened but nothing would happen to that dark window for me. But then I had heard my dad telling everyone to stand for prayer, and I knew that I would be in real trouble if I wasn't standing there beside my mother when he looked up. So I had to force myself to run off and leave the ladies while they were still talking.

Now, after all this time they were again standing and looking at the dark window that was in the house where Jorje lived. They were reminiscing with long faces, staring at the curtains which turned the dark window even darker. Their eyes seemed desperate to see through them. I think they wanted really bad to see Jorje naked again. I would have liked to see him too, just once to know if it was true or not.

But when nothing happened, Reba Boone said, "at least he has the decency to keep his curtains closed."

"Yeah," said Mrs. Boone with a voice full of disgust.

I watched them as they finally turned and walked like good Christians to their pew. I walked in behind them and could hear them whispering as I walked by. But then I saw Studs Gatlin sitting beside Jack and his mother.

Studs waved and smiled as though we were old buddies. He looked at me as though he thought I was supposed to come and sit beside him. I waved because I didn't know what else to do. But I didn't smile. I just walked on past wishing in my heart that I were bigger, and that I could just start beating him until I could make him cry.

In front of the Gatlins sat old Larson and Annie Smith. They had been married for 60years. Old Larson's face was smooth and his cheekbones stood out boldly but his eyes looked as old and gray as his hair. He would always look at you like he didn't care whether he saw you or not. He always seemed to be tired and would start dozing as soon as the singing was over. When he left the church each Sabbath, he would just say "howdy" and keep walking when he passed my dad standing on front steps trying to talk to everyone. He would walk ahead and wait on Annie, who would talk until my dad would start talking to someone else.

I heard Reba Boone say once that old Larson was jealous. And Mrs. Barnes had replied, "yes, he only comes because she makes him, and so he can keep an eye on Annie."

Old Annie's face had so many wrinkles that you couldn't take your eyes off them because they were always jumping around, especially when she started getting excited in the Lord. When she said amen, they would leap and quiver with joy, but when she said "bless him Jesus" or "have mercy on his soul," they would sag and become long with sorrow.

Mr. Barnes and Butch Boone would usually sit in front of their wives so that they could whisper man talk before the sermon.

Mr. Barnes had a shaggy head of gray hair and a rough, weather beaten face. He and his wife had come to Florida with their little girl Robin a couple of years before. They had come from a ranch in North Dakota.

Robin had an older brother who somehow got killed by getting caught in a wheat combine while harvesting wheat in the field.

"Before that happened," Mrs. Barnes had told my mother once, "Albert never went to church. I had warned him all along."

"Yes, the Lord works in mysterious ways," my mother had agreed. "It was God's way of bringing Albert into the fold."

Robin didn't come to church back then. I once heard Mrs. Barnes telling my mother that "she was just too young to understand." I could tell by looking at my mother's face that she was disagreeing with her.

I sat down beside Charlotte. She tapped my arm with her finger. I looked at her large dark eyes staring back at me. They seemed so full of something, and I thought maybe she was going to cry. I didn't want that. She threw a glance over her shoulder as though to acknowledge Studs' presence.

"He made me marry him when we were picking flowers in India," she whispered. A large tear rolled down her cheek.

"He can't do that," I whispered back, "you gotta have a preacher to get married."

"But he did," she insisted.

"Did you tell Mother?"

"No," she whispered fiercely. "Please don't tell her Bobby."

"Why?"

"Because when he married me, I caught the Devil from him."

We couldn't talk after that because everybody started singing "When the Roll is Called up Yonder". I sang too but Charlotte didn't. She just stared around behind Agnes Everbe, who was singing from the pulpit, at our dad, who's face beamed from the darkness and sang like everybody else's.

When Agnes Everbe sang, she would always get really thrilled, and her voice would get louder and louder until she started to sound like somebody screaming.

"When the roooolll is called up yonder, when the rooooolll is called up yonderrrrr, when the roolll is called up yonder I'll be there."

Then Father preached. He looked at Charlotte. She looked at him. He looked at me. I looked at Charlotte. I always started to feel guilty when he did that.

He preached about evil thoughts. "Even the thought of, or desire to commit a sin such as adultery or fornication is an abomination before God," he had thundered, firmly.

I had turned around to look back at Mrs. Barnes and Reba Boone. Their faces looked hot and their lips were moving really fast, but their eyes were closed so they couldn't see what my dad was saying.

Agnes Everbe was sitting on the other side of my mother and kept shouting "praise the Lord". Her face was glowing as though it were perfect. Agnes Everbe had so much faith that everyone envied her. She would testify every Sabbath about it. She would testify in a loud authoritative voice about how "if you just believed hard enough in it, that God's will would be done." Then she would say amen in a voice that sounded like some kind of musical instrument, and her face would look like an angel's face that had just dropped out of heaven. But it would look best when you looked at it from the side and couldn't see the big holes on the front her nose.

And on this Sabbath, my dad couldn't even finish preaching before she leaped up off the pew as though she had suddenly got hit by a bucket full of the Holy Ghost.

"If ye had faith as a grain of mustard seed," she screamed with an ecstatic cry. "ye might say unto this sycamine tree, be thou plucked up by the root and be thou planted in the sea; and it should obey you."

Her eyes suddenly flew open, and she had looked wildly around like she was trying to see if what she had said was true. Her voice had been so strong that I was looking where she looked. But then everything turned back to normal and she sat down. She opened her purse and got a handkerchief out of it. I watched her as she blew her nose loudly. The holes got bigger and turned red and ugly, and there was something sticking to one of them.

So then my dad said, "praise the Lord," and started preaching again.

I heard someone snore. I turned around just in time to see Annie Smith jabbing old Larson in the ribs. I couldn't help but look at Studs. He gave me a big grin as though I knew his secret. I turned around and just sat and hated him.

My dad finally stopped preaching, then dropped his head and began to pray. He blessed everyone in the church and then stopped. After this everyone said amen, and they all started talking at once. My dad then walked to the front door so he could stand on the porch and shake everyone's hand as they left.

Agnes started to tell Mother how wonderful the sermon was, but Mother had suddenly noticed Charlotte just sitting there looking straight ahead and didn't hear her.

"What is the matter Charlotte?" my mother said in a worried voice.

"Nothing," Charlotte responded as tears started flowing down her cheek.

"My, my," cried Agnes Everbe, smiling brightly at Charlotte. "Put everything in Christ's hands dear, in Him our burdens are light."

Charlotte quickly wiped the tears away because Melba Gatlin was walking towards us, and Studs was right behind her. And when I looked around for Jack, I saw him running out the front door like he was looking for the toilet.

"Why, hello Melba," cried Agnes. "It is so good to see you again. Is that backslidden husband of yours finally letting you come to church again?"

"No, Agnes, but Studs, here..." she reached up and patted him on the shoulder. "and my other son Jack, have promised not to tell him."

"And Martha," she turned to face my mother, "Studs wants to get right with the Lord and start coming to church again. He says that Reverend McGee convinced him that it was the right thing to do."

"Praise His Almighty Name," screamed Agnes in a voice so loud that everyone stopped talking so they could turn and stare at her. Agnes just beamed at all the inquisitive eyes and shouted "praise the Lord," again.

She then ran over to give Studs a big hug in the Lord. Studs got so red that he looked like red paint but he hugged her back anyway.

Suddenly Charlotte was beside me and she put her hand in mine and whispered, "let's leave and go out to the car, Bobby."

As we walked out, I glanced back over my shoulder and saw that Studs was staring at us like he wished that he could go to. He seemed to be ignoring Agnes, who was still hollering in ecstasy. I noticed that Mother was picking up Jonathan who had fallen asleep on the hard pew. And Eddie was following Charlotte and I at a distance. But Melba Gatlin's face looked really proud as she stared at the back of Studs' head.

Out in the '49 Packard, we all sat in silence as we waited. I didn't know what to say, but I was worried about the Devil part that she had told me.

During all the next week, Charlotte didn't want to play Little Car. And there was just not enough people with only Eddie, Jonathan, and I.

On Friday, the Gatlin boys and their mother came traipsing out of the woods again, marching in single file, like criminals, towards the porch. Charlotte had seen them coming and ran to her bedroom.

While the big folks talked, Studs sat on a rickety old stick chair, his eyes roaming restlessly around the room. He went to get a drink of water to see if Charlotte was in the kitchen. He went to the toilet and peaked into the boys' room, hoping it was Charlotte's. Charlotte's door was closed, but he stared at it anyway. When he had finished walking around, he came back and sat on the floor beside my chair. Then he got up and whispered into my ear.

"I want to play 'little car'," he whispered.

"I don't want to play," I replied.

"Where is Charlotte," he finally asked, still whispering, while he fidgeted about, still standing up.

"She doesn't like you anymore, and she doesn't want to play either," I said curtly.

"Well fuck her, then," he responded in a furious whisper. I could feel the spit coming out of his mouth, landing in my ear.

I just got up and walked to another chair where I could watch my dad talking about the Kingdom. I watched Studs walk over to Jack's chair and whisper in his ear. And I saw him point towards the door. Jack came to life and they both walked out.

I sat and listened to my dad talking about the Kingdom for a long time to make sure they were gone before I went out on the porch and looked around. I couldn't see them anywhere, so I decided they had gone home. I heard the screen door slam behind me, and I felt Joe licking my leg. When I turned around, Eddie and Jonathan were standing there.

"Why don't we play 'little car' anymore?" Eddie had asked, after staring in the direction of the Gatlin house for a long time.

"Because Studs is mean," I said in a low voice so no one behind the screen door would hear. "He forced Charlotte to marry him."

"Is she going to have a baby?" Eddie asked in a voice that was too loud.

"I don't think so, she is not big enough," I told him.

Before long Melba Gatlin walked out to check on her boys.

"Where are Studs and Jack?" she asked, when she saw us boys just standing there.

"I think they went home," I said as Eddie and Jonathan turned and began staring vacantly at the silent woods.

"Why didn't you kids play with them?" she asked as though she thought it was all our fault.

I just stared at her. I knew better than to say anything, because my mother and dad had walked out and were standing there on the porch watching me to see what I was going to say.

Melba Gatlin said, "I had better go check on them, hard tell'en what they are into."

She kissed my mother on the cheek and shook my dad's hand. After that we all stood and watched her disappear into the woods.

"How come the boys went home, Bobby?" my dad had asked.

"Because we wouldn't play 'little car'."

"Why was that?"

"Because Studs said 'fuck', in a whisper," I said, hoping to get Studs into trouble.

"Bobby said Studs forced Charlotte to marry him," piped Eddie, while watching me closely.

I was embarrassed and wished that Eddie would keep his mouth shut. I turned back to stare at the path where it first disappeared into the woods.

"Is that true Bobby?"

"Yes."

I turned to watch my dad as he went back towards the screen door.

"I'll have to have a talk with Melba," he said, before he opened it.

When the screen door slammed behind him, we boys rushed over to look through it, and we watched as he walked towards Charlotte's room.

At supper that night, Charlotte just sat crying and wouldn't eat while Jonathan sat and stared at her with his mouth open.

# THE FIRST DAY
# OF SCHOOL

School started that year, and I went for the first time. Mother had taught me at home through my first four years of school but when three of us had reached school age, she said it was too much and sent us all off to school.

The school was on First Street, and the playground went all the way to the edge of the swamp. There were two buildings, one for the high school kids and one for first through eighth grade. Up by the highway was the football field which belonged to the high school kids. Sometimes at night, kids from other schools would come and play with them. All their families would come and watch, and everyone would have a lot of fun and do a lot of yelling.

Across First Street from the football field was the gas station where kids would hang out a lot. In the summertime they would stand around and eat Baby Ruth candy bars, drink sodas, make sure the air pressure was right in their bicycle tires, and get into fist fights.

On the morning of the first day of school, I couldn't eat my breakfast. My insides had felt so empty, as if there were no bottom and it seemed as if school were somewhere down there in the emptiness. Also floating around down there were the words I had heard Charlotte say when she had woke me up screaming the night before. She had been begging Studs not to marry her, and it had been so terrifying and real to me. I had almost felt ugly Studs breathing his hot breath on my face.

"Eat your breakfast Bobby, Charlotte," Mother said turning towards the table. She had been fixing our lunches.

I looked at Charlotte. Her eyes were glued to her untouched plate. I had heard both my parents talking to her in the night after she screamed. Charlotte almost seemed like a stranger sitting there. I simply couldn't understand what had happened to her.

"Ok," Mother said, glancing at Charlotte, and seeing that nobody was eating their breakfast, "I can understand the excitement of your first day of school, but if you don't eat your breakfast you will probably be awfully hungry by lunchtime."

My dad drove us to the big school grounds that morning. It seemed like he drove faster than usual because we got there too soon. Before I could get my wits about me, the three of us and our dad were walking across the schoolyard toward the big white wooden building. I noticed Charlotte's face was too white and her little hand was clinging tightly to one of Father's fingers. My dad and I climbed the steps. The emptiness inside me seemed to get deeper. I glanced around at Eddie who stood whimpering and clinging to Charlotte at the bottom of the steps.

"You two wait there," my father said as he led me into my new classroom.

I stood, nearly in a panic, as I glanced frantically around the room. Then my dad spotted the teacher. She didn't look too bad. She was really old. She had hair that was white like snow, and her face was full of wrinkles.

"This is Bobby McGee," my father said.

She smiled at me as she stooped over to hold out her hand.

"Welcome to fith grade, Bobby," she said with a pleasant voice, "my name is Mrs. White."

Her name sounded just like her hair, I remembered thinking, as I held out my hand. I then followed her to a seat, and I sat in it. And when I looked back to see if my dad was still at the door; he was already gone.

I sat nearly motionless, nearly frozen to my seat through most of the first period, afraid to move. I didn't want to get Mrs. White's attention for fear she might ask me a question, and I would have to answer her in front of everybody.

First she asked everyone to introduce themselves. Everyone else was saying their name loudly and boldly, but when she came to me I was tongue tied. But then I took a quick glance around the room and was shocked to see Robin Barnes. Then I knew I had to say it.

"Bobby Mc.. Mc.. Gee," I stammered.

We had been to the Barneses' place several times for a visit. They lived just a mile further up the road from our drive. Robin was my age but always acted like she knew more about things than I did. She would never ask us kids to play with her when we went over. But it still made me feel more at ease to have someone in the classroom that I knew. And I didn't want to act like a coward in front of her.

My first day at school had been a tiring and confusing day. Mrs. White talked in a way I had never heard people talk before. She gave us "assignments" from our new school books. She talked about what we would do "upon completion" of the assignments. When she came to arithmetic, she had several students, including Robin, come to the blackboard and solve problems that they should remember from last year. While this was happening, I was terrified because I didn't have any last year to remember!

Suddenly a loud bell rang, and all the students jumped out of their seats and headed for the door. But I just sat there for a minute, to weak to move, until it dawned on me that I was free to go out onto the big playground.

Outside at the bottom of the stairs stood Charlotte and Eddie waiting on me. I had almost forgotten about them, and I was relieved and overjoyed to see them. Eddie's face was still tear streaked, but he had stopped crying. Charlotte had whispered in my ear asking if I could see Studs over on the high school grounds. We both looked over there, but it was too far to see who anybody was, so I said I couldn't. The three of us then had walked over to the edge of the swamp to sit under a shade tree and watch the other kids play.

# ROBIN

THE GRAY SPANISH moss hanging from the trees had turned white overnight. The brown weeds in the garden had also turned white in the clear crisp morning air. I looked from my window and imagined that it was snow, but I knew that it was only frost and would melt with the rising sun.

I hugged Joe, who had looked up at me with sleepy eyes and gave me a sloppy kiss. He had sneaked into my bed in the dark of night. The old blanket beside the front door where he was supposed to sleep was a mess, like he had been trying to chew it up or something. Now he didn't seem to want to get out of bed. But when I got up, he reluctantly followed as I tiptoed quietly into the kitchen and looked at the presents, wrapped and laid out on the kitchen table.

We weren't allowed to have a Christmas tree like they did at school. My dad had said it was a heathenish tradition. But that was ok with me as long as I got my presents.

Back in the living room, Joe stretched and yawned. He looked at the door then back at me.

"Ok Joe," I said. "But hurry up before Daddy sees that you are gone and won't let you back in the house."

I quietly opened the door, and Joe was gone. I had watched from the window as he ran down the drive, raising his leg to every tree he came to. He squatted and crapped in the garden just as the rays of the rising sun hit it.

It was then that the excitement of the day ahead hit me. Not only would we kids get to open our presents when everyone got up, but the Barneses were also coming over for Christmas dinner. Robin was coming too, and I had high hopes that she would play with us kids.

Finally, overcome by inpatience, I ran in and woke up Eddie and Jonathan. The three of us then went back to the kitchen to stare at the presents.

Joe whined and scratched at the front door, and I ran over and quickly let him back in.

Then Charlotte came in and looked at the presents with the rest of us. Even Joe stared at them with his tail wagging expectantly.

We then heard footsteps a coming towards the kitchen. It was Mother, and she came walking in.

"My goodness," she said, as she stared at all of us kids and Joe standing around looking at our presents. "What are you kids doing?" she asked, as her lips spread into a little smile.

"We are waiting to open our presents," piped Eddie a grin of excitement spreading across his face.

"We want to open our peasants," mimicked Jonathan, looking at our mother and smiling broadly.

"Ok," she said. "Go to it, but be sure to get the one that has your name on it!"

We had all of us looked them over very closely in advance and knew exactly which one to grab. So when we heard that we all started grabbing for the one that we each had staked out. While we were opening ours, Mother went to the refrigerator and got Joe's Christmas present. It was a nice big bone, but he had to go out on the porch to chew it.

We had each got something for our 'little car' game. I got a new Cadillac. Eddie got a new dump truck. Charlotte got a little cheap Plymouth because she also got a doll. And Jonathan got a train with three cars on it. All of us together were given a deck of Rook cards to play with when it was raining.

Finally after we had tried out our new toys and looked over our Rook cards, I remembered that Robin was coming and started watching the drive expectantly for their big shiny car.

Robin was a small girl with a plain face and brown hair. But when she smiled, she looked really good. Back then it wasn't that I particular liked her because she was a girl, but I wanted her to act like she knew me when we were at school together. Up to then she would always look the other way or straight ahead when I was around, as though she didn't know me. And the way she would smile at the big boys would make me wish so bad that it was me. Now it was Christmas, and I was hoping to get in good with her.

So I felt a thrill racing up my back as I saw their car come out of the woods down along the distant drive. When Mr. Barnes parked the car, and when Robin got out, she looked right at me like she had never seen me before. Then another thrill ran up my back. After that everybody was too busy talking, and Robin didn't look at me anymore until it was time to eat.

At the dinner table, Robin sat across from me, and she kept on looking at me while she ate. So I looked back at her, and then she smiled at me like she did to the big boys at school, so I smiled back and started feeling really good!

But then her smile was drowned out by my father's voice, talking about the Second Coming to Mr. &. Mrs. Barnes.

Mr. Barnes just ate and looked down at his food while he ate it. Mother listened but kept on eating while she did it. But Mrs. Barnes had stopped eating. Her food was getting cold, and the flies were buzzing around it. She started to get excited at what my dad was saying.

"It should be just about seven years from today," he said, as he scooped a spoonful of lima beans into his mouth.

"Praise the Lord, how wonderful," chortled Mrs. Barnes. "Then the wicked of this world will get their just desserts," she said with finality. She licked her lips and then with her fingers peeled off a piece of cold chicken meat from a leg bone, stuck it in her mouth and began to chew it.

At this point my dad stopped talking and started filling his mouth up with food. He stuffed his mouth using his teeth to pull the meat off of a chicken thigh. He filled his mouth up several times with lima beans and a bunch of times with mashed potatoes and gravy. He then swallowed it all and burped. He looked at his plate like he was looking for something he could eat real quick before he had to start talking again. He saw a little crispy chicken gizzard lying at the edge of his plate and stabbed it through and through with his fork. He then popped it into his mouth and ate it in the blink of an eye.

"Yes," my father said, "God has revealed to me His means of transportation He intends to use when he returns to take us to Zion."

Mrs. Barnes just gasped and stared at my father in suspenseful silence. I had heard it all before so I just kept on eating. I glanced again at Robin who was staring at her food but was peaking at me from the corner of her eye. Mother had heard it before too but stopped eating anyway so she could see what Mrs. Barnes would do when my dad said it. Mr. Barnes stopped putting food in his mouth, but he already had enough in it to last for a while. He turned and stared out the screen door, where Joe stood looking in with his tongue hanging out in great joy as though he knew exactly what my dad was going to say and believed every word of it, especially if someone would just let him in to where the chicken was.

But my dad looked back at his plate where he discovered a baby lima bean lying by itself. He again stabbed it with his fork and popped it into his mouth. But this time he just kept on chewing it while everyone sat and waited for him to say it. Finally he swallowed the poor little bean and was about to say it, when in the silence everyone could hear Jonathan chomping his food and smacking his lips together, oblivious to what my dad was about to say.

"Close your mouth when you eat, Jonathan!" my mother said.

Then my dad said it. "He is going to return for us in his divine chariots," he said. "Today we call them flying saucers."

Suddenly Mr. Barnes dropped his fork and with a loud clatter, it fell on the floor. He then started staring at the top of the screen door where the flies were coming through the hole in it, so they could fly down and get a taste of the chicken before it was gone.

"I don't know about that, Reverend McGee," he blurted out loudly while still staring at the hole that the flies were coming through. "Sounds awfully far-fetched to me."

"Oh yeeeee of little faith," Mrs. Barnes hollered as she stared with closed eyes at the ceiling. She then opened them and stared accusingly at her husband. "When are you ever going to learn, Dear?"

Mr. Barnes' eyes had dropped from the hole in the screen to his black shoes and his fork that lie beside them, and he mumbled something that no one else could hear.

She then turned to my father and said, "What a wonderful revelation Brother McGee, and what exciting news it is! How hard it will be for us to have to wait for that glorious day when we as overcomers have the privilege to watch God's chariots descending from the sky on His rapture day, Hallelujah . . . praise His Name."

"Yes praise His Name," my father said.

"Yes praise His Name," my mother said.

And then the food was gone.

I glanced at Robin. She was looking at me, and she smiled real big so that I started to think that she liked me. But before I could get excited about it, my mother said "Bobby take the dishes off the table and take them to the sink and wash them."

My heart sank. I had forgotten about the dishes! I just hated to do them when company came. I would always miss out on all the fun of listening to them talk! And this time was even worse. Robin would be going out to play without me! She looked over her shoulder at me, and she looked like she felt sorry too, but she just went on walking out the door to the porch behind my brothers and sister.

"Mother!" I whined in my misery, "can't I do them later?"

"No," she said, "but if you hurry it won't take very long at all."

But when I looked at them, all piled full of bones and leftover food, I wanted to go hide under the bed and cry because it felt like it would take all eternity to do so much work. I felt like it was the end of time, and there was no future as I began to slowly carry all those dirty dishes into the kitchen sink. As I methodically washed them, I dreamed about how much fun it would be if I could simply walk out onto the porch and play with Robin.

But then suddenly Mrs. Barnes' voice penetrated my thoughts. She and my mother were sitting on two old wooden chairs at a table just outside the kitchen door so I could hear what they said.

"I bought Robin some clay for Christmas," Mrs. Barnes had said, "to show her how God can mold us according to his will, if we will just put our lives into His hands."

"That is a wonderful idea!" my mother said.

But then I suddenly noticed to my astonishment that the dishes were almost done! My heart leaped for joy. I quickly washed the last dish and raced for the porch, but as I ran, I suddenly realized I had forgotten to drain the dirty dishwater, but there was no way I could turn back then. I think my mother did it for me since she never came and got me.

Out on the gray porch where the sunshine made it warm, everyone was playing with Robin's clay. Robin was making people out her clay. She was telling my brothers and Charlotte that she was "God" and that she was "molding people according to her will so that they could all go to heaven when they died."

When I saw her people, they looked like they were already dead to me. They didn't even have eyes or a mouth, though some of them looked like they had a nose.

Then Robin saw me and grinned. "This is you, Bobby," she said. "I have molded you according to my will so when you come to heaven you can work for me because I am God."

She looked steadily into my eyes and grinned even bigger, and I liked it. I knew she wasn't God, and it wasn't very nice to lie that way. But I decided not to tell her so because it was too much fun pretending that it was true.

It was then I noticed Eddie groaning in frustration. He was trying to make a dump truck out of clay, and it wouldn't stick together in the right places. Charlotte was feeling sorry for him and trying to help him. Jonathan was in a dream world and was just beating his clay like my mother beat the bread before she baked it. Robin then started holding "me" up so that I could look at it. I didn't think it really looked like me, but I sat down real close beside her anyway so that we could look at each other and smile.

"Do you like school?" I asked.

"Yes," she said and sighed. Her eyes grew distant as though she were looking at something far away. She turned her head and stared at the woods that went to the Gatlin place. "I just wish I was old enough to have a boyfriend," she said.

She suddenly turned back to me, to lean over and kiss me on the end of my nose. And I started to wish that I was older too.

Then I heard my father's voice coming out through the screen door, and he was saying, "Yes it will be seven years from today when Christ returns in his flying saucers to take us to Mt. Zion to set up his kingdom on earth. Shortly after that, Armageddon will begin."

And I just sat there for a long time listening to his voice, trying to get the courage to kiss Robin on the nose. But then suddenly it was time to go, and she had to start smashing all her people back into regular clay. And before I could even think about it anymore, they all got into their big shiny car and left.

# THE ANNOUNCEMENT

IN OUR CHURCH almost everyone liked my dad. They knew that he was getting revelations from God about the end times, and the date when it was to happen. They knew he was reading the holy bible scripture over and over again trying to get its exact meaning. So on that Sabbath morning on the day of the announcement, no one said a word as they watched with anticipation as my father walked out of the shadows in the back of the church toward the pulpit.

In the churchyard before the service began, I had stood with my back toward Reba Boone and Mrs. Barnes as I listened to them talking about it.

"The date has been set!" Mrs. Barnes squealed, barely able to contain herself.

"So when is it?" Reba gasped breathlessly.

"I can't tell you that Reba!" Mrs. Barnes said sternly.

"Well I hope it is not too soon," Reba had said as she looked up at two birds singing in the tree that I was standing under. "There is a lot of stuff that needs to be done before we leave," she continued.

"Don't worry Reba, you will have plenty of time to do what needs to be done."

"But I don't want it to be too far off either," worried Reba. "I don't want to have to die first!"

"Stop worrying Reba! You will live long enough if you don't die worrying about it first! But I will give you a hint," continued Mrs. Barnes, and then she was silent for so long that I had to peak to see what was going on. She was looking around her to see if anybody was listening. I began to panic and began to stare at the singing birds in the tree above me. And then I heard her say it. "Our Lord is returning on Christmas Day."

Reba let out a whoop of joy. "How like Him to come…," she began loudly.

"Shhhhhhhhh," whispered Mrs. Barnes.

They glanced around them, but I guess they didn't think I was important. Then they heard Agnes Everby, somewhere in the church say "praise the Lord," and they started walking toward the front door.

As my father had stood silent behind the pulpit, one could have heard a pin drop. No one wanted to miss a single word of it!

"Praise the Lord," my father shouted.

"Praise the Lord," screamed Agnes Everby.

My mother said it too, but not so loud.

"Praise the Lord," my father shouted again. This time he lifted his arms like an angels wings and looked up at the ceiling.

This time the congregation took its cue, and they all shouted "praise the Lord," in unison except old Larsen Smith who said it after everyone else had shouted it.

I figured that old Annie had probably jabbed him in the ribs to get him to say it.

Now everyone was silent again, all eyes looking up at my father standing behind the pulpit.

"Today I have some wonderful and important news from God on high to report to you," he said. His voice sounded excited and thrilled. It usually didn't sound that way.

"God on high," he said even louder, "has revealed to me the date of the second coming, the date that Jesus is coming back to earth again." His voice became intense and passionate. "In First Thessalonians Paul tells us that for those who live in darkness His return will be like a thief in the night, but we of the 144,000 will not be taken unawares by his coming. We can have knowledge in advance. Hallelujah!"

"Hallelujah," screeched Agnes Everby.

Then most everybody else said hallelujah, but they said it quick and not to loud, because they didn't want to miss out on what came next.

As I listened, I became excited too and believed it.

"Only seven short years!" he cried, in a voice that sent shivers up my back.

The people in the pews became electrified and went wild shouting all kinds of things like "praise His Name," "hallelujah," and "thank you Jesus, blessed be your name."

"Seven years," my dad shouted again as he looked out over the happy faces.

Then Agnes Everby's voice started getting louder and louder. She was speaking in another tongue so that nobody knew what she was saying except God. Everyone else started getting quiet and thrilled because they knew that whatever it was that she was saying had to be wonderful.

"Bless her Lord."

I turned just in time to see the wrinkles on Annie Smiths face jumping all over the place.

"Yes bless her," said Mrs. Barnes and Reba Boone in unison. And then everybody in the congregation said it.

"Hallelujah," shouted my dad, even louder then Agnes Everby's other tongues. But when he said it, Agnes Everby came to her senses and stopped shouting so that she could listen.

"He is returning in all His glory to pass judgment on this wicked earth exactly seven years from this past Christmas day. Praise the Name of the Father, Son and the Holy Ghost!"

Again the congregation erupted in shouts of praise, stunned by such miraculous news straight from the mouth of God on High.

"But I have even more wonderful news!" cried my father, looking out over everybody with eyes that looked like he was staring at God Himself.

"Hallelujah," he hollered as silence suddenly returned to all the uplifted faces full of hope and wonder as they stared expectantly at the man behind the pulpit.

"Our Father in Heaven has revealed to me the mode of transportation that He will use to transport His people to Zion."

He was suddenly silent as he reviewed the uplifted faces that were staring back at his face.

"Return, O backslidden children says the Lord," cried my father as he quoted the scripture from the bible! "For I am married unto you. And I will take you, one from a city and two from a family, and I will bring you to Zion. Bring you," he repeated.

He was silent for a moment so that the congregation could shout with joy at the wonderful news. And Agnes Everby just kept right on shouting after everyone else had stopped. My dad stood and watched her with a smile on his face until she finally said amen and took a hanky from her bag and blew her big nose into it.

"Then we who are alive and remain," he began to quote again, his voice shouting so loud that it bounced off the walls of the church. "Shall be caught up together with those who have been raised from the dead," he continued.

"Caught up together," he repeated. "Caught up by what? Hallelujah.........His chariots. And he has revealed to me that these very same chariots of God are the UFO's that numerous witnesses have seen flying around our country and the world. Hallelujah," he said again.

"It is in these divine chariots of God that we, the 144,000, will descend onto Mt. Zion in, to stand with the Lamb of God. Hallelujah!"

Then my dad went silent and looked out over the congregation waiting for the shouts of "amen," "hallelujah," "praise his name." But no one said anything. I turned around and started looking to see what had happened.

All the faces looked like they were saying it but had died before they could get it said. Only Annie Smith's face was moving, but her wrinkles were jumping around in silence. Mrs. Barnes' smile was frozen, her hallelujah hung in silent suspension. Reba Boone was staring at her smile, her mouth hanging open. I couldn't tell what she was trying to say. Then Agnes Everby began to gurgle and gag like she was trying to throw up. I figured she was trying to shout in other tongues.

I glanced quickly back to my dad behind the pulpit. He was staring way up at the ceiling at the cobwebs that glistened in the sunlight. Then I saw it, a spider hanging on the end of one of the webs and making it longer. The stringy web was coming right out of his tailbone. At least that is what it looked like from where I sat.

But then I quickly turned as a cry came out of Annie Smith's throat but stopped before she could say anything because a tall skinny man named Gregory Picklesworth stood up and walked out of the church.

"Satan, get thou behind me," screamed Agnes Everby, suddenly able to talk and then a bunch of amens began coming from around the church.

Now no one knew very much about Mr. Picklesworth, and he wasn't very friendly with anybody. So people were always gossiping about him. He would always sit at the back by the door as though he wanted to be ready to leave really quick, if necessary. Once he had started bellowing in a loud gruff voice, "praise the Lord, Brother McGee, give'm hell Brother McGee."

After that everyone said he couldn't be that close to God if he said hell, that way. Then once he had suddenly jumped up really angry-like and told Agnes Everby to "stop shouting glory while Brother McGee is speaking! Can't you hold it until the end of the sermon?" he had said in a voice that croaked like a loud bullfrog.

My dad had stopped preaching and had looked at Mr. Picklesworth with a kind smile on his face. But everyone else started looking around in all directions, like they were pretending they didn't hear him say it.

After that service, I heard Agnes Everby tell my mother that she had felt the presence of Satan in the room when Mr. Picklesworth had so rudely said that to her.

Once I had heard Reba Boone tell Mrs. Barnes, "that Mr. Picklesworth was probably living in sin because she had drove by his house once after dark and saw him going into his house with a woman. I'm pretty sure he is not married." she had added.

And I overheard Mrs. Barnes saying once, "she had smelled alcohol on his breath when he had hugged her in Christ."

After Mr. Picklesworth had walked out, my dad had started preaching again about the stupid virgins who fell asleep with no oil in their lamps, and everyone started acting normal again.

But after church service, everyone stood around stunned and silent as they listened to Anthony Parshams shouting at my dad as they stood on the front steps of the church.

Now no one was surprised by the rude behavior of Mr. Picklesworth, but everyone thought that Mr. Parshams was a good Christian. No one had ever seen him or his wife do anything wrong. His wife even wore her long skirts all the way down to her feet because she did not want to tempt anyone by showing too much flesh.

Mrs. Barnes had once said, "no one could ever accuse her of exposing the evils of the flesh."

"Brother McGee," he was yelling, "how can you be so audacious as to claim that you can get inside God's mind. Why don't you leave Christ's second coming to Christ?" He then raised his voice even more and shouted, "this borders on blasphemy! Isn't it enough that He has promised to return soon?"

"Come Helen," he had said loudly, turning to his wife who had been standing behind him, her face aflame with embarrassment. "Let's get out of here and go find us a more humble preacher."

He stomped down the steps dragging his wife, Helen behind him. The poor lady almost fell as she was tripping over her long skirt.

The rest of the congregation politely, but silently shook my father's hand then left. Only Agnes Everby had hung around to offer my father encouragement.

"Keep up the faith, Brother McGee," she had said, her face abeam with joy. "Blessed are those who are persecuted for My Namesake, sayeth the Lord."

My dad gave her a silent but gentle smile.


It was years later on a chilly January day that we attended our church on Third Street for the last time.

"We can no longer afford the rent," my father had said.

The only people present beside my family were Agnes Everby, Betty and Albert Barnes, Butch and Reba Boone and old Annie Smith. Robin didn't even come. Everyone else had drifted away over the years because they didn't like the flying saucer part. At least that was what my father was always saying.

Old Larson had died the summer before. He had died peacefully in his sleep, Annie said. But he hadn't liked our church anyway. I figured he had just got tired of having Annie poke him in the ribs. They had buried him beneath an old dead tree covered with Spanish moss behind the house that he and Annie had lived in since they married more than sixty years before.

Annie just stood there, on that hot sticky summer day, over the closed casket waiting to be buried, while a clap of thunder penetrated the hot stillness. Her tears had welled up in her eyes to roll down and mingle with the sweat, through the labyrinth of wrinkles that creased her old face, and made her look as old as dirt.

"If he could have lived a few more years," she had said quietly, her wrinkles jerking with grief, "he wouldn't have had to die."

And after our church closed, we met every Sabbath at Annie Smith's house because she had a big living room with a church piano.

As for the Gatlins, they never returned to our church after my father had disappeared into the woods that day on his way to have a talk with Melba Gatlin. When he had returned, his eye was big, bruised, purple and almost swollen shut.

"What happened," my mother had cried when she saw him.

But when my dad stared at her with his good eye, she shut up and said no more that we kids could hear. We kids had figured that Studs had beat him up when he had accused him of raping Charlotte.

# RUSSELL DUKE

I WENT TO the school on First Street for three months before anyone took the time to talk to me, and it was Reggie Smithers who did it. His father was a Catholic who wore a beard that was starting to turn gray. Reggie also had a friend named Russell Duke. So he became my friend too, at least for a while, but mostly because he tagged along with Reggie all the time.

Before I met Reggie and Russell. I would spend all my recesses and lunches out by the swamp. I would just sit there and watch the other kids play. At first Eddie and Charlotte would join me. but after a while they found some friends, so I would sit there alone watching the frogs sneak out of the water and stick their tongues out to grab a mosquito that would be a humming in the air above them.

Sometimes when I would eat my peanut butter sandwiches that my mother fixed for lunch. I would watch the brown water that was hidden in the shade of the old moss covered cypress trees, real quiet like, hoping to see a snake silently slither out to try and catch a frog for its dinner. I once saw one swallow a frog with one gulp! And then there were the days that I would become so lost listening to the humming mosquitoes as they hovered above the stale water that I would forget my class and have to try to sneak in late while all those eyes were staring at me.

In early December, I was watching the distant figures of my classmates play, when one small figure separated itself from the rest and came rapidly toward me.

"Hi Bobby," he said as he gasped for a breath of stale autumn heat. Sweat poured down his face, and his shirt was wet with perspiration.

"You must be pretty smart," he panted. "My dad says quiet people are usually real smart and you are awfully quiet!"

I looked at him in silence for a minute, thinking he might be making fun of me. But then he smiled really friendly-like.

"Well, I ….don't know." I replied. I had never thought about anything like that!

"Where did you come from before this year?" he had asked.

"Up north," I answered, not wanting him know this was my first year of regular school.

"Did it snow where you came from?" he asked.

But before I could answer, Russell Duke came running up and out of breath.

"Reggie," he said, as he gave me a long look from head to toe, "we need you in the game. It is your turn to bat."

"Ok," Reggie replied and as he ran off he looked back over his shoulder and said, "why don't you come and play with us Bobby? Playing ball is fun even for smart people."

Russell also threw a stare over his shoulder, but he only gave me a long victorious grin.

"Maybe," I responded, "but recess is almost over today."

I had felt a warm feeling of self-confidence come over me that day as I walked back to the classroom. Reggie thought I was smart. Such a thing had never entered my mind before. Reggie gave me a big smile as he entered the classroom, but Russell had stared at me with a long face, probably because the bell had rang before they could finish the game.

Later that year Reggie tried to teach me how to play softball. At first he would stand behind me, both of us holding onto the bat. But neither of us could hit anything that way, and one day the ball hit Reggie square on the forehead. It knocked him down and stunned him. After that he didn't help me anymore, and I could almost never hit the ball. I would strike at it violently, hoping for a home run, but I would usually miss it. Sometimes the bat would go flying, everyone around me running to keep from being hit.

"You are a hopeless case," Russell once said. And after that he would point to me and call me hopeless every time I missed the ball.

Finally I became frustrated and lost interest. I had more fun on the sidelines cheering Reggie on. He was always hitting home runs.

I was better at football, because I was little and skinny and could run really fast. I could dodge around the big guys and jump over them when they would fall in front of me in an attempt to trip me.

After a while, though, I began going back to the swamp again, and Reggie would sometimes come over to sit and talk with me. It wasn't long before Russell was joining us also. Russell followed Reggie around like a loyal hound dog. So I had no choice but to be his friend too.

So Reggie and I had grown quite close over the years. and Russell and I had become more or less acceptable to each other.

It was a warm, sunny late April afternoon when Reggie, Russell and I had rode our bikes over to Russell's place from school. Russell led us into the kitchen of his big house. There on the kitchen table, as usual, was a big stone jar that said "cookies" on it. He gave one to Reggie, then one to me. From the refrigerator, he took out a big jug of milk and poured it into three tall glasses. It was cold and delicious when I drank it to wash down the soft, sweet brown cookies.

Russell's house was so big and nice. The floors in the living room were polished wood and so clean that I was almost afraid to walk on them. The kitchen floor was white and hard like stone, and the refrigerator was chock full of good things to eat. There were things in it that I didn't recognize and other things too good to imagine. When I was in Russell's house, I could not help but wish that my dad wasn't a preacher. and that he could have a job that made lots of money. And I would think about my house sitting out there in the woods with nothing on it but gray siding.

Even Reggie's house was a lot nicer than mine. It was painted blue and sat on a nice street with a big grass yard so nice and green with the grass cut short. Only weeds would grow around my house. There were too many trees with big roots growing out from them. I had never invited Reggie or Russell out to my place because I had always figured that Russell would make fun of it.

But then I forgot about my place in the woods when the three of us went out the kitchen door and headed for the pasture gate. We were just finishing a third cookie when we climbed the fence and walked over to watch a cow licking from a block of yellow salt. She turned and looked at us and went "ooooh", then turned to bite at a big black fly that was buzzing around her tail. Her udder was hanging low. Russell said it was filling up with milk. He said it was the grass she ate that made it, but of course, we all knew that because he told us that every time we went over and looked at the cows.

Russell suddenly turned and looked at Reggie. "I heard all the girls a giggling at school," Russell said. "They were teasing Julie Pendleton about you being her boyfriend...is she your girlfriend Reggie?"

It had become a fad among the boys at school to have a girlfriend. For some it was just an imaginary girlfriend, for others, they really had one who would admit it and sometimes kiss them in public.

"Sure," Reggie had replied.

"How come I didn't know about it?" Russell had whined.

"Does she let you kiss her?"

"Sure," Reggie had replied again.

"Wow," said Russell as his mouth dropped open and his eyes got bigger to stare at Reggie in awe.

Reggie had just kept staring at the cow.

"When are you going to get a girlfriend Russell?" Reggie asked as he looked out into the pasture to see a whole herd of cows that had stopped eating grass in order to stare at us.

"I already have one," Russell said while throwing me a defiant glance with a face that was starting to turn red.

"Who!?" Reggie had said loudly while turning to his friend with sudden interest.

"Robin Barnes," Russell said with a voice that began to sink and become weak so that I could hardly hear it.

But I did hear it, and my heart sank because I had secretly fantasized Robin as my girlfriend. I had never forgotten her kiss on my nose that Christmas Day. After that I had really hoped she would be my friend at school. but she wasn't. She acted like she had forgotten all about the kiss. Sometimes she would glance at me with a small smile around her lips, but mostly she would just laugh and talk to the bigger boys.

In the early years of high school, Robin's breasts had started to protrude behind her flimsy little dresses, and finally, by the time we reached our senior year, they were soft and full. Sometimes I could see most of them, and they made me want her close so I could touch them to see how soft they really were. But she always seemed to be out of reach. At home, I would stand and stare at myself in the mirror trying to figure out why she didn't like me. I finally decided that I was just too skinny and small for my age.

But as long as I could not point to anyone and say he is her boyfriend, my jealousy rested below the surface. But now Russell had let the cat out of the bag and had identified himself as Robin's boyfriend. The very words had stunned me, nearly taking my breath away. They made my stomach sink into my gut. For a moment I thought I was going to throw up Russell's cookies.

Robin's bright smile that she used to flirt with the big guys flashed before me, and I vividly remembered the kiss on the nose, as a child. But then with a sudden surge of hope, I suddenly realized that I had never seen her flirting with Russell. In fact I couldn't even remember her ever smiling at him.

"I have never seen you talking to Robin, Russell," Reggie had said in disbelief.

This gave me more hope. If Reggie didn't believe him, Russell was probably lying, I thought.

"We talk secretly," Russell had almost whispered.

I was beginning to get my second wind and get angry. How dare Russell lie about something as important as this?!

"I think Russell is just talking and don't have any girlfriend at all," I had said while glancing at Reggie for support.

"You better not call me a liar, Buster Hopelessness, after you ate my cookies and drank my milk!"

He stood in front of me with his fist doubled.

"Don't start a fight, Russell, you are bigger than Bobby," Reggie said. "Besides I have never seen you around Robin either."

"And I ain't seen you around Julie, either," Russell said, "but I aint calling you a liar!"

"I wasn't calling you no liar, Russell," I said. I sure didn't want to get into no fistfight with him!

"That's alright, we will ask Robin tomorrow," Reggie said.

At this, the blood drained from Russell's face and his mouth fell open again.

"No," he said almost violently. "I will let you see me talk to her."

"Ok," Reggie said, "but you have to let us hear what you say and what she says back to you."

"This is your fault!" Russell shouted turning on me. "You go home and don't come back no more!"

"Bobby is our friend, Russell, we three have been doing things together for years. Besides it was you who started all this about Robin, not Bobby!"

"Don't pay any attention to Russell, Bobby" Reggie said as he laid his hand on my shoulder.

Russell hung his head to stare at his feet, angry and embarrassed.

"I got to go home," I said, "before my mother gets mad at me for being so late."

"Ok, Bobby, see you tomorrow," Reggie said.

I felt them, their eyes, piercing my back as I made my way over the fence and through the gate to the front yard to my bicycle.

The next day at school Russell's face was really white, and he looked sick as he approached Robin, who was being pushed on the swing by Albert Rotterbaum. He was one of the bigger seniors. Reggie and I stood back a ways, watching. He stood there for a moment to build up his courage, then he walked resolutely toward her.

"Robin, I want to talk to you," he said quite clearly.

Suddenly I was afraid again. What if she really was his girlfriend, or what if she became his girlfriend because of this?

"Ok," Robin said.

She spread her legs and dragged her feet in the dirt to stop the swing. The dust climbed up between her legs to get her white panties dirty. She turned and gave Albert a big bright smile, then jumped up and walked right over to Russell and looked him in the eye.

"What?" she asked.

But Russell's courage had failed him. He glanced at Albert, standing there real tall, a grinning. He glanced back at Reggie and I, and his face was so white it looked like a ghost. He again momentarily met Robin's bold stare before looking at his feet.

"Nuttin," he said, before turning and running towards the swamp.

Reggie followed him and I started to follow Reggie, but he stopped me.

"I need to talk to him alone," he said.

I watched them from a distance until the bell rang. Neither one of them returned to class that day.

For awhile after this Russell would give me nasty looks and sit and sulk when he joined Reggie and I out by the swamp.

Then one day Reggie brought Julie with him out to the swamp. Russell came behind them at a distance. When we all sat down on the ground facing the swamp, Reggie pulled Julie over close to him and started kissing her. Russell and I watched . Finally they started sticking their tongues in each other's mouths, Reggie had called that 'French kissing'.

Then Russell leaned over and whispered in my ear, "I'm going to make Robin my girlfriend, you just watch!"

I just tried to ignore him as I continued to stare at Reggie and Julie. And when the bell rang, I ran as fast as I could to get into the classroom so I could look at Robin.

# THE BLACKBERRY PATCH

ONE SABBATH ROBIN was with her parents at Annie Smith's for church. She sat between them pouting and looking really angry. I watched her closely for a hint that she was noticing me, but she wasn't.

After everybody finished praying, I heard Mrs. Barnes talking to my mother as they stood by the front door getting ready to leave.

"Robin is becoming a sex crazy young woman," she was complaining. "She is always going over to one of her girlfriend's house. Well the other day, Albert gave her a ride over there in the car and then drove down the street and parked and watched the house. Sure enough, a short time later she left and walked several blocks down the street and knocked on the door of another house. Albert had turned the car around and followed her, and this tall young man opened the door for her. She walked right in like she knew him. So Albert went up and knocked on the door. It turned out it was the Rotterbaum residence. Albert was angry and brought her home. She claims she was running an errand for her girlfriend, but we don't believe her. So we have decided it is time for her to get closer to God, one way or another."

"Yes, I don't blame you," my mother had said sympathetically.

I glanced at Robin. She was standing at the piano looking back at me, like she had just noticed me for the first time again. I started feeling the thrills go up my back like before but I couldn't bring myself to go closer. I was really angry at myself for the rest of the day.

That night I dreamed that Robin was running naked through the house, and that my father was chasing her with a keen switch. I suddenly awoke in alarm. My thing was hard and dancing out of control. I grabbed for it, but it was too late. Later I sneaked silently out of the house, making my way across the yard through the sultry dark night to the edge of the woods where I dug a hole and buried them.

At dawn I wanted her and didn't want Russell Duke to get her. I swore to myself, as light began to pervade the crevices of my bedroom, that if she was at Annie Smith's the next Sabbath that I was to going to talk to her. I was going to get her somewhere where I could get her naked, like in the dream.

The rest of the week, her naked image burned a hole in my brain as I waited impatiently for Sabbath to come.

Then Sabbath came.

At Annie Smith's, I sat in my chair nearly breathless, stewing with desire, as I watched the door for her to enter with her parents.

Suddenly the screen door flew open and in walked Mr. Barnes. I stretched my neck, desperate to see who was behind him. Yes, there she was! She walked in proudly behind him, with Mrs. Barnes behind her. My excitement knew no bounds. I will talk to her today, I told myself.

The service had dragged on. They sang the hymns, the same ones they had sang last Sabbath and the Sabbath before. My dad had some new information on the second coming. I heard it already, but he had to tell everyone else. He moved the date up two days, to the twenty third of December. Then, of course, Agnes Everby had to get excited and start shouting, "praise the lord", and when she did it everyone else had to do it too.

My dad preached on and on about the "eye of the needle" and how hard it was to get into God's Kingdom. After that everyone had to kneel and pray, and it took such a long time! And then just as I was beginning to think it was all finished, Agnes Everby lost control to the Holy Ghost and started running around the room with her eyes closed while speaking in tongues. I think she was peeking, though, because she managed not to trip over anyone's legs or feet that were sticking out behind them while they prayed.

The service finally ended, and I got up off my sore knees. I looked for Robin. She was walking over toward the piano. I started to follow her but stopped in my tracks. I was listening to all the loud voices of the folks around me. I looked at their faces and they all seemed to be looking right back at me. I looked back at Robin. She was looking at me. I suffered pure torture! How was it possible for me to go over there and start talking to her while everyone was watching? I turned and walked out through the screen door. My heart was pounding wildly in despair! How was I possibly going to wait for another Sabbath to see her?

I went and sat on a big root that wound out under the shade of an old tree, my brain swimming in agony! Then someone tapped me on the shoulder. Startled, I came to my senses and turned quickly to see Robin standing there with a bright smile on her face. I smiled back at her in relief, my heart melting like butter on a hot stove.

"Mama and I are coming over to your house on Wednesday," she said, "and we will do something, okay?"

I stared at her breathless and speechless.

She cocked her head coquettishly to one side kind of like Joe did sometimes. A sexy smirk hovered around her lips. She put her hands on her hips and stood there like a suspended question mark, waiting for an answer.

"O…o…ok," I stuttered.

"Okay," she repeated, and then turned and ran back into Annie Smith's house.

I couldn't trust myself back inside with all those people in my euphoric state so I went and sat and waited in the car.

Wednesday morning I was up with the dawn and could hardly contain the thrill of my anticipation. After breakfast even more good news came.

"Bobby, I want you to hurry up with those dishes," Mother had said. "Robin and Mrs. Barnes are coming over at nine o'clock."

I did the dishes in record time, then waited on the front porch. I had not expected them to come so early.

When they arrived, Robin had on long baggy pants, a loose shirt and carried a pail. She climbed the steps, crossed the porch and entered the house with her mother, without even looking at me, as though I hadn't existed.

My feelings were hurt. She is ignoring me again, I thought. I slowly got up and followed them in. Inside I quickly became curious. Why was she carrying that pail? Why was she wearing those baggy pants? I had been hoping that she would wear some little shorts. .

Inside I found Charlotte, Eddie, and Jonathan congregated around Robin. Mother had just finished giving Mrs. Barnes a hug. Robin, then glanced at me with a smile that sent the courage surging through my veins.

"Mama thinks it would be a good idea for us to go blackberry picking, Bobby." When Robin said it, her smile got even bigger. She then looked at my brothers and sister for approval.

"I think that is a wonderful idea," my mother had said.

Everyone agreed, including me. Although I was not sure how I was going to get her naked in the blackberry patch, especially with Charlotte, the boys and the rattlesnakes and all.

"Go change your clothes," Mother said. "Sticky blackberry vines are hard on clothes, so wear your old ones."

As I was going to the bedroom, I overheard Mrs. Barnes saying to my mother, "It is such a relief to have Robin with a good Christian young man, Martha. Maybe it will take her mind off them sex maniacs in town. Bobby is about her age. Maybe they can have some good Christian fun so she can take her mind off sex for a while."

I wished that I didn't hear that. I felt guilty, like someone had poured a cup of cold water on me.

We had all piled into Mrs. Barnes' car in our baggy clothes, carrying buckets and pails. The back seat was full of us so Robin sat on my lap and she felt really good bouncing up and down on me as we drove out along the bumpy driveway. And she kept on bouncing up and down on me even after we got onto the smooth road. So I soon forgot my guilty feelings as Mrs. Barnes took us to the blackberry patches in the fields just west of our place.

"Watch out for snakes, now," Mrs. Barnes yelled, as the five of us ran down the embankment on the side of the road and over or through the barbed wire fence into the fields.

"We will Mama," Robin hollered back over her shoulder, her face beaming with joy.

Robin and I stopped to watch the smoke pour from the tailpipe of her mom's car as she drove back to spend the time visiting with my mother.

When we turned again, Charlotte and the boys had already crossed the field and were busy picking berries. Robin and I started walking slowly toward them.

"Bobby," Robin said as she came to a stop.

"What?" I asked as I walked a little bit ahead before stopping and turning to face her. I felt my blood boiling with anticipation. But it felt so good that I was afraid of it. Her eyes met mine boldly.

"Do you know how to fuck?"

I felt my boiling blood rushing to my face. I looked quickly at my feet to keep it from showing. Though everyone at school, including Reggie and Russell had said "fuck" all the time, I never said it because my dad had warned us that Christians just weren't supposed to talk or think about things like that. But when I heard Robin say it, it left me breathless, and my whole body on fire with desire. The thrills were racing one after the other up my back.

"Sure I can fuck," I said.

I felt like a giant then, and I boldly stared back at her, not caring that my face was red and hot and not caring how evil the thrill of my desire was.

"Did you ever fuck before, Bobby," she asked.

"Well…." I said, and then looked down to see it standing out hard against my baggy pants. I looked at Robin, and she was staring at it too and that made it get even bigger.

"I have," she volunteered

"Who?" I asked

"Albert Rotterbaum. His dick got hard real easy and I think yours would too" she said as she continued to stare at it standing there.

"My dick is already hard," I said, as flames of jealousy joined the flames that were already consuming my face. "Can't you tell?"

"Yes," she said, as she began to slowly move towards me.

"Is Albert your boyfriend?" I asked, in jealous fear of her answer.

"He used to be, but not anymore," she said as she came close to me and took my hand in hers.

"Come," she said, quietly, "let's go to a different berry patch where the kids can't see us."

"Charlotte," I yelled, "we are going to a different berry patch to pick, so don't come looking for us, okay?"

"Okay," Charlotte's voice came back to me faintly.

Robin's grip tightened around my hand as she led me, running, across and through the tall grass of the field. My feet were like wings beneath me. Soon we couldn't see my brothers and sister. We stopped where some big juicy blackberries hung from the vine.

She turned to me, her breath hot on my cheek. Our eyes met at close range. My blood throbbed, like my heart had climbed into my face, and it rushed violently into my cheeks. She reached down to grasp my arm and guide it around her waist as our lips met.

At first my kisses were harsh pecks placed on her cheeks and wet, passionate lips. But her wet open ones soon loosened mine into a passionate and wet response. I held her tightly as she gently pushed me back into the briars.

Pain seared my arm as in a fading dream. I was falling and a blackberry vine was taking my shirtsleeve with it as it went by. Then she was on top of me taking my breath with her kisses as the mosquitoes swarmed around us in the muggy hot summer sun.

She rose above me, her nostrils flaring, her cheeks glowing with beauty as from an unquenchable fire. Her eyes seemed to glaze as they riveted me with wild desire. She quickly unbuttoned her shirt, took it off and threw it to one side. Her breasts were firm and her nipples tight. She played with them, squeezing them so that her nipples stood up boldly with goose bumps popping up all over the place. She laughed wildly, while again riveting me with her bold gaze.

She stood, then, casting her shoes to one side. Her baggy pants fell in billows over me. I pushed them to one side and stared hungrily up at the wrinkles and crevices between her legs. Thrills came in waves as they raced through my body. I gasped for air and gulped in stale heat. The mosquitoes hovered in swarms around me, but I didn't hear them or feel their bites.

She dropped to her knees and crawled over me and beyond me toward a lone mulberry tree giving shade to the scrubby briar thicket. I frantically followed as sweat poured from my hot face and the vibrating thrill left my body weak.

The nakedness between her legs bulged enticingly beneath her white bottom and beads of perspiration ran seductively down her soft legs as I followed her on hands and knees. Reaching the shade, she turned and sat, her legs spread before her in the hot sand.

"You will get it dirty," I admonished in a barely audible voice, my gaze riveted to where it was hidden beneath her.

"My pussy?" she whispered in a hiss of passion.

"Y…y..yes,"

"Don't worry, we will wipe it off later."

I continued to crawl towards her, my body permeated with sticky heat.

She unbuttoned and took off my torn shirt. Next my belt slithered from me. Then quickly I became barefoot. She made me lie flat on my back as she squatted at my feet and with a violent tug pulled off my pants. I was naked and wildly free.

Exposed, my cock suddenly shriveled as though fearful of its newfound freedom.

"I don't know why……" I said, embarrassed, as we both stared at it.

"Don't worry," she said, "it is just not used to the fresh air, that's all." she stood and deftly flicked and wiped the sand from the open lips between her legs. She turned and knelt above me. It was just above my lips. It was so close that I wanted to help clean it with my tongue.

"I will make it hard for you," she said gently as she took hold of it and threw a smile back between her legs at me.

The boiling sun begun to invade the shade of our mulberry tree. Sweat was pouring from my body. The knats and mosquitoes began to bite, and the earth became harder beneath me as Robin continued to jerk and push at my stubborn dick.

"You are not easy, Bobby," she said with a sigh.

But then her wet lips and tongue enveloped me and coaxed me. It became as hard as a rock in a moment and blink of an eye. She leaped up, her face on fire to squat over me and face me. She grabbed and inserted my organ before its hardness could go away. She went up and down in rhythmic motions until my dick, again, began its dance, shooting liquid fire into her body. The ecstasy of my dream had become reality.

Robin simply sat on me, then, her face peaceful. Her eyes were closed, and her head was lifted toward the heavens where her sex god lived. We communed our happiness in our own private silence as the fluid seeped slowly from her.

Suddenly a crack of thunder ripped through the silent heat. Robin jumped to her feet.

"Oh Bobby!" she cried, "we must pick some blackberries so no one will know."

I grabbed my clothes and followed her naked little butt through the briars that were creating streaks of blood on her white legs, but they didn't seem to bother her. A sharp vine grabbed me, and I looked to see the blood running down my skinny leg.

Robin disappeared in the briar patch ahead of me, and I caught up with her just in time to see her white butt slip quickly into her baggy pants and to see her bloodied boobs slip beneath her shirt.

Lightning cracked like a whip across the darkening sky, followed almost immediately by the ominous roar of clapping thunder. A big raindrop hit my forehead as I looked up at the gray-black turmoil in the heavens and wondered if God was going to strike me dead for fucking Robin.

"What are we going to do?" Robin asked in anguish as she looked into her empty bucket. "Mama is going to want to know why we didn't pick any berries. What are we going to tell her, Bobby?"

I quickly put on my clothes, noting again, with some apprehension, my torn shirt. I wanted to get out of there and not tempt God too much, with that lightning flashing around like it was, but Robin was right, we had to do something about our empty pails. Glancing around, I noticed big juicy blackberries were hanging everywhere. I quickly picked some and smashed them around the sides of my pail.

"Now let me do yours Robin," I said. "We will tell your mother that we tripped and fell over each other trying to get out of the berry patch when the storm came."

The thunder became a steady roar with the louder claps becoming more ominous all the time. Lightning was beginning to hang like zigzagging fire ropes from the churning black cauldron above.

Through the din of the storm, we both heard the feint sound of a distant car horn.

"It's Mama!" Robin had cried, running into the sudden downpour.

As we ran, it felt as though we were running along the bottom of the sea, the rain drops so thick that one needed to gasp for breath. But at least, I thought, it is washing the blood away.

Charlotte and the boys sat dry in the car. They each had picked nearly a gallon of berries. Jonathan was gripping his proudly and possessively.

"Where is your bra?" Mrs. Barnes had asked sternly as she watched Robin climb in out of the rain.

Robin glanced down in horror at what her soaked and clinging shirt revealed.

"I forgot it," Robin responded weakly, "and this shirt was so big...."

"You might as well be naked now!" said her mother.

Robin bent over, folding her arms while her cheeks blazed.

Then Mrs. Barnes noticed our empty berry pails.

"What on earth have you two been doing?"

She frowned and looked at my torn shirt.

"We were running," I began bravely, "and we tripped over some blackberry vines. Robin was behind me and fell on top of me. The vines ripped my shirt, and we spilt all the berries on the ground. The storm was coming fast, the lightning was scary, and we didn't have time to pick them up or pick any more."

Robin glanced up, giving her mother a victorious glance. Mrs. Barnes just grunted, turned around, started the car and started driving through the downpour.

It was quiet in the back seat, but everyone was staring at Robin and I. I looked at Charlotte, and she returned my look with a penetrating stare. I started to feel guilty as we turned on to our long driveway that went winding through the woods.

# 'NEPAL' IN THE
# UNDERBRUSH

I DIDN'T SEE Robin again until Charlotte's birthday party two months later. In the intervening period, I had grown confident in my power over Robin. I convinced myself that we were almost as good as married. Surely she would be nice to me in public now, at least, and hopefully acknowledge me as her boyfriend.

Mother planned a party for just my brothers, Charlotte and I and Robin, but in my newfound confidence, I asked her if I could invite Reggie Smithers and Russell Duke.

"I don't mind," she responded, "as long as you do things that include your brothers and sister as well as Robin Barnes."

"Ok," I said, "we can all play hide and seek down in the woods."

"Whatever, it will be up to all of you though."

In my excitement, I rode my bike to town that late July day. I rode to Reggie's place but Reggie wasn't home. His father met me at the door to tell me he was at the Duke farm.

I really didn't want to go to Russell's farm but decided Russell couldn't be too angry if I invited him to come also.

The sun above was relentless and showed no mercy upon my head and shoulders as I stood astride my bike, contemplating upon what I should do. Sweat dripped into my eyes and the salt irritated. What if Russell was rude to me and ordered me off his property? I would just have to take that chance, I decided. It would be worth it just to see the look on Russell's face when I told him that Robin was my girlfriend, especially when I promised that she would admit it in public.

The Duke house was quiet but Reggie's bike was parked near the front porch. I stood a full minute or more at the front door before

I could get the courage to knock. I jumped, startled when the door opened almost before I was finished knocking and there stood Russell's mother Patricia Duke.

"Where's Reggie . . .err Russell?" I stammered.

"Out in the pasture, somewhere," she said.

I was gone, over the fence and through the pasture, to a small pond that was surrounded by trees, a cool place to sit in the summertime.

"Reggie, Russell," I shouted .

As I approached the shade of the willow trees, I saw them standing there watching me come. I slowed down to determine what their reaction was going to be.

"Hi Bobby!" Reggie shouted, "come over to the shade."

It was as though a burden had slipped from my shoulders. Reggie's voice had been disarming and friendly. I ran up to them, only looking at Reggie. I was afraid to look at Russell, just yet.

"Guess what?" I said in an unnaturally high voice. And before anyone else could speak, I continued, "I'm inviting both of you to my house for my sister, Charlotte's birthday party."

I then looked at Russell, but he was looking at Reggie.

"That's great!" Reggie said. "I always wanted to come out to your house."

This reminder dampened my enthusiasm somewhat, but I was refusing to let anything disturb my great plans.

"Guess what else," I continued.

"What?" queried Reggie

"Robin is my girlfriend, now, for real. I have even fucked her!"

I said the word proudly and gloried in my worldly knowledge as I glanced back at Russell.

"You lie," Russell accused, harshly.

"You just wait until the party, I'll show you."

"Is Robin coming to your sister's party?" Russell said in surprise, unsure of himself then.

"Yes," I responded in triumph.

"Looks like you have opened your big mouth once too often, Russell Duke," Reggie said as a big grin began to play around his lips.

Russell just hung his head and said, "okay, I'll come," in a weak voice.

"After cake and ice cream, we can do 'hide and seek' in the woods," I said excitedly.

"Then we can watch and see if you make out with her or not when you go off and hide together, ha…. ha ….ha," laughed Russell.

A small mischievous grin continued to play around Reggie's lips. I began to feel uncomfortable and started to wish I hadn't said anything about fucking Robin.

The three of us just sat in the shade by the pond, while Reggie told us that he had fucked Julie Pendleton two times. Russell's eyes bugged out in awe. He threw an envious glance at me but bit his lip, and looked at his tennis shoes lying in front of him in the dirt and was silent except for a sigh that escaped him.

It was a hot August morning, hot even before the sun came up, and it was day of Charlotte's birthday party. I awoke when there was only a touch of pink in the east with the trees of the woods standing like black silhouettes before it. But there was nothing that I could do at that hour. Everyone slept. I wandered restlessly into the kitchen. I stared at the birthday cake, outlined in the first light that had begun to slip in through the kitchen window. Mother had baked it the day before.

Out on the porch, Joe greeted me joyously, his tail wagging so hard that it threw his rear end off balance.

I began to pace the wooden porch restlessly with Joe running along beside me when it came to me that there was something I could do to kill the time until daylight. I ran down the drive with Joe close at my heels. Then about half way down the drive, near the spot where we had played "Little Car" as kids, I turned and ran into the dark woods. I would find a place where I could hide with Robin when we played "Hide and Seek" . I went to all the old places that had been different countries for me when I would go flying around the world as a child. They were just memories, part of the woods now, though a little spooky in the half light. The thrill and make believe of flying to foreign lands was gone now. And no place seemed adequate for what I wanted to do with Robin, but then I remembered the spot that used to be "Nepal" and went there.

There were two different ways you could get to "Nepal" which was at the end of a small path beneath some underbrush. One way was to crawl. Going this way, you had to cross a tiny stream. You could do this by squatting and stepping across. However, if you were to approach this small country from the other direction you had merely to slide down a small embankment, crawl beneath some underbrush and you were there, on a bed of Spanish moss beside the small stream.

It was still very dark, there on the moss, sitting beneath the woody thicket. Joe sat beside me staring and panting as I contemplated how I was going to get Robin there without anyone seeing us. Reggie and Russell would be watching our every move. It would be a disaster if they busted in upon us when we were fucking. I was beginning to wish I hadn't invited them. Suddenly a beam of sunshine showered the little stream I sat beside. I climbed back up the embankment into showers of sunlight streaming down into the forest of trees. I then rushed back to greet, with great anticipation, the activities of the new day.

As the late morning approached, I became fidgety and restless. The sun was already blazing when I went out and started pacing at the head of the driveway as I watched intently for the first car to show itself. A rush of relief came over me when Reggie's father's Cadillac came out of the distant woods along the drive.

"Is Robin here yet," yelled Russell, before he had covered half the distance between us.

I was embarrassed, enraged at his loud voice. "No," I hissed.

As they walked up, I tried to be more pleasant. "You must be quiet," I whispered, "I don't want my mother to hear you talk that way."

"Why not?" Russell had asked, while glancing defiantly toward the distant screen door.

"Because," said Reggie, firmly, "old adults don't want people our age to have fun, and if they find out, they'll make life miserable for you. Now, keep quiet dummy!"

"Okay," whined Russell, bowing his head in acquiescence.

The glance he threw me was sharp, like he would get me later.

"You have a nice place," Reggie said, smiling excitedly as he looked around. "I wished I lived in the woods like this. You should invite us out more often, Bobby."

I was taken aback at this. It had never occurred to me that he might like my place since his was so much nicer.

"It's okay," I said proudly, as I glanced around, looking for what it was he liked about it.

I glanced at Russell, but he was just looking at his feet with a red face.

We then went up and sat on the front porch waiting for Robin to come. Eddie and Jonathan stood back by the screen door and watched us for a while.

Finally Eddie walked over to me and asked, "why do we have to wait on Robin anyway."

"Yeah," seconded Jonathan, emphatically as he stepped forward.

"Because we want to see . ." began Russell.

"Shut up!" hissed Reggie, cutting him off with a long hard look.

"Because Mother wants us all to stay together," I answered, trying to sound authoritative.

I looked at Russell again. He was hanging his head and pouting. And I was now wishing I could get rid of him someway.

Suddenly the Barneses' car came around the bend, out of the woods and up the long driveway. And all eyes focused intently upon it.

Robin leaped out of the car, slamming the door shut behind her. She ran quickly up the steps, across the porch and into the house, brushing Russell with her bare, tanned leg. He had refused to move an inch to make way. She had not so much as even glanced in my direction. I felt like a worm and glanced furiously at the woods that went to the Gatlin place and then turned my gaze back down the driveway. Helplessly, I continued to sit, trying to avoid the faces of Reggie and Russell.

Finally I looked at Russell. He was staring at me with a victorious grin that ate at me like a cancer. I glanced at Reggie. He was sitting and looking at his shoes, saying nothing. Eddie jumped up and went into the house, the screen door slamming behind him.

With great effort I turned and whispered into Reggie's ear, "Mrs. Barnes doesn't want Robin to have a boyfriend, so she has to act real secretive about it."

"That is the way older people are, they are afraid of a little fun, so don't worry about it Bobby." Reggie whispered back.

"What are you guys talking about?" Russell asked in his whiney voice.

"Sh.h.h.h," hissed Reggie, he then put his mouth to Russell's ear and told him what we said.

Mrs. Barnes had gotten out of the car and went into the house with Robin, but now she went back and got into the car and was heading back down the driveway. Robin was staying by herself.

Suddenly I felt Russell's hot breath on my ear, "you lie," he whispered fiercely. "If she were my girlfriend I bet she would be nice to me in front of her mother."

"Fuck you!" I whispered back. "I live in a very religious family and besides the last time she got near you, you ran like a jackrabbit."

"That is because she is so ugly," he said menacingly, his voicing rising as his glaring face got into mine to breath hotly on my nose.

"She is not as ugly as you are, wimp!" I shouted back.

Russell made a fist and drew back to hit me but Reggie grabbed the drawn arm and held it. I stared at the drawn fist and then looked at Reggie.

"I'm sorry Reggie, but Russell is a troublemaker," I said.

"Yeah, Russell is too hot-headed," Reggie agreed.

After a while the three of us got up and went into the house to stand around and throw not so discreet glances at Robin as though looking for an answer.

As we were walking in Robin was giving Charlotte a kiss on the cheek, she then said, "Happy Birthday, Charlotte," she then turned and gave me a big smile.

I came to life and smiled back at her.

After that we all started eating our cake and ice cream.

Robin came over and poured me some Kool Aid. And then she kept looking at me and smiling. So I started smiling at her as well. I glanced at Russell, but he acted like he didn't notice and he started looking angry and sullen.

When I finished eating my cake and ice cream, I went out and sat on the porch to wait on the others to finish. As I sat, I began to wish more and more that Russell hadn't come. I began to worry that Russell was going to spoil my fun. He was a troublemaker.

"Don't worry Bobby," Reggie's voice startled me. I had not heard him come up behind me. "I believe you, about Robin being your girlfriend, but women are funny that way. women like to have fun too. But not as bad as guys . When they are in front of us, they pretend they are not interested. But sometimes I listen to them talk to each other when they don't know I'm listening, and guys are all they talk about."

"I know," I said.

The screen door slammed and Russell approached us. He was soon followed by Eddie and Jonathan. We then all stood around looking at each other while we waited on Charlotte and Robin.

Robin came out and looked directly at Reggie and gave him a big smile. This caused something in my heart to jump around painfully. Then Charlotte came out and also looked at Reggie and smiled.

As we started down the driveway, I noticed how sexy Robin's little green shorts were. Her white bottom seemed to escape in all directions from the edges as if there were no panties to control it. I hung back to watch it and listen to everyone else talking. Robin was trying to talk to Reggie, but Jonathan kept interrupting with a list of perfect hiding places in the woods. Eddie was running ahead. Then I noticed Russell trying to talk to Charlotte, but she was listening to what Reggie was saying to Robin and ignoring him.

"Who is going to be seeker, first?" Eddie asked, shouting over his shoulder.

Robin then turned and looked at me, the dark of her eyes steady upon me. Her soft eyes thrilled me and caused me to get hard in my pants.

"I'll be the seeker," Robin said, her lips parting into a seductive smile as her eyes continued to penetrate me.

My blood surged wildly from the thrill of it!

"Okay," I shouted, "Robin is the first seeker!"

A bright idea came to me then as we congregated at the edge of the woods. I would make sure Robin knew where I was going to hide.

"Come Robin," I shouted. "I'll show you the starting point where you are to close your eyes and count to ten."

The group followed me as I took them to a big tree beside the embankment, just above the den that used to be "Nepal." This place was my secret that no one else knew about.

When Robin closed her eyes and started counting, everyone scattered to find a hiding place except me. I waited a minute and then whispered to Robin to peak and watch where I hid. I again looked about to make sure everyone was out of sight. And then I saw movement in the woods and detected Russell, but he was running toward the driveway. Finally I decided it was safe and quickly slid down the embankment at Robin's feet. Lifting the dead branches, I squirmed into my den. I looked back up at Robin and at the soft leg that seemed to climb back up into her green shorts. Then the leg moved and she was looking furtively around her. The next thing I knew, she slid down the embankment, joining me on the soft cool Spanish moss.

She grabbed me, putting her lips against mine. We kissed with passionate gasps, not having time to stop and breathe. Then suddenly, she pushed me away.

"We must hurry," she said. "We can't leave the rest of them up there hiding for too long. Please, Bobby, pull my shorts off for me."

As they slid off, the blood ran hot in my cheeks. I could hardly contain my excitement as I reached frantically to feel the warm nakedness between her legs. She grabbed my finger and stuck it in, thrusting her body forward with rhythmic strokes. Then, just when she was getting really wet she screamed, her legs drawing tightly together, clasping my arm between them. She sat up and pointed. I looked up just in time to see Russell's face disappearing from the brush above us. Then we heard his voice shouting through the woods like a town crier.

"I saw Robin naked in the underbrush.….I saw Robin naked in the underbrush!"

We fled the long way out of "Nepal" on hands and knees. Robin crawled half the distance naked, getting soaked in the stream before she put on her dirty green shorts. We ran together to the edge of the woods. She wouldn't talk to me, and at the driveway, she just turned and ran toward the main road. I supposed that she run all the way home.

I wanted to kill Russell Duke and stood at the edge of the woods scheming about how I might do it. As I turned back toward the woods, I remembered my pocket knife and pulled it out and looked at it. I could stab him in the heart, I thought. Then another thought raced through my mind, like a nightmare in broad daylight. How would I be able to keep my mother and especially my dad from hearing about this? Then an even more terrible thought struck me. Would I ever see Robin again? If her parents found out, they might not let her come over anymore. I put my knife back in my pocket, my heart sinking with its burden of despair.

Suddenly I heard the voices of the kids in the woods behind me, coming toward me and panic seized me. I just couldn't face my brothers and sister. I turned to run, but then quickly realized I had to face them if I was to have any hope of keeping them quiet and not telling Mother.

When they walked out of the woods and stopped to look at me their faces were long with mock solemnity. Jonathan was picking at his nose and looking at my feet. Eddie was contemplating my stomach. Charlotte was looking back at me with a steady, serious gaze that made me look down at my feet in disgrace. Russell's face was insolent, mean-looking but silent. Reggie looked angry but was staring at Russell.

"Please don't tell Mother, Charlotte," I whispered pitifully as I lifted my eyes to look into hers.

"I won't, Bobby," she promised.

Eddie and Jonathan were not so easy. I begged them, with a flaming red face not to tell Mother. Eddie finally looked at me with a face that beamed with importance and demanded to know what had went on down there in the bushes.

I told him, "Nothing, except that Robin had had to go to the bathroom and couldn't wait to go to the house."

"That's not what I saw," Russell shouted .

"Shut up, stupid," Reggie said, turning on him. "I think you are lying to get Bobby in trouble. You are simply a troublemaker."

"No I ain't," he said, hotly.

"Don't listen to Russell, kids," Reggie said confidentially. "He lies and besides older folks don't understand stuff like this."

"You promise, she just went to the bathroom?" Eddie asked in a dubious voice.

"I swear," I said hopefully.

They finally all agreed not to breathe a word to anyone after Reggie promised them some candy that he had in his dad's car that he would give them when his dad returned to pick them up.

We then all walked in silence up the long driveway to the house. But I hung back, reluctant, listening to my feet drag in the dirty sand. Reggie and Russell walked to one side, looking at their feet as well.. When we got to the porch, Reggie and Russell sat on the steps and waited for Reggie's dad while I followed my brothers and sister in where they stood around eying each other and our mother who sat on the couch reading her bible.

"Okay," Mother said, "what is it? Where is Robin and your two friends, Bobby?"

"They are on the front porch," I said.

"Robin isn't," Jonathan blurted out, eying me apologetically.

"Where is Robin?" Mother asked looking at Jonathan.

"She ran home." Eddie answered, refusing to look at my intense stare upon him.

"What do you mean, she ran home?" Mother's voice was now rising in alarm.

"It's not that far," I said in a pitiful voice of defeat but hoping against hope to avoid the inevitable.

"I want to know what happened! Mrs. Barnes was going to come back and pick her up."

Silence followed as all eyes turned on me.

"Russell caught….." Jonathan had started to say.

"Shut up!" I shouted, "it's a lie!"

I ran out of the house past Reggie and Russell, down the driveway to the woods. I sat where I could watch the driveway without being seen behind a big cypress tree. I waited there in pure torture, knowing that they were telling everything.

Then out of the woods Joe came to sit beside me. He lay his head on my lap and looked up at me like he understood everything. I was pretty sure Joe had lots of girlfriends all around the countryside. And I told him there was nothing wrong with it.

I saw Reggie's father come and go. I saw my own dad come home, driving slowly by with white paint on his face. He was painting one of the Duke sheds white. Finally starved for dinner, I slowly walked back to the porch. On the porch, I stood and stared at the warm light coming dimly from the kitchen through the old screen door. Then with a determined step, I walked through it to the kitchen table where I sat without looking at anyone. I just looked at the food and ate it.

Late that evening before bed, my dad asked me to come to the porch with him. On the porch, Dad sat on the steps and stared at the stars for awhile. I knew that Eddie and Jonathan were evesdropping somewhere but couldn't see them through the darkness.

"What happened today," my father asked soberly, like a judge.

"Nothing," I said. "Robin and I were hiding together, and she had to go to the bathroom, that's all."

And then he started staring at the stars again. When he spoke again he told me that 'he understood the power of the attraction of sexual desire on young people, but', he continued, "you must maintain strict control of these desires, because they can lead you into great evil"..

"Oh, I will!" I responded with great enthusiasm. I couldn't believe I was getting off so easy. But I knew that I would never associate with Russell again!

# THE CHICKEN
# LIVERED COWARD

ROBIN STOPPED COMING to Annie Smith's for church and I was looking forward with great anticipation to seeing her in school again. I had ridden my bike up the hot sand road in the summer dawn with the blazing sun already shining across the treetops down on me.

Hot and wet with perspiration, I had parked my bike then waited and watched.

Then I saw her. She was coming toward me, her head was down, looking to the ground as though she was in a daydream.

"Hi Robin," I said in a cheerful voice then started moving toward her.

Her head jerked up but that was the only sign of recognition as she walked coldly past me.

I was devastated, embarrassed. I could have melted into the earth as I looked quickly about to see if anyone else had noticed. The first person I saw was Russell Duke. He was jerking his head to one side as though he didn't want me to know that he had witnessed the whole thing. I had hated him so much that I thought I was going to throw up on the hard sidewalk beneath my feet. So my worst fears had been realized, I thought with a sigh. She was too ashamed to speak to me anymore.

. Ice needles of pain would stab my heart when I would hear her distant laugh from my observation point by the swamp. Then one day I caught her kissing Albert Rotterbaum behind some trees not ten yards from me. I knew then that she was not my girlfriend any longer. The heat waves danced deceitfully in front of my squinting eyes when I tried to watch the kids play softball on the distant ball field.

Reggie would still say hi to me, but he wouldn't come over and talk to me by the swamp like he had done in former years. I knew that this was Russell's fault. "His day was coming," I would tell myself, it was just a matter of time. Anyway who needs friends, I had thought to myself. They are a pain in the butt…that was what Reggie had always said about old people .

It was early November when my chance to even the score with Russell came.

The Saturday before it happened, Robin had come back to Annie Smith's house for church. She had on a long face and a pout around her lips. After watching her awhile, I decided that her mother must be worried about her soul again otherwise she wouldn't be there. She was there when I had arrived, and I could not resist the old thrill of having her near me outside of school.

I tried to catch her eye, but she would just look at the ceiling as though something of interest was hanging there. I followed her gaze but this irritated her even more so she started staring at the floor. I had to sit in front of her so was unable to watch her while the singing and the preaching was going on. I turned around a couple of times to look at her, but she would just stare real hard at me until it hurt my feelings, so I quit doing it.

I was so restless that I started concentrating on Agnes Everbe's ugly nose while she led the singing. I daydreamed after that about a trip to China. While my father preached on how one could determine God's will, I was trying to figure out how I could get enough money to go to China.

And then everyone turned and knelt for prayer. I was still thinking about China until I suddenly noticed Robin kneeling for prayer behind me. She bent over and her short dress had climbed up above her underpants. They were white and real silky and looked really good with the white skin of her bottom hanging out. Suddenly she turned and looked at me, catching me in the act of looking at it. My face became hot like fire, but I kept on staring, refusing to be intimidated. I noticed that the pout around her lips had softened some. She scratched her bottom, her fingers slipping beneath the panties so that she could scratch all of it. But then she turned around and continued to pray.

Agnes Everbe started to scream. God's wrath sounded like it was flowing through her, almost like she was describing hell in other tongues.

So I started to pray as I continued to concentrate on Robin's panties and finally got to feeling so good that I thought for a minute that I was going to start shouting like a Christian full of the Holy Ghost but I didn't.

When I heard my father say amen, I quickly jumped up and looked to see what Robin was going to do. Our eyes met. I turned and went out the door and over to the knarled old roots of the shady cypress tree and sat to watch the screen door, hoping that Robin would follow.

My heart jumped three times only to flutter in disappointment when other people came out, but the fourth time it flew open it was Robin. She came running as she looked several times over her shoulder.

"Let's go to the other side of the tree," she said, "so we can't be seen. Mama doesn't trust me anymore."

She sat on a big root. Her panties were right in front of me then but I tried really hard to look at her face anyway.

"You know Bobby," she said in a hurt voice, "Russell Duke really insulted me that day at your place. I was willing to forget it at first but not now. He has been real mean to me at school the other day, Bobby, when you were sitting over by the swamp," she then cocked her head coquettishly, as I looked into the hurt that shined out of her dark eyes.

A surge of anger started climbing out of my gut.

"I'll kill that bastard yet," I said. I felt good after saying this and confident, like I could beat up anybody. "What did he do to you, Robin?" I had asked boldly. I put my hand on her soft white leg, and she let it rest there.

"I was with some other girls on the other side of the schoolhouse when Russell and Reggie came up."

She looked at me again with hurt beaming from her soft brown eyes. I couldn't face their intensity and looked down at my hand resting there on her leg and then at the knarled root that twined along beneath the white skin of her almost bare bottom.

"Russell said 'will you fuck me, Robin?' right in front of everybody. He then started to giggle like a jerk and looked back at Reggie. Reggie just grinned. So I said to my friends, 'let's go somewhere else and get away from these rude guys.' But as we walked away, Russell shouted that you had told him that you had fucked me, Bobby."

"I told him no such thing, that son of a bitch!" I nearly shouted, breathless in my anger and embarrassment.

"Sh......h....h, don't talk so loudly, I know you didn't."

"Of course not," I interrupted again, "he just saw us in Nepal....
uh......the bushes and thought we did."

"I think Russell Duke should be punished," she said, flashing
seductive pain from her dark eyes. "After all, I don't want a coward
for a boyfriend." Her voice had become soft and low, like a whispering
promise.

"I'll kill him!" I shouted.

"Robin!" it was a high pitched voice coming from behind Annie
Smith's screen door.

Robin's dark eyes flashed at me once more with the heat of her
passion, then she was gone.

I waited, hidden by the cypress tree, and gloried in my newfound
excitement. Robin was my girlfriend again and that made me strong.
I was going to beat Russell Duke to a pulp! Robin would be proud of
me, kiss me in public and would fuck me anytime I wanted out in the
woods somewhere.

I couldn't understand Reggie, though, why would he let Russell do
such a thing? Maybe he wasn't my friend anymore. Fuck him, I thought,
who needs a friend with Robin as my girlfriend?

I spent the rest of the weekend building up my courage and
determination. I worked out several plans on how I might confront
Russell.

At first I had simply planned to get him when we both went out to
get our bikes from the bike rack after school. But with so much time
to think about it, I devised a more dramatic way of confronting him. I
would humiliate him in front of the whole class.

Every morning after all we students had taken our seats, Mr. Eustis,
one of our twelfth grade teachers that year, would ask, "does anyone
have any questions or comments before we begin class?"

He would always ask this, even though almost never did anyone
have anything to say. He would look around, above his glasses hanging
low on his nose, "no, then let's begin," he would say.

I decided I was going to raise my hand on Monday. I could just see
Mr. Eustis saying, "yes Bobby?". I was going to stand, stare right into
Russell's eyes and say, "Russell Duke is a wimp and a coward; he is
afraid of girls but he is always jealous of everyone else's girlfriends and
is rude and nasty to them."

At the same time, I was going to try and get a glimpse of Robin from the corner of my eye. I was sure she would be looking at me and smiling proudly.

Russell would probably just sit and look at his feet, saying nothing. He would be afraid to leave the classroom during the break or during lunch for fear that everyone would laugh at him. I probably wouldn't even have to fight him. I would just grin and look straight ahead when I walked by him.

While I was making my public announcement, Reggie would probably motion at me, desperately trying to get me to shut up, but I would just ignore him, and if he said anything to me, I would simply tell him that he should have controlled Russell when he was talking nasty to Robin. After that the two of them would probably sit around whispering and looking in my direction. After school I would stare boldly at their dirty looks and say, "fuck you both," then walk over to where Robin would be waiting for me. She would give me a big kiss, while the other girls stopped and watched. Then we would walk hand in hand toward the bicycle rack.

Monday morning I left for school with a lofty purpose. I felt like a knight and professional boxer wrapped into one. I was the first to take my seat in the classroom and was able to watch as the others filed in. When I saw Russell, I was shocked at his size. He seemed so much bigger than I had remembered him and Reggie, beside him, looked so confident.

Suddenly I felt fear, like it had sneaked in to erode my confidence. I shook my head and tried to stare down Russell's bold glance in my direction. Then the two of them started chatting like I wasn't worth a second look.

A battle began within me then, between my fear and my anger. At first I bolstered my anger, cheering it on. But then I noticed Mr. Eustis had taken his seat and was staring over the rims of his glasses at me like an evil judge. Those staring eyes sort of took the wind out of me. I could see, as I sank almost into a panic, that fear was gaining the upper hand.

I looked back at the door in time to see Robin enter. She was all smiles and chatting rapidly with Albert Rotterbaum. The two of them took their seats side by side without so much as a glance in my direction.

"Does anyone have any questions or comments before we begin?"

My courage evaporated completely. Empty of all but my helplessness, I looked up at Mr. Eustis. He was looking directly back at me as though it was just me he was talking to.

"No," I replied, shaking my head.

"Then let us begin," he said, getting out from behind his desk and going to the blackboard.

My self-esteem was gone. I was the wimp and the coward.

During the lunch break, I walked back down to again sit on the old fence, my lunch untouched, and stared again at the tepid, stale water that stood at the edge of the swamp. The humming mosquitoes floated in the heat above it. The tall trees made the shade look like the dark heat that made me sweat. And the red ants climbed the fence post to get me. Suddenly Robbins voice penetrated my misery.

"What's the matter, Bobby?" she asked, in a sympathetic voice that stung like rubbed salt on raw flesh. "Are you afraid of Russell? If you are, I don't blame you. After all he is bigger than you."

"Of course not!" I said, turning on her almost violently and nearly falling off my perch.

It dawned on me, at the same time that no one knew of my cowardly defeat except me.

"I just haven't had a chance yet, but I'll get him before the day is out."

The anger surged, rebuilding my self-confidence. My fear seemed to have fled into the stale heat of the swamp.

Robin looked at me, her gaze, steady. She could see right through me, and I was hoping she could see my newfound resolution. I knew then that I had to confront Russell, or Robin would never speak to me again.

"Good," she said, "will you fight him after school this afternoon?"

"Yes," I said, my heart sinking with the finality of it. But I was resolved even if it meant I had to take a beating.

"Great!" she said. "That big overgrown wimp needs the shit beat out of him, and I think you can probably do it, Bobby. You are stronger than you think. I ought to know," she said, raising her voice slightly and throwing me an encouraging wink.

I looked defiantly back toward where the boys were playing softball. "I'll do it by the bicycle rack," I said.

"Oh boy," she gloated as she bent over and gave me a kiss on the cheek. "I'll tell my friends."

She then turned and ran back across to the high school grounds.

Back in class I was miserable as I watched Russell take his seat. I noticed Robin chatting excitedly with Albert. She was probably telling him what I was going to do. I couldn't get mad at him, though, he was even bigger than Russell.

I picked up my heavy feet to take one tortured step at a time as I followed Reggie and Russell from the classroom with a sinking heart. The school day was over. In the western sky, the sun was hanging hot and the damp heat flowed down my forehead. I slowed down to watch them unlock their bikes. They just continued to talk, ignoring me as I approached them. Through the corner of my eye, I noticed that Robin and Albert stopped to watch me. I quickened my pace and walked up behind Russell to stand, speechless. I did open my mouth to speak, but there was no sound coming out. I felt the stares of Robin and Albert on my back and figured they were probably laughing by now.

Suddenly Russell had turned and looked me.

"What do you want, asshole?" His voice was full of contempt, and he almost ran me down with his bike as he backed it out of the rack.

It was then that I felt it coming out of my throat like a gust of wind.

"You are the asshole and the coward Russell Duke!" Hearing myself say this gave me courage and a second wind.

"What ....did you call me?" Russell screamed, caught off guard. His face turned livid and his bicycle fell to the ground. He nearly fell over it as he started moving toward me. "Son of a bitch!" he swore.

I stood there silent, my mouth and fist clenched tightly as I prepared for the beating I thought was coming. But then Reggie was between us.

"Don't hit him Russell, he is smaller than you."

Then Reggie started pushing Russell back toward the bicycles.

"But he called me an asshole and a coward!" Russell whimpered.

"He is just jealous," Reggie said as he gave me a dirty look.

It was Reggie's dirty look that had enraged me then.

"You called me one first but now I think both of you are assholes!" I had shouted at their backs.

Russell almost wrecked his bike as he tried to look back at me over his shoulder, but they continued to pedal off towards the street. But I noticed Robin and Albert still standing and watching and knew that I had to act quickly.

"You are both cowards!" I screamed, "and Russell is a wimp who is afraid of girls!"

Russell stopped on the street, but Reggie had kept riding.

"Come on Russell," Reggie had shouted.

Russell dutifully got on his bike and started to ride in an effort to catch up with Reggie. Meanwhile I started racing toward him as fast as I could pedal. I caught up with him near the filling station on the highway. I ran my bike into his, knocking him over.

"I tried to save you!" shouted Reggie as he stopped near a gas pump at the filling station.

Russell came at me like a Mac truck. I didn't get a chance to hit him, but he hit me so hard that I saw stars that weren't even there. I fell, grabbing my nose where he had hit me. It was wet and I figured it was blood coming out. I became even more angry, but when I tried to get to my feet, I saw two of him coming at me again. In my desperation, I grabbed a small rock that was lying by the side of the street. I threw it at him just as he lunged toward me. It hit him hard in the jaw and he fell, screaming bloody murder on the street.

"Why, you chicken-livered coward," Reggie screamed over by the gas pump. "I'll get you for this!" he yelled as he started running towards us.

I raced past him on my bike as he arrived and dropped to his knees to bend over Russell. Reggie flashed me the finger as I looked back at them, but I just kept on riding out towards my house in the woods.

As I rode, I wondered how much Robin had seen. Maybe she would think it was my fist that hit him and be proud of me. But I also hoped that Russell wouldn't die. He didn't deserve that.

On the driveway by the woods, I stopped and ran into the woods to the stream that ran through old "Nepal" and washed the blood from my nose so my mother wouldn't know. But she could tell anyway.

"Did you get into a fight, Bobby?!" she asked.

"No," I replied. "I fell off my bike and hit my nose on a rock."

"You have got to be more careful," she said as she turned back to reading her bible.

The feud between Russell and I continued through the rest of the year. And Reggie turned against me too. But nothing ever came of it because we did all our shouting at a distance and did our dirty looking in the classroom. Besides something else was about to happen that would make our little squabble look like a love affair.

Furthermore my reason for fighting Russell in the first place seemed to evaporate. Robin never once mentioned the fight to me, and she started to ignore me again at school. She and Albert would talk and laugh together as though they were discussing a secret that they held between them. I figured they probably knew what I had done and thought that I was a coward as well.

Robin did start coming again to Annie Smith's for church, but she would ignore me there as well. And she also started wearing long dresses that covered up her underpants so that there was nothing to get excited about when I prayed. So when she again stopped coming, I got so I didn't care anymore.

At school I started avoiding everyone as much as possible. I just didn't care who knew that I was a coward. After school I would wait on the others to get their bikes before I would go out to the bike rack to get mine and ride home. But if it hadn't of been for this habit, I would have missed witnessing the horrible thing that happened on that chilly mid-January afternoon up at the filling station on the highway.

# HORROR AT THE
# FILLING STATION

I HAD NOT seen much of the Gatlins since my dad had had a talk with Melba Gatlin years before. My brothers and I had sometimes spied on their activities from thickets near the edge of their clearing. But mostly all we would see was either Mrs. Gatlin or one of the boys doing routine chores around the yard. One time we did hear a really loud fight going on between Studs and Jack while their mother was screaming at them, pleading with them to stop. "You are two brothers," she screamed helplessly.

"Fuck you and Jack both," Studs roared back.

Then the screen door flew open, to expose Studs' ugly, mean and red face. And to our shock, he stared right at our faces as we watched him from the thicket. So we turned and ran back through the woods as fast as we could run and heard no more.

Rumor had it that Studs flunked out of high school or had been kicked out several years before because he was so mean. No one seemed to know which for sure. And everyone talked about how he picked on his brother Jack.

But then suddenly Jack had gotten almost as big as Studs. I had seen them walking together after school one evening, and I could hardly tell the difference from a distance.

I was alone that evening, as I rode my bike out onto First Street and up toward the highway. The wind blew chilly across the high school grounds and into my face. My lips were chapped and dry, and I licked them to make them wet, but I was then distracted by shouting voices that were carried to me on the cold wind.

"Fuck no, ya ain't getting my car and ya just might as well shet up, cause ya ain't talking me into it!"

"I'll beat the mother fuckin shit out of ya, ya little wimp, you're probably trying to date my chick anyway!" came the reply like the bellow from an angry bull.

"Go ahead and try, low life, I'm most as big as you are now," the first voice responded in a frenzy.

I saw them then, as they came out into the street ahead of me. It was the Gatlin brothers, and I was afraid to go any nearer to them, with them a hating each other like that.

Studs' voice turned into a hiss. I couldn't hear what he was saying, but his white teeth glared cruelly from his ruddy red and angry face. It looked like the face of a pirate. As I watched it, adrenalin pumped fear into my gut. I wanted to run, but I didn't want to attract Studs' attention because to get home I had run right by them. So I was still like a mouse, silent like a stone, as the drama unfolded itself before me.

Studs shoved Jack; Jack shoved Studs. It quickly became a shuffle. Studs fell, Jack gave him a hard kick in the ribs.

"Take that, motherfucker!" Jack yelled. His voice made me shiver and made the wind feel colder.

Jack then turned and walked back toward the filling station. Studs lay breathless in the street but not for long. As I watched, almost breathless myself, I noticed that one of his bloodshot eyes had started to focus on me. My fear began to turn to terror and my state of being to one of paralysis. He lifted himself to his elbow, his face contorted and purple with rage. He was still gasping for air, but he was jabbing his fuck finger at me. I wanted desperately to run, but my shoes stood on the pavement like there was glue stuck to the bottom of them. Then Studs, with great effort, got to his big feet and started walking toward me. His shoulders were hunkered, his head lowered. His dull eyes pulsated with hatred. His mouth was open in his purple face and his tongue twisted wildly as though trying to talk. The brute was moving closer. But then suddenly he stopped.

"I raped your sister," he croaked and a horrendous laugh escaped through his lips. I could almost smell the evil on his breath from where I stood glued to the pavement. "Do you want to do something about it?" He was hissing and it was deadly.

I could do nothing but to continue to stare at the violently distorted face on this creature. He started toward me again. He was going to kill me, I thought, if someone didn't stop him.

"So the mother fucking lowlife bully is at it again, huh?"

Jack stopped at the filling station and was watching us. Studs stopped and slowly turned as though suddenly remembering the real object of his anger. Jack saved my life, I thought.

"Ya couldn't whip me so ya had to go find sompin littler to whip, huh?" Jack goaded.

Studs' body grew taut and he shuffled like a sick cat, determined to get its prey, toward Jack.

"I'll kill you," he hissed.

He pulled a knife from his pocket and opened it.

"So you're going to play dirty, huh?" Jack said cool-like as he picked up a tire iron from the grease covered floor of the garage.

They moved slowly toward each other. I moved a little closer in morbid fascination.

Jack started swinging the tire iron and hit Studs' hand knocking the knife from it. Studs didn't move or cry out. He just glared and held his hurt hand.

"Now are you ready to fight like a man?" Jack asked, as he put the tire iron to one side.

Studs continued to glare and say nothing, and they stood that way facing each other for what seemed like forever. Jack's lips were twisted into a snarling grin as he stared down his bully brother. But then he turned and walked toward his car that was sitting beside the gas pump. Studs came to life, springing like a cat and grabbed the tire iron. Without any warning, he gave Jack a terrible blow to the back of the head. Jack fell forward hitting his forehead on the pump glass and breaking it. Studs ran to him and took the car keys from his pocket. He ran around and got into the car.

I suddenly became aware of my own danger. I dropped my bike by the side of the road and ran for my life. But Studs wasn't interested in me. He hit the highway going north, in a storm of screaming, burning rubber.

I moved up the street a bit to watch Jack lying there in a pool of blood. The filling station attendant had come out to stand over him and look frantically about. I hunkered low so he wouldn't see me.

Then a car pulled in for gas. The driver got out of his car to lean on his hood and stare at Jack lying there in his blood.

"Oh, thank goodness," cried the attendant, throwing his hands in the air while looking at the stranger, there leaning on the hood. "Can you help this man?"

The attendant's face was white like a washed sheet but perspiration was running down it and he began to tremble violently as he walked back and forth stumbling over things.

Some chattering school boys came walking up but became deathly silent as they stood and stared at Jack lying there.

I heard the distant wail of a siren.

The stranger, still leaning against the hood of his car, lit a cigarette and continued to stare at Jack. Finally the attendant ran up to the stranger and gurgled, like he was trying to swallow his adams apple.

"For Christ's sake man, don't just stand there, do something! That bastard just murdered him in cold blood! I saw it, saw it with my own eyes!" His voice grew loud and hysterical.

"What do you want me to do?" the stranger asked in a calm cool voice, blowing cigarette smoke into the face of the attendant.

"My God, I don't know!" cried the attendant.

The staring boys got closer.

The wailing sirens soon turned into the revolving red lights of a speeding highway police car. It pulled into the station and a big cop got out slowly and looked at the stranger staring at Jack in his blood.

The attendant ran to him, throwing his hands about wildly and shouting incoherently. The big cop pulled a radio phone through the window and talked into it, ignoring the attendant. The cop then turned and gave the school boys a cold piercing stare. They began to cringe and melt into the background across the highway.

He walked nonchalantly toward Jack lying in his pool of blood. He knelt and felt for a pulse then shook his head and stood, to turn his bold gaze back on the stranger, who was now crushing his cigarette with the heel of his shoe.

"Dead," the cop said with finality. "Did you see what happened?"

"No," was the cool response of the stranger as he boldly returned the cops stare.

The cops eyes grew hostile as he attempted to stare down the gray eyes of the stranger.

"I just stopped for gas and this is what I saw." said the stranger with a voice like grating ice.

The attendant, who had been clutching at the empty air, could contain himself no longer. He began clawing at the cop like a cornered cat. His voice shot from him like the voice of an idiot.

"I saw everything," he screamed but then it was like his tongue got twisted around a marble. "ut…ut..wa..was tur..tur…rible." His head dropped and he began to pant, his white face streaked with blue marks.

The cop freed himself from the grasping attendant. "If you don't get a hold of yourself, I'll have to put these handcuffs on you," he said scornfully.

"Now you wouldn't do no such thing," drawled the stranger coolly. "the poor jerk hasn't done nothing 'cept lose his cool."

The cop's body grew taut and his head riveted toward the stranger like the head on a puppet. His face started to look real mean, and he started to walk towards the stranger. But then he was distracted again by the attendant.

"This…is….is," then his tongue seemed to come free, "is what he did it with," he said, while holding the tire iron above his head.

"Put that down!" yelled the cop, his voice leaping out of his mouth like spiteful spit. "You are destroying evidence!"

The attendant dropped it like a hot potato, then stood whimpering as he did a slow dance in a circle, like he was trying to keep from pissing in his pants.

The wail of many sirens came through the pale and premature twilight of the cool winter afternoon. Crowds began to gather. They stood in small bunches, whispering while they stood and looked at Jack in his pool of blood. Two more cop cars pulled up. Then an ambulance pulled in beside Jack, its siren wailing eerily. Two paramedics jumped out and rushed to Jacks side and bent over him. And then they shook their heads like the cop before them had. But they brought the stretcher anyway and put him on it, putting a pillow beneath his bloody head.

"I could have told you as much," said the cop, as he threw another threatening glance at the stranger.

Another cop walked up and began to speak to the first one, and while they were talking, the stranger quietly got into his car and drove away without ever having bought any gas.

The cops then started spreading out as though they were looking for something. They were coming in my direction so I ran back to my bike on the street. I got on it and stood with one foot in the dirt while I agonized over whether I should ride through all those cops and staring people. I finally took a deep breath and held it while I raced through all the commotion. To my surprise, no one seemed to notice the boy racing through on the bike, and I continued to race toward home.

Just before I got to my road going east, a highway cop car passed me, his siren was wailing and his revolving light was an eerie red in the growing dusk. He was going south at a high speed. He is probably looking for Studs, I thought. But Studs went the other way.

I told no one about what I had seen. I didn't want to take a chance on having Studs come looking for me. It was a good thing that I didn't too because at his trial two months later in Tallahassee, it was decided that he was crazy. So they sent him to an insane asylum instead of jail. Then the following summer, he was released because they said he got his sanity back. But I was afraid, anyway, that he might go crazy again and come after me.

When my dad heard about Studs, he just shook his head and said, "Now she has lost both of her sons because she wouldn't listen to me and rebelled against God. I warned her that she was inviting tragedy." As he said this, he stood on the gray porch and stared at the path that led into the woods between the Gatlin's place and ours.

I always wondered what it was that she wouldn't listen to but he never told me.

Mother said, " I feel sorry for Melba," but said no more.

At school no one talked about anything else. They talked out loud about it outside and in whispers in the classroom. There were nearly as many versions of the story as there were students. One story that was propagated by Russell Duke, had it that Studs had cut out Jacks heart with his hunting knife and had stomped it into the pavement with his big boot.

I gloried silently in my superior knowledge, knowing that I was one of only two witnesses. I did kind of wish that Reggie was still my friend so that I could tell him, but as it was he did not deserve to share my secret. I also longed to tell Robin, but she never gave me a chance. She was always hanging out with Albert Rotterbaum.

# DEATH BY FIRE

So the months of winter slipped into spring, and beneath the hot sun, the talk turned to more pleasant things. Gradually everyone forgot about the Gatlins. My aloof self-importance began to melt in the heat of the coming summer, leaving me with nothing but a lonely image of myself, separated from the many voices of happiness. The voices chatting with loud exuberant joy across the schoolground, joy that competed with the singing birds in the swamp. Sitting on my perch, out by the stale pool where the insects played, I listened to both of them. Silently I tried to remember Robin in the blackberry patch and her white bottom when she scratched it while praying at Annie Smith's.

But this also was soon to come to an end because in April my father pulled me out of school, preventing me from graduating with my high school class.

It was in late May that another tragedy hit the Gatlins, and I was, again, there to witness it. This tragedy was so horrible that I completely forgot about myself for awhile. I even told Robin about what I had seen this time.

A very strange thing happened to me that sultry, warm and sticky dawn in late May. I awoke in a sweat and threw back the sheet I had wrapped around me. I felt that something had awakened me so I laid there listening to the silence, wondering what it could have been. And then I heard it. It sounded like bells tinkling in a distance. I looked around my room at the familiar objects that now looked strange and indistinct in the half darkness of my bedroom. Eddie and Jonathan laid on their mattresses sound asleep. They apparently heard nothing. I continued to listen intently, but the sound faded again. I began to relax and drift back towards my slumber. I must have dreamed it, I thought drowsily. But then I heard it again, distinctly and sat bolt upright in my bed. It sounded like an ice cream truck. But that couldn't be out here in the woods in the half darkness before dawn!

I carefully got up and dressed, careful not to wake my brothers.

The bells faded as though moving away but then increased in intensity like they had turned around and were coming back. I thought about Charlotte's jewelry box where she kept the small trinkets that she had saved. I tiptoed down to her bedroom and found her door open but immediately knew the sound was not coming from there. It was coming from outside, probably over on the highway that went by the Gatlin place.

I quietly made my way out to the dark porch. Joe's tail thumped the gray porch boards in greeting. But it was a slow thump, and I noticed that he too was staring off toward the dark woods that lie between us and the Gatlin house. The musical bells were fading again, but they definitely were coming from over there.

An irresistible urge began to come over me from the dark woods to go look and see what it was that was making such noises in the darkness of an early dawn. So I followed it along the path that wound its way among the dark trees. Joe stayed near my feet, sniffing the ground loudly, his step cautious as though afraid of the smell that touched his black nose. A touch of foreboding came with a sudden breeze that shook the leaves in the dark trees above. But I continued to follow the urge that pulled me, like one tempted by fate into an abyss.

I stumbled on a root that had sprung up on the dark path in front of me, causing me to step on Joe's toes. A short yelp escaped him. We both stopped. The breeze died as suddenly as it came, and we felt bathed in the ominous and heavy silence that surrounded us. Joe let out a short whimper which sank into a low and steady growl, and I could feel him looking up at me through the darkness as if to say "Bobby, what am I supposed to do?"

This is stupid, I thought to myself. Though the bell was strange, surely there was nothing to worry about. But then I shivered as a bolt of fear raced up my spine. I decided it was best just to go home, and I was torn between running for the safety of my bedroom and following the urge that pulled me on. I glanced over my shoulder to be reassured by the deepening pink as it boldly outlined the dark trees that were behind me in the woods. It is almost light, I thought, and this gave me the courage I needed to go on toward the Gatlin place.

Stealthily we had moved forward, Joe's hot breath on my leg, until we could see the Gatlin yard spread out before us silent in the half dawn. A dry twig cracked. I froze in my tracks with terror racing up and down my spine. It had come from somewhere off to my left. Joe forgot his fear and took off barking at the top of his lungs. I guess the noise had given him courage. I stood paralyzed in my tracks and listened to the underbrush popping beneath fleeing feet.

"Oh Joe!" I whispered, fearing for his life.

I saw it then, the fleeing figure and Joe was right behind it lunging at its legs.

Suddenly it occurred to me that the fleeing figure might be Studs out to get me. Terror gripped me. I wanted to run but now I couldn't leave Joe. And then Joe cried out in pain. When I heard Joe, my terror had turned to anger and surged like a shot of adrenalin through my body. I turned and ripped a tree branch from a dead tree and stepped boldly into the clearing. The bastard had hurt Joe, and I was ready to kill him!

But then I saw Joe's dark, silent form racing towards me across the Gatlin yard. When he got to me, he practically leaped into my arms, nearly dragging me to my knees. His kisses were slobbers of pain. He had sighed deeply and through a hurt look back over his shoulder towards Studs, somewhere over on the dark road.

We had turned to go back through the woods when I caught a whiff of the pungent smell of smoke. Faintly at first, but then a stronger whiff hit me. Yes! It was coming from the Gatlin house! Joe and I were standing at the edge of the woods looking back. A sliver of pink had started climbing a corner of the white house, and in the pink light, I saw gray smoke coming from around the Gatlin's back door. I stared at it unable to believe my eyes.

The Gatlin house must be on fire! I just kept standing there unable to move, wondering what I was supposed to do while the smoke got thicker. Then I heard the popping of breaking glass and before I knew it, the house was burning out of control. And I just kept standing there as my curiosity turned into horror. I must do something to save their lives, I thought, but continued to do nothing but stare, hypnotized by the leaping crackling flames. The plate glass window blew, with an earsplitting crash, into a million splinters.

She came, then, running from the house like a ghost in pajamas, her face an eerie white, contorted in horror and lit by the leaping flames.

"Help me, please help me!" She cried, her voice coming in gasps of panic, thrown with helpless random up at the pink of a new day that was spreading across the sky. "Helllllp me!" she cried again, "he is still in there!"

She fell, then, groveling in the dirt beneath her maker, somewhere up there beyond the pink sky.

I wanted to help her, but I was overcome with fear. besides what was I supposed to do? Then it was like the voice of God that said it, "get your father." I got a hold of myself and was about to turn again and run home through the woods when I saw something so horrible that my legs dropped out from under me, and I fell to the ground with Joe there kissing my face.

It was a surreal dance of death and took the wind from me. My weak body was shaking from the horror of it. It was the flaming dance of a demon, and it came running from the house. It was silent like an apparition out of hell. It danced to a beat that I could not hear. It ran and leaped, twisting, in a ballet of terror. It came towards me then, as though it had a purpose, as though it thought I was its savior. I heard a scream escape from my mouth as though someone else had done it. But it stopped again, then twisted. And then I heard it. It was uttering a scream that was horrendous, all enveloping; a scream that floated like Devil music to climb up into the pink dawn.

I tried to get up on my feet, but they were like jelly. I gagged, the vomit shooting from me to splatter on the dark earth beside me. I could not move then. I was paralyzed by the scene I was watching.

And then the bloodcurdling scream was cut off as the hot leaping flames devoured it. But the flailing arms and clutching fingers were still grasping as though desperate for something beyond them, as though reaching for life that was somewhere out there beyond the pink heavens. The ball of flames then crumbled and stretched, for one last effort, for what, I could not tell. I knew then that it was Mr. Gatlin, wrapped in flames dying on the ground. And then I felt the heat from him like I was on fire as well.

I looked back at Mrs. Gatlin. She was on her knees, her mouth open like a scream was frozen in her throat and her unblinking eyes were staring at her burning husband.

Suddenly I came to life and regained my strength. I ran like a bat out of hell through the increasing light of the darkened woods to get my dad.

God sure got even with Mr. Gatlin, and I shivered at the thought of it!

# THE FUNERAL

THE BIRDS WERE chirping and squawking wildly in the trees above, and the sun was already hot in the late morning.

An urn rested on a table, standing on the spread out green of Annie Smith's yard.

I sat on the root beneath the old tree that Robin and I had sat on when we talked. I now watched the people talk at each other in low monotones.

School was out now, and it was the beginning of the long empty summer. And it was the day of Mr. Gatlin's funeral.

Everyone was sitting or standing around, waiting on the law to bring Studs Gatlin to the funeral.

Melba Gatlin didn't talk. She just sat over by herself and stared at the urn as though puzzled and uncertain what it was. My dad sat her on the chair that Annie Smith had brought from the house. Everyone else threw her sympathetic glances but stayed clear.

My dad said, "Melba completely lost her mind and that Satan had taken over."

An attendant brought her out from the hospital in big black car that followed the hearse. He now sat on the hood of the car, smoking a cigarette, as he waited down by the end of the driveway.

Then a police car came and slowly pulled up to the house. Two cops got out and opened the backdoor and helped Studs out and led him, handcuffed, to the chair that Annie Smith had hastily brought out and placed beside his mother. The cops took his handcuffs off and then went back to sit in their car and watch him somberly.

I wasn't afraid of Studs then. He didn't even look in my direction. He mostly kept looking at his father's urn but kept throwing quick glances at his mother. Finally he hung his head and began to cry. I knew because I could see the tears flowing down his cheeks. And then he sobbed out loud, and I started to feel real sorry for him.

Finally he turned and looked with steady eyes at his mother.

"Did he go to hell, Momma," he asked in a pitiful voice.

Slowly the poor woman seemed to come to her senses when she heard her son speak.

"No" she said, "he repented while he was a burnin."

"Are you sure, Momma?" I heard Studs whisper quietly.

"Hush," she said as she began to cry in helpless silence.

After this, my father did the eulogy. I couldn't hear, though, much of what he said. It wasn't so much that I couldn't hear, but the sultry heat that lay heavy upon the summer morning made it hard to listen. The birds stopped singing when he talked, and one of the cops sitting in the car began to doze. I caught a whiff of cigarette smoke and looked down at the hospital attendant. He was lighting up again just as my father was beginning to pray.

As I watched him, a crack of thunder rumbled across the sky. Everybody started looking up and getting restless. The cops got out of their car and started inching back towards Studs. Studs saw what they were doing and whispered something into his mother's ear. She looked at him but said nothing. Her face looked too tired to talk.

My dad finished praying, and everyone started moving quickly toward their cars parked on the other side of the driveway. Studs kissed his mother on the forehead before the cops put his handcuffs back on and led him away.

Meanwhile, for several days, men had been swarming all over the burnt out Gatlin house. We watched from the edge of the clearing. And my dad made me talk to the police that came down from Tallahassee after I told him about the intruder in the woods. I had to tell the cop about the ice cream truck after he demanded to know what I was doing there in the woods at such an hour in the first place.

Finally they made me go to their office in Tallahassee where they exhausted me by asking me the same old questions over and over again, like they couldn't remember nothing! I can't even remember all the things they asked me. They harped a lot on the musicals bells and "how did I know it was an ice cream truck?" I tried to explain to them that I didn't but that it sounded like one. They asked me over and over again "what did the person look like that ran from the woods?"

And I just kept telling them that it was too dark. And besides, I reminded them, "I was too scared to look at him."

So then they wanted to know how I knew it was a him. I told them I didn't, but what else was I supposed to call him?

They even asked me some real stupid questions like, "did you hate Studs for raping charlotte?"

"No," I answered, "I don't hate him." I was becoming uneasy. I didn't want them to think that I had started the fire. "I hated Studs once," I said, " but not anymore, I'm mostly just afraid of him now."

They finally let me go after telling me that if I remembered anything else to call them. I didn't tell them about what Joe did though. I was afraid they might lock him up for evidence or something.

Two months later they finally caught some stranger, or rather Mr. Beezley did. They said that he was some tramp, and he had tried to set fire to Mr. Beezley's house. Mr. Beezley lived just two miles down the road from the Gatlin's place. He had just let his old dog out early in the morning to do her thing. The old dog had surprised the guy and lunged at him while barking really loud. Mr. Beezley ran and got his gun, so he could hold the man at gunpoint while his wife put out the flames with a garden hose and then went and called the cops.

I never did find out what made the sound of an ice cream truck. I finally thought it was just maybe that God wanted me to see Mr. Gatlin die that way.

# THE DOLDRUMS

THE LONG EMPTY summer went by. I daydreamed a lot. I would go deep in the woods, sit on a log, and dream that I was traveling to far off places. Other times, I would dream that I was married to Robin. I would dream that I was fucking her every day, and she was having babies. Once I fell asleep and dreamed that my father was the President, and he ordered the Russians bombed because they didn't believe in God. At times I would simply despair at the sheer emptiness of the long summer days and wish that somebody, anybody would come to see me.

My sister Charlotte stayed in the house and helped Mother while Eddie and Jonathan stuck together and played their own games that didn't much interest me.

Soon the long empty summer days stretched into and became autumn. Nothing much changed though. My dad had forced us all to quit school in the spring. He said it was too close to the Second Coming.

"You kids have no further use for worldly learning," he said.

Charlotte had been very unhappy about this. I could tell. She went around with a long sad face and didn't smile anymore. She had a lot of friends at school. Eddie and Jonathan were excited about it. I would have been out of high school anyway. Besides I had given up all hope for Robin, and my only friend Reggie had long since deserted me.

As autumn advanced, a sense of excitement did begin to invade the atmosphere around our little place there in the woods. First Father decided that the few remaining in the congregation should meet at our place for Sabbath services.

"Most sightings of flying saucers have been in isolated rural areas," he explained. "I think God would be more pleased if we would wait for him out here in the woods.

Agnes Everby shouted, "Praise His precious name."

And it was exciting, at least, at first to have the attention centered upon our house. Secondly, Agnes Everby's thrilling existence of warbles and shouts was beginning to rub off on everyone.

In October Robin started coming out to our place for church, but she was usually mad and would sit and pout and stare at the ceiling or straight ahead and wouldn't even look at me. I figured that maybe Mr. Barnes had caught her over at Albert Rotterbaum's place again. And besides now she always wore shorts or jeans so that nothing much really showed when she knelt to pray. But if I got the chance I would stare at it anyway and remember.

Before long though, my frustration and loneliness began to grow again, becoming almost intolerable. I got bored at the same old people, especially Agnes Everby, always shouting and praising.

My dad quit working except to tend the garden, so all we had to eat was vegetables. So I started longing for fried chicken and good old down to earth talk, where people talked to each other instead of God. At least at school I could listen to the kids talking to each other and watch them play from my perch by the swamp.

Finally I started sneaking off on my bike and riding into town on weekday afternoons hoping to get a glimpse of the kids at play on the school grounds. However the fence around the school grounds and the tall trees kept me from seeing much .

One day, in my frustration, I rode right past the school grounds to Third Street and down it to the old church where my dad used to preach. The grass was tall and uncut in the church yard. The glass was broken where windows were supposed to be and the wood was turning black from lack of paint.

As I had stood staring at the old church, I suddenly remembered Jorje Carlyle who lived across the street. I quickly glanced toward his house to discover him sitting on the porch looking at me. He, himself, then glanced at the old church.

"Much more peaceful, now," he said with a smile playing about his lips. "Why not come sit a spell?" he added, "you look hot and thirsty."

It was a hot autumn day and his invitation tempted me. His voice was so relaxed it made it feel like time was standing still. But then I remembered that he was an atheist.

"I have got to get back to school," I said apprehensively.

I tried to quickly mount my bike in an effort to get away from him, but in my haste, I fell into the street, my bike on top of me. I could hear his quiet chuckle behind me and felt the blood rushing to my cheeks.

"Relax son," Jorje said calmly, "I'm not the evil asshole you may think I am. I'm sure rumor has it that I'm evil incarnate, but really, I'm just a free spirit living in a sick little Florida town full of hypocrites." "Besides," he continued, "school can always wait. Often it is not much more than a propaganda machine anyway. Come have a beer or a coke or something."

I got to my feet and looked again at his smiling face. His smile was broad and relaxed, and his voice was gentle and pleasant. The idea of a beer sent a thrill up my bored spine. And it grew on me as I stood there in the hot sun on the street.

"Okay," I said, "just one."

I sat down on his old couch that stood on the porch while Jorje went into the house for a beer.

In front of the old wooden chair where Jorje had been sitting, stood a folding coffee table, and on it lay part of a newspaper neatly folded. The rest of the newspaper had been thrown to one side and lay on the couch where I was sitting. Beside the coffee table stood an ashtray with legs on it. A really short cigarette butt was held in one of its clips, and on the floor, four Budweiser bottles were sitting near the couch. At the far end of the porch, a fat gray cat was licking his rear end contentedly, and not far away, a little white dog with a black eye was crying in his sleep from a bad dream.

Jorje walked out, the screen door slammed behind him. He had two beers. They both said Budweiser on them. He handed one to me. I took it and it was cold and heavy. The word Budweiser looked evil, and the thought hovered in the front of my brain that I was about to do something awful. I was about to decide not to taste it.

"Would you like me to pour it into a glass?" Jorje asked as he watched me.

The question had startled me, leaving me embarrassed as though he were looking right through me.

"No thank you," I said as I bravely took a long swig.

I involuntarily cringed, like I had expected something to happen but didn't. It did taste a little bitter but I decided that it wasn't bad at all.

After all, I thought, it is not that different from water. I took another long swig and began to feel pretty good about it.

"What is your name, son?" Jorje asked.

I told him and he said, "Wasn't McGee the name of the preacher that used to preach over at that church?"

I followed his gaze over to the dilapidated old church.

"Yes, that was my dad." I said.

"I'll be a horses ass," he said and chuckled softly. "Bet your father would skin you alive if he knew you were here at my place playing hooky."

I gulped another swig of Budweiser and threw a guilty look in his direction. He was looking at the ceiling with his lips twisted in a grin.

"I'm not really supposed to be in school," I said, "my father wouldn't let me finish high school last year and he won't let any of us go this year." The beer was beginning to loosen my tongue.

"What! The man of God's son doesn't need a worldly education?"

"Well you see," I continued glibly, "the second coming is next month...er...ah..that is what my father says anyway, and we don't need to know what this school teaches us on Mt. Zion."

A wave of guilt and embarrassment swept over me, inundating my good feelings from the beer. And I couldn't figure out why I had told Jorje that! I watched Jorje for his reaction and took another long swig from the brown Budweiser bottle.

Jorje just mumbled something about the second coming and stared at the ceiling for awhile. Then he looked back at the church and chuckled again.

After this, he reached over and took the little cigarette butt from the clip and lit it. He sucked in several times real hard until I thought it was going to burn his lips. Then he used a little pair of tweezers to hold it with and sucked some more. The smoke smelt sort of funny, like a skunk in the woods. I was beginning to think it wasn't an ordinary cigarette but decided that I wasn't smart enough to know such stuff.

"I'd like to witness the second coming," he said suddenly, almost making me drop my bottle of beer. "Where is it going to be?"

"At our house," I said, again wishing I had kept my mouth shut.

"Do you mean the place out there in the woods south of town?"

"Yes," I responded and drained my beer bottle.

"Hummm," he grunted reflectively, then noticing my empty beer bottle he asked me if I would like another beer.

"No," I said to loud, getting to my feet. I was suddenly dizzy and leaned against the porch railing. "I got a go home," I said, half to myself.

I was beginning to feel afraid that I was going to be left behind when the flying saucers came. Drunks probably wouldn't be allowed in, I thought.

Then Jorje noticed my plight. "Have a seat Bobby," he said. "I'll get you a Coke. You drink that and you will be fine."

He was right, after the Coke I wasn't dizzy anymore. And rode my bike home. But not before he had warned me not to get too close to either of my parents because they might smell alcohol on my breath.

I lie wide awake in bed that night, thinking about Jorje. He seemed so relaxed and happy. He didn't seem to be worried about anything. I decided that if Christ didn't come, or I got left for some reason, I was going back to see Jorje Carlyle. I was also still curious about the funny smelling cigarette that he had been smoking.

"Whipper will…..whipper will…whipper willllllllll." It came to me out of the silence in the dark, still night, resting my heavy eyelids, coaxing me into sleep.

But then it hit me suddenly with a thrill up my spine. I was wide awake, staring into the silent darkness, forgetting the song of the night birds. What if Christ took everyone but Robin and I? We could both go live with Jorje. We could drink beer, and fuck while he was asleep! I figured that Robin didn't have much of chance at getting into one of them flying saucers anyway because she was bad already. All I had to do was make him mad at me too. And that was the nice thing about God, it didn't take much to make him mad. I decided I would buy a package of cigarettes at the filling station the next day. I would ask if they had any of the stinky sweet kind. Robin would be impressed, and God would be angry. With the decision made, I promptly fell asleep.

# THE SECOND COMING

As the day for the second coming grew closer, Agnes Everbe spent more and more of her time out at our house. She would walk in without knocking, praising the Lord before we had gotten out of bed.

"Thank you Jesus for the glorious new day and for the wonderful times in which we live!" she would cry in a brittle operatic voice that could have awakened one from the dead. And in case someone was still asleep, she would follow that with, " Rise and shine my beloved brothers and sisters, rise and shine to God's lovely new day!"

After a while I got tired of hearing it. But knew that I didn't dare say anything. Later I was to find other ways to get even with her. Once when she and my parents were having one of their marathon prayer sessions, and I was slipping between them in order to get to the kitchen to get myself a glass of water when she turned on me between one praise the Lord and the next to demand a glass of water. When I got to the kitchen, I drank two glasses of water, one for her and one for me, then ran out the backdoor and down the kitchen steps to the freedom of the outdoors. I guess later she complained to my dad because he asked me about it.

"I thought she was asking God for water," I replied. He gave me a long look but said nothing.

Then one night I heard my mother's voice coming loudly from my parent's bedroom. "She is taking over this household!" my mother was saying. "She tells the kids what to do, she tells you and I what to do, soon she will want to be sleeping in here and asking us to take the couch!"

I could hear my father's voice as he answered but couldn't understand what he was saying. I strained my ear, putting it to the door knob. Then

I heard some of it. He was saying "in Christ's presence all of us will be perfect."

But then Jonathan had noticed what I was doing. He gave me a push into the door, and it made a loud noise. At that, Jonathan and I both ran out of the house.

"Are you trying to get me into trouble?" I panted as I turned on him once we were outside.

"No, but you're not supposed to listen in that way!" he said, with a grin on his face.

As the last week of our wait began, Mother's concern came true. Agnes Everbe stopped going home to sleep. She slept on the couch at first, but then after a night or two, she asked if she could sleep with Charlotte. Charlotte had said okay, but she had said it with a long face.

By this time, Agnes was in a constant state of euphoria. She would constantly cry praises to God, then run around the house talking in ecstatic half sentences. She didn't eat much, but when she did she ate our food. She would wake up in the middle of the night shouting revelations in a different language that she didn't even know. Since it was God shouting through her, there was nothing we could do about it except grin and bear it. I would put my pillow over my head, but I could hear her anyway. My brothers would just lie and listen with their eyes wide open. But I sure felt sorry for Charlotte.

My mother started locking herself in her bedroom to pray most of the day. My father would sit in the living room with his eyes closed to pray, until Agnes' screams would get too loud, and then he would go walking in the woods.

Agnes Everbe's voice finally got hoarse, and she sounded like a sick rooster who kept right on crowing anyway! I got so I hated her and was determined that I was not going to spend eternity with the likes of her!

Two days before the expected end, Robin Barnes and her mother came over. Now I hadn't seen Robin since I had rode to town on my bike and stole a pack of cigarettes from behind the counter in the filling station. I did it while the attendant was out putting gas in somebody's car. I had felt guilty about it, but I didn't know what else to do since I wasn't getting any money any more.

Robin had her head up and looked haughty and angry. Mother came out of her bedroom just as Agnes had began to maneuver Mrs. Barnes toward it. She had tried to include Robin in her enveloping grasp, but Robin ducked under her armpits to escape and turn to look back at her with a face flushed with anger.

Charlotte was already in Mother's bedroom. My dad was out praying in the woods, and my brothers were out playing somewhere, so I found myself alone with Robin.

"Robin," I said bravely, " I have something to show you." "What?" she asked, as she turned her dark eyes absently upon me.

"That woman is crazy!" she added, throwing a frowning glance back over her shoulder at the closing bedroom door.

"Be careful that she doesn't hear you say that," I said.

"I don't care if she does!" she said loudly. "I'm almost nineteen now, why does everyone insist on treating me like a kid"?

I decided not to say anything else, or I might get into trouble if Mother should walk back out through that bedroom door.

"Come," I said.

"Okay," she said, "anything is better than this." She turned again to throw one more fleeting scowl at the bedroom door and followed me out onto the porch.

I decided to take her to the woods to smoke cigarettes. I was pretty sure that she knew how to do it. By this time, I had smoked half a pack. After smoking the first one, I had become very sick and I had kept getting sick until I smoked three or four. But after that it wasn't so bad. After the last one, I just had to sweat a little.

After following me about half way down the driveway, she started to hang back.

"Where are you taking me? We are not going to do THAT again, are we?"

"No," I said, "but I have to take you to the woods to do it."

"Just tell me!" she demanded, "and I will decide whether I want to do it or not."

"Okay," I said, glancing around to make sure that we were alone. "I'm taking you to the woods to smoke cigarettes."

"Alright," she said in a half-hearted voice. "I'll smoke with you."

In the woods, we sat on two logs facing each other. Her short shorts were loose around her legs. Robin could never hide her sexy body. I saw it again, most of it anyway. It had fallen loose from the side of her panties. I started getting excited again and remembered it in the blackberry patch. Robin saw where I was looking, but did nothing to hide it.

"Let's light up, Bobby," she said in a more gentle voice.

I fumbled for my cigarettes and matches, now too excited to really want to smoke. But I got two of them out and lit hers then my own. It was exhilarating, and it didn't make me sick. Robin sucked the smoke in deeply and spread her legs further apart as she blew the smoke back out, glimpsing up at the warm winter sky.

Beside my foot I noticed a small yellow daisy flower that was growing. It looked wild and it was all alone. On an impulse I picked it.

"Here Robin," I said, as I held it out to her.

She took it and held it, then twisted it between her fingers and stared at it absently. She then looked up and smiled at me.

"If your dad wasn't the preacher," she said, "I might fall in love with you."

"But," I said, "the flying saucers might leave me, and I could stay with you."

"Bobby, there ain't going to be no flying saucers!" she said with finality, as she blew the last puff of smoke in my face and crushed the butt into the earth with her foot.

"You want my pussy, don't you Bobby?" Her voice sank to almost a whisper and her dark eyes had turned moist and sexy.

She then dropped the daisy flower on the ground beside her.

"Yes, Robin, I like you," I said as I tried to look deeply into her eyes. But they were too dark to see much.

"I know," she said in a voice full of stoic resignation. "All you guys want is to get into a girl's panties." She sighed. "But that is alright, fucking is kind of exciting when everything else about life is so boring."

With that she came over and started kissing my cheek passionately. I returned her kisses and groped wildly, attempting to strip her little shorts from off her body. Losing our balance, we fell backwards into the wild brown grass of last summer. I entered her then and we fucked. Our emotions became one in orgasmic contentment, each of us taking from the other the sustenance of life.

"You really ought to use a rubber, Bobby, Albert does." Robin said, as we lie wrapped in each others arms beneath the warmth of the noonday sun.

A stab of pain had cut through me then. Why did she always have to bring up Albert?

Little did I know then, that this would be our last time together.


It was in the predawn hour that I awoke on that day, awoke to the moans of Agnes Everbe. Her cries were pitiful. She was begging God to forgive her for all her evil deeds.

"Oh my God, forgive me for not being a better wife to Rudi. Oh my God, oh my God, ooooh my God, don't leave me here in this cruel world where the wicked rule and lord it over us good folks. Oh my Savior, oh sweet Jesus take me away with you, take me swiftly when you come like a thief in the night."

Gradually the dynamics of her humble prayer created within her psyche, victory out of defeat, and she began to sing in a very beautiful voice that was tremulous in its victory. It was a voice that warbled like the music of a bird that had just laid a golden egg.

She sang, "When the roll is called up yonder, I'll be there."

Shortly other voices joined her. I heard the voice of my father, then that of my mother. The voices became powerful and hypnotic. I found myself being dragged from my bed. I heard Charlotte singing. I looked at my brothers. They were twisting in their bed. I walked like a somnambulant, a puppet on a string, toward the living room. At first I sang in a whisper so as not to be heard, but the power of the voices overwhelmed me. I began to shout and run through the house praising God. Agnes Everbe almost went through the ceiling with joy. I opened my eyes, then and saw my brothers staring at me, awestruck. I got a hold on myself then and was just glad that Robin was not there to see it.

Then Agnes came over and put her hand on my head and shook it.

"Just let yourself go!" she cried, " don't resist God's power. Just let yourself be a vessel in his hands."

I just stood there, letting her rattle my teeth. I half heartedly said "praise the Lord" a couple of times, hoping that it would appease her. She finally wondered off in a trance and left me alone.

Shortly after daylight, Annie Smith came and everyone got excited and started praying again.

I began to watch the driveway for the Barneses' car to round the bend coming out of the woods. The next person, however, to show up at our door was Reba Boone. She was alone and her face had tear streaks on it. When Agnes saw her, she rushed to the door, her arms open wide.

"My dear sister," she cried, "this is our day. Where is Butch?"

Tears began to flow down her cheeks like fresh water on an old riverbed. Uncontrollable sobs began to escape through her trembling lips, shaking her slight frame in the process.

"He...he...he's not coming," she said with great difficulty and fell with a loud sob into Agnes' arms.

"Why?" gasped Agnes in disbelief.

Reba was sobbing then, so uncontrollably that she couldn't answer.

"I think I can answer that," my father said, as he looked through the window down the long empty driveway. "He has decided that it is all a joke, and he doesn't want to feel like a fool when it is all over. Isn't that right Reba?"

Reba nodded, her sobbing becoming even more uncontrollable.

I was beginning to think she really believed it!

"Now, now, Reba," my father said soothingly, "you will find that life in God's kingdom will more than compensate for the loss of family and friends here in this world. Reba, you cannot imagine the glorious life we will have living there."

"Praise the Lord," cried Agnes, as she shifted under Reba's weight.

"Praise the Lord," mimicked Annie Smith.

"Yes, praise the Lord," affirmed my mother.

"Yes, praise the Lord," said my father in unison, "but I can't help but feel sorry for Butch," a slight smile was playing around his lips as he stared down the driveway again. "Because he is going to know what it is really like to feel the fool."

Reba Boone's sobbing stopped. She sniffled several times as she followed my father's gaze down the long empty driveway as though she had suddenly taken note of the ironic humor in it all.

Then suddenly the driveway was not empty because the Barneses' car came out of the woods and into view. I started to get really excited because I was hoping to get Robin down into the woods so we could discuss a plan of action, in case God came and left us. While I was thinking about it, they pulled up near the porch and parked.

"Oh, there is Betty and Albert!" Reba said excitedly. She then took her weight off Agnes, who promptly shouted "hallelujah".

Only the two front doors opened so I started trying to see into the backseat to find Robin. I couldn't see her anywhere. My heart began to sink, but I could only hope that she was just mad and refusing to get out of the car. But I couldn't see her, unless she was lying down.

Mr. Barnes was somber, only nodding and grunting greetings to everyone.

The moment they had entered through the screen door, Agnes asked, "Where is that darling daughter of yours, Betty?"

A sob that seemed to shake her whole body escaped through Mrs. Barnes' throat and tears started flowing like a river down her face. She choked on the words but she said them anyway.

"She ran away!"

"Oh, my poor baby," cried Reba Boone as she ran to her with fresh sobs of her own. So they sobbed uncontrollably on each others shoulders.

I was overwhelmed by my own disappointment. My heart was sinking, any hopes of getting left with Robin were gone now. But this shed new light on the situation. A sudden and terrible realization struck me. What if I got left alone? The thought of it struck terror in me! So I went to a dark corner in my bedroom and began to pray feverishly, asking God to forgive me for the cigarettes and for fucking Robin and for everything else I could think of. I prayed on and on until I got bored of it and began thinking again. Robin might just be at Albert Rotterbaum's place. If I got left, she might just come looking for me. I finally decided to leave good enough alone. If I got to go, so be it. If I didn't then I would just go looking for Robin.

"........many are called but few are chosen," I heard my father saying. "As I was telling Reba, here, God will compensate beyond our wildest dreams for the loss of our dear ones."

"Huh!" Mr. Barnes grunted as though in disbelief. My dad gave him sharp look but said nothing.

"But my Robin," she said with a tremulous voice, "she didn't even tell us where she was going! She was just gone this morning when we awoke."

"My Butch didn't come either," said Reba, another sob escaping her.

"Oh my God, I hadn't noticed," gasped Mrs. Barnes. "I was so wrapped up in my own heartache that I was thinking of no one else." The two of them started to whimper on each others shoulders, but I was thinking that by this time they should both be tired of crying already.

Suddenly Agnes started singing, "We shall overcome, we shall overcome, when the saints shall come rejoicing we shall overcome!"

Father and Mother joined in. Shortly, Betty and Reba gave up their sobbing and begrudgingly joined them. Mr. Barnes didn't sing though. He just went over and stared out the window down the long driveway. I didn't sing either. The shock of not having Robin there on the last day left me empty of any desire to sing.

As the day progressed, the praying, the singing and the shouting continued. Nobody bothered about anything to eat. I thought maybe we wouldn't need food where the flying saucers were taking us, but I didn't know if I could make it to then. I went and looked into the refrigerator, but all I could see was some green beans in an old canning jar, so I decided that maybe I could wait after all.

Even Reba Boone and Betty Barnes finally began to cheer up. Mr. Barnes, however, remained restless. He would pray quietly kneeling in front of an old rickety chair in the corner for awhile then he would go out and pace back and forth along the gray boards on the porch.

My brothers and I checked the refrigerator again around noon time. We took the green beans out, divided them up and ate every last one of them. While we were eating, I suddenly became aware of Mr. Barnes standing in the doorway watching us as though he were hungry too.

It was in the late afternoon, darkness was already climbing above the woods in the eastern sky, when I suddenly became aware of a big black car making its way up our driveway. This sent my adrenalin to pumping excitement out of my stomach. No one else was expected for the second coming!

The singing and shouting were intense, loud and desperate. My brothers were napping in the bedroom. Charlotte was praying and shouting like everybody else. Mr. Barnes sat in a corner on an old rickety chair with his eyes closed, just listening to it all. So no one noticed the big black car as it came to stop out front except me. I strained my eyes in order to recognize our company. He stood and slammed the car door shut and looked up at the house. Suddenly a spark of recognition came with the adrenalin pumping out of my stomach. It was Jorje Carlyle!

I was near a panic as he climbed the front steps and came toward the front door. The sounds of his steps as they crossed the gray boards of the porch and approached the front door seemed to shake the house like an earthquake. I ran quietly to the far corner of the room and squatted beside the old rickety chair that Mr. Barnes was sitting on.

Suddenly Mr. Barnes stood and said, "Here kid, do you want a place to sit?" and then walked off towards the kitchen. So I sat and grasped wildly in my mind for something to say in self defense in case Jorje told on me.

I think Father was probably the first to be distracted by the tall quiet figure standing at the front door. I saw him glance through the screen door and then become quiet with his eyes closed. I thought he was probably asking God to identify the stranger.

Jorje didn't knock or say anything, he just continued to stand there and watch.

Dusk was rapidly gathering and twilight shadows played around the room as no one had turned the lights on yet. Jorje's dark silhouette became almost sinister as it continued to stand there silently, framed by the doorway. Then finally my father began tiptoeing towards him like he was sneaking up on a shadow. I heard him say something quietly through the screen door but could not hear what it was.

Then Agnes espied him and shouted, "Bless me, do we have another saint prepared for travel?"

Prayers began to die on everyone's lips. Only my mother continued to pray as she watched. Then my father, with reluctance, finally opened the door for him. It was then that I heard the shocked whispers coming in gasps from the lips of Betty Barnes and Reba Boone.

He continued to stand there, his glance racing around the room. He is looking for me, I thought and cringed, hoping the shadows would conceal me. Then at that moment my father, with the flick of a switch, turned the lights on, and Jorje looked right at me. I thought it was all over for me as I had stared back at him, my eyes begging for mercy. But he only smiled and turned his gaze back to the open gasping mouths of Reba and Betty. When he saw them, his smile twisted at the corners and became a smirk.

"I'm Jorje Carlyle," he began, "you probably remember me as the strange man who lived across the street from your church." He paused and turned his eyes back upon Reba Boone who turned pale under his scrutinizing gaze. "I have come to you with a message from God," he said boldly so that I almost believed it. He looked my father right in eyes and said, "an angel has come to me with a warning, that I must be at your home tonight, Reverend McGee, if I am to witness the second coming of Christ."

He threw me a furtive glance, and I felt the blood rushing to my head in embarrassment.

"I know that I am an evil man and cannot hope to go with you. And I told the angel this, but the voice of the angel became more urgent. 'Jorje, my son,' it said, 'you are not as evil as you think. Sure you smoke funny cigarettes and nip the bottle occasionally, but God needs a witness, one who will faithfully report the events of the second coming throughout the world so that the world might prepare itself for the third coming.'"

"Praise the Lord," shouted Agnes in an unsure voice as she glanced at my father for confirmation. But the glance my father threw her was one of rebuke.

"Jorje, we neither want nor need a witness," my father said sternly, in a voice that hinted of anger under control. "I have lived and prepared for this moment all my life and will not tolerate a disruption by the Devil now. This is private property, my property and I am asking you to leave immediately!"

The door still stood open, Jorje just inside. Jorje threw another smile in my direction, sending me again into near panic. I glanced at my father to see if he had noticed but he was using his eyes to direct Jorje out the door.

"If that is the way you feel, Reverend McGee, but what shall I tell the angel when it comes for my report?"

"You tell that angel, Jorje, that he is Beelzebub, Satan's own and that he cannot deceive nor tempt me."

Father then walked out on the porch and held the screen door wide open for Jorje to walk through. Jorje's scheme had failed. He underestimated my father. But I was overwhelmed with relief and felt really good about Jorje because he hadn't told on me.

"Get thee behind me Satan," Father shouted at Jorje's tail lights as they moved down our driveway and into the rapidly darkening twilight. Everyone started crying to God then with a vengeance as though to make up for the Devil's interruption.

At the window, I watched Jorje's taillights move slowly down the driveway, but they went out too soon and I knew that Jorje hadn't left. A shiver went up my spine as I stared into the black of night and wondered what he was doing down there on the dark sand road.

But I was soon distracted by the loud prayers and intonations coming out of the mouths of uplifted faces, prayers and intonations that after a while just became noise. And it seemed like many boring hours later that I was again distracted by my father's voice cutting through the increasingly desperate prayers, praying voices that were strained, full of self-pity, voices that sounded like the beggars on the street corners of Tallahassee.

"Come," my father said, "it is time to go out into the night and watch the sky."

"Hallelujah," Agnes' voice crackled, in a high squeak.

We all went out and stared up at the star studded sky. And then the voices from the uplifted faces began to pray, voices that seemed to fall flat on the heavy dew laden, chilled night air. The voices seemed insignificant as they shouted into the darkness that lay between them and the sky. I then stared out into the twinkling infinity that had no end, a distance that made me shiver with cold. The coldness that enveloped me left me breathless and with doubt that God or any other living thing existed out there. I shook my head and began to pray, determined to hold out a little longer.

Then out of the distant night, a bright object moved towards us rapidly. Agnes and my father saw it at the same time. Father just pointed. Agnes just gasped in a cracked exclamation of ecstasy.

Annie Smith startled everyone with a cry of joy, "Oh my God!" she cried, "He's coming, He's coming, I'll soon be with my Larson in heaven!"

All of us stared for a long moment, marveling, hoping. But it disappeared, far from us and there were aaahs of disappointment.

"Maybe it has stopped to pick up other saints," Mrs. Barnes said hopefully.

"No, my dear, it was just a shooting star." said Mr. Barnes, a note of incredulity in his voice.

Father said nothing, he just continued to stare at the black point where it had disappeared. I could see that his lips were moving rapidly. I think he was praying for miracle to prove Mr. Barnes was wrong.

I don't know how long we waited that way, but I remembered Jorje again and wondered if he was watching us somewhere. It was around midnight and the prayers fizzled. Disappointment and depression had taken over. They hung, like the heavy chill of the dark night over the little group. As I watched them, contemplating what I was going to do next a feint whiff of something disturbing came to me. I tried to identify it but couldn't. But it came from down the dark driveway, and I just knew it was Jorje doing it. I moved stealthily into the dark towards the driveway. Suddenly Joe was beside me, then ahead of me moving off rapidly. A strong whiff of it hit me again and I knew what it was. I stopped in my tracks. Jorje must be nearby I thought.

"Joe," I said in a harsh whisper, "come back here!" Joe ignored me and moved off into the dark.

I stood paralyzed. I knew the smell came from Jorje's funny cigarettes.

"Do you know what that smell is?" My fathers voice had startled me and I nearly jumped out of my pants.

"No," I responded with a shiver, hoping that he would believe me.

"I think it is marijuana," he said, "but I can't be absolutely certain. I only had a smell of it once before."

He moved off into the dark ahead of me. I was afraid to follow, but my curiosity overcame my fear. I ran to catch up as he began to disappear into the dark. His footsteps fell heavily on the sandy road as we made our way down the driveway. Then a form began to take shape in the distant darkness in front of us as we got near the spot where our "little car" town used to be when we had been little kids. I could tell what it was but held my tongue.

"It's a car," my father said, grimly, as we neared it. "It looks like Jorje's car! He has been here all along, watching, as the Devil's witness." He opened the door. The inside reeked with the smell of marijuana. The pungent smell hit me. I thought it smelled kind of good myself but didn't say it in front of my dad. Father looked quickly around the inside of the car then slammed the door shut violently as though to prevent the pungent smoke from polluting his fresh air.

We then made our way across the garden. It was mostly dead weeds now as the first winter frost had already come. In the dark, I kept stumbling over the broken ground and rotting weeds.

Suddenly, the light from a rising moon broke upon us as it rose above the trees. It created an eerie glow for us to walk by.

"Wasn't Joe home tonight?" asked my father.

"Yes," I answered, "but he ran on ahead before you came."

"I, thought he was supposed to be a watchdog!" he growled in disgust.

"I think he is," I said, "it is just that he is out looking around right now."

"A watch dog is supposed to stay with those he is watching," my father said. So I decided not to say anything else.

At the head of the garden, we walked into the Gatlin woods but saw no movement or anything suspicious. We then made our way back toward the front yard. As my father's gaze moved intently from left to right, he saw a movement in the dark shadows. He threw his hand out in front of me to keep me still. But then it was Joe that materialized out of the eerie moonlit dark and came running to me, his tongue hanging out in a hard pant.

"You good for nothing mongrel," Father admonished. "Listen!" Father hissed.

Sure enough, it was the grinding of an automobile motor, trying to start. My father started running for the clearing of our yard. I followed, my heart beating a mile a minute. Just as we reached the yard where we had a view of the distant drive, the motor jumped to life. The moonlight was reflecting off Jorje's black shiny top momentarily before the two tail lights disappeared around the bend into the dark woods.

"The Devil has most certainly won a battle tonight," my father mumbled to himself as he stared after them.

"Do you think it was him that scared the flying saucers off?" I asked.

"No," he replied as we both turned and walked back towards the house.

As we approached, we spied a figure standing alone in the dark wet grass staring up at the newly risen moon. It was Agnes Everbe. All the others had gone in now.

"It is getting kind of chilly Agnes," my father said. "Might as well come on in now." But Agnes didn't hear him, and he just walked on by to go up the steps and through the screen door.

But I stopped and watched her, struck by her silence. It sounded good. There were no praises to God now, there was no singing, and there were no shouts of joy; just a normal lady staring at the moon in silence. I stared at it too and felt peaceful. The moon looked full of something but all the darkness around it was empty, except for its light. I looked again at Agnes, standing like a ghost in the moonlight. She had really believed and now it was all over. I now knew that Robin was right, there wasn't going to be any second coming. I then moved quietly over beside her and tapped her on the shoulder.

"What is it?" she asked calmly, showing no emotion whatsoever

"It is after midnight," I said. "The day is over, you can come in now."

Her head dropped and she sort of shook it like she was trying to get her senses back. She looked at me as though trying to remember something, as though she didn't recognize who I was. And then in the squeaking crack of a whisper, almost like the throb of a death rattle she began to sing, "We shall overcome, we shall overcome, we shall come rejoicing, we shall overcome."

She then put her hand on my shoulder like a blind lady and followed me across the dark grass, up the steps onto the gray porch, through the screen door and into the dimly lit sitting room all the time continuing to sing, "we shall come rejoicing…" when the room light hit her eyes she became silent. She stumbled, then fell exhausted into the big sofa chair and stared vacantly at the ceiling as though searching for the moonlit night she had left outside.

"I'm convinced," I heard my father saying, as Agnes and I entered. But he broke off and all was silent as Agnes stumbled like a blind lady for the chair.

"I'm convinced now," my father repeated as Agnes sat breathing heavily in her chair, "that God let the Devil win a battle tonight to test our determination and faith. How Jorje knew the time of our rendezvous with the flying saucers is beyond me. But it must have been God's will that he knew because nothing happens that is not God's will. He has not left us stranded here." His usually calm and cool voice had become intense, taut, like a tightly wound violin string that has been scratched by the tips of one's finger nails. Then his voice rose into a high pitched whine. "Besides, God has promised that all things work for the good of those who love the Lord. God will not let us down." His voice suddenly dropped as though to emphasize the finality of it. He then continued in the old cool calm voice of certainty, "I know he will come soon. There can be no doubt about the approximate date. But we must remember we are dealing with six thousand years since creation, and I suppose I could be off by a day or two."

"My dear friends in Christ," he continued, his voice now getting louder and shrill again. It almost sounded desperate, like he was pleading. "We must continue to pray and wait. His coming is but momentary. But I do suggest that we rest our exhausted vocal chords and get a little sleep. I'm sure that if he comes in the night, someone will wake us with a knock on the door."

I dropped my head to hide my embarrassment because I knew that I was the one that had scared the flying saucers off that night. If I hadn't of told Jorje, I would probably be in a flying saucer eating flying saucer food. As it was, I sat there starving knowing that there was nothing in the refrigerator.

When I looked up again my father was sitting silent, scratching his chin and trying to look confident that it was all settled. He looked at my Mother as though as to ask what is keeping us from going to bed. But it was not to be. Mr. Barnes had been sitting restlessly in his chair listening to my father talk. I guess he had detected human weakness in it and was about to strike.

"No, Reverend McGee," Mr. Barnes had said in a firm and controlled voice. "Betty and I are finished with this nonsense. I have felt from the beginning that you were wrong in setting a date for the second coming."

"Now, Mr. Barnes," my father interrupted, "I refuse to let you be the Devil's mouthpiece by trying to instill doubt in the minds of the believers."

"Just you wait a minute, McGee!" Mr. Barnes' self control was beginning to erode and his voice was rising. "If anyone is instilling doubt, it is you by setting false dates and telling your followers that you can't be wrong."

"Mr. Barnes," my father interjected sharply, but before he could continue Mr. Barnes interrupted loudly.

"Mr. McGee," he bellowed, "it is my turn to talk! I have listened to you these last few years without a peep, though I disagreed with you. I did it for Betty's sake, who believed in you. Now you have grievously disappointed her, and I'm going to have my say."

"No, Mr. Barnes!" Father's voice had become extremely sharp and vitriolic, "not on my property, I will not let you instill doubt…"

"YOUR PROPERTY!" roared Mr. Barnes, "this is church property! You wouldn't be here if we hadn't of supported your ministry. You have gradually alienated most of your congregation, the humble people who bought this property for you. How dare you try throw me from your property!" The room shook with his anger!

Agnes sat staring right through Mr. Barnes with a vacant expression like she was seeing Annie Smith who was sitting behind him with a long, sad face and closed eyes.

"Peter," my mother said with a calm fortitude, "let Albert say what he has on his mind."

"Thank you, Mrs. McGee," said Mr. Barnes, glaring at my father. "Uh..h..h, because of your rude interruptions McGee, I have forgotten what I was going to say, however..."

"Praise the Lord!" my father shouted, "that is because God didn't want you to say it in the first place!"

"The essence of what I was about to say," continued Mr. Barnes, ignoring my father's latest outburst, "can be paraphrased by God's own words, taken from the scripture, 'He shall come as a thief in the night,' I have never heard you quote this passage, Reverend. Now a thief does not pre-warn anyone of the date and place of his coming."

My father's face looked haggard and drops of perspiration stood out on his forehead.

"Mr. Barnes he started condescendingly.

"Reverend McGee," Reba Boone said suddenly, "I think Albert has a point, I have never thought of it that way before. Why don't you just admit your error, and we can go on with our lives like before. We all make mistakes. I do believe that you are a good man and sincere. We all understand your desire to bring Christ back to earth as soon as possible, but maybe He wants to make a surprise out of it. After all most people just love it when something good happens and comes out of thin air, as it were."

"Yes," said Mrs. Barnes, "that makes sense, God probably wants us to be on the lookout for his second coming all the time. That way we wouldn't have to waste so much time praying, begging and hollering for it." With that she glanced hopefully at my father.

Father glanced at my mother as though expecting a comment from her. She said nothing, but looked directly back at him as though to say: well?

"It breaks my heart to hear you, the last of my disciples, say this," my father began, in a tired voice, "but it reveals to me how really few there are that God has chosen. Furthermore, it reveals to me that none of you have really listened to my sermons, for I have explained all these things to you many times."

"Enough, enough," said Mr. Barnes, getting to his feet. "Come Betty, we have to make up for lost time in trying to find Robin. She is our only child, you know."

"Yes, yes, my Robin," said Mrs. Barnes, getting to her feet. She went over and kissed my mother on the cheek. They then gave each other a big kiss and hug.

"Oh, I must get home to my Butch," cried Reba Boone, suddenly coming to life with the realization that she was going to get to see him again after all. A thrill seemed to vibrate through her voice. "I hope he will forgive me for walking out on him this way." She threw an apprehensive look at my father as she jumped to her feet.

"Butch probably knew you would be back." Mr. Barnes said with a hint of sarcasm in his voice.

Reba quickly ran over and gave a hen peck of a kiss on my mothers cheek. Then the three of them quickly exited into the night.

I never saw Reba again, but as far as I know, she and Butch still live in their little white house with a big green yard in Woodlake, Florida.

Several weeks later, Mrs. Barnes called my mother to tell her that Robin had hitchhiked in the dead of winter back to North Dakota and was staying with her grandmother there. During the following summer, the Barneses' sold their place there in Woodlake and went back to North Dakota themselves.

As for the rest of us left there, that night, back in the Florida woods, we continued to wait for the second coming.

# THE WAIT
# CONTINUES . . .

"Annie, is your faith firm? Are you a faithful and loyal servant? Will you wait a little longer with me?" My fathers voice turned quiet and gentle but full of self pity.

"Yes Peter McGee, I have nothing to lose, my hubby is up there. However tonight I want to go home to get some bacon and eggs, vegetables and other good things out of the refrigerator and bring them back in the morning for breakfast. I bet your kids are starved."

"That is really nice of you Annie Smith," my father said, "and I'm so thrilled that you will continue to wait with us." His voice sounded self-confident again. He patted Annie on her wrinkled old hand and walked her out into the bright moonlight to her car.

And after what she had said about the eggs and all, I was really starting to like her too!

When my dad came back into the house, his attention turned to Agnes. He put his hand on her head and started praying quietly, but fervently. I couldn't hear what he was a praying about, but soon mother joined him.

"Oh Jesus," my mother prayed out loud, "please bring poor Agnes out of her lethargy, give her the strength and courage to hold on."

Agnes started to stir then. I got closer to hear what she was going to say.

"Praise the Lord," came out of her like the cross between a whisper and squeak.

My father put his ear down near her mouth so he could listen.

"Praise His Holy name," he said, then straightened up. "Agnes is going to be okay. She needs to rest her voice now though."

They put Agnes in my bed so Charlotte could sleep for a change, and I had to go sleep on the couch. Daylight, however, was already starting to invade the room when I fell asleep.

The wait for the second coming went on for two more days. And on this the first day, I awoke about noon to the sound of my father's voice.

"I feel very strong and certain, now," my father was saying, "that this is God's way of weeding out the weak and insincere. Only the very strong, the courageous and those who are absolutely loyal to God's will are destined to be rulers in God's kingdom. And Annie, that is what this coming is all about; to prepare his rulers to lead the repentant and fleeing masses of the coming Armageddon. Our strength will be really tested then."

"I don't know if I'm up to leading so many people," Annie replied tiredly. "What I want is a little peace and tranquility with my Larson in heaven."

"You shall have that Annie, but we first, with God's help, must prepare a place where tranquility can exist for all eternity."

"I suppose you are right Peter," she said with a sigh.

As I lay there listening, I had suddenly got a whiff of food and remembered Annie Smith's promise of the night before and jumped from beneath my blanket and off the couch, totally famished. I didn't have to dress as I had slept with my clothes on. As I moved hurriedly toward the kitchen, I noticed that Annie and my father were heading out through the screen door toward the porch. In the kitchen, the smell of frying eggs and bacon were overwhelming. The smell of such good things thrilled me and gave me reason to live. I noted that Charlotte, Eddie, and Jonathan were already eating, and Agnes Everbe was standing there absently nibbling on a piece of bread. Mother was cooking, but neither she, Annie nor Father were eating as they were fasting.

I ate as much as my mother would let me have. She said we had to save the rest for another day. After I had stuffed my stomach, I felt sleepy again, and I dozed as the afternoon passed more peacefully than the day before. Everyone just sat around with their eyes closed, praying in a whisper. I think they were just trying to recuperate their voices.

As the afternoon sun sank toward the treetops separating us from the old Gatlin place, I noticed that Annie Smith had stopped praying. She started just sitting and staring with her eyes wide open as though she were looking at something that couldn't be seen. But Agnes seemed to regain her enthusiasm, though she still didn't have any voice left. She would walk back and forth, staring silently at the ceiling, but she was jerking her head back and forth like she was thinking just as loud as she usually shouted. My parents both sat praying in a whisper.

Then in the evening when Agnes and we kids were having some split pea soup, Annie announced that she was breaking her fast and joined us for a bowl of the delicious soup. She finished her soup, wiped her lips with a napkin and then turned resolutely to my father. Her wrinkles were like stone and her old frame was straight and stiff.

"I neither have the will nor the strength to hold on any longer," she said in a bold, determined voice. "I'm going home for a good nights sleep."

"Are you sure about this Annie?" My father asked, trying to sound surprised. "Won't you spend just one more night with us?"

"Yes, please!" rasped Agnes hoarsely.

"No, I think your date must be in error, my dear Peter, I'm going home. If God should come, have Him stop by my place. I'll be waiting."

She gave a kiss to each of my parents. My mother had tears in her eyes when she gave old Annie a big hug.

When she got to Agnes, Agnes leaped up to grab for her but her sudden movement caught the table cloth and pulled her hot bowl of pea soup off the table and spilt it in her lap. She leaped into the air letting out a croaking scream. She forgot about Annie as she danced around the table holding her crotch. Annie's wrinkles on her face began to twitch in disbelief as she turned and walked out through the screen door and into the coming darkness. A moment later the tail lights of her old chevy moved off down the long driveway, to flicker once and then disappear into the woods and around the bend.

Less than a week later, Annie Smith had a stroke that paralyzed her. She lived on about a month in a rest home in Tallahassee before another stroke killed her. My mother visited her once at her rest home, but my father sat in the car and wouldn't go in.

On the third day of our vigil, my mother quit fasting and started going about her business. Now only my father continued to fast, but he and Agnes continued to pray. Agnes started getting loud again as her voice was coming back.

Then, it was in the dusk of the evening as the intensity of the moment began to build again that the headlamps of another car began to make their way up the long driveway.

"Now what is it?" My father asked of no one in particular. He became quiet and watched with apprehension. The lights moved slowly and came closer as though they were ghost lights feeling their way alone through the darkness.

"Nothing is going to stop us now, Peter," Agnes said quietly as she laid her hand on his arm lightly.

"The Devil is an ingenious trickster," my father said in a tense voice.

The person on the porch when he got there was a cop, a really big one. His head was out of sight when you looked out the screen door, but I saw a big badge shining on his chest. I was really surprised and excited. Maybe Father was right about the devil part, I thought. No cop had been to our place since Mr. Gatlin had burnt up, and for one to show up now at this particular time was unbelievable! He walked boldly across the gray wooden porch and looked down at my father through the screen door.

"I have been told," he said, "that Agnes Everby is here."

"Who wants to know and why?" My father demanded in frustration.

"I have something that I must speak to her about...." His voice trailed off as he ducked his head to look beyond my father around the room.

"I'm Agnes Everby," Agnes said, almost defiantly, stepping forward toward the door. "What do you want?"

"I have some news......bad news......about your husband Rudi."

"What has he gotten himself into this time?" she asked, scorn surfacing in the tone of her voice.

"He's dead Mrs. Everbe," the cop said flatly.

Agnes' face turned as white as a ghost's face is supposed to be and she staggered as though about to fall. She looked into the faces of all of us present as though pleading for someone to tell her it wasn't true. My father ran to her and grabbed her under the armpits so that she wouldn't fall.

"How?" she whispered imploringly, throwing a desperate glance at the cop standing outside.

"He hung himself Mrs. Everbe. Would you like to come with me, now?"

"No," my father had snapped we will take care of it here."

"Mrs. Everbe?" the cop said, ignoring my father. He was still looking down through the screen door at Agnes.

"Maybe I should," she said, hesitantly. Her eyes were pleading and dark as they glowed unnaturally from her white face. Even her big twitching nose looked pitiful as she looked at my father for guidance.

"Can you wait a moment officer?" My father asked as he turned back toward the screen door and to the form of the big cop and the black night beyond it. His voice became less harsh it seemed.

"I suppose," the cop said, "but not for long."

Father practically carried poor Agnes by the armpits into the kitchen. I followed, unnoticed, so I could hear what he was going to tell her.

"Agnes," his voice was low and urgent. I had to strain hard in order to hear. "This is the Devil's last trick, his guise to deny you the glory of the second coming. Don't go, Agnes! Pray a little longer with us. Rudi is dead, you can't help by going to him now. If you stay, victory is yours, for Christ should be here soon."

"Oh, my Rudi!" her voice cried out. She began to sob, but at the same time she seemed to be getting her strength back. She pulled away from my father, standing on her own two feet. "I will go to my Rudi!" she shouted in a voice that had become brittle like cracking ice. "I should have been with him all along, then maybe he wouldn't have done this terrible thing. You are a fake Peter McGee!" Her voice turned into a hysterical scream. "It is your fault that my Rudi is dead. You caused me to neglect him. I told him I was leaving him for a better life, and it is your fault Peter McGee!" She just screamed then with no words coming out of her mouth, and she slapped my father across the cheek.

My mother ran to get the cop.

Father just looked confused and turned to stare at the drip…. drip…..drip falling from the faucet above the kitchen sink.

I then heard a commotion behind me and turned to see the big cop, with a big gun hanging at his waist, ducking his head to enter the kitchen. Father just ignored him as the cop took Agnes by the arm and led her out through the screen door into the dark night.

Agnes had been breathing heavily, her big sore nose inflating and deflating rapidly as the cop led her through the dimly lit sitting room of our little house in the woods. Her dark eyes were moving rapidly from one thing to another. She seemed to be constantly trying to look over her shoulder as though to get one last look at my father before she finally walked through the screen door and was swallowed up by the darkness beyond.

After Agnes and the cop were gone, Father went into his bedroom and shut the door. He stayed in there for three days and three nights. Mother said he was praying all that time.

The rest of us started eating and acting normal again. We began to eat the vegetables my mother had canned during the last summer. We also had some potatoes and lima beans to soak. We had some flour that Annie had brought. And lima beans are pretty good with fresh baked bread. But I had to soak the bread in bean juice because we had no butter.

I started going back to the woods again to dream dreams. I had more fun dreaming then because there was more of a chance that they would come true now. I didn't believe in the second coming anymore. Robin had been right all along.

# JORJE CARLYLE

THE SHARP CALL of the whippoorwill came out of the dark woods. The sharpness of its call was almost startling, surrounded, as it was, with the predawn silence. The darkness, attempting to be cool, brought its voice through my open window and left it hanging with suspended clarity.

The adrenalin racing out of my stomach left me sleepless, wide awake to think and plan, to mull over the events of the day before, a day that I had spent with Jorje Carlyle.

But the light thoughts that brought thrills and restlessness were soon to be invaded by heavy ones, thoughts that hung like anchors on my brain. The image of my father paraded before me, with an evil grin twisting the lips on his face.

After the aborted second coming, my father spent three days and three nights in his bedroom then emerged a changed man. He came out a tyrant, determined that he was not going to lose any of his family to the wily Devil. We had to stand by him and wait, no matter how long Christ delayed his second coming.

Shortly after he emerged from his three days and three nights of prayer, I made the terrible mistake of telling him that I didn't believe that there was going to be any second coming. He became almost hysterical in his own stern way. He ordered me, on the spot, to my knees and had, with a firm hand on my head, dictated my prayer of repentance to God. I rebelled at first, refusing to repeat what he was saying. But the pressure on my head became intense, and he began to twist my head until I didn't think my neck was going to support the pressure any longer. I began to pray then, following his dictations. I, then found relief from the twisting pressure, like the rat in Pavlov's cage. But unlike a rat, my brain remained active, and I denied each word uttered in repentance as fast as I said them.

I didn't have much faith in my defiance though. God was omnipotent, and you just had to learn to live with Him.

My voice continued to follow the long dictation, "Forgive me, the weak moments in my hour of disappointment and frustration.".

The next several months had been a nightmare of determined prayers and long waits beneath the cold winter stars for flying saucers that never came.

It was in August that the breaking point finally came. The heat had been intense that summer day. The sweat poured from my body as I lay naked, propped up against a log, the one deep in the woods where Robin and I had spent our passion fucking on that warm day of the winter before. That day seemed so long ago now, as the mosquitoes swarmed and the bees hummed around it, dripping, sticky and wasted to the damp earth. I tried to remember Robin's pussy more distinctly as I jerked harder, hoping for a little more pleasure before I had to return to the impotency of my father's world.

I couldn't get far from his world, however, because my father had locked up my bicycle back in January when I had doubted the second coming. Things had improved, somewhat, in the spring when the second coming still failed to materialize because Father became more reclusive, spending more and more time in the bedroom, again, praying. I started spending hours in the woods thinking and planning.

Then one evening as I had walked up the long driveway, sweat dripping, damp, beneath my old shirt, a brilliant idea occurred to me. It was like a breath of fresh air in a hot mosquito-infested swamp on late August night. The undulating chorus of the cicadae cheered me on in the evening stillness. I could walk to town and visit Jorje Carlyle! Father wouldn't miss me as long as I was home for supper. He was too busy the rest of the time praying in his bedroom. I looked up at the steamy kitchen light that shone through the window of our little house in the dark woods and knew that it was a good idea.

I climbed the steps to the front porch with newfound buoyancy, even though I knew that we were out of bread, and all we would have for supper would be some of last summers dried lima beans and fresh vegetables from the garden. I was hungry for meat, and the hope came to me that maybe Jorje would invite me to eat some of his food. It wasn't that far to town. I could walk it, maybe even catch a ride. The gray boards beneath my feet seemed to announce my arrival too loudly as I crossed them and opened the old screen door.

"Where have you been, Bobby?" demanded the stern voice of my father as I walked into the steamy light of the hot kitchen. He stood at the window, looking out, as though he had been watching my approach. "You have been gone nearly all day which is inexcusable."

I looked at his angry face as he turned it toward me and my newfound purpose in life began to disintegrate. I wished he would just disappear and be like God.

"I was praying in the woods," I said, as I looked past him at the big bowl of yellow lima beans that stood steaming on the table.

"It is honorable that you spend your time praying," he said, coldly, "but from now on I want you to pray closer to the house and in sight so we can keep an eye on you, and where you can hear us when we call. Is that understood?

His voice grated on me, like sand on a raw sore. I knew that I should keep quiet for my own good. But I felt my voice coming out of me like it was talking by itself.

"No," my voice yelled, "I'll pray where I please!"

He grabbed my arm and was trying to hold me and take his belt off at the same time. I jerked free.

"I have had enough of you!" I screamed, "both you and Go….. God….there!" I said it out loud and I was still alive!

I attempted to get past him and out the front door but he grabbed my arm again and held on. So I just stood and let him whip me with his belt. The anger inside me hardened, and I was determined that this would never happen again. I would have to delay, though, my visit to Jorje.

My father would be watching me closely for awhile. He raised the strap to sting my arms because I was ignoring the sting to my butt. I ignored that pain too.

At the supper table Father watched me closely while my anger smoldered quietly. I was not hungry anymore, but I put a spoonful of beans in my mouth anyway and took my fork and reached for a quartered tomato.

"Pass the salt," I said, as normally as I could.

"We are out of salt," my mother said while throwing a glance at Father.

So I bit my tongue and ate my tomato without salt.

"I got a letter from Betty Barnes today," my mother ventured.

"She has a lot of audacity writing here. What did she want?" Father growled.

"She wrote to say goodbye to me. They left for North Dakota this morning."

"Good riddance," my father mumbled as he gulped down a large spoonful of beans. "The likes of them desecrate holy ground," he said, as he reached zestfully for another helping of beans.

I continued to smolder and nibble at my tomato, but my mind had come alive, to envelope itself around the thought of North Dakota. I mulled over it as I absent mindedly took a helping of beans and began to eat them.

The solution hit me with the force, simplicity and suddenness that comes with the enlightenment of a Zen monk. I began to relish my beans and tomatoes. I would run away and go find the Barneses in North Dakota. My purpose in life had returned! Mr. Barnes would be good to me because he hated my father too, and he didn't know about Robin and I. I ate more beans and more tomatoes. Fuck father and his whippings; they didn't hurt that bad. Tomorrow I was going to town to see Jorje Carlyle!

"Wha.......what town in North Dakota are the Barneses going to?" I asked, trying to sound casual as I had glanced at my mother and shoved another spoonful of beans into my mouth.

"What difference does it make?" she had asked. "North Dakota is North Dakota." She sounded like someone talking to herself. She was picking absently at a quarter of tomato with her fork.

"I want to look it up on my roadmap," I said. Everyone knew about my old US road atlas. The pages were worn and torn, but I had used it for years to chart fantasy trips and lately, to look for places that I could run away to.

"Oh," she said in an unsuspecting voice, "Far....Far......Far....or something...Fargo, that was it," she said as she continued to poke absently at her tomato.

I lowered my eyes and didn't respond. I dare not let anyone guess my thoughts. I rapidly cleaned up my plate and ran to my bedroom to find Fargo on the map. It turned out that half of my map of North Dakota was missing, and Fargo was missing with it.

I couldn't sleep that night. I tossed and turned in my restlessness. I lay scheming as to how I might get away the next morning. It all depended on what my father did.

The next morning, early, my father come out of his room when he smelled the frying potatoes Mother was fixing for breakfast. He ignored me as though he were preoccupied with more important things. He probably thought that I would be too scared to do anything so soon after getting whipped.

We ate the fried potatoes with a helping of hot cooked tomatoes.

"We are almost out of gas for the cook stove," Mother said as she sat down at the table.

"God'll provide," my father said. "I got a letter from a church up in Tallahassee yesterday. They want me to preach on the second coming tomorrow night. Maybe they will take up an offering for me. The guy said he would pay for my gas."

"I hope so," Mother said.

I said nothing. I just took another helping of tomatoes. The fried potatoes had already vanished. It seemed that Eddie and Jonathan always ate more than their share, and they ate so fast! On this morning though I really didn't care what I ate. I had my mind on town and Jorje Carlyle.

Father just went back to his bedroom after breakfast. He was probably trying to figure out what to say at the church in Tallahassee.

I was thrilled, restless, and anxious to get away but overly cautious. I hung around the house impatiently pacing as the summer heat of the morning began to come through the doors and windows. Father did not reappear, so I finally got the courage to leave the house. I went into the woods that separated our place from the old burnt out Gatlin place. From there I watched and sweated in the shade for almost an hour. I saw nothing of my father, and no one else seemed to miss me. I made my escape!

I cut through the Gatlin place to the narrow, deserted old dirt road that went to town. I walked along it beneath the hot Florida sun. It seemed forever that I walked, the sweat dripping, my clothes clinging to me in the damp, intense heat before I heard the humming motor of an approaching automobile. It came from behind and stopped when it got up even with me. I turned to see an old pickup with Mr. Beezley driving it.

"Jump in," he shouted above the hum of his engine. I could hear his gear shift grinding. "Aint you one of the McGee kids?" He shouted into my ear as I jumped in beside him. The clutch slipped from beneath his foot and the old truck jumped forward as though someone had pinched it in the butt.

"Yeah," I said meekly. I hoped he would wouldn't say anything to my father.

"I heard your old man has been having some kind of strange visions or sumpin." He had thrown me a funny glance as though we shared a secret and he hoped I would elaborate.

"No sir, he didn't see nothing, though he sure was a looking for something, but I best not talk about this or I might get into to trouble." I said.

So he changed the subject and mumbled something about how hot it was and how he couldn't keep the fleas and ticks off his dog.

"By the way," he said, raising his voice just as we were arriving at the filling station, "you better start keeping that old dog of your'n at home. I caught him humping my old bitch the other day. I thought she was too old for that sort of thing but she was a standing there like she liked it. I ran'em off but I 'magin he'll be back unless you keep'em home."

"Ok," I said, thanking him for the ride and jumping from the truck. He pulled along beside the gas pump where Jack got killed.

But when he had mentioned Joe, a wave of sadness had swept over me. If I ran away, I would have to leave Joe forever. But I got to thinking some more about it as I had walked up the highway towards Third Street. Joe had sort of grown up like I had. He had girlfriends all around the countryside, and I figured he stole the food the neighbors fed their dogs. Besides we didn't have much food for Joe anymore, at least the kind he liked. But I still felt the hot tears well up in my eyes, and then roll down my cheeks.

But then my grief was distracted as I arrived at Third Street and turned down it and soon could see Jorje's house up ahead. I strained my eyes in and effort to see if Jorje was sitting on his porch. A wave of disappointment swept over me when I couldn't find him. As I got closer, though, I spied his garage door open and could see his big black car sitting there.

When I arrived and walked boldly onto his porch, I could hear the hum of a fan somewhere in the dark behind the screen door. As I raised my fist to knock I hesitated, suddenly overwhelmed by uncertainty and shyness. What if he was busy and didn't want to see me, or maybe he was drunk and wouldn't recognize me. He might even run me off in anger, after the way Father had run him off our place last winter. As I continued to stand there, my face began to burn with acute embarrassment! What if he was watching me? I had just about decided to turn and walk away.

"Just open the door and come in, son." A voice coming out of the dark behind the screen door said.

"Ok," I said, feebly as I grasped for the door knob then entered.

Jorje sat naked in a big armchair. The fan hung from the ceiling and was spinning rapidly, creating a cool breeze, or at least a breeze that brought relief from the stifling heat. The room was dark, he had the blinds pulled. There was a coffee table in front of the couch, and there was a nice soft carpet on the floor. I didn't notice this at first though as I was too stunned by Jorje's nakedness. I remembered what Reba Boone said a long time ago while standing across the street on the church grounds. So now I figured that she had told the truth after all!

"I never wear clothes when I'm alone, and it is hot like this in the summertime," he said, evidently noticing my gawking eyes and mouth, agape. He stood. I could make out his long dick and hanging balls. They seemed so much bigger and longer than mine. "Sit down on the couch there while I put on a pair of shorts." When he walked away, his butt looked hairy and kind of old.

I then began to notice the room as I sat there alone. It was cozy and pictures hung on the walls. One I could make out was a girl. In the dark she looked like a beautiful girl, but I was too shy to go look closer. He might return and catch me looking. Then I felt a cold nose shoved against my ankle. Jorje's little dog was doing a smell analyses. I reached down and petted his little head. He was a lot smaller than Joe, and he gave my fingers a dainty kiss of appreciation.

Jorje entered with a pair of baggy shorts on. With a little jerk he pulled the blind up, exposing the room to the light of day. Jorje needed a shave and his hair seemed more gray then I had remembered. As I had suspected, the girl who's picture hung on the wall was beautiful. She had dark olive skin with black hair.

"Well, what can I do for you son? What did you say your name was?"

"Bobby McGee," I replied.

"McGee...?" He hesitated, giving me a long glance. "You mean preacher McGee? I'll bet you're preacher McGee's son aren't you?"

"Yes sir," I responded.

"I guess your father is still here, isn't he?"

"Yes sir," I replied again.

He chuckled, then stared off into a dark corner of the room for a moment.

"How is he taking his defeat?" There seemed to be a glint of mischief in his eyes when he turned them back upon me.

"Okay, sir, but he still thinks that the second coming is going to be any day now. He has quit work, and we can't afford meat anymore." I immediately knew that I said the wrong thing and felt my face blush with embarrassment.

"Huh," Jorje grunted, ignoring my frustration. "So he won't admit defeat?" His voice became distant as though talking to himself. "I have seen the symptoms before," he said, "but never so blatantly obvious." Jorje stared at the floor but his eyes didn't act like they saw it. "It's what we call schizophrenia," he said, then glanced at me as though to share a private thought. "The symptoms are present in all Christians in varying degrees, but most manage to appear rational, but it sounds like your father has really gone off the deep end."

"How about you, Bobby, what are your plans? Do you also believe that God is going to be returning at any moment?"

"No, not anymore," I responded, "I'm planning to run away."

"That is one solution," he said, as he turned his gaze to stare thoughtfully into the dark corner of the room again.

"There are roses everywhere," he said, "when we want to see them." His eyes seemed to moisten a little, but I didn't know what he was talking about. "And one does not have to go elsewhere to look for them," he added.

I still didn't know what Jorje was talking about but it sounded important, like someone reading poetry. I then remembered a man with a beard who had come to the school and read poetry to our class.

"The problem with the rose is ..." Jorje continued as though talking to someone hidden in the darkness in the far corner of the room, "we try to touch it, hold it, yes even absorb it into the depths of our hearts. But that is when we discover that the rose is protected by thorns that scratch and tear at us to leave our hearts bleeding and broken." He looked back at me then like that he suddenly remembered that he was supposed to be talking to me.

"But you know Bobby," he continued, "it seems that we never learn for as we heal from the scars of one encounter, we grasp again for the compelling beauty of another."

He turned his gaze from me then, to stare at the picture that was hanging on the wall. Near the picture of the girl, hung something else that caught my eye. It looked like a painting and was full of distorted figures that looked like screaming dead people. There was a horse in it with a sword coming out of its mouth. Jorje, glancing back at me, followed my gaze.

"That is a print of *Guernica*," he said. "Picasso painted that in memory of the civilians slaughtered by Franco's forces during the Spanish civil war."

I would, I vowed to myself, study about such things as this someday, so that I could be civilized. For the moment though, I had looked back at the pretty girl.

"Was she your wife, once?" I asked.

His gaze went back to her picture. but it quickly turned away as though what he saw was too painful.

I watched him staring back at *Guernica* for a moment, but then looked out the window to see some red roses growing on the fence. They were big and beautiful and climbed to the top. Then I thought, maybe the girl was Jorje's rose.

"No!" he suddenly said, with a force that startled me. "I never married. The women that I have loved were like those roses out there." He said, glancing through the window. "They were beautiful at a distance, but I brought them too close to me, and they left scars in my heart that will never heal. There are lots of things like those roses, Bobby McGee."

I thought I knew then what he meant by "only smelling the roses" and said, "I love a girl too. She ran away to North Dakota, though, because she didn't want to be bothered by the second coming. And she knew before it happened that it wasn't going to happen."

"Is that so? She sounds like a spunky kid. Is that where you are planning to run away to also?"

"Yes sir."

He was quiet for a while as he stared out at the roses twisting in the late summer breeze.

I was hoping that he would offer me a beer and just as I thought it he turned back at me as though reading my mind.

"I was going to stick to beer, but what the hell, I'll offer you something even better. The marijuana plant can harm no one when used in moderate amounts. It is a mild and healthy hallucinogen. I'll share a joint with you Bobby, if you would like."

His words had nearly taken my breath away. The excitement nearly choked me. I just stared at him speechless, my mouth agape.

"I know," he said and grinned. "those who are at war with nature will tell you it is evil and wrong. But true evil comes from the wag of their tongues, so relax Bobby."

I looked out at the roses again, and in the breeze, they looked like the color red dancing, and my heart was throbbing with the thrill of committing such an evil deed.

"I'm going to have a joint myself," Jorje said casually, then stood and walked into the kitchen. When he returned he had a small wooden box. He sat and poured the stuff on a small white piece of paper. He rolled it, and licked it and then lit it. He inhaled deeply and held his breath for a long time, it seemed. He blew the smoke out, finally, and the sweet smell was tantalizing.

"Want to have a drag, or do you want a beer instead?"

He held the little cigarette out to me. My arm lifted and my hand reached out to take it while my body sat shaking. I bravely put it between my lips and puffed, gingerly.

"No," he laughed, "You waste it that way." He took it and inhaled deeply again, "like that," he said. I took it, and with determination I inhaled deeply. I almost gagged but held it bravely. Jorje laughed at my discomfiture.

"Good…..good, Bobby," Jorje said as he took the joint back for another go at it.

I decided that it didn't feel so evil after all. And as the afternoon passed, I noticed the roses out the window were getting bigger and becoming more beautiful than any rose that I had ever seen. I began to feel so good that I decided that what I felt like was probably like what I would have felt when the flying saucers took off going to Zion, if they had come.

"I ran away from home when I was about your age." Jorje began, after he had lit a second joint. "My father was a gambler, a whisky drinking Irishman. He won a small farm down in Cuba in a poker game. He moved there where he met and married my mother."

"The earliest thing I can remember about him was him yelling at and beating my mother. When he got drunk, he was a tyrant. And it seems he was always getting drunk. Finally he started trying to beat me as well but my mother would have none of it. She would get between us and end up getting a beating for protecting me."

"When I was nine or ten years old, he lost our place in another poker game while on a drunken spree in Havana one night. I think he was also in trouble with the law because the next morning he rushed my mother and I in a taxi to the airport where we caught a plane for Miami."

"As I got older in Miami, it got so my mother couldn't protect me anymore, and I have got the scars to prove it. My father couldn't hold a job, and he would come home drunk in the middle of the day. By the time I was fifteen, I was getting beat up trying to protect my mother. Finally at seventeen, I ran away, with a promise to my mother that I would get a job somewhere, and she could come live with me to hide from my father. 'I'll support you Mom,' I remember promising her."

"I went to Jacksonville," he continued, then paused. "I bet I'm boring you, aren't I?" A smile started to play around his lips.

"No," I said, "I want to hear about it." I had the joint and tried to suck on it more deeply.

"Well, while in Jacksonville, I worked for a veterinarian as a kennel boy. I always liked animals, but the only one I ever had was an old blue tick hound in Cuba. My father kicked him to death in a drunken rage once for growling at him when he was trying to beat on me."

"I got me a room and wrote my mother, asking her to come join me. I warned her to hide the letter and not to give her plans away to my father."

"I guess I'll never know what happened, but several weeks after I had written the letter, I found my father waiting for me when I came home from work one evening. I saw him just in time to keep from being grabbed. I started running then with him in hot pursuit. It seemed we ran for miles, and he stayed right on my tail. I was growing exhausted! For a drunk that old man sure could run! Finally, just when I was beginning to think it was all over he gave up and started to scream and curse at me."

" 'No god dammed son 'o mine is going to run from me!' he screamed. 'I'll take you home, you fucking brat, if'n I have to do it dead in a plastic bag'."

"I left him screaming as I rounded a corner, turning up another street. He didn't follow, but I was still terrified. I made my way back to the animal hospital, hoping he wouldn't find out where I worked. I slept on a cot with a bunch of lonely and sick dogs barking and howling around me for nearly two weeks, afraid to go near my apartment. When I finally did return, I found a letter in my mailbox. It was from the police in Miami."

" 'We are sorry to inform you,' it began and then continued, 'that your mother is dead, she died from an assault, and your father is the suspect, but he has disappeared,' it continued, but I could not bring myself to read anymore and the tears were blinding my eyes anyway. I collapsed on the steps leading up to my apartment gasping at the emptiness I felt inside me. But I knew that my father had killed her and was still looking for me, and the sudden thought that he might be upstairs waiting for me now left me no choice but to leave and go on the run. So I left my apartment and my few belongings never to return."

"Though my pangs of hunger had turned to grief, I knew that I should eat before taking to the road so I went to a small café where I often ate, but as I ate I glanced through the window to see my father standing in the parking lot. I was gripped with terror even though I couldn't be certain that it was actually him. I ran behind the counter and through the kitchen, while the cooks stared in disbelief, to slip out the back door."

"I first fled to my cot in the animal clinic, but couldn't sleep. The possibility that he had followed me was pure torture. I felt like a trapped animal so finally ran into the dark streets in a panic to run like a somnambulant fleeing his own shadow. I was terrified of every movement and every dark street held an imminent threat. Not only did I imagine the dark ghost of my father right behind me, but I feared the thieves and murderers waiting in the dark shadows ahead of me. I ignored the exhaustion that was beginning to creep over me. My mouth opened to gasp for air as I stumbled, plunging to get to the end of the street beneath my feet only to struggle and plunge to get to the end of the next street that I must cover."

"Finally, the thunder of the ocean surf penetrated my terrified brain. I increased my efforts as I frantically ran toward it. Suddenly the street came to an end, and I was alone on the cool sand. I looked behind me and no one had followed. I ran to be closer to the sea then fell exhausted to sleep like a baby until I was doused by the incoming tide in the darkness before dawn."

Jorje hesitated again, giving me a keen glance.

"Still not boring you?"

"Oh no!" I responded, "I want to hear what happened next."

But he was quiet for awhile anyway. He stared out through the window again.

The red roses seemed to twist with pleasure in the gentle breeze and had become so big and beautiful that I could hardly stand to look at them without crying out for joy!

"I don't know about you, Bobby, but I'd like a beer now," he said suddenly as he stood and looked at me.

"Okay!" I said with a joy that I had never felt before.

He returned and handed me an open bottle. I took a long contented swig from it and then waited for Jorje to start talking again.

"Now where was I? Oh yes, on the beach," he said, resuming his story. "I was disoriented when I awoke with the salty sea swirling around me and dragging the sand from beneath me with it. I couldn't remember why I was there. Then I noticed a distant figure coming down the beach in the half light of the dawn and remembered everything. I started running again, only now I was trying to get off the beach and back on the road. I turned to watch the lonely figure as it trudged along on the sand right past me without so much as a glance in my direction."

"I came to my senses then. I knew that I could not just keep running around the city of Jacksonville. I had to plan. I sat down on a bench that stood by the concrete walkway that stretched along the beach and concentrated on my dilemma. I finally decided that I was going to leave Jacksonville and Florida and go far away. But with this decision made, the grief from my mother's death again hit me, leaving me nearly breathless. I began to sob uncontrollably until my body began to shake. I only brought my sobbing to an end by concentrating on my hatred for the man who had killed her, my father."

He was quiet, again, his eyes seeming to stare and follow the carpet that stretched off across the floor. But after awhile he began again.

"The realization of my immediate plight again invaded my consciousness. I got up, wiped my eyes dry, brushed the sand from my clothes and walked off into the uncertainty of the new day."

"On the street, I had no more than lifted my thumb then an old lady had picked me up and took me to downtown Jacksonville."

Jorje laughed then as he contemplated the memory.

" 'Son, you look like you slept on the beach all night,' she said and laughed. When I told her that I had, she gave me a long hard stare and asked if I was homeless. I told her that I was and after that she was silent until she said, 'this is far as I go.'"

"I got several rides around Jacksonville before I finally ended up on the highway north to Waycross, Georgia. It was an old man who picked me up on the highway going north. He had on overalls and chomped on a big cigar that was so chewed up on the end that it looked like he was eating it. His face was wrinkled, and he had an ancient smile that seemed glued around his lips.

"'There aint much work up in Georgia,' he had said, friendly like."

"But he didn't take me far before he dropped me off in a little place called Folkston, Georgia. I especially remember the mosquitoes as I walked by the side of the road that ran up along beside the Okefenokee swamp. They were so big that when you squashed them, blood would splatter, and you would wonder who's blood it was while hoping it wasn't yours. When I would hear the hum of an automobile behind me, I would stop and hold the thumb of one hand out and slap mosquitoes with the other hand. Fear of my father had faded with the miles I had traveled after leaving Jacksonville."

"I think I must have been walking along for an hour when I turned to see an old Studebaker with a loud muffler approaching me on the hot pavement. Sweat was pouring down my face, and my thumb pleaded for it to stop. It passed me without slowing down, and my hand dropped to my side in disappointment. But then I heard the screaming of tires up ahead and turned to watch it grind to a halt beside the pavement. I ran up to it, clutched and jerked open the front door. I was about to jump into the front seat when I noticed my father sitting behind the steering wheel. An evil grin twisted the corners of his lips. I stared in terror unable to move."

"'Howdy son,' he said, 'come on, get in, les lut bygones be bygones. I ain't goin to beat ya no more.'"

"His smooth quiet voice only caused the terror to sink in more deeply because that was the way he used to talk to my mother before he would give her the worst of his beatings.

"'I said get in son,' he said, and this time I could detect the anger and violence that was just beneath the surface. He had never begged anything of me before, but he had used to do it with my mother. The thought of how he had probably killed her raced through my mind and how he was probably using the same method with me that he had with her. My mind was on the verge of panic, but I knew I must have a plan of action and have it quick. Plans of action began to race through my brain in succession, but my body seemed disconnected from them. He suddenly opened his door and shifted the old car into neutral."

"'I guess you need some help getting into the car,' he said."

"This galvanized me and put my legs into motion, I started running back towards the town I had come from. I could hear the roar of the old Studebaker as he turned it around and came racing back toward me. I have never felt more helpless in my life," Jorje said and began to stare silently at his feet.

"What did he do to you when he caught you?" I asked, unable to sit silently with my suspense.

Jorje turned a long and silent gaze upon me before he began again.

"Well," Jorje said, "it wasn't so much what he did to me as what he tried to do. As I continued to run, he pulled up beside me and when I looked at him, my terror nearly paralyzed me. My worst fears were realized. He had a gun pointed directly at my head."

"'I warned you,' my father yelled above the clatter of the noisy engine, 'that I was going to take you back, even if I had to do it in a plastic bag!'"

"I stopped in my tracks, the taste of death on my tongue and faced the terror of certain oblivion."

"'Now get in!' he roared again."

"I walked slowly toward the pointing gun. He then opened his door and for a split second the barrel of the gun was taken off me. I turned and ran behind the car. Then I ran across the highway and started screaming at the top of my lungs."

"'Someone please help me, someone please help!' But in the midday heat that surrounded me, all were asleep or maybe all were dead. I couldn't tell, but no one came to my rescue."

"On the side of the road leading toward the swamp, the roof of a house shimmered in the midday heat, but it was at the end of a long and secluded driveway. I could see a short distance up the driveway what appeared to be a partial clearing with huge stumps and scattered piles of brush, and I could see a bulldozer sitting idle amongst them beneath the hot sun."

"I quickly glanced back at my father who was now standing beside his car with the gun again pointing directly at me."

"I don't know what made me do it, maybe just the survival instinct, but I quickly dropped flat and rolled into the drainage ditch beside the road as I heard the gunshot and the bullet whizzing over my head. I scrambled, first frantically crawling then running bent over from one group of trees and bushes to another along the secluded drive as my father continued to take shots at me. He was running along the drive behind me. Soon I came to the clearing and frantically crossed the drive as a hail of bullets came flying over me and around me."

"When I think back on it," Jorje said, interrupting his narrative, "the actions I took that day never cease to amaze me. After the gun came out, none of my actions were planned, they were simply instinctive. I guess that I was simply an animal in the 'fight for survival' mode."

He was again silent for awhile and took several swigs of beer from his bottle. But I sat nearly breathless, my bottle of beer sitting on the table in front of me, waiting to hear what was going to happen next.

"When I entered the clearing, I had a moment of respite, out of my father's line of fire. And the first thing I noticed was a row of venerable old cypress trees loaded with Spanish moss and behind them was nothing but darkness, but they were on the other side of the clearing. I figured it was dark swamp land and felt that if I could just make it over there, I would probably be safe. But then I heard his voice almost right behind me, it seemed, and instinctively knew I did not have time to cross the clearing."

"'You are a fucking bastard,' he was screaming. 'Your mother screwed another man to get you, and that is why I had to kill her. Now I'm going to kill you, her bastard son.' His voice had become almost hysterical and the horror of his words had sapped some of the strength out of me. But in the split second battle between the horror of the words he spoke and my desire to live, the latter won and I moved in a panic for the first pile of brush. Dropping to my knees, I scrambled to crawl under it, lifting dead limbs and shoving rotting stumps to one side. I crawled as far as I could go beneath it."

"'I know you are in there!' he yelled. And he was standing right beside my pile of brush. I simply flattened to the ground in silence, my heart like a stone gripped with terror. But then to my amazement, he moved on into the clearing. Suddenly he started shooting, but he was shooting somewhere else, probably into a different pile of brush, and the thought that he would probably return and do the same to my hiding place left we weak, my body profusely sweating. I felt then that it was probably all but over and that I was going to die."

"The gunfire went off several times though his voice had become silent. It was then that I suddenly heard a clicking sound, and I knew he was out of bullets. And then I prayed, dear God don't let him have more with him! I think my prayer was answered because I then heard his footsteps approaching. When he stood beside me, he suddenly yelled, 'if you are in there bastard, I will be back to get you!' He then started poking my pile of brush with a stick. I could hear it hitting the ground around me, and then it hit my leg. I figured he knew that I was there. But if he did, he didn't let on. He just walked away, but I knew that he would be back."

"I lay there on the damp earth beneath the brush until I was as certain as possible that he was gone and then I wiggled my way out. I had to do it feet first because I couldn't turn around, so I expected at any moment that he might be there to grab my feet. But I decided since he probably didn't have any bullets, I still had a chance to escape. Nothing happened and I was soon standing on my feet looking frantically around, and I again decided the swamp was my best bet so I ran across the clearing and jumped the fence."

What I saw was a dark impenetrable jungle with what appeared to be black mud beneath it. One step into it, and the black dark muck stuck in gobs on my foot, and I knew that this was no escape. I quickly climbed back over the fence and crossed the clearing where I peeked around a tree back down toward the highway. I saw nothing, so I began to make my way back, moving from one clump of bushes or trees to another. I crawled back into the drainage ditch then half stood to peek across the highway to where my father's old Studebaker still sat. To my shock and surprise, he was sitting in the driver's seat with his head resting on the steering wheel! He appeared to be asleep!"

"The sight sent hope surging through me. I ducked down to consider my course of action, but then it suddenly dawned on me that he might be pretending to be asleep as a trap. So I thought about it some more and peeked over again. He had not moved. It was then I decided to move down the highway a ways in the drainage ditch then cross over and crawl along that drainage ditch to the right side of the car and let the air out of his two right tires."

So I proceeded to carry out my plan. When I had moved some distance down the highway, I again peeked back, and it appeared that he still had not moved. So with my heart in my mouth, I quickly ran across the highway and into the other drainage ditch. I quickly moved back towards the old Studebaker. When I was even with it, I moved right up next to the rear right tire and bravely, with a stick, started letting the air out of the tire. The hissing sound was so loud that it nearly made me jump, but I continued anyway with the thought that this was my only hope. I let out a gasp of relief when the tire was empty. I then very slowly rose to peek into the car to note that my father had not moved. With a little more self-confidence, I stood up to look more closely. But just as I did, he sat up and looked back down the dirt road I had just come down. I quickly fell to the ground realizing that he was trying to set a trap after all!"

I knew then that he was sitting there, waiting on me with his gun loaded. I half stood, just enough to see his head looking down the road, and I saw him take a long swig of whiskey. I heard him mutter something, and I rose a little higher to see him put his head back down on the steering wheel. I moved quickly to the front tire and began to let the air out with my stick. The hissing noise was so loud that I could not believe he did not hear, but I bravely continued until this tire was empty. I then quickly rolled back into the drainage ditch and made my way back down the road.

I had not gone far, but I was regaining my self-confidence. I was just about to stand and run when I heard the blood curdling scream of my father. I flattened myself in the ditch and slowly twisted around so that I could see. He was standing beside his car with a whiskey bottle in one hand while violently kicking his flat tire. He started looking around wildly, and I could only hope the grass was high enough to hide me.

I watched while he crossed the highway as though he were going to walk back down the drive, but changed his mind and walked back to stand beside his car and look back down the highway towards me. He then turned and looked the other way. He then violently threw the whiskey bottle onto the highway where it splintered into little pieces. He opened his door and got his gun and started pointing it in all directions, and a shot flew over my head. He finally decided to get back into the car, and I started to crawl again frantically away from him."

I crawled, with the mosquitoes eating me alive, until I could take no more. I jumped to my feet and looked back at the distant Studebaker then turned and ran as hard as I could run."

It was as though my brain was hardwired with fear and terror, and I could hear or see nothing, but then through the mental fog came the blare of a horn. I came to myself and found that I was standing in the middle of the road with a strange car stopped in front of me blowing his horn. I ran to him, begging loudly for a ride."

"'Settle down son,' the gentle voice said, 'and go around and get in.'"

"I nearly collapsed with exhaustion on the seat beside him as he took off down the road. But then the terror again climbed into my throat as I saw the old Studebaker up ahead. Suddenly my father had jumped from his car and started waving frantically for my benefactor to stop."

"'Might as well give this guy a ride as well,' he said, slowing down."

"'Mister, no!' I screamed, 'that man is trying to kill me!'"

"So my benefactor moved on past my father, but moving slowly."

"'Why would you think he is trying to kill you, son? I fear you are delirious. The man needs a ride'. And with that he pulled over and stopped by the side of the road."

"In a panic I looked back to see my father rapidly approaching the car and I turned, desperate, towards my benefactor. 'Sir' I said, using all the power within me to sound calm, 'that man is my father and he is trying to kill me. If you let him get in, he will not only kill me, he will kill you because you will be a witness.'"

"'Huh,' the man said. Then suddenly just as my father was reaching for the door handle, he took off, burning rubber on the pavement. I think I fainted then or simply fell asleep because the next thing I remember was the late afternoon sun on my face and the man shaking me to ask me if I was hungry."

Jorje stopped talking as though he were finished. He took several long swigs of beer and sighed contentedly.

After a while I asked, "Did your father ever catch you?"

"No," he said. "I never saw him again. And I didn't stop running until I got to Chicago."

Jorje then looked at his little dog who was patiently standing at the door looking back at him. "Do you have to go pee, Patch?" Jorje asked him.

Patch seemed to nod and show his teeth in a smile. Jorje went over and opened the door for him.

I was suddenly aware of how fast the afternoon was advancing. But I felt so mellow and relaxed that I didn't want it to end. I took the last swig from my beer bottle.

"I got to go home," I said, "or my father will miss me."

Jorje had glanced at his watch. "The time has flown," he said. "I'll give you a ride home, if you want," he offered.

"Thank you very much, Jorje!" I said. My only disappointment was that he had not offered me anything to eat, and I was starved.

A short time later he was letting me out at the old Gatlin place.

"Jorje," I asked before slamming the door behind me, "Will you tell me about the girl who's picture hangs on the wall?"

"Yeah, maybe," he said, "if you don't run away before I get to it."

I ran through the tall grass, growing unkempt, in the Gatlin yard, then through the woods that separated their old place from ours.

At home my father was nowhere to be seen and my mother never even looked up when I entered. She sat on the couch reading the bible. Why do they just keep reading it over and over again, I suddenly wondered, since it always said the same thing?

As daylight gradually seeped through my window, the cry of the whippoorwill stopped. The fading darkness was silent. I rolled about restlessly in my bed. I wanted to go back to Jorje's house to hear about the girl. I wanted to smoke his pot and drink his beer, and the thought of it thrilled me. But I didn't dare go two days in a row, I reasoned. First Jorje would get tired of me coming so often but mostly it would be pushing my luck to expect my father not to miss me a second day in a row. But I decided I was going to visit him once more before I ran away.

In the late morning, I went to the woods and dreamed of the sweet smoke rising from a marijuana joint and the pink pussy lip that hung from Robin's panties in the winter woods.

# THE RUNAWAY

In early September, I knew that if I was going to run away to North Dakota, I had to go soon because I figured the winters came early and were cold up there. It had been almost a month since I had spent the day with Jorje. I had not had another chance to visit him, or at least I had been afraid to take one.

My father had a new revelation from God in which to him a new date for the second coming.

"None of you," my father stated firmly, "are to reveal this date to anyone outside our immediate family." He looked at my mother accusingly. This announcement had been just two days after my last visit with Jorje.

After the announcement, he didn't spend as much time in the bedroom. He would walk around staring at everyone, making you feel miserable and guilty. He seemed to notice everything. I didn't even dare go to the woods.

Christ was supposed to come in October. This time but I was not about to wait around to see if He actually came.

At first I just planned to disappear like Robin had, but then I started feeling sorry for my mother. She might think I was dead or something. I could just see her quiet tears and pleading glances at my father and I started feeling guilty. My father deserved to suffer, but he would probably just be angry and not suffer at all. I decided to tell my mother, then run out the door before my father could stop me. I would do it at night then hide along the road until I could get to Jorje's house. I could just see my father searching the dark countryside with his old flashlight, that he had to shake every so often so that it would keep shining. I would spend the night and next day at Jorje's house then start hitchhiking early the next morning to North Dakota.

After making the decision, a week went by while a battle raged within me between my desire for freedom and my fear, not only of my father catching me but of being alone to fend for myself. I had no money but started harboring a secret hope that Jorje would loan me some. I would get a job in North Dakota as soon as I found Robin.

I finally set a date. It was to be the next Thursday night. My father would be looking for me on Friday while I was at Jorje's house, but on the next day, the Sabbath, I was almost certain that he wouldn't go out looking for me. I would have a whole day to get away.

As the time for my departure approached, I became nervous and jumpy. I avoided my father as much as I could for fear that he might read my mind. I stayed near the house, but at a distance, watching everyone.

In the wee hours of the morning on Wednesday, the night before I was supposed to leave, I awoke from a nightmare. I dreamed that it was Thursday morning, and I had forgotten to leave. I hastily jumped from my bed and ran to the door, in a last ditch effort to escape but was too late. Father had installed bars in front of the door. I then frantically ran to the other door, then to each window, only to find that iron bars had been installed in front of them. I did not sleep after that.

I resisted checking the doors and windows, knowing it was just a dream but I had to lie there wide awake listening to the blood pounding in my forehead.

After a breakfast of potatoes cooked with boiling water because we were out of grease, I volunteered to hoe the late summer weeds from the garden to hide my restlessness.

My father looked stunned and said, "I hope this indicates that you have gotten right with God." I had just nodded the back of my head at him as I fled out the door.

After dinner in the evening, I volunteered to do the dishes and went to work on them, ignoring the amazed stares from my mother. Then sitting in the living room looking out the window into the gathering darkness, I waited for my opportunity. My father was reading his bible and taking notes at his small study table in the far corner of the room. Mother was reading an article by some preacher. My brothers were playing some sort of game beneath the floodlight on the front porch. Charlotte was in her bedroom. My father slammed his bible shut, and I jumped, startled. He cleared his throat.

"Charlotte…boys," he said loudly in a stern voice, "it is time for bible reading."

Charlotte appeared and the boys came in, slamming the screen door behind them. When we were all there, he began to read from Job, 38.

"'Then the Lord answered Job out of a whirlwind, and said . . .'"

But I heard no more. My stomach was becoming bottomless with fear and nervous excitement.

My father finished the bible reading. We each said a prayer while kneeling. I then sat with my tongue paralyzed while everyone moved off towards their respective bedrooms. But then the perfect opportunity presented itself when my mother went alone into the kitchen, and my father moved away toward the bedroom. I got up and followed her. Then I stood and watched while she drank a glass of water.

"Turn the lights out when you leave," she said, throwing me a non- suspecting glance as she walked out of the kitchen and toward her bedroom door. I watched as the door closed behind her.

Switching the lights out, I made my way through the darkness in near despair toward my bedroom that I shared with my brothers. I just couldn't leave my mother without telling her. But then a new thought hit me and the burden was lifted. I could leave her a note on the kitchen table and leave in the early dawn before anyone got up.

"Dear Mother," I wrote from the lamplight beside my bed, "I'm running away tonight, but don't worry I'll be fine. I'll write and tell you where I'm going. Love Bobby."

Feeling lighthearted, I climbed into my bed, vaguely realizing that it was for the last time, but I was soon fast asleep, the note under my pillow.

I awoke suddenly, too much light was invading my bedroom. I leaped out of bed, dressing in a feverish haste. I have overslept, I thought and was angry with myself. I didn't have much time to get to Jorje's house before the sun came up. I tiptoed rapidly to and out through the old screen door with nothing but the clothes on my back. Then as I hurriedly crossed the porch, I remembered the note for my mother. I had left it under my pillow. I hesitated, started to return to retrieve it and put it on the kitchen table. But just as I opened the door, I heard something fall with a loud bang somewhere in the house. Panic seized me. I turned and ran from the porch, across the clearing and into the Gatlin woods.

In the woods, I became aware that my old dog Joe was running along beside me with his tongue hanging out. Pangs of regret began to race through my heart. I didn't want to leave my old black battle scarred buddy, even if he was a womanizer. I gave him a kiss on his damp black nose and told him to go back home. He just wagged his tail and stared at me with eyes that shined with his desire to please, but he stayed at my side anyway until we reached the dirt road that ran by the Gatlin place. When I turned north, old Joe stopped and watched me for a spell, but then he turned south towards the Beezley place. He was probably remembering Beezley's old hound, I thought. But I felt the hot tears surge into my eyes, then their wetness on my cheek as I ran down the sand road that went toward Woodlake. I would probably never see Joe again, I thought, he was getting old.

I gasped for air from running, and my tears dried from the rays of the rising sun. When I saw the blackberry patch off to the right of the road my heart leaped again with the old memories that hurt, but I kept on running. I didn't want to think about that no more; besides, I would see Robin again in North Dakota, I hoped. And the thought lent new buoyancy to the rapid clip of my flying legs.

I was almost to the main paved highway when I heard the hum of an approaching automobile from behind me. It gave me a start, and I quickly fell to lie motionless among the dusty weeds beside the road. I didn't recognize the car that passed. Maybe it belonged to the people who had bought the Barneses' place I remembered thinking. On the highway there wasn't much traffic, but when I heard a car approaching from behind, I would quickly drop into the drainage ditch by the side of the road.

As I neared the filling station in Woodlake, I noticed a car parked by the side of the road just beyond it. It was parked beneath the branches of some big tall trees that made shade on the highway. A man was sitting behind the wheel, and I hesitated. I felt uneasy at having to pass and be noticed. I looked over at the filling station. Behind the window, the attendant sat reading the paper. When he glanced up at me, I saw that he was the same one who had watched Jack get killed. A long cigarette drooped from his lips and smoke was pouring into his squinting eyes. I felt safer then and walked boldly forward. I was almost beside the car before I realized that it was Studs Gatlin sitting there. A wave of fear swept over me as I quickly looked down at my feet and quickened my pace to get past him.

Then just beyond his car when I was beginning to feel more at ease again, a movement in the woods to my right caught my eye. The shock at what I suddenly saw caused my jaw to drop and sapped my energy, leaving me unable to do anything but stand and stare in disbelief. I stood and stared at a naked woman who had arisen from a squat and moved out from behind a tree! She was wiping herself with a handful of green leaves that she had pulled from off a tree branch. And then she was coming at a fast trot toward me! Her big boobs were jumping and the inside of her nose was red and she was breathing hard. It was Agnes Everbe! My shock was complete, and I was horrified! I wanted to sink into the earth so she wouldn't see me standing there. She kept coming and didn't see me. I looked at her white stomach, it was fat, fatter than it had been with clothes on. Her pussy was big and loose and red on the inside like her nose. Suddenly she stubbed her bare toe and screamed. I jumped in spite of myself.

"Ouch, fuck!" the words hit me like the splatter of wet shit! That couldn't be Agnes Everbe! I must be mistaken. She suddenly jumped sideways behind a tree at the sound of a passing car that I didn't even hear until she jumped. Her butt was big and white, and she didn't even know that I was looking at it. But then she turned and looked directly at me.

"What are you staring at, kid," she asked calmly. "Haven't you ever seen a naked woman before? No, I suppose not. Well my advice to you kid, is to get out and get a taste of life while the gettin's good. Get out there before you have wasted as many years as I have."

Her boobs bulged out firmly, and she pulled her stomach in proudly. She didn't act like she recognized me so I just went on staring in disbelief. Actually, I thought, she didn't look too bad considering that she was suppose to be a nice Christian lady. That part stunned me, left me breathless.

"This is the way God made you," she said. But she finally put her hand over her big pussy because I couldn't stop staring at it. "I just wished I had showed it off more when I was younger, and it still looked good," she said defiantly.

She then turned and ran towards the car that Studs Gatlin was sitting in. She opened the door and jumped in. Studs Gatlin quickly turned his car around and sped off south with a smooth roar, out of town. I watched as the roar faded into the distant heat of the summer morning.

Then, out of nowhere, the attendant stood in the road in front of his station staring with bugged out eyes, almost like when Jack got killed at the shimmering blacktop going South.

"My gawd, did you see that?" he asked, like he knew that I was there all along, like he could see me through the back of his head. "She didn't have nuthin on!" he said gesturing wildly toward the empty road heading South. "Hot dam, ha…. ha….. ha," he croaked with a horny laugh. "must have been a scumbag whore from Tallahassee." He grew silent as he continued to stare into the shimmering heat. "She did have some purty boobs," he added reflectively as he turned with a sigh and went back to sit and wait for somebody to come along and buy some gas.

I turned towards Third Street and Jorje's house.

Boy, the Devil had sure gotten into Agnes Everbe I reflected. Maybe my father was getting even with her for walking out on him last winter. Maybe he had asked God to turn the Devil loose on her. But Agnes Everbe had loved God too much to suddenly be this wicked. I twisted my tongue around the word "wicked" and relished it. It probably wasn't Agnes Everbe's fault, I thought. God and my father were probably to blame, and it made me angry that they should have so much power.

"Fuck you God," I said in a whisper and then glanced timidly at a dark cloud racing across the azure sky. But then I thought better of it. I was not far enough away yet. "Forgive me," I said loudly and glanced again with relief at the red hot sun that hovered as it climbed into the sky.

As I turned down Third Street, I could hear the black children playing on the street across the highway. They all were so poor, yet they always seemed to be having so much fun. A wave of regret passed over me then, and I wished that I could have been black, so I could have grown up having that much fun. But then I saw Jorje eating breakfast on the porch and forgot about everything except food.

"Good morning to you. Bobby, are you hungry?"

"Only just a little bit," I said modestly as my mouth watered at the sight of hot grits, eggs and sausage with big slices of toast covered with melting butter.

"Good," he said and grinned, "I'll fix you just a little bit to eat, then."

Patch, his little dog, was thrilled to see me. I let him jump in my lap and while I petted him I fought the tears and tried to get Joe out of my mind.

"Come in," Jorje said.

The three of us went into the house. I carried Patch in while he was kissing me.

Jorje broke several eggs into the skillet and threw in several pieces of sausage.

"I had expected to see you back before this," Jorje said, throwing me a questioning glance.

"Yes, I know," I said, "but my father has set another date for the second coming and has started staying out where he can watch everybody."

"You don't say," Jorje chuckled. "I see you got away quite early." He again threw me a questioning glance.

"I'm running away from home," I said, "and I got up and left while everyone else was asleep."

"Is that so?" His voice was quiet and reflective as he put the sausage and eggs on my plate beside two large slices of toast. "With nothing but the clothes on your back?" He started towards the door with my plate of food.

"Can we eat in here?" I asked quickly.

"Sure," he stopped and looked at me. "Do you think your father is going to come looking for you?"

"'He might," I responded.

I ate his food like a starved wolf, embarrassed but helpless before the power of my hunger. When I had finished, Jorje went and fixed another plate of food without saying a word. I ate in silence, and when I finished, he took the dirty plate and put it in the kitchen sink. He opened the window so that the heat that filtered in would smell like roses.

The first thing I wanted to tell him was about Agnes Everbe, but I was afraid he would think I was making the story up, so I bit my lip and stayed silent.

Jorje went and stood by the window looking out, and a light breeze started to ruffle his gray hair. He glanced back at me again like he was trying to think of something to say. Finally I decided that I just had to tell him about Agnes Everbe.

"Jorje," I said, then hesitated.

"Yes," he said as he turned around to face me.

"Do you know Agnes Everbe?" I asked.

"No, can't say that I do. Should I?"

"Well… she was there for the second coming that night when you showed up."

"Oh yes, what did she look like?"

"She has a big nose," I said, "and she came up and asked you if were another traveler, or something like that."

"Yeah…it seems I do vaguely remember someone like that, why?"

"Well….it's kind of crazy," I said, looking at Jorje for encouragement.

"It is alright," he responded, "go ahead get it off your chest."

"Well . . . I saw Agnes Everbe squatting naked, like she was taking a pee, back in the woods down by the filling station. Then she jumped up, ran out and got into a car with Studs Gatlin, and then they sped away off to the south together."

"I understand what you mean," he said, "about it being kind of crazy." He laughed softly and was quiet, like he was thinking about it. "I can see how it would have shocked you to see someone you highly respect, someone who you have always thought of as a pillar of Christian and moral rectitude, behave in such an extremely unsocial fashion." He shook his head, chuckled and looked out through the window.

He stood and opened it and when he did the cheerful voices of singing birds came floating in and made me feel like singing too.

"I bet she was the one who prayed the hardest and yelled the loudest," Jorje said, as he looked out a bluebird sitting on a limb his mouth open and singing loudly.

"Yes," I volunteered. "She was so noisy sometimes that you could hardly hear my father preaching, and sometimes he would just quit and listen when she was shouting under the power of the holy ghost."

"Aha," Jorje said as he again sat down and looked directly at me with eyes that seemed to get intense. "You see, Bobby, when we abdicate our natural ability to think and substitute it for the dogma of faith we are trading common sense for the promise of security. But since this security has no bases in natural reality, since it is simply a verbal promise, the mind must obsessively cling to it in order to eliminate natural doubt.

It is like choosing to be blind because you don't like or you fear what you see. The faithful are encouraged and warned to keep their eyes shut tightly or they will suffer an end like Lot's wife did when she couldn't resist looking back and turned to salt. Only the faithful today are promised much worse.....nothing less than Hell. So you can imagine the shock when one of these obsessed and blind believers have their eyes forced open to witness the natural truth that exposes the emptiness of their faith based blindness."

"Most faith based leaders are too cunning to put their religion to a test like your father did. Most know, whether they are true believers or not, that their leadership is also their bread and butter. So they know that it is to their advantage to keep stringing their blind parishioners along not only with a lingering fear and future promises but to also keep them fat and happy while they wait. Once in awhile, however, the obsessive nature of blind belief will drive one mentally into insanity, and it is my guess that it is this that has happened to your father and Agnes Everbe."

"Agnes Everbe feels betrayed, and she is fighting back, defying the god-bigot that she feels betrayed her. Yet there is a glimmer of hope for those such as Agnes Everbe because they have the will to move on after defeat even if their movements could be better described as violent lurches forward. But people like your father will simply will their own death as their defeats continue to accumulate."

"I guess I have said enough," he said after a moment of silence. "I'm not surprised to hear about Studs Gatlin. I have always thought of him as a sociopath after he killed his brother down at the filling station. But people like this are unpredictable. I guess Agnes Everbe thinks he is fun to be around so who am to question the judgment of Agnes Everbe?"

I looked at him then and saw that he was grinning and looking at me slyly. "But let's quit jawing, Bobby and contribute a little ourselves to criminality by sharing some powerful hash that I have to spice the weed up with?"

"Sure," I said, trying to sound nonchalant but rather showing too much readiness for my own satisfaction.

I was soon inhaling deeply, and this time it really hit me, making the birdsong coming through the window sound like an orchestra coming off a mountain top! I then jumped up to look and see what the roses would look like, but to my surprise they seemed to be singing too! And when I sat back down on the couch it had turned soft like a pillow!

But then Jorje began to talk again. It came to me gently across the room. His voice had turned to music and seemed to be cooled by the quiet hiss of the ceiling fan.

"So you want to know about the girl, do you?" I heard him say, though it was hard for me to hear above the music.

"Yes," I said and was startled by the clarity of my own voice. It was like I was hearing myself for the first time speaking!

"Her name was Natalie," I heard him say. Then he stopped and softly repeated it to himself, "Natalie," his voice seemed to softly caress the word as it rolled softly off the surface of his tongue. "I loved her one hundred times more than any other woman that I have ever known. She loved me too...I think." he said and then became silent as though reflecting upon it.

Inhaling deeply, he was quiet for a moment, then exhaling he began again.

"Natalie was born in Hawaii, a Japanese girl, raised according to a nineteenth century Japanese social structure, a way of life that I could never master."

"Have you been to Japan?" I asked, when he suddenly became quiet again as though relishing the contentment of the moment.

"Yes," he said, "I traveled all over Japan after I lost Natalie. I went there to learn Japanese and to learn about the Japanese people and also in hopes of finding another Natalie. I learned the language and a lot about Japanese society and its people. But I was never able to find another Natalie."

At this moment, Patch stood and yawned, wagged his tail a couple of times then ran to the door and began to bark.

"You had better go into the bedroom," Jorje said in a low voice, "in case it is your father out looking for you."

I ran into the bedroom and peaked beneath the curtain at the front porch. It was then that I saw the mailman standing on the porch lifting a letter to put in the mailbox. His head was held high, and he looked like he was trying to identify whatever it was that he was sniffing. I went back out to the living room and sat on the couch and Jorje soon rejoined me.

"The jerk!" he said, "he would love to get me in trouble for smoking this stuff. But he knows better than to say anything because he knows that I would know that he was the one who did it," he continued with a chuckle.

"Anyway," he said, as he began again to relate his story, "I was attending the University of Hawaii, working on a history major. I was a devoted student and a hard worker and had very little time to concentrate on anything other than my studies. Then one spring day after I found out I had received an A on my final history exam, I decided to spend the rest of the day on the beach. I remember I went down to the beach that fronts the old Queen Surf Restaurant and hotel. I took a book along and even remember which one it was. It was *The Idiot* by Fyodor Dostoyevsky. But I didn't get much reading done that day!"

"Before I could open my book, I saw her coming down the beach. She was a slim and petit slip of a thing but her bulging boobs revealed that she was definitely a woman. And she was walking right at me. But then as she had approached within steps of my towel, she turned revealing a skimpy little bikini that seemed to be withdrawing into the crack of her butt as she had walked a short distance and began spreading her blanket on the beach."

"I had then opened my book and tried to read but my eyes and mind kept straying to where she lie, her tanned body soaking up the heat of the Hawaiian sun. She appeared restless as she was constantly tossing her raven black hair and her legs kept swaying back and forth in a chaotic clutching restlessness. Then I noticed the occasional glances that glistened, dark and seductive, that she was throwing over her shoulder. I turned and glanced about to see who else she might have an eye for, and there appeared to be no one except me."

"And then she got up, her butt twisting in a daring seduction, as she slowly made her way to the water. I lost my power of resistance and got up to follow, like a zombie. About waist deep in the water, she stopped her forward movement, and I stopped a little behind her where we both stood staring out to sea. A wave, larger than the rest that had managed to get over the reef, hit her with enough force to knock her over backwards and into my arms. I grabbed and held her as close as I dared. She did not resist so I went right on holding her and began to talk."

"'What is your name?' I asked, but then became so distracted by her little belly button that kept revealing itself out of the undulating sea that I missed her answer. 'What?' I asked as I glanced down at the flaming blush that had started to spread around her cheekbones."

"'Natalie,' she responded more loudly. She squirmed gently against me and again looked out towards the reef where the booming surf was pounding loudly. Then I felt her hand start to push gently against my bare chest. I put her on her feet then, and we walked back toward our blankets on the beach. She invited me to sit on her blanket, and so there we sat while the gentle trade winds made pleasant the heat of the afternoon sun."

"We were still talking when the rays of the late afternoon sun became slanted as they spread out on the white sand beach. We were still there when the white sand became cool and the sun as a ball of fire began to sink into the Pacific somewhere out beyond Barber's Point. We were still there when the warm dusk, in its half light, hovered silently around us, and the distant boom of the surf began to take on the loudness of the night."

"We sat and talked of everything, Natalie and I, her, me, but mostly of other things, the majestic Pacific ocean, the beautiful islands of Hawaii, the world in which we lived, philosophy, religion. I even told her that I was an Atheist."

"'Come, now, Jorje,' she said, giggling with one of her thrilling little laughs, 'aren't you afraid that God might strike you dead?'"

"But then as dusk became darkness and the rising trade winds began to rush down from the rugged mountain peaks behind us, to carry our mortal words out into the darkness above the sea, I allowed my hand to slip beneath her bikini bottom, to quickly find her passion that so infinitely separates girl from boy yet brings them together so desperately. She gasped as our lips met and the violent surf pounded loudly against the distant reef."

"It was like a moment in eternity, a moment suspended, before she jumped to her feet, leaving my finger wet to feel the chill of the damp wind rushing down from the mountain peaks."

Jorje began to stare at the picture on the wall again and was silent. "It was simply not to be," he mumbled more to himself then to me.

"Why?" I asked, "what happened?"

"Well," he responded, "love and life are really all about sex. And I became obsessed with my need for it. But also in love and life, everything is layered in the rituals of propriety. In other words, I had decided that the next natural step in our relationship was sexual. But for her it was simply much more complicated. She was torn by her desire to be with me and her need to honor her parents wishes to choose a man that they approved of and go through the ritual of marriage first."

"While this was fine with me, there was a sticking point. She doubted that her parents would approve of me, and she was afraid to introduce me. So we were at an impasse that seemed to have no resolution. Finally she revealed to me that her parents had already set their hearts on the man they wanted her to marry, though she wanted nothing to do with him."

"So Natalie continued to keep me away from her parents, but we continued to see each other in secret without resolving the need to share our passion."

"'Let's elope,' I once suggested to her, 'go to the Big Island, get married then come back and announce it to everyone.' But she wouldn't hear of it, she wanted a big wedding with her parents blessings." It was here that Jorje's voice trailed into silence

Jorje inhaled deeply and handed the joint to me.

"It is incredible," Jorje began as he exhaled, "the length people will go to, at throwing up barriers to their own happiness. This is the ritualistic barrier, a barrier that is held over our heads to prevent us from seeking our individual happiness at the expense of our social existence. But happiness is always an individual experience and to the degree we allow our social existence to interfere with it, we pollute the individual and become creatures of habit, creatures afraid to be who we are as individuals. The uninhibited passion of sex becomes terrifying without social acceptance, without the absurd institution of marriage."

"At any rate, she finally took me to meet her parents, after a lot of badgering on my part. As soon as she had introduced me, I knew it had been a mistake. I could feel the chill behind their pleasant smiles and polite chatter. And the realization also dawned on me that Natalie was not going to forsake her parents for me. With a sinking feeling, I knew in my heart that it was over, but I stubbornly refused the intuition that had overwhelmed me with that meeting."

"Three days later I received a letter from Natalie, it was a diplomatic little 'dear John' letter that tried to hide the brutal facts. She 'begged off' seeing me for 'awhile' because 'she would be busy at school and all'. I knew what had happened. Her parents had either forbidden her from seeing me or the price for doing so was too high for her to pay. My attempts at reaching her by phone were fruitless. Her mother always answered day or night, and I would silently hang up in despair."

"I did not see Natalie for three months after the letter. She seemed to have disappeared from the face of the earth. I did not return to classes that autumn. I spent my days searching for Natalie, peeking in classrooms where she should have been, but to no avail. On some days I would walk the beaches of the Island hoping that I might find her again like I found her before. My mind would wonder back to the happy summer we had spent together with the rambling discussion in philosophy and world events. And sometimes it would occur to me that this happiness could have continued if I simply could have been satisfied and not demanded more."

"And yes, I would remember more thrilling moments when I came tantalizing close to having more, such as when in the gathering dusk on the North Shore at Sunset Beach I chased Natalie naked over the white sand dunes, and when I caught her, we rolled in the sand before racing out into the surf that rumbled on the beach out of the dark Hawaiian night. But I also remembered her gentle voice that forbid us from going further, 'not just yet'. Words that I would repeat to myself over and over again, looking for something that I had missed."

"Then one night when my emotions were at their lowest ebb, I drove out to her home on Ninth Avenue and parked across the street in the dark. I watched her house until the last lights were gone. I didn't even know if Natalie was there or not. I had repeated this performances for nearly two weeks, just sitting there with my flicker of hope waiting until the lights joined the dark night around them."

Then on a night in early December, I watched the lights fade again into the nothingness of the dark. The flicker of hope was gone. I was mouthing the words 'goodbye Natalie' and was reaching for the keys to start my engine and drive away when I saw a slight figure approaching. She came quickly and stood there by my window."

"'Natalie,' I gasped."

"'Sh.....sh......sh......sh' she responded, putting a finger to her lips. She ran around to the passenger side and slipped into the seat and said, 'Let's go Jorje.'"

"I stared in silence, paralyzed by her presence, in ecstatic disbelief."

"'Let's go Jorje,' she repeated in a voice hardly above an urgent whisper."

"Without the need for further urging, my engine leaped to life, and we were gone."

"That is very romantic," I said, when Jorje was silent again. "I just wished Robin had come back to me that way."

"Don't worry," he said. "All is not as it seems." And he looked again at the wall where Natalie's picture hung.

"What happened then," I prodded.

"I got what I was after," he said, "she fucked me that night at my place. But in retrospect I can see that in my victory lie the seeds of my defeat."

He looked out the window, silent again, as though trying to choose his words.

"To this day I'll never understand the woman, any woman for that matter. It was as though she were offering herself as a sacrifice to my passion, yet it was a sacrifice I was supposed to refuse. On the other hand," Jorje sighed deeply, "maybe she was simply torn between her individual desire for happiness and the demands of her social existence, and she was simply unable to break the chains that bound her."

"Oh yes," he continued, after another moment of silence, "I fucked her like an over sexed dog. Like a hungry beggar, I took her virginity. And oh yes, she squealed and cried in her pleasure and pain at its loss. And yes, the rest of that winter was a sex maniacs dream fulfilled."

"The passionate lust of her frantic lovemaking appeared almost as if it were itself the very struggle to break free from chains of her social restraints."

Then one day I realized that she had failed in her attempt to break free. Our lovemaking had reached a feverish crescendo. I was in the throes of a wild ejaculation, drawn out by her warm tongue, teased by the soft coaxing of her lips when she suddenly collapsed beside me on the bed, sobbing violently."

"'I can't do it anymore Jorje you have taken everything from me,' she cried, 'you have violated my trust.'"

The outburst to me was like a kick in the ribs. I had not dreamed that such terrible thoughts were going through her mind.

Just as suddenly, the sobbing had stopped. 'I'm pregnant,' she said to me in an accusing voice, 'how could you have done this to me, you have treated me like a whore, and I have acted the part for you, all for you!'"

She was rapidly dressing as she talked and when she was dressed, she ran from the room. I heard the front door slam behind her."

"'Natalie', I cried out, 'I will marry you,' but it was too late, for she was already gone."

Jorje's voice lowered then as he asked, more to himself then to me, "I don't know how she could have thought that…..that I had violated her trust. Surely she knew that I would take what she would give. I tried to give as much in return. I didn't think of her as a whore! We were lovers satisfying a mutual desire. I would have married her at anytime had I thought she wanted it or had suggested it. I think it was her that knew she couldn't marry and the whore part was of her own making. We were just in different worlds…I guess."

"It was the next day, though, before I truly realized the gravity of the situation. I had clung to the hope that it was a temporary fit of anxiety, and that she would come back and make it up to me. It was just a lovers quarrel. But then she called me."

"'Jorje,' she said, in voice, cold like ice, the music was gone. Dread came with the sinking feeling in my heart. I instinctively knew that my stay in this heavenly paradise had come to an end. 'I'm not coming back anymore, Jorje,' I heard the distant and strange voice saying. 'Our affair is over. We have had our fun. Now it is time for each of us to stand like adults and say goodbye. This is the price we must pay for our moment in the sun.'"

"'It can still be our moment,' I heard myself saying. My voice sounded as distant and strange as did hers. 'I'll marry you,' I heard myself mumbling weakly."

"'No,' I heard the distant voice say, 'we both have always known that that can't be. I allowed myself to slip into self-denial and to pretend that my love for you mattered. I allowed myself to wallow in the pleasure of the moment. But you are not guiltless Jorje you also knew that WE couldn't be.'"

"'What about the baby?' I had asked in a barely audible voice."

"'I'll have it aborted,' she said, 'before my parents find out.'"

"'Natalie,' I heard myself screaming in an eerie surreal voice, like the cry of a distant ghost. But like hell itself, it was heard by no one, for the clicking sound on the other end told me that Natalie was gone and I was alone. Those were the last words that I heard her utter and not long after that I was on a plane leaving my Island paradise for Japan."

He looked again at the picture that hung from the wall.

"I've said enough, Bobby, about the lady," he said quietly, "let's smoke another joint and talk of other things."

"You plan to leave today?" he suddenly asked. "It might be better if you spend the night here and get an early start tomorrow."

"I think so too." I said, relieved and on cloud nine.

The afternoon faded into evening as we talked, or rather Jorje talked about philosophy and the evils of religion. He talked about people and things that I had never heard of before. But somehow I liked what he said, and it made me feel good because it all seemed to make sense. And the pot made me feel good as well.

My hunger began to overwhelm me when I smelled the rich smell of roasting pork coming from Jorje's oven, and when I tasted it, with the potatoes and all, I could hardly contain my pleasure because it was the best tasting food that I had ever eaten!

I awoke from the soft couch early. Jorje had the motor going out front. I thought we were going without breakfast, but Jorje assured me that we would eat on the road. We did and I stuffed myself up by the Alabama line.

After breakfast at the roadside café, Jorje drove up through Dothan, Alabama to the city limits and pulled to the side of the road.

"I guess this is as far as I go, Bobby. I doubt that your father will come this far looking for you."

I opened the door and listened to the big black car engine idle by the side of the road, and I felt empty, in spite of all the food in my stomach.

"Bobby," Jorje said, as I stepped from the car.

I turned and looked back at him as I had began fighting the tears rushing towards my eyes.

"Here," he said, as he handed me a hundred dollar bill and five twenties. "Stick the hundred dollar bill in one shoe and four of the twenties in the other and use it sparingly. It should get you to North Dakota."

I felt rich and tried to control my shaking hand.

"Good luck, Bobby," he said.

But the tears welling up in my eyes had choked me when I tried to say thank you. I closed the door behind me and stared off into the sticky Alabama morning. I then turned and silently watched the black car and its engine fade into the distance back towards Florida.

I let the tears flow freely then, unabated as I walked north along the highway.

Finally I heard the birds and insects chirping as they blended with the heat of the summer day. "you are free, you are free," they seemed to be singing to me.

I turned, then with newfound courage, wiped the tears from my eyes and stuck my thumb out boldly to the fast approach of an automobile.

# PART 2

# JOEY AND THE
# BLIZZARD

THE COLD WENT right through my overcoat that I had bought in Fargo, grabbing me like it was going to freeze me to death as I stood out along the empty highway desperately seeking a ride that did not come. But thanks to Joey, I had shelter now.

It had been in the middle of the afternoon when I first saw Joey as I stood beside the highway just West of Mandan North Dakota. He had come walking out from town, a dark stick figure wearing a big black coat, bent over as he leaned against the wind of the approaching storm.

I had been waiting in the silence, interrupted only by the howl of the wind, long before I saw Joey. I stood, my coat tightly wrapped around me, staring back towards Mandan, hoping to detect the first movement of an approaching automobile. But there were very few coming in my direction. I stood for what seemed like hours waiting, straining my eyes. I would feel a thrill race up my spine when I detected an automobile coming my way, then would feel the emotional collapse of disappointment when the car would turn before they reached me or simply pass me by, ignoring my freezing thumb standing naked in the wind.

After a while I didn't care where I went. I just wanted to get in out of the cold. It was about a mile back to Mandan so I started watching for cars that were heading back towards town as well.

I had a chance to get out in Mandan, in fact the old farmer who picked me up back in Fargo had warned me, that that was the safest thing to do.

As I stood freezing beside the highway, I remembered the toasty warmth of the heater inside his big gray Buick. I had dozed a lot while we had made our way across the open flatlands of North Dakota. In no time at all it seemed, we were in Bismarck, crossing a river of solid ice.

"That's the Missouri," the old farmer said. "Mandan is just up the road a ways and that is where I call home."

I guess I had wished that the North Dakota plains would go on forever, and that I could have stayed in that big warm Buick all the way across them. But I had to soon pile out into the bitterly cold wind.

"You had better get out here in town and go to that motel over there," the old man had said as he pointed to a forlorn sign that said Plains Motel. "I hear a blizzard's a coming."

"No, thanks," I said, "I'll go as far as you go."

Suddenly a snowflake hit my cold cheek with a sudden gust of cold wind and a wave of panic swept over me. I searched frantically for movement in the distant and lifeless town. I glanced fearfully at the growing darkness climbing into the northwestern sky but turned my eyes away, searching for movement on the empty highway. Suddenly a powerful gust of wind hit me from behind, jerking and pushing me east along the road, like a warning to seek shelter at all cost.

It was then that I saw the distant figure coming, and soon I saw that it was a man in a big black coat. I watched him as he came closer; he was carrying something over his left shoulder. His struggle was strong against the wind, and he faced the dark sky with determination.

As I watched him, he slowed and seemed to be looking at me, then he stopped and stared. The wind shook him as though trying to knock him down. He began to motion, then, as though trying to draw me toward him. I ignored him at first, but his hand movement had become quite violent. He pointed to the dark sky that was climbing, ominously, behind me.

I glanced over my shoulder, and its icy approach stung my face. Snowflakes began racing past me, in earnest then. Something told me that there would be no more cars coming by that afternoon.

I then turned my gaze back in search of the man in the big black coat, but he was already walking away from the highway up a side road toward some bluffs that rose above the river. I felt a pang of disappointment come over me for I had started to hope that he had a solution for my predicament. As I watched him move off toward the north along the road, he slowed, turned and motioned for me to follow. Relief swept over me as I ran, driven by the wind pushing at my back, down the road to then turn north to catch up. I had no idea what he could do for me, but I guess just the thought of company was enough to give relief.

The man in the black coat kept walking, and as I turned north, I had to fight the challenge of the cold wind in my face. I panted, sweated and pulled myself against its awesome power. The snowfall had become heavy, at times obliterating the dark figure ahead of me. Once I saw him turn and shout something over his shoulder at me, but the wind swept his words away into the cold whiteness of the blizzard. Finally he stopped and waited on me and watched as I struggled to eliminate the white distance that separated us.

"There's a barn just up there, on the left, beside the road." he yelled into my ear as I walked up along beside him. "We got to get to it soon, or we are going to lose it in this weather."

He then resumed his steady plodding and desperate struggle into the blinding white fury of the blizzard. I followed as I leaned into its numbing howl.

In spite of my effort, I soon found myself falling behind, losing ground to the steady pace of the man in the black overcoat. I began to feel the cold beneath my coat, and I began to tire and the urge to stop and rest became overwhelming. Then suddenly out of the white wind loomed the dark barn by the side of the road.

"There it is!" I heard his scream as it went by me in the wind.

Hope surged within me then as I ran behind this man toward the dark promise of a barn. Then suddenly it was gone, obliterated by a gust of wind, like the end of the world, swept away in a whiteness that took one's breath away. I couldn't even see the man who had been only a few feet in front of me. I screamed into the blizzard, but its howl swept away my voice. Leaving my mouth opened in silence. Then briefly, out of the cold white fury, I caught a glimpse of the dark figure in front of me. He saw me and grabbed my arm, pulling me to him.

"Stay close!" he screamed into my ear, "we are too close to lose it now."

Then it was there, solid, but invisible in the blowing gloom. We felt our way along its solid wall until we found a door. The man fumbled with his frozen fingers, attempting to open it. The latch sprang free. Suddenly we were inside, staring in disbelief at our good fortune and the island of dark quiet warmth that surrounded us.

"The first thing we gotta do is get a fire to goin,' the man said, matter of factly.

At first it was dark as night in the barn, but soon light began to creep through the cracks and crevices to reveal the tall haystacks that seemed to stand in piles around us.

Then suddenly, we were again joined by the howl of the wind. A gust of it grabbed the door and threw it open. With a crash it hit the outer wall. The invading blizzard swept away the darkness around us with its white violence. The man dropped his shoulder bag and ran out into the storm. I stood watching his desperate attempt to close the door. I must help him, I thought. And I shivered violently as I ran out into the blowing snow. Together we had managed to close the door. Then the man securely latched it from the inside. And again we felt separated from the blizzards cold song of death.

We then moved away from the violent rattle of the door and into the welcome silence of the haystacks. There was a pathway through the stacked hay, and when we followed it, the roar of the wind became distant and muffled.

Exhausted, I sat on a bale of hay beside the path, and the man turned to face me. He looked haggard and old in the dim light. His face was creased and weather beaten, and his shoulders slumped beneath the weight of his dirty old bag.

"I'm a hobo and they call me Joey Kline," he said in a voice that made one feel that it really didn't matter who he was. "What's your handle?" He then turned and looked up into the haystacks as though he had forgotten that he had even asked the question.

"Bobby McGee," I said, then tried to get a better look at his face in the dim light.

"Come on," he said, seeming to ignore my name. He turned and started walking away so I followed.

"We gotta fix us a little somthin to eat." He said, throwing a casual glance back over his shoulder.

I followed him into the gloom and quiet. The muffled roar outside seemed to explode, in its effort to get around the barn that was our shelter.

"Watch out!" Joey had said sharply as he staggered and nearly fell. "The wooden floor ends here and you have to step down." I stepped down and found myself on solid dry earth.

"Good," Joey said, "Now bring us a couple of bales of hay, Bobby, so's we'll have something to sit on." I dragged and carried two bales of hay from a nearby haystack.

Joey Kline had his big heavy bag open when he sat on his bale of hay. He pulled out a small charcoal cooker and a bag of charcoal. No wonder the bag looked so heavy, I thought. He cleaned the earth of loose hay with his boot and then put a dozen charcoal cubes in the cooker.

"All I got to eat is some pork 'n beans," he said, "less'n you got something to eat in that bag of your'n." He eyed my bag like he was hopeful about it.

I felt real sorry then that I didn't have some kind of food in my bag, but I only had some underclothes, a pair of pants and other stuff like soap and a toothbrush that I had bought in Fargo.

"I only got some clothes in there," I said as I watched him start a fire with some loose hay. He then hovered over the infant fire, protecting it from any wayward wind gust that might drift across the open area where we were. Finally the black charcoal began to turn red.

Joey Kline worked silently. He reached into his bag and pulled out an old beat up aluminum pan and two cans of Pork and Beans.

I started to feel real hungry, but I also was feeling real guilty and helpless. Joey Kline was doing everything as well as providing the food. But he then broke the silence, easing my guilt, somewhat.

"Maybe in the morning, the storm will let up enough so's we can get out and get us a chicken to eat," he said as he pulled out a big dome like cover and put it over the pork and beans so that they would get hot faster.

Joey sighed and stretched himself out to lie on his bail of hay.

"Walking in that blizzard was enough to tire the best of us," he said.

His jaw fell open, and he seemed to doze for a moment. His face was grizzled and gray from a half grown beard. And in the silence, I began to relax some and felt warmth again inside me as I huddled close to the dim glow of the charcoal. I smelled the sweet steam coming off the cooking beans and felt my stomach churn.

"Where 'ya coming from, Bobby?" His tired voice startled me as it broke the silence coming out of the half light where I had thought he was dozing. I then felt his gaze as it penetrated the dark space between us.

"Well," I hesitated. I didn't know if I trusted Joey Kline or not. I knew that if I started talking, I would probably say too much. I didn't dare tell him about the money that I had left. He might rob me, taking it from me while I slept.

"You ain't beholden to tell me nothing," he said. "I ain't curious, jus being friendly."

He sat up and took the lid off the pot of beans and found an old spoon to stir them with.

"I'm from Woodlake, Florida," I said, "but the last two months I have been staying in Fargo, North Dakota."

"I'm a hobo," he said as he scooped a huge helping of beans into an old aluminum pan and handed it to me. "One of the last of a dy'in breed," he continued. Then scooped up a helping of beans for himself. "I work sometimes when someone'll hire me, but I mostly just keep on a moving. Sometimes I steal my food, sometimes I buy it. It all depends on if'n I got any money or not."

We were silent then as we shoveled the hot beans into our mouths and let them warm us down to the pits of our stomachs.

The roar of the wind came closer in the silence and tore violently at the roof above us.

"And I ain't got no money, now," he said as he swallowed the last of his hot food then used his finger to wipe his pan clean of bean juice.

I bit my lip and tried to ignore my guilty feeling as I licked the juice from my pan. I felt sorry for him but was afraid to mention my money yet.

"Kinda dangerous ain't it, out hitchhiking at this time of year, in this godforsaken place?" I felt his eyes again coming at me, now unseen, across the charcoal coals that glowed brightly between us. The coals had suddenly glowed with an increased intensity as a cold wayward draft whipped up dust from the dry earth around us.

"Well," Joey said, pulling his feet back away from the warmth of the coals, "it is getting dark and what little heat we have left will soon be gone, why'nt you stay here and warm your feet a little longer while I go see if'n I can find us a good place to hole up for the night."

"I guess you don't have a blanket in that bag of your'n?"

"No," I said, embarrassed again.

"If you want, you can share mine," he said casually as he walked off, to disappear into the dark shadows of the barn.

I felt uneasiness in my stomach as I watched him disappear. Not once since I had run away had I spent the night with a stranger. I had either stayed in a motel or in my own bedroom while staying with the Barneses.

These thoughts took me back to the night in Indiana when this strange guy had wanted me to spend the night with him. He had given me a ride all the way up into Indiana from Kentucky. He kept talking to me funny-like, as though I were a little kid or something. He had called me "honey" all the time and told me that I was a "fucking cute young man". When we neared Vincennes, Indiana, where he said he lived, he not only asked, but begged me to spend the night with him. He made me uncomfortable and very uneasy. "No thank you," I responded as politely as I could. But he continued to insist and told me loudly that I was "stupid" to spend good money on a cheap hotel room when he was offering me a comfortable bed in a nice home.

I became afraid of him, and he started to look creepy and sound dangerous. Finally he got so angry at me that he suddenly stopped the car about mile before we reached Vincennes and ordered me out of the car.

"The audacity," he croaked, hoarsely, "to refuse my hospitality after all the miles you have ridden with me! You can just walk the last mile to town!"

I jumped out, breathing a sigh of relief as I slammed the door shut behind me but then he pulled off to the side of the road up in front of me and continued to sit there, his motor idling as I had walked past him and on ahead, his high beams made me uneasy as to what he would do next. But I continued to walk boldly on ahead. Suddenly with a roar, he passed me and the red points of his tail lights gradually faded up ahead on the distant highway.

Alone in the falling darkness beside the strange highway, I felt a pang of fear run up my spine. At this point, a bolt of lightning above the road ahead revealed a huge thunderhead cloud that was climbing high into the sky. And I walked as fast as my legs would carry me with my load toward the distant town. As I walked, the lightning became more frequent and the roaring thunder grew louder and creeped closer.

Finally, exhausted and gasping for air, I saw the distant neon sign that flashed "motel". Big heavy raindrops began to splash onto my hot cheeks. Hard, intense claps of thunder were rocking the fire streaked darkness. I literally ran the last hundred yards into the musty, dimly lit motel lobby.

In my room, I laid awake long into the night wondering why the angry man had been so insistent that I spend the night with him. It hadn't made any sense to me then. It was like the tip of something ugly but was hidden from me. It had made me remember how I felt when Studs Gatlin had raped Charlotte.

"Well Bobby, I think I've found us a sheltered niche where we can keep warm." His voice brought me back to the present, and I jumped, startled from my reverie.

It was almost completely dark and the coals in the charcoal burner were rapidly fading. Joey dumped them on the ground and stomped them into the hard dry earth with the soles of his boots.

"We gotta make sure," he said, "that no fire gets started."

Joey picked up his bag, switched on an old flashlight that I hadn't noticed before and walked off, leaving the charcoal burner sitting there.

"Follow me, Bobby," he said.

I followed him up a path, deep in between two haystacks. At the end, we came up against a third haystack. Here Joey had spread his old tarpaulin and then his blanket. Then over this, he had broken up two bales of hay.

"This ought to keep us warm," he said.

The howl of the blizzard, far above me, was muffled, and its vengeance seemed far away. I was suddenly overwhelmed by my exhaustion. I got beneath the hay and the blanket, too tired to care where Joey was. The hay was warm and heavy above me. Then I heard Joey getting beneath the blanket too.

Suddenly from Joey's side came the music of the French harp. I knew what it was because my dad had played it once in awhile. The notes thrilled me and softened my drowsiness, turning it into sleep. The music of *Way Down upon the Suwannee River* wafted up into the darkness to meet somewhere with the roar of the blizzard above .

The horrendous howl of the blizzard woke me. It was dark and warm beneath my blanket, but it felt like it must be morning. I peaked out into the dim light of another day. Though it was warm beneath the hay, the roar of the blizzard above me sounded more terrible than it had the night before. I looked over at Joey's corner, but he was gone. I counted my money to make sure it was all there. It was. Joey was not such a bad guy after all, I decided. But then a new fear gave me a start. What if Joey had deserted me? I looked quickly about for some of his belongings, but as I looked with growing alarm, I was suddenly aware of Joey's blanket keeping me warm. So I pulled the blanket back up over my head and went back to sleep.

Suddenly I was awake! I could smell the blizzard, I could smell it fresh and cold and taste it like ice cream, and I knew that Joey was standing above me before he ever said a word.

"Might as well get up boy," he said in a matter of fact voice. "I got a chicken a roastin', be awhile before it is done, but there is no need to go on sleepin."

I threw the blanket back and sat up. The cold air had hit me like the sting of an icy whip. Again I became conscious of the wind tearing at the roof above us.

"How long do these blizzards last?" I asked as I wrapped my coat around me.

"Oh, they can go on for days at a time." He responded casually, "but I think this one is almost petered out. The wind is a blowin' awfully hard, and the snow on the ground is a blowin' up real bad, makin it hard to see, but there ain't much snow a fallin'."

"C'mon," he said coaxingly, "let's go get close to the heat, while the chicken is a cookin'."

The smell of roasting chicken was enough to set my stomach to growling wildly. I got a whiff of it as it penetrated back into the haystacks. And it was difficult to be patient as I sat on my bale of hay, waiting and warming my feet by the charcoal burner.

"I don't think we have to worry much about anybody discovering us here or running us off or anything as long as the snow is a blowin' like it is," Joey Kline had volunteered. "The drifts are ten feet deep out there and the road is buried as deep as everything else."

I was glad but hadn't thought of the possibility of anyone chasing us off until Joey had brought it up. Now I watched Joey as he sat and stared up at the roof. A violent gust of wind was tearing at it.

"There is a farmhouse near by, though, with smoke a comin' out'n the chimney. Course there isn't nothing we can do about it until the snowplow clears the road."

I did not understand his concern. In fact, I was kind of hoping someone would find us and invite us in out of the cold.

"How did you find the chicken, Joey Kline, with the blizzard blowing and all?" I asked.

I noticed his eyes; they looked old, faded and blue. They seemed to light with appreciation at my question.

"Well," he said, "to the lee of the barn is a clear area where there is no snow, or very little anyway. I figured as much. I went out that door over yonder." He pointed at some cracks of daylight behind an old wooden corral. "I was a hopin' I would find a chicken house to the lee of the barn and sure enough it was there alright. I didn't have to worry about the squawkin' the chickens 'ud make because the wind 'ud drown it out. I went in amongst them quiet like and caught me one before the rest of 'em knew what happened. I cut off it's head with my huntin knife before it had got the first squawk out of its mouth."

As I sat there on my bail of hay warming my feet and smelling the chicken cook, the need to go to the bathroom became urgent. I held off mentioning it from embarrassment but just before the chicken was ready, I asked Joey where I could do it.

"Well," he had said, "it don't make much difference in a barn but if you want to hide to do it you can either go out'n that door over yonder and do it in the snow or you can go back over there somewhere." He waved his arm at the empty corrals at the far end of the barn.

I went outside, why I don't know, I guess it was because I didn't want to take a chance on Joey seeing me. The cold outside nearly took my breath away. A gust of wind grabbed me, twisting me in its vortex. I withstood it by clinging to the side of the barn. Out in the barnyard, the snow was seething and twisting violently. Beyond the blowing and twisting snow, I could make out what must have been the chicken house that Joey talked about standing brutally black in the blowing snow. My bare butt had become numb as I squatted, then hovered above the subzero ice. I worked hard to hurry up and complete my task.

I had never tasted chicken that good, though some of the meat was still bloody by the bone. The two of us had finished it off, silent as we wolfed it down and then continued to sit with our feet extended to the hot coals.

"Mr. Kline," I said, then waited respectfully for a moment, for Joey to say "yes" or "what is it, son."

But then he said, "Just call me Joey. 'Mr.' is for educated city folk. But if'n you don't like Joey, then just call me Kline because I ain't educated nor city folks."

"Joey," I asked. "What is a hobo?"

"Well," he said, and was quiet so long that I was beginning to think he had forgotten my question. "Well," he started again, "a hobo is a free spirit who likes to roam and be on the move most of the time. It's not that he is lazy or afraid to work but it is just that he doesn't want nothing a tying him down."

"Times are hard now for the hobo," he continued, after a pause. "All the old hobo jungles are gone now. They arrest us and call us vagrants."

He stared at the fading coals which glowed brightly then pulsated into a dull gray ash. The wind was whistling through the roof top again, and I was getting cold.

"There are only two things people today really value," he started again. "One is religion and the other is money, and you are considered strange if'n you aint chasing one or the other. And you are considered a pillar of your community if'n you are greedy for both of 'em. Everybody considers me a quack, but the only quacks that get any respect in this country is the religious ones. Common folk will look at them funny like but if you look at them up real close you will see the awe a shining out'n their ignorant eyes."

"Now I ain't a sayin that I ain't ignorant but my ignorance is doin to my lack of education and not for a lack of common sense."

Joey shook his head and sighed, and I shivered. It felt like the cold was a creeping in closer.

"They say we are free, even us misfits, but we are dirt under their feet because we do not worship the behinds of fat preachers. We do not contribute to their war against the people nor do we vote for the bigots that rule us. We ignore their bigoted values and their attempts to impose them on us. In their smugness, they pretend to pity us, but in reality, they hate us because we are the proof that they are hypocrites. We are the poor people that their religion says to give to and it makes them feel real guilty and angry. Take this chicken here. I could go to jail for stealing it and you son for eating it. And look at the Injuns," he said, "they were herded up like cattle and put on reservations and their religion was taken away from them by the people who were our forefathers."

"I would rather be a Black man with no past," Joey continued, his rambling voice rising an octave, then to claim heritage to some straight faced puritan with a powdered wig. But you just wait," his voice climbed another octave, "someday this society is going to have a rude awakening. They are going to wake up to find that they have destroyed their land with their smokestacks, cigarettes and car mufflers."

I shivered, unable to control myself, but not because of what Joey said. I wasn't really certain about what he was talking about.

"Let's go get under the blanket and the hay," Joey said, "We can't go no place today no how. You go ahead Bobby, I'll clean up a little here."

I started walking toward the haystacks. I was freezing in the clammy cold of the barn. I glanced back to see Joey stomping the hot coals into the dirt floor. I was hurriedly wrapping myself in the blanket when Joey walked up carrying his charcoal burner.

"Somebody might come while we are a sleepin and steal my hibachi," Joey said when he saw me a looking at it.

"It's a getting a lot colder," Joey observed after he got beneath the blanket on his side. We both concentrated on getting warm after that. The silence between us brought again to my attention the howl of the wind, raging, cold against the rooftop.

"Well, where was I?" Joey's muffled voice began again, more to himself, it seemed, then to me. "Well, anyway, I have been a freedom loving hobo for more than forty years now, ever since the great depression. Back during the depression, there were crowds of us. There was no welfare back then. Everybody was on his own and people was a starving to death right and left, and those of us who lived did it mostly by stealing and spreading out over the prairies from Kansas to North Dakota and helping the farmers harvest the wheat fields when we could find the work. Back then we worked hard for a bite to eat. But today they have too much machinery, and there are no jobs for folks like me."

"Back in the thirties, we always rode the rails to get from one place to another. Back then cars didn't go very far. Nowadays I'll catch a freight train sometimes, at other times I'll try my luck a hitchhiking. But most of the snobs who drive cars don't take a likin to my looks. But the railroad never treated us right because even though we would catch our rides in empty cars, they was always a looking for us and throwing us off' their trains, so riding 'em was a dangerous proposition. You had to time it right and jump on 'em just as they were beginning to build up speed. They were always a watching for us. I got thrown off's a train twice and both times it was the Great Northern. One time the train was a movin', and I got bruised up real bad. Course we didn't think much about it back then, just counted ourselves lucky to be alive. I guess it was kinda like the slaves that just took it when the white folks was a shoving them around. Course, like I said, the hobo is a dying breed, and we have no rights that do us any good, anyway."

"Now the black folks are up and coming. They are a defying the cops, the judges and the bankers and Ku Klux..uh..uh...Klan, that's it. And I say, more power to 'um. But I'm too old to fight now and besides there is not enough of us. Back in the good 'ol days, we never thought of fighting. We were just doing what we had to do to survive."

"But you know, son," he continued after a lull, in which the howl of the wind on the roof was beginning to make me sleepy. "The black folks are a getting white washed ...er...uh...I mean brainwashed by white folks and their sneaky religion."

"Are you an Ath..Athe.ist, Joey Kline?" I asked.

"Never much thought about it, Bobby, but I shore's the hell ain't no Methodist or born aginer. My sister who lives in Minneapolis in Minnesota is a born aginer. I stayed at her house once't when I was down and out. And believe it or not, she talked me into goin to church with her one Sunday. I guess I felt beholden to her since I was eaten her food. But you know what she did when she got me there, son? She got up and started this long spiel about how I was a lost sinner a looking for God and salvation. And pretty soon, the preacher started a shouting with closed eyes and a long face, 'help'em Lord, help'em Lord, help'em find your salvation!' then you know what that skinny fellow did? He suddenly jumped up and ran down the aisle toward me, his eyes a squinting so he could see where he was going, and he was heading right toward me. And then all the congregation started a shouting 'bless'em Lord, bless'em in your name, hallelujah'. And then they all began a closing in on me. But that skinny preacher got there first. He put his hand on my head and started to shake it. I never saw nothing like it. The preacher then started to shout 'come out'n him Satan, come out'n him!'

By this time, I was starting to get suffocated with all them shouting people a crowding around me so I ducked low beneath the hands of the praying preacher and made my way through all the praying blind people to the front door."

"On the way home, my sister told me that she was not concerned because 'she knew God was going to save me in the end because she had asked Him to,' and that 'God always answers prayer.' So's I said to her, 'then Sis neither one of us has anything to worry about so's just leave me be.' She didn't have much to say about it after that."

In the distance, we heard the hum of a pulling motor. "That'll be the snow plow a coming," Joey Kline said. "I think I'll go out and have a look around." He pulled out a long hunting knife from a sheath in his bag then disappeared from our shelter in the hay.

He's going to kill another chicken, I thought, then dozed, warm beneath the hay. I could hear the snowplow getting closer, but its steady hum added to my drowsiness and I slept.

I awoke. It was sometime in the night and very quiet. The darkness was intense. I could nearly feel it about me. I was disoriented and couldn't remember where I was. I felt out into the thick darkness but could touch nothing. Why was it so quiet? I sat up. The bitter cold grabbed the fragile warmth protecting my body. It was going right through my winter coat. I slithered back in beneath the blanket and the hay. Suddenly I was startled by an inhaled snore coming from somewhere near me. It all came back to me then. It was Joey snoring, and I had been sleeping for a long time. Then in the silence it suddenly dawned on me that the wind was gone. The blizzard had moved on to leave behind a death-like silence. How could I have slept so long? The road must be clear for us to leave now. I wondered why Joey had not awakened me. Did he eat another chicken without me?

I tried to go back to sleep and pulled the blanket and my winter coat tightly around me and curled up beneath the heavy warm hay. Boy, was I glad that I had taken Mr. Barnes' advice and bought a winter coat before leaving Fargo, even though it took too much of my money. And with the thought of Mr. Barnes, other memories began to flood my brain.

I remembered the relief I had felt the morning that I had left Vincennes, Indiana on my hitchhiking trip from Florida. I had been apprehensive that the strange guy that had given me a ride to the town the day before would be outside waiting for me, but he wasn't. Nothing much stood out about my trip after that. Except, maybe, the car accident I had seen near Chicago with the headless dead body that I had seen lying in the road. It was still vivid at times in my mind's eye.

It had been rainy, windy and cold when the old man in the Oldsmobile Ninety Eight had said, "This is Fargo North Dakota, son, where do you want to get out at?"

"Right here," I finally said, when it looked like we must be downtown. We were stopped at a red light and a gust of wind had nearly taken the door off when I opened it to get out.

"Good luck, son, hope you find your girlfriend," the big man with the weather beaten face, sitting behind the big round steering wheel had said, friendly like.

With extreme effort, I slammed the big door shut against the wind. The rain was slanted and cold as it hit my face. I made a beeline for a coffee shop that I had seen just down the street.

I ordered my coffee black and splurged on a ham and egg breakfast. The warm coffee and food felt good in my stomach after running through the cold wind and rain.

The waitress was a sharp-eyed old woman who watched me like she thought I was going to steal the silverware or something. I wanted to ask her for a phone book, but each time I was about to get up enough courage to ask, she would turn and penetrate me with a hard look that would leave me speechless. Finally a big cook with a smile on his face walked out, wiping sweat from his face with an apron.

"Sir," I said quickly as I glanced around to make sure that the hawkeyed old waitress wasn't watching.

"Yes, son," he responded congenially.

"Do you have a phone book I could borrow?"

"Right over there, son," he responded as he pointed at a phone booth over in a dark corner of the café.

I finished my breakfast and drank the last of my coffee as my nerves gradually grew taut with my growing excitement and my attempt to control it. Many different scenarios were going through my mind as I got up from my table and walked toward the phone booth. Goose bumps raced up my spine when the possibility that Robin could answer the phone occurred to me. What if I would see her before sunset tonight?! What if she was married or dead? These thoughts also occurred to me.

In the phone booth, I could find no listing for Albert or Betty Barnes but I finally decided to call a B. Barnes that was listed. A squeaky old voice of a lady answered to inform me that B. Barnes was her husband who had died twenty five years ago. "I just ain't gotta round to changing the listing yet," she said.

In my disappointment and desperation, I started randomly going through the phone book looking for nothing in particular, but then the bold numbers 411 caught my eye. At the same time, it occurred to me that it was probably a new listing since they had not been back in North Dakota very long. 411 was the number for information so I called it.

"Wendy, may I help you?" said the voice that sounded like a pretty girl.

She answered so quickly that I was not prepared to respond. The words stuck in my throat driving me to near panic that she would hang up before I could say anything.

"Wendy, may I help you?" she repeated.

"Yes, mam," I finally blurted out in relief. "Do you have a phone number for Albert Barnes..." There was a long pause in which I had suffered pure torture. What if I couldn't find the Barneses at all? What would I do then?

"Yes," Wendy's voice said as it came back over the wire, and I nearly collapsed with relief. She read the number off quickly, and I nearly forgot to write it down. "Just a moment mam," I yelled frantically as I reached for my pencil and wrote it down as she repeated it.

Finally it was time to dial it, and I stood with my heart in my stomach. What if Robin were to answer, what on earth would I say to her? I would have to say something!

"Hello," the voice said. I did not recognize it. It sounded weak and tired and I knew, at least, that it wasn't Robin.

"Is this Mrs. Betty Barnes from Woodlake, Florida?" I asked, in a voice that I feared showed to much emotion.

"Why yes it is," she responded in a voice that had become more lively and anticipatory. "Who's calling?"

"This is Bobby McGee, Reverend McGee's boy."

"Reverend McGee's boy?" her voice turned real excited then.

"Yes mam," I replied modestly.

"Well, I'll be…..what are you doing way up here in North Dakota?"

"I'm just a going through," I said, "and I stopped by to say hello."

"Why that is very sweet of you, Bobby, you didn't run away or anything like that did you?"

"Oh, no mam," I said with solemnity, but a wave of fear had put a damper on my rapidly beating heart. "My father gave me permission to leave, I'm almost nineteen now.

"Good," she said. "Your father must of changed a lot since I knew him. I couldn't have imagined him letting his kids run off at eighteen. But I guess you kids needed to get out and see some of the world after growing up out there in them Florida woods like you did. Why don't you come on over and visit awhile. We are at 1508 Oak Avenue. I would love to hear how your family is doing these days. I haven't heard from your mother in ages."

She gave me directions and my pumping adrenalin kept me from feeling the cold rain in my face.

It was a very pleasant looking whitewashed house on a street lined with trees, now full of leaves that were brown in the rain from autumn frost, leaves that were falling and scattered in heaps upon the ground. Some of the houses had raked their leaves into piles while others had left them scattered on the ground. All were soggy now from the cold rain.

My heart pumped violently and my cheeks felt hot and flushed as I had run through the cold rain, but the rest of my body had suddenly felt cold, and I had shivered violently. What if Robin had died or had gone away. Mrs. Barnes hadn't sounded to happy on the phone.

"Hello Bobby," she said as she met me at the door, in the same tired voice that I remembered on the phone. She opened the door widely. Her face had more wrinkles on it than I remembered, and it looked tired like her voice.

"Gracious me, come in out of the cold rain, Bobby, you are all wet." She led me into the bathroom and told me to take a hot shower.

About this time, my memory faded into a dreamless sleep.

It was dark, very dark and the silence was bitterly cold when Joey Kline shook me awake.

"We must be a moving, Bobby, before a hint of daylight brings out the farmer who owns this barn. They get up early on the farm, and some of them don't take kindly to vagrants sleeping on their premises.

We gotta walk to Mandan where we can catch a train or a ride or something. If we can wade through the snow around the barn, the road has been cleared by the snowplow."

I wanted to stay beneath the blanket, but Joey was throwing the hay off me. I noticed that his sack was all packed except for the blanket. I sat up and shivered violently.

"Let's go, Bobby," Joey coaxed. I yawned and continued to sit, shaking with chills in my coat, my arms folded tightly against my chest. "You should run around a bit to get your blood circulating. It is going to be cold out there! Let me see that coat of yourn." He opened it and felt inside it. "I don't know….that's not a very heavy coat for this weather, but I guess it will have to make do."

He finished packing his old bag, after which we made our way through the dark toward the front of the barn.

"If'n you got any business to tend to you had better take care of it now," he said casually as we neared the front entrance to the barn. "It must be thirty below out there."

I ran to the corner to pee, the steam coming off of it like from a boiling teakettle!

When I joined Joey again, he was pushing with all his weight against the barn door, but it wouldn't budge. So I through my weight against it also.

"No use," he said. "The snow is piled to high agin it." And we had went back to the door on the lee side of the barn.

Outside you could feel the cold as it climbed your nostrils and descended into your windpipes in gasps that seared your lungs like cold fire. I turned my collar up in an attempt to hide my nose from it as we turned and made our way through the deep snow toward the roadway.

The moon was big and cast weird shadows from us with it's eerie silver light upon the soft, dry snow. I could see our weird shadows struggling, in an effort to get over the snow banks to the dark road beyond, which like a black ribbon on white moved off ad infinitum into the silvery moonlit darkness. The white expanse on either side was the package, a gift of the north, frozen, lifeless, endless.

Even after the struggle to get into the roadway, I was cold, like a naked boy exposed to a cruel joke, thrown out with flippant disregard by the ice woman of the north in heartless laughter.

We walked then, Joey and I, along the black ribbon through the moonlight, a cruel shadowy light exposing a world in deep freeze that hung over us suspended like frozen eternity. It pricked me like a thousand syringes fitted with ice needles. But we plodded on with the knowledge that we had no other choice.

I hardly remember the details of that predawn odyssey. I walked on and on like a zombie. At one point, I remember that Joey stopped me and dropped his bag on the cold blacktop and ordered me to take off my coat. He had taken his off, and we traded. The extra warmth from his dirty, but heavy old coat, brought some life back to my forced march through the bitter cold of that winter dawn.

Once again, I awoke to the awareness that we were on the highway to Mandan, but the dark and bitter cold stretched on like a trip to the North Pole. It was a forced march, not only through space but time as well. The march itself became the time, the space, the end in itself. A frozen moment, in a cold hell of eternity.

Joey stopped me. I the zombie awoke again. We again traded coats. My coat seemed defenseless then. The cold was going right through me to leave my nakedness numb. Vulnerable, it seemed, to be raped by the ice woman of the north. Her teeth were like frozen pearls, and they bit down harshly as she had bitten and sucked, in her frozen passion, from my nakedness.

Oh Robin, my Robin, I remembered then, in an attempt to flee the cold and create time out of eternity. I remembered that while taking the hot shower, my stomach began to sink while dread began to climb out of it. Where was Robin?

Back in the warm living room, Mrs. Barnes led me to a seat and had me sit. I looked around for other entry ways from which Robin might suddenly enter the room. My brain had become feverish in its anticipation as I frantically searched for a glimpse of her. Then the thought dawned on me that she might possibly be in school. She would probably be a senior in high school now. Relieved I turned my attention to the chatter coming out of the puzzled face of Mrs. Barnes.

"What's the matter, Bobby?" I heard her asking. "You look as though your thoughts were miles away from here. You don't look like you are hearing a word I say!"

I felt my cheeks grow hot with embarrassment. "Uh….uh….uh," I heard myself stammer. "I'm just a little homesick, I guess."

"Oh, how sweet, bless you," Mrs. Barnes crooned. I detected a tear in her eye and was about to give myself silent congratulations, but then she continued, "I wish my Robin would become homesick and come back home to us."

Her words hit me like a bullet to my heart, a bullet that then sank as dead weight to leave my chest cavity empty and in despair, helpless against the onslaught of her words which were to follow.

"Oh my Robin," she said, her voice becoming gentle and introspective, "if only she would come home, I would forgive her, and so would Albert."

Then as though suddenly aware of my presence again, her voice became harsh and accusative. "Robin turned bad," she said. "When Albert and I got here to North Dakota, she was living in sin with this guy who was twice her age. He was a bartender, a no good 'rounder who not only sold whiskey, but he drank it and cussed." She shivered then as though horrified at her own words. "That man would say horrible things that I can't repeat. He would say them right here in front of Albert and I. Robin would sit there where you are sitting, Bobby and just laugh as though she thought such wickedness was funny. I begged her to come home, practically on my hands and knees. When I finally saw that my begging wasn't going to do any good, I asked her to marry the guy so at least she wouldn't be living with him in sin."

"But do you know what she did? My God, I shiver in horror at the thought of it. She told me to my face, something that she had done. She and the evil man that she was living with were at a party where they were drinking whiskey and other evil drinks that I don't even remember the names of. And she must have gotten awful drunk, otherwise she couldn't have done what she did. Wild heathens don't even do such things anymore, or so I hear. It shows you how alcohol is the tool of the Devil. Anyway she and the other wicked women at this party got into a contest to see who would be brave enough to dance naked."

"I just couldn't believe it when she told me. And how could a girl tell her own mother a thing like that anyway? If it was me, I would be too ashamed to tell anyone something like that let alone my own mother."

My brain was starting to become feverish again as an image of Robin's nakedness flashed boldly through it. I listened intently to hear what Mrs. Barnes was going to say next.

"She danced naked without a stitch on," she gasped as though shocked by the sound of her own voice. She shook her head in disbelief and pulled her own dress down firmly around her ankles. "But that's only the half of it," she continued, "this rich fly by nighter, a stranger, came up and danced with her while she was still naked. Robin said she fell in love with him at first sight, and they got real close." Mrs. Barnes dropped her head then and whispered, "it just makes me sick at my stomach."

But then her voice again rose in anger, "Her bartender boyfriend got real jealous, and he and the rich stranger got into a big fist fight. To hear this stranger tell it, the bartender boyfriend got beat up real bad and had to go to the hospital."

Mrs. Barnes' words seemed to take the wind from her, and she started gasping for air or maybe she was just trying to keep from sobbing, I couldn't tell. But they made me feel like I got hit in the fist fight as well. I felt like that rich guy had hit me in the stomach.

"The next day Robin and this fly by night character walked in without knocking," Mrs. Barnes continued, her voice becoming soft and whiney, like a defeated old lady. "When Albert saw this strange man, he just walked out of the house in disgust. I tried to be nice and asked them to take a seat. But it was then that Robin had told me the whole thing, and how she was madly in love with this stranger. I finally had to put my hands over my ears and motioned that I could take no more."

"'Oh, Mom,' she said, 'it is not as bad as all that, what is wrong with being the way God made us? Life is too short to get bent out of shape over loose ends.'"

"Loose ends, she called it! After the way Albert and I raised her! I guess we should have been more strict with her, like your parents were with you kids." She wrung her hands and stared out through the window at the falling rain. But I don't think she saw it.

"Anyway," Mrs. Barnes said, her voice now subdued, "Robin told me that she had really come over to tell her dad and I goodbye, and that she and Edgar, her new boyfriend, were going to Europe together to spend the summer at his villa on the French Riviera. She looked at me," Mrs. Barnes said, her voice becoming incredulous, "as though she had expected me to congratulate her or something! It was like a slap in the face, my own daughter. I looked at her then, sitting beside that wicked rich man, and I could only see a stranger. I could take no more of it!"

Mrs. Barnes turned her pained expression once more toward the cold gray rain out beyond the window that was now fogging over.

"I told 'em to leave then and told Robin not to come back with this man. But I remember her face. It seemed so innocent and happy. Why it is that I keep remembering that I'll never know. She started to protest, but I told her to shut up and then I told 'em both to get out again. Then this guy grabbed her by the arm and dragged her out of the house without a word. And I slammed the door behind 'em."

"I'm sorry, Bobby," Mrs. Barnes suddenly said as she turned her gaze back on me. "I shouldn't have said all this stuff to you! What could you care about it? How's your mom?"

I was suddenly jarred from my reverie, I was sitting on my butt on the cold hard pavement, Joe's voice hovered over me. "You gotta get up off's the cold pavement, Bobby," it was saying, "before you freeze your asshole solid!"

Then he was pulling on me by the coat collar. When I managed to get to my feet, we traded coats again and walked on into the frozen moment.

"We gotta find someplace to get in outta this cold," I heard Joey say, but his voice seemed so distant.

I looked for his voice and saw the cold outlines of buildings looming ahead of us. Like in a mirage, they stood as pale shadows in the dawn. But soon they became warm windows that twinkled and beckoned in the light of the new day. But they stirred in me a new consciousness and a restless desire to walk faster.

As we approached them, I heard Joey's distant voice again, "First we'll try to find a public place that is open." I looked for him again and was shocked to find him right beside me. "Be a shame to impose upon the privacy of these people," he said. His voice sounded like where it was supposed to be then.

But then we saw what we were looking for, the blink of a neon sign, a blink that was so slow that it looked frozen like everything else around it. But it blinked: café.

"Come, Bobby," Joey urged gently. I stared at the frozen blink for a moment and then stumbled toward it on my numb feet.

Inside, it looked all blurry, and I stared at its warmness in disbelief. It had come as a shock to my freezing brain. It must be a dream, I thought. I shook my head to make sure I wasn't imagining it. Suddenly the soft warm air smelled like stale bacon grease, and I became aware that I was very hungry.

"Are you alright, Bobby?" and I realized that Joey was shaking me on the shoulder.

"I think so," I heard myself responding as reality began to flicker on again, like a loose light bulb that someone had tightened in its socket. I stumbled to the counter with Joey helping me. My feet had no feeling in them, like they were another man's feet. Sitting on the stool, I heard my own voice say, "Boy am I hungry."

"Food'll be here in a jiffy," Joey said, then yelled, "anybody here?"

Sitting in the warmth of the café, I remember my money and told Joey about it. Any fear I had of him was gone now.

"Good," he said, his old gray eyes beginning to sparkle. "Now we have an excuse for warming up and eating without imposing on anyone. We'll drink lots of coffee and eat our breakfast real slow like, so's to stretch the time out and warm up a bit."

"Hey," Joey shouted, with new found confidence. "is anybody here? We are hungry!"

A big woman appeared, surly like. "Wha'd juz want?" she asked with a voice full of suspicion.

"We want you 'juz' to take our order," Joey mimicked boldly.

"Juz tell me what you want," she said coldly.

We ordered bacon and eggs while the woman continued to stand in the back.

Joey loved the strawberry jam that came with the toast. He kept yelling at the surly woman to bring him more jam until she finally told him she was going to charge him extra for it if he didn't stop yelling.

We drained our coffee cups when the rays of a sick hazy sun cut its arch through the dead frozen land to bounce off the back of my neck and onto the dusty counter top.

The railroad station had been bleak and empty when we got there. It stood beside the cold steel tracks like a strange hump on a moonscape. I squinted off toward Bismarck where the sick sun hung like a cruel joke played on summer.

# JOEY AND THE OLD COP

THE CONSTANT CLICK-CLACK.....CLICK-CLACK of the wheels on steel, beneath us, had turned our dimly lit afternoon into sheer boredom. It was warmer though, we were somewhere west of Billings, Montana. Joey talked himself to sleep and was snoring loudly beside me. I was warm and beginning to fade off into sleep myself.

Back in Mandan, we had finally hopped a freight train but not before our exhausted bodies had been severely numbed by the cold again. We stared down those two long cold ribbons of steel for nearly an hour before we saw something that moved. It turned into a freight train and then stopped at the station.

Earlier a car had pulled up. "That'll be the station master," Joey said, "and hopefully that means a train will be here soon." Upon the arrival of the station master, we went around back behind the station out of sight to wait.

"These railroad people aren't as watchful as they used to be, but you still can't trust'em." Joey said.

The train came to a slow stop while Joey watched intently, saying nothing.

"Aha!" he suddenly exclaimed, excitement creeping into his voice, "I think I see our ride down there, the railroad is getting lax in its old age. Do you see that unlocked car?" he asked as he pointed down the track. I followed his finger and stared hard into the cold sun, but all the boxcars looked the same to me.

"C'mon," he ordered as he took off in a trot down the side of the tracks. At the side of one of the boxcars, he stopped and looked back at the station. Shortly, I came up huffing and puffing beside him, nearly out of breath. I was beginning to feel the blood burning into my numb feet. I followed his gaze back toward the station but could see no movement.

Suddenly the train jerked forward then stopped.

"C'mon, Bobby," I heard Joey say in an intense whisper, "either they ain't seen us or they don't care."

Joey grabbed a wrung on the ladder that hung welded to the side of the boxcar. He pushed on the sliding door until his face turned red with exertion. I started pushing too, from the ground. The door moved. An opening appeared, just big enough for a man to slide through, and it was just in time too.

"C'mon," Joey yelled excitedly as the train jerked forward again, and this time continued to move. I ran to keep up with the ladder and finally got a grip on Joey's outstretched hand and then a hold on the ladder itself. I pulled myself upward, and we were westward bound.

Inside it had been bitterly cold and dark. But Joey had soon warmed a corner up for us with his charcoal burner. We sat close to each other beneath his blanket while Joey had roasted another chicken and the cold North Dakota miles slipped noisily beneath us.

The train stopped only once, and Joey assumed it must be Billings, Montana. It had been in the pre-dawn hours, and no one bothered us.

Now another day had nearly gone. The long hours stretched out on the slow train across Montana. After awhile, the boxcar was comfortable. We roasted and finished off a third chicken that Joey had killed and cleaned before stuffing them in his bag back on the farm in North Dakota. So now my stomach was full, but Joey was out of food.

"We'll worry about it later," he said, then promptly falling asleep he began to snore. I'll buy some food with my money, I remembered thinking as I began sinking into a sea of contented sleep.

She was there, it seemed, naked, squatting. The lips of her pussy seemed to quiver with her passion. The nipples of her boobs stood out firm, surrounded by goose bumps of excitement.

"Robin!" I cried, attempting to leap to my feet, but I was helpless. I couldn't move. She stood, then came slowly toward me, her naked hips swaying seductively. My eyes riveted upon her. My passion climbed, obsessed, out of my gut, totally seduced by her hypnotic sway.

"Bobby, I think that you are impotent again," she said, laughing as she stood over me. Her blood dripped to sooth the fire on my tongue.

"I didn't want to fuck anyway," she said, "with my period and all…and besides, I have another boyfriend now."

"It's only a dream," the dream told itself. "only for her is it real." Becoming aware of my passion, I grabbed for it, bittersweet, unfulfilled, yet fulfilled, frantically I held it with a knotted fist. I must not get my underpants dirty on such a cold night, especially with Joey there…but where was she? All I could see was the empty darkness.

"I'll never see her again," I said, softly to nothing but myself, and the darkness that surrounded me. I again heard Joey snoring beside me. I didn't want to wake him up. So I turned away from him and remembered.

My stay in Fargo had been miserable with no Robin. The Barneses had tried to make me comfortable, but I had been ill at ease around them and felt guilty for my lack of empathy. Their grief held no meaning for me. It looked to me like it was their fault that she was gone. I just spent my time wishing that I were the one that she went to France with.

Mr. Barnes had been quiet and seemed so much older than I remembered. He would get up early every morning to get his coffee pot "a boilin" and to get the paper read before he had to go to work. Sometimes while he was reading, he would get distracted by something and would just sit and stare off into space.

A little later, Mrs. Barnes would just be there, silent, starting to fix breakfast. Soon you would hear her crack an egg.

I had been loath to make an entrance at these times. I hated to disturb their silence and their sorrow. I felt like a third leg of grief. Their grief had seemed stupid to me. After all, everyone had to grow up and leave home someday, and since Christ wasn't coming back no more why did parents have to always have things their way? Of course, I also thought, if Robin listened to them, she would have been there when I arrived. But that would have been even worse if she had been there with her boyfriend. So what was the use?

"Sleep well son?" Mr. Barnes would ask each morning when I would exit from my bedroom. Without waiting for an answer, he would go back to reading his paper.

"Help yourself, Bobby, there is plenty of everything," was Mrs. Barnes' greeting as we would sit down for breakfast.

"Thank you," I would respond and begin to eat in silence.

Mrs. Barnes would eat slowly and very politely with her mouth closed. But Mr. Barnes had false teeth that didn't fit well, and they would rattle and grind as he tried to chew his food. Mrs. Barnes would watch this as though fascinated, and I would watch her watching. It helped keep the noise of his teeth from spoiling my appetite.

Several days after I arrived at the Barneses, Mr. Barnes suggested that I come work at the *Daily News* where he worked. They needed a dock worker.

"Can you drive a forklift, Bobby?" he asked.

"Yes," I answered, not even sure what one was. "But it's been a long time" I added, "I'll need some practice."

"That can be arranged," he said, "be ready to go to work in the morning."

I had been with the Barneses for nearly two months, going to work daily with Mr. Barnes. I saved up another two hundred dollars. I felt real good about this. I just wished Robin had been there to share it with me.

Then like a lightning bolt out of the blue, I had received a letter from my mother. I wondered if my mother had told Mrs. Barnes that I had run away. The thought had sent slivers of fear through my heart. What if Father was on his way to North Dakota at this very moment to take me home?

"Your father promised to forgive you," Mother wrote. "He has promised me he won't punish you if you come home, and we both really miss you. And old Joe, he keeps going through the house like he is looking for you."

Why did she have to mention Joe, I thought as the memory of him had raced sorrowfully through my mind. In the moment of weakness, the thought of returning home tempted me. There was no Robin in North Dakota, what was the point of going on or staying here. But then memory of the second coming came back to haunt me, and I didn't trust my father not to punish me.

With my decision made, the thought that my father might be on his way to get me alarmed me and I decided I had to leave the Barneses as soon as possible. I was tired of living with them anyway.

"I'm leaving," I said abruptly, breaking the awkward silence of breakfast the next morning. Neither of the Barneses had shown any surprise.

"Are you going home?" Mrs. Barnes asked as she gave me a sharp penetrating look.

"Yes," I said, "Mother misses me."

"Oh how sweet!" Mrs. Barnes exclaimed, her long face widening slightly into a sad smile.

"Son," Mr. Barnes began as he swallowed the food he chewed with difficulty. "I think you owe us a little something for the food and lodging."

"Sure," I said, a little taken aback. I hadn't expected him to say something like that. "How much?"

"Fifty dollars, with your promise to also buy a winter coat before you leave. You could run into some very cold weather before you get back to Florida."

Mrs. Barnes helped me find a coat at the Salvation Army store.

One more night went by at the Barneses, but I didn't sleep very well. I was too excited about moving on, this time to destinations unknown. This time I was just moving on.

We ate breakfast in silence. The glow of the kitchen florescent was surrounded by the dark corners of the room, the lingering darkness of a winter dawn before daybreak.

"You just be real careful about who you get in with now," Mrs. Barnes said as I walked through the door into the cold with Mr. Barnes.

Mr. Barnes took me to a big intersection and pointed off to the east. "That's the way you got to go," he said. And I looked up at the big green road sign that said Moorhead.

"Thanks for everything, Mr. Barnes," I said as I got out of the warm car and faced the orange winter sun climbing up out of the east. I slammed the door on him before he could answer. I had been disappointed that he had taken so much of my money. I turned and watched as his car had disappeared into the distant traffic. I then turned towards the west to see the sign that said Jamestown….Bismarck and walked that way.

The click-clack, click-clack of the wheels on steel slowed several times in my sleep but never stopped. They moved on, ever turning into the dark and strange country.

I awoke suddenly. The darkness was black and unrelenting and silent. It was disorienting and unexplainable. I remembered Joey first and felt into the darkness with my eyes for him, then with my hands, but he was not there. I was afraid and became aware of the reason for the silence, the click-clack of the moving wheels had stopped. I was afraid that Joey might be gone as well. But then a figure loomed in the darkness and moved toward me.

"Joey is that you?" I whispered fearfully.

"Yes," came the whispered response.

"They have dropped this car," he said as he sat down beside me. "They probably intend to put something in it come daylight so we gotta get out'n here before the break of day."

He pulled the blanket up around him and promptly began to snore again. I huddled close to the old man and stared into the blackness until it began to turn light.

We were in Helena, Montana. The city sat on a gentle slope of a big basin. You could see for miles to the distant mountains. But the miles looked barren, and they looked cold. They looked like they ought to be colder than North Dakota. But it wasn't so bad. My coat was nice and warm again, the cold did not come creeping up beneath it like it had in North Dakota. By the time we had walked up to a city grocery store, I was sweating underneath it.

"Joey," I said, breaking the silence, punctuated only by our heavy breathing as we made our way up toward the town center, "why is it so much warmer here in Montana than back in North Dakota?"

"Don't let it fool ya, boy," Joey replied. "It can get just as cold here or maybe colder. We are just lucky so far. Here in Montana a nor'wester blizzard can come out of nowhere on a warm day and turn it bitter cold in a matter of minutes. So we better not waste a lot of time taking care of our business. The quicker we are movin' toward the west coast the better."

Back in the railroad car when I had volunteered to buy some groceries, Joey had said nothing. But as we approached the corner grocery store, Joey took my arm and pulled me to one side.

"Now looky here, Bobby, we'll go in there, and you can buy a quart of milk and some potatoes, but I'm goin to put some chops and things in this here bag of mine. You have gotta be real sparin' with that money of your'n."

"But what if they catch you?" I asked worriedly.

"Well that is just a chance you haf to take, livin the life of a hobo but it is not likely, boy, I'm purty good at this sort of thing. So c'mon let's go in there and do like I say. Actually, it might look good if'n I was the one that paid for the milk and potatoes," he added. So I gave him five dollars as we entered together.

"It's kinda early for shopliftin'," he said as we glanced around the near empty store. "There's not many people around, but we'll have to make due 'cause we can't afford to waste any time."

At the produce section, Joey pointed and said, "There's the potatoes."

I grabbed a five pound bag and put them in the basket that I was carrying. Joey found the milk and put a quart in my basket. At the meat counter, Joey began to rummage.

"Ya gotta be awful careful these days 'cause they got hidden cameras around taken pictures of ya," he said in low voice as though he were a speaking to the package of pork chops that he had picked up and was looking at. He threw them in my basket as though he meant to pay for them. "We need some charcoal too, but we will pay for that. The store'll still come out ahead, the way they mark things up."

We moved up an empty aisle, then, with rows of canned goods on either side. Joey glanced quickly around us, twisting his bag around on his shoulder to make it handy. He reached to the shelf and took two cans of pork and beans and shoved them into his bag. He then quickly grabbed the pork chops from my basket and shoved them down on top of the pork and beans. He then walked coolly toward the front of the store.

We found the charcoal up by the checkout counter, and Joey put a bag in my basket. The total for the milk, potatoes and charcoal came to $4.86. Joey gave the clerk my five dollar bill and then put the fourteen cents change in his pocket.

Up to this point, I had been fidgety and nervous. Stealing could be a terrible crime if you got caught. But with the change in Joey's pocket, I was beginning to feel quite proud of the way Joey had handled it all.

But then before we could get to the door, a tall, ugly man, with bulging muscles beneath his red flannel shirt, stood in front of us. A big livid scar started at his nose, went across his cheekbone and then disappeared into his long sideburns. The grin that exposed his dirty yellow teeth was evil and had stopped Joey cold in his tracks.

"Mind if I take a look in that bag of yourn?" His voice was harsh and stupid. It sounded like an idiot's voice.

Joey stared silently at his dirty and evil grin for a moment or so as though sizing up the hulk that stood in front of him.

"Yes, friend," Joey said, calmly, "I do mind, what I have in there is my business and not yourn. If'n you didn't want...."

What happened then was almost to quick for the eye. The bully, with a quick step forward and a twist of the wrist, yanked Joey's bag from off his shoulder and dumped its contents on the floor.. The charcoal burner had clattered loudly, one leg breaking off as it went gliding across the freshly polished floor.

"Aha," exulted the bully, his evil grin broadening, "I caught you red handed! Ya old good for nothing tramp."

He bent over to pick up the package of pork chops. "Look at this way," he continued, his idiot voice rising in glee, "in jail you'll get a chanc't to take a bath, ha...ha....ha....ha!"

At first my anger smoldered quietly inside me like coals from Joey's charcoal burner, but when the brute had reached for the package of pork chops and began to laugh at Joey, it was like a gust of wind had swept through me and my smoldering anger had leaped out like flames from a forest fire. I quickly stepped over and quietly kicked the package of pork chops from the grasping claws of the bully.

His eyes found me and began to pulsate in stupid surprise.

"Why you punk!" he roared, his idiot voice throbbing with rage. He stood, his shoulders slumped forward so he could see me better. His bloodshot eyes bulged like devil eyes, and he started toward me. "Maybe ya want a lesson taught ya." he croaked in a harsh choked whisper.

I ran back to the checkout counter as the bully continued to come at me slowly, methodically, but steadily.

"I want my five dollars back!" I screamed at the clerk, "you can keep your fucking potatoes and milk!" I dropped the bag on the counter. But while I was screaming at the clerk, I noticed from the corner of my eye that Joey was rapidly putting his charcoal burner and the pork chops back into his bag.

"There ain't no refunds in this store, leastways not for you, punk!" His voice was getting closer. It became hoarse and tense, like the disharmonic growl of a sick tuba.

"Fuck you!" I shouted over my shoulder at the approaching brute, but I knew that I had to act quickly. I turned on the checkout clerk. She was counting out change to another customer and was just starting to hand him a five dollar bill. What luck! I thought as I quickly snatched it from her hand. I felt the hot breath of the bully on my neck as I leaped over the bars separating me from an adjoining check out stand. The bully leaped also, and I felt his big clumsy hand trying to get a hold on my coat tail. He growled in his rage as I ran back into the aisle where the canned stuff was.

Halfway down the aisle, I turned to watch him approach. He was panting and coming at me with an awkward gait. His face was red, so red that the livid scar had disappeared into it. Suddenly I felt fear, he intended to kill me! I had to act quickly. I looked around in desperation for a way out.

My eyes fell on a can of peaches that said "freestone" and "in heavy syrup," I would steal these, if I had a chance, I thought, but instead I picked it up and threw it at the bully. It hit him between his legs where his balls were supposed to hang. He bellowed like a bull and doubled over and grabbed the stuff that hung there. I felt real good so I picked up another can of peaches. This can said "no sugar added." I threw them at the bully harder than I had thrown the first one. This one struck him between the eyes where the top of his nose joined his head. Stunned, he stood up, staggered and shook his head. He put both his hands on his forehead, forgetting about the pain between his legs.

"Punk!" he screamed, his voice rising to the pitch of an opera singer, howling at the moon.

I turned and ran to the end of the aisle then back up another one toward the front of the store. I was a coming back to my senses and knew that I had to get out of there. And I was a hoping that Joey had made his escape by now. Suddenly I was aware of two stern faces coming toward me. They looked dangerous, but it was too late to avoid them so I tried to run between them. But they both grabbed me and held me up by my armpits, one on each side. I twisted violently, desperate for my freedom. Images of prison raced through my mind, and they terrified me. The two men had grips like iron, but the terror added strength and cunning to my violent effort. The image of the bully clutching his balls gave me an idea. I managed in my violently twisting to turn enough to kick one of these men between the legs. I think it hit him just right because he groaned, released me, then bent double and began to hold on for dear life. I then swung on the other one with my free arm and whacked him soundly in the jaw. He released me and stood rubbing his jaw and looking stunned.

As I ran toward the front of the store, with a dull roar the hobbling bully tried to cut off my escape, but I was too fast for him. I noticed that my bag was still sitting at the check out counter so grabbed it as I ran toward the front entrance. Outside I frantically looked around for Joey, but he was nowhere to be seen.

"Over here son, over here, the cops are a coming!" It was Joey's voice, and it was a coming from down the street.

"Ok," I yelled in response but at the same time I heard the cop sirens wailing eerily. They were coming after me! The thought paralyzed me, taking the strength from my legs. I stopped and stared helplessly at Joey's fleeing figure.

The sirens got louder, and I saw Joey throw a glance back over his shoulder.

"Watch out!" he screamed, but it was too late.

As I started to run, the bully grabbed me with such violence that it took the wind out of my throat. He then held me with such a tight grip that I couldn't inhale any new air. I thought I was going to die and twisting only made it worse. Black spots were popping up in front of my eyes, and I gasped like a silent fish in my attempt to cry out. Then when everything was starting to fade the cops were there, prying his fingers loose.

"For God's sake man, let loose of the boy," the old cop said. Then the young cop hit the bully on his crazy bone with a night stick. The bully dropped me, and I fell to the ground like a sack of potatoes.

"Now wha'd ya go do sompin like that fur," whined the bully, "I was a doin ya a favor by a holdin 'um for ya!" but the two cops then ignored him, so the bully sulked.

"Now what is this all about?" the old cop asked, but only his lips moved. His long narrow face was covered with wrinkles, but they looked like they had turned to stone. They were hard and wouldn't wiggle when he talked. It was as though they weren't real or were just a mask.

"These here riffraff was a tryin' to rip us off," whined the bully in a voice saturated with his hurt feelings. He then pointed halfheartedly toward Joey, who was now shuffling slowly back toward us.

Up to this point, the old cop had stared at a parked car so he wouldn't have to look at the bully, but when he caught a glimpse of Joey, he turned his stare upon him.

Suddenly from the store came a bald-headed man who was walking brisk and business-like. His bald head was polished red like an apple. He strutted like a boss and tried to look big, but he was too short to look very big to me.

"I'm the manager here," he quipped curtly, "this old tramp was trying to steal some pork chops from my store." He then pointed at an old man who was standing nearby.

"No, it's attin," said the bully, as he pointed, importance beginning to creep back into his hurt voice. Though he pointed at Joey, he turned to glare at me. "This punk threw a can of peaches at me and hit me in the......." he added lamely.

"Oh yes," said the manager as he adjusted his bald red head so that the front part faced Joey, "my mistake."

"He hit me in the balls," the bully's voice trailed again, and his scar-marked face reddened into a fresh flush.

The young cop snickered softly. And the bully turned to glower at him, his flush getting deeper and duller.

After that everyone began to ignore the bully like he didn't exist. They must be Christians, I thought, because they all looked so uncomfortable when the bully talked about his balls. The bully continued to stare helplessly at the boss, as though begging for his support, but the bobbing red head of the boss was trying to hold the eye of the old cop.

"I want to press charges against the old tramp," the boss was saying, "for shoplifting," he continued, "I think you will find the evidence in that dirty bag he's got over his shoulder."

"That's right," screamed the bully victoriously, "he put them back in his dirty old bag!" But everyone continued to ignore him.

"I also want to press charges..." the boss began again, but then he stopped to stare at the parked car that the old cop was staring at again with his stone face. "Sir," the boss said, trying to get the cops attention by showing some respect.

"I'm listening," said the old cop roughly, as he threw an impatient look back at the boss.

The boss then stared into the momentary glance that the old cop had threw him but still acted as though he were tongue tied.

I figured the boss was having a hard time talking to someone that was always a looking somewhere else.

Finally he said it anyway, "I also want to press charges against the old tramp's young partner over here." He then paused and threw me a smug look of authority "I want him arrested as an accessory. He needs to be taught a lesson that crime doesn't pay."

"Don't tell us what you want," said the old cop, "just tell us what happened, and we'll do the rest."

The old cop turned toward Joey then, his shoulders hunkered over like he was about to attack. His big gun looked heavy and hung low on his hip. "Get over here old man," he said in a cold, harsh voice.

The boss looked victorious then and beamed a red grin down at the crowd of onlookers who had gathered just down the street.

"Get a move on ya, old man, you are a wasting my time!" the old cop roared, sounding like a dried up sergeant in the US Marine corps.

"What you do with your time is your business, and if'n you want to go wasting it on an old hobo like me then don't blame me if'n the old hobo is slow." Joey said it while he stared coolly into the face of the old cop. But the old cop looked down at his big gun for support.

"In a minute I'm going to make you wish it was your business old man, if you don't get over here and open that bag of your'n." The old cop continued to stare down at his gun while he talked, and his voice seemed to lose some of its authority.

But then Joey stopped in his tracks. "You ain't a touchin' this bag without a warrant." Joey's voice turned cold like ice, and he spit words out boldly like they were ice cubes.

At this, the old cop came to life, and he stared right back at Joey, and he looked like an old rattler about ready to strike. I was starting to worry about Joey, but I was starting to worry even more about me!

"Are you defying the law, old man?"

"You know, sir, that the old man is right," the young cop said, in a quiet and calm voice. He was standing over beside the gloating red face of the boss.

The old cop turned to look at the young cop, and his voice came out of his throat like someone was trying to strangle it out. It was strained, rough and angry, "Your education is going to be the ruin of you, yet, young man." The eyes in the old cop's face looked mean and they squinted. "Now, you just go back to the station, young man, I don't need you here any longer."

He then glanced at the bully, who was wringing his hands and licking his chapped lips. The bully's eyes were pleading in anticipation, and they were focused on the boss's red face which was still split widely in a victorious grin.

"I'll talk to you later," he added, throwing another threatening glance at the young cop. The young cop then turned without a word and got into his car and drove away.

The old cop started marching toward Joey. The red head of the boss was ablaze beneath the winter sun, and it bobbed in step beside him. The bully, in his excitement, began to shuffle toward him also. But with the movement, he felt the pain between his legs and grabbed it with a curse. He continued to shuffle forward as he gently held onto it. The shiny head of the boss turned slightly, reflecting the sun like a red mirror. He saw what the bully was holding onto. He jabbed an authoritative pointing finger at the offending hand. The bully yanked it away. Then he turned a purple stare back at me.

"I'll kill you yet, you little punk," he whispered tersely, but his attention was again diverted by the harsh voice of the old cop.

"You are under arrest, old man, for shoplifting," he was saying as he pulled out a pair of handcuffs from his pocket.

Suddenly, with a twist of the wrist, he yanked Joey's bag from his shoulder. It fell with a clatter to the ground.

The bobbing head of the boss looked more like a sugar beet now, as the old cop dumped the contents of Joey's bag onto the sidewalk.

"Aha" he croaked in a voice that was almost ecstatic, "there's my pork chops and pork and beans!" He reached for them affectionately.

"Don't touch 'em," said the old cop, but in a more gentle voice as though touched by the reunion, "they're evidence."

He snapped the handcuffs on Joey's wrist.

"But they will spoil," whined the boss.

"We'll keep them in the refrigerator," said the old cop, emphatically.

"I take it ya ain't goin to read me no rights," Joey said boldly

"You're a trying my patience, old man. I'm sure you have had them read to you a thousand times before, probably memorized them. Besides tramps ain't got no rights in this town. We don't take kindly to vagrants and shoplifters."

Suddenly Joey looked at me and jerked his head back and forth a couple of times. It looked like he was telling me to run. So I started moving backwards toward the parking lot. The bully was watching in fascination as the old cop was snapping the handcuffs onto Joey's wrist, so I picked up pace, moving like a sidewinder backwards toward the parked cars so that I could continue to see what happened.

Then out of the blue, Joey yanked free from the old cop and started running in the opposite direction. I stopped and stared in disbelief.

"Stop!" the old cop bellowed hoarsely, "or I'll shoot," he then pulled his heavy gun from its holster.

"I don't doubt you will, you God dammed ol dried up piece of shit!" Joey yelled over his shoulder as he kept on running away.

"Why you bastard!" bellowed the old cop in a voice that cracked in its rage. "You just wait until I get a hold of you!" He then shoved his gun back in its holster, after throwing an ominous glance at the crowd of onlookers. He yelled something unintelligible at the crowd then took off running after Joey.

"Ha..ha..ha…ha," the bully guffawed loudly as he also took off in pursuit, seemingly forgetting about the pain between his legs.

The boss just stood and stared longingly at his pork chops lying there on the cold sidewalk.

It dawned on me then that Joey was probably running to give me a chance to get away. I continued to stand there and hesitate. I wanted to help Joey someway, but I was also terrified of prison. And it worried me that the bully's balls seemed to stop hurting, and he would probably be able to run a lot faster, Besides once that old cop locked his eyes on me, it would be over. There would be no place to hide. First I ran over behind a parked car and watched from behind it.

The old cop finally caught up with Joey, and I watched with a sinking heart as he hit Joey on the back with his night stick. I wished then that I had a rock to throw at the back of the old cop's head so that I could watch his brains spill out onto the pavement. But I didn't have one.

"Help!" I heard Joey screaming, "this cop is a beatin the shit out'a me!"

The crowd started surging forward so that they could see better. The old cop noticed them and got off of Joey.

"Scat," he hissed loudly and ran at them as though he could shoo them off like so many kittens.

I could see Joey lying on the sidewalk where he had fallen from the force of the blow. Some of the bystanders stood their ground and stared sullenly back at the old cop.

"You're interfering with the law," he spat at them, but they just went on looking, so the old cop went back to deal with Joey.

"Get up!" he shouted at Joey, "you ain't hurt."

Joey slowly got to his feet just as the bully had run up, his scar marked face all aglow with self importance.

"Want me to hold him for you, sir?"

"No, I can handle him," snapped the old cop.

"Hey, Panhandle," yelled the boss at the bully, taking his eyes off his beloved pork chops, "stay out of the policeman's way."

Panhandle(the bully) turned with a confused look and tried to focus his eyes on the boss, but before he could focus, he suddenly jerked as though to attention and began to look wildly about.

"Where's the punk?" he screamed in alarm.

All was silent as they looked frantically around the parking lot. Panhandle bolted forward, running toward my hiding place.

"I'll find 'em sir and hold 'em sir 'till you can get the handcuffs on 'em sir." Panhandle croaked magnanimously as he lumbered with a slight limp towards me.

"Ok," the old cop said as he began shoving Joey towards the flashing lights on top of his cop car.

With Panhandle coming toward me like a lumbering ox, I was galvanized into action. I jumped up and ran while bending double, between and around parked cars. I ran for my life.

"There he goes!" I heard Panhandle scream from behind.

"Can any of you bystanders give us a hand?" I recognized that as the voice of the old cop again. I felt terror in my stomach. He was trying to sick a whole mob on me!

"Hey, where are you punk?" Panhandle was just a few cars lengths behind me.

I was near panic as I ran from one car to the next looking for one that was unlocked so I could get in and hide. Then I yanked violently on the door of a big silver Cadillac. The door flew open, nearly knocking me off balance. I climbed in, locking the door behind me. I crouched low on the floor behind the driver's seat. I made it just in the knick of time. I heard heavy breathing and felt a cold shadow creep over me while my heart thumped against my ribcage, sounding as loud as the methodical beat of a voodoo drum. I felt like a wild animal trapped in a cage. I almost prayed as I held my breath and waited for the shadow to pass. Then something shook the big Cadillac. Was he trying to shake me out of it?!

"We gotta find him sir, he stole five dollars." It sounded like Panhandle's face against the window. I tried to lie flat against the locked door but my heart just wouldn't be still!

"It seems like you guys are making an awfully big deal over five dollars and a package of pork chops," I heard a strange voice say.

"But the punk hit me in the balls with a can of peaches," Panhandle whined. The two voices faded, they were walking away. My heart started to lie flat against the door then, like the rest of me.

"He couldn't have gotten far," yelled a distant and harsh voice. I recognized it as the voice of the old cop. "Did you look under all the cars and check for unlocked doors?" I couldn't hear what Panhandle said after that.

It seemed an eternity that I remained frozen against the back door of the Cadillac. My legs had fallen sound asleep, and when I moved them, they felt full of hot needles. And I was feeling sorry for Joey. As I silently waited, I started hating the old cop and wishing that Joey would escape. Finally I decided I had to move and started to lift myself when I heard footsteps coming. I again flattened myself in frozen silence. But the footsteps traipsed by without stopping.

Finally I got the courage to pull myself up to the back seat and peak out the window at the winter sun that was sinking behind the gray mountains to the west. As I looked, I suddenly became aware of an old lady making her way across the parking lot with a bag of groceries. I squatted down again when I saw that she was coming right at me. But now, not only was my heart thumping, but my stomach was growling, and I knew that I was getting hungry.

I heard the trunk door unlocked where I assumed she put the groceries. Then a key opened the front door, and the old lady sank into the seat with a sigh. The motor started and the Cadillac moved slowly backwards. It coughed slightly as though in protest before moving forward.

My legs slept, cold, bombarded by the needles as we made our way at a steady clip along the open highway. Finally I managed to sit, putting my butt on the soft velvety floor so I could stretch my legs. I relaxed a little then, feeling certain that the hum of the engine would keep the old lady from hearing me.

"I wonder if Marcus is home yet." It was the voice of the old lady! I quickly withdrew into a fetal crouch.

"Boy, it is a good thing that I always lock my car doors!" she suddenly exclaimed, hardly above a whisper, "especially after that incident with those bums in the parking lot today. Tom said they never did find one of 'em. It's a getting so it ain't safe to leave the house no more." She sighed and was silent after that as the click of the tires took us on down the highway. Then she slowed turned and stopped.

I crouched, flattened against the door, silent, waiting for what I figured would soon be the inevitable. The old lady laboriously got out and walked off leaving the motor running and the door open. I quickly peaked out, my heart racing with indecision. But I had to duck quickly, because the old lady was already walking back from a mailbox by the side of the highway. She got back in and turned up a road that felt like it was full of potholes. One threw me with such force against the back door, that I lie down flat and stopped breathing, in fear that she might have heard me!

When the old lady stopped again she turned off the motor, got out and slammed the door shut behind her. I heard the trunk door open and heard it slammed behind her also. After a long wait in silence, I peaked out at the darkening sky. Silhouetted against it was a lone one story house. One window was alive with light. The stark, bare branches of two small trees shook in a rising wind. Surrounding them was nothing but short brown grass. The winter night was coming quickly. I decided that I had no choice but to escape into it. Especially after what the old lady had said about the bums in the parking lot.

I quickly got out, locked and shut the door. As I had closed it I heard a door slam up at the house. So I ran down the driveway and into the Montana cold that was a blowing in with the dark. When I got to the highway, I was not even sure which way I had come from. But I turned away from where I thought it was and headed towards the faded mountains that were disappearing into the night, ignoring my exhaustion and my growling stomach.

I thought about Joey then and missed him. And for a moment, I almost wished I was with him in jail so they would give me something to eat and a blanket to keep me warm.

I shivered against the wind coming out of the strange Montana darkness. I wrapped my coat tightly around me and started walking fast to keep warm. After awhile, the wind got harder and I had to lean into it to make headway.

Suddenly I heard the hum of an engine coming from behind me. I turned to see the two pinpoint beams from headlamps plowing rapidly through the darkness. I thrilled at the thought of being in a warm car again. I flailed the darkness in an effort to slow its fast approach and cried at it to stop as I leaped from its speeding path. As it passed, I turned to smell and hear the scream of burning rubber and ran desperately toward it.

A man stood between the two tail lights as I approached, and he was staring intently at me through the darkness.

"For Gods sake," he said in a disbelieving voice, "what are you doing walking along the highway in this wind and cold at such an ungodly hour?" I stopped and stood while he looked me over from head to foot.

"I caught a ride to a farmhouse, and then it got dark." I finally said, lamely.

"It does get dark awfully early at this time of year," he said, "go around and get in."

We climbed into the mountains where one could see dark trees rapidly passing by the side of the road. We went through McDonald Pass, at least that was what the stranger called it. He never said much, and I never did get a look at his face.

Late in the night, we came into Deer Lodge where the stranger dropped me at a motel with a sign above it that said "Dewy's Mountain Inn." Inside I got a room that was warm. I fell on the bed to rest a moment while I stared at the heater which looked like a car radiator. Before I knew it, I slept, too tired to eat.

# JESUS, BUDWEISER AND JACK DANIELS WHISKEY

THE BLUE GREEN hills were coniferous and climbed high to become mountains. They looked wild, then turned cold and forbidding like steel, as gray clouds came off the peaks to trail snow behind them. Among the evergreens were the lifeless trees of gray and black, the branches stark and bare, boldly reaching skyward as though to welcome the swirling trails of snow that raced toward them upon the wind.

Then it had come to us, white and obliterating against the windshield, blown in from the vastness of the distant peaks. At first it just melted against the windshield as it fell against the warm glass, carried away by the windshield wipers, but as we climbed higher, it began to stick. And the highway in front of us began to turn white, and it became difficult to tell just where it led.

Albert Standing Tree stopped by the highway along a curve at a lookout point and exited from the cozy warmth of big white Buick to scrape excess snow from the windshield. We were on Highway 10 and had just crossed into Idaho.

"We've got to try and make it down into Coeur d'Alene." Albert said with a frown starting to wrinkle his forehead. He then threw his head back and drained the last of the beer from the Budweiser can before bending forward to concentrate on the rapidly disappearing highway ahead of him.

Russell, Albert's brother, took a long gurgling swig from his Jack Daniels bottle.

"Driving in this kind of weather makes you glad that all is right between you and your maker," Russell said as he shivered violently and also tried to see into the heavy snow ahead of us.

He then turned to look at me closely as though he were looking for traces of fear in my face. I wasn't afraid, I assured myself and I refused to return his analytic glance, rather, I too, stared ahead into the gray-white gloom.

Suddenly, just ahead of us, two burning red coals of light leaped out of the falling snow. They had looked like they were fastened to a moving snowdrift shaped somewhat like an automobile.

Albert slowed, sighed a sigh of relief and leaned back in his seat. "Good, thank you Jesus" he said, "that car's a melting a trail on the highway for us to follow."

"Open me another beer, Bobby," he continued. I popped one and shoved it into the hand that hovered expectantly in front of me.

"Have another one yourself, Bobby," Russell said as he took another gulp from his Jack Daniels bottle.

I opened a can and drank slowly. I wanted the blurred vision of the snow storm ahead of us to remain steady.

I had been standing on the highway just outside of Missoula, Montana with my thumb standing out against the bright morning sunshine when the Standing Tree brothers had come to a screeching halt about a hundred yards up the highway from where I stood. Out of breath, I had climbed into the back seat of the big Buick over two cases of Budweiser.

It was good to be in a warm car again. I spent the whole day, the day before, by the side of the road, facing the raw wind, my thumb boldly freezing, to no avail. I stood beside a road sign that said 55, just outside Deer Lodge, Montana. The cars would pass me seeing how fast they could get to 55 it seemed. Some of the drivers would look at me as though they were afraid I might somehow get in with them without them even stopping! Others looked the other way as though they were afraid that my smile might captivate them. At the time, it had been beyond my understanding. I never had trouble catching a ride before.

Finally, baffled, I had walked back into town and found the bus station where I bought a ticket to Missoula.

On the bus, I had to sit with a man who had a long black beard and a runny nose. He wouldn't wipe it, and it kept piling up in his mustache.

Everything on him was black, including his long black coat and the tall black hat that stood on his head. He looked like an ancient Israelite or something. I even went and checked the toilet and found that there was plenty of toilet paper, so I decided that there was simply no excuse for his snotty nose. He was just lazy, and I fervently wished that there were another seat available, but there wasn't so I ended up having to sit with him all the way to Missoula.

"There is a state prison at Deer Lodge," Albert said with a chuckle, when I had told him of my misfortune and inability to catch a ride.

Albert and Russell were Indians. They came from a town "on the other side of the divide" where Albert was a Pentecostal lay minister.

"I preach when the preachers sick," he said, with a jovial grin and a long swig from his Budweiser can.

I had been puzzled and charmed at the same time by this. How could a preacher drink so much beer and still be a preacher? At first, I thought they might be joking about Albert being a preacher, because they were drunk or something, but I soon changed my mind about this.

At first, as we made our way toward the distant mountain peaks, the Standing Tree brothers had only made small talk.

"The weatherman says it is going to snow in the mountains west of here." Albert said this as he glanced at Russell as though seeking his advice.

"Yeah," Russell responded as he took a swig from his tall Jack Daniels bottle. "This stuff'll keep you warm though."

It did look good, alright, and I kind of wished he would offer me some.

"Whiskey's not good for you," Albert said, as he looked at the bottle. "It'll make an alcoholic out of you. I'll stick to beer."

I glanced at the two cases of beer on the seat beside me and decided that Albert was probably right, and besides Russell hadn't offered me a swig anyway.

"You either are or are not an alcoholic when you are born," Russell responded, "And I am not one, besides God has promised to heal the sick and alcoholism is a sickness."

"I'm not sure about that," said Albert

"You mean about God healing?"

"No, about alcoholics being born that way."

"Have a beer, Bobby, there's plenty. I have more in the trunk," Albert said, throwing a reassuring glance over his shoulder.

"Where are you heading to, Bobby," Russell asked, turning sideways in his seat so he could devote more attention to me.

"To Seattle, Washington," I replied on the spur of the moment, having remembered seeing it on the map.

"Good," Albert said, "that is where we are going."

"We are going to a Pentecostal revival there!" Russell added his voice rising in excitement. "The revivalist has a reputation for divine healings, and we are just dying to see it."

"My minister wanted me to check it out." Albert continued. "The evangelist is a guy by the name of William Baker. He is supposed to be a great healer. They say people are healed instantly, simply by the touch of his hand."

"Albert is usually skeptical of divine healers," explained Russell, "oh I don't doubt that there are fakes. But I don't doubt for a moment the validity of Reverend Baker. I have heard that his closeness to God is beyond doubt."

"Russell attended a Baker revival once before," Albert said, as he poured some more beer down his throat.

"Are you born again, son?" Russell suddenly asked as he turned and stared hard into my face.

"I was only born once, as far as I know," I said, trying to sound innocent, but I actually knew exactly what they were talking about.

"He isn't going to know what that means," Albert said his voice rising. He had thrown a sympathetic glance over his shoulder. "What he is asking you son is, are you a Christian?"

"That is not what I'm asking!" Russell insisted, stubbornly, "and you know darned well that there is a difference between being a Christian and being born again, Albert!"

"Yes, Russell, I know that there is a difference, but Bobby here might not, and we should take it a step at a time so we won't confuse him." Albert explained as he tried to sound long suffering and patient.

"Are you a Christian, Bobby?" Russell asked half heartedly as though asking simply to humor Albert.

"I don't know," I responded, "I used to be but……"

"Good," Russell said matter of factly, "now let me tell you what it means to be born again." He focused his eyes on me then, and I noticed that they were starting to get bloodshot. "After Christ died on the cross, He ascended into heaven and became one with the Father. It was then that….."

"Just a minute, Russell!" Albert interrupted, "you have left out the most important part! The resurrection!"

"I was getting to that," Russell said but he lost his focus and turned to take another long swig of Jack Daniels whiskey. He burped contentedly and turned back to me, and again after some effort, he focused on my face again.

"So after the resurrection, He poured out His spirit on those who believed."

"No," Albert interrupted again, "you haven't got the sequence right. He poured out his spirit after he ascended into heaven!"

"That is what I said the first time!" Russell said in an incredulous voice. "There is no point in repeating myself!"

"Russell," Albert, said in a loud commanding voice, "I think you are drinking that Jack Daniels whiskey too fast. It is not helping your thinking process." Then Albert turned and threw an apologetic glance back at me.

"What Russell is trying to say is that after Christ resurrected, he suddenly ascended into heaven and showers of the Holy Spirit fell on all those that were looking up at Him as He disappeared. And this was his sign to all the onlookers that they had been born again."

"And don't forget," Russell added "that everyone who believes that this happened is also born again."

"But what if you believed once, and then changed your mind about it?" I asked.

"You can't change your mind about this," Russell stated emphatically. "Once you have been reborn you can't go back and be unborn!"

"Praise the Lord!" piped Albert, "once saved, always saved!"

The thought was alarming to me. What if I couldn't change my mind and had to go on believing whether I wanted to or not? But then I thought, that had to be nonsense! How could you be forced to believe something? But after that, I decided to just keep my mouth shut and just listened all the way into the mountains as they, like a team of used car salesmen, tried to sell me their formula of salvation. I didn't believe most of it, but I didn't want to be kicked out into the cold mountain weather, and I didn't want to be told again that I couldn't change my mind. But finally, I started to enjoy all the attention, anyway, especially after I drank some more beer, and I began to encourage them now and then to keep them going by asking stupid questions.

But after awhile, I wasn't even hearing most of what they said, but two different feelings were beginning to sweep over me as the two voices, two distinct monologues, in their life and death urgency, tried to save a lost soul from hell. One was my feeling of importance, the second was the feeling of freedom and independence. The second was the most powerful. In spite of the urgency in their voices, the choice was mine. I could reject the words of these strangers with impunity. I had no fear of words anymore. So I started to enjoy listening to the noise that came with them. I started to watch the scenery, as I listened. We were climbing into the mountains, racing toward the descending clouds that soon would bring with them the winter gloom.

"Jesus loves you, Bobby," I suddenly heard Russell say. He was trying to sound poignant, like Jesus would have sounded. "He is infinitely patient, but even God's patience has limits."

"When Christ returns, He will cast the hard-hearted and those who refuse to repent into Hell. You should read Dante's *Inferno*. He gives you an idea of what Hell will be like."

"You mean you read that trash," Russell gasped in a shocked voice. "Dante was a Catholic. Most of them are Hell bound themselves unless they stop worshipping the Pope and ordinary people like Mary."

"I know," laughed Albert, "but that in itself might give them more insight into the nature of Hell."

"Never thought of it that way, ha…ha…..ha….," laughed Russell.

Suddenly Albert slammed on his breaks and swerved into a paved parking area, by the side of the highway. It was just after a sign on the road had said, "scenic view ahead".

"Anyone got to piss," Albert asked, loudly. He glanced back in my direction, but I just sat there and said nothing.

A precipice fell sharply just beyond us to one side, and the mountains climbed above the approaching gloom in a panorama, even though some of them were already being obliterated by trails of falling snow.

"Well," Albert said, "I definitely have got to go." He unwound his tall frame and climbed out into the cold air. He stood by the side of the car facing the curve in the highway just ahead of us.

I watched the curve in fascination, holding my breath as I waited for a car to suddenly round the bend and race towards us. Could Albert finish in time? No! he had just kept on standing there, and the approaching car just kept getting closer. My eyes were fixated on it! Would it be a woman driver? I wondered if that would be against the law, if she saw him, that is. Then the car was right there, and the woman was looking right through her glasses at Albert! Albert didn't seem to notice her. He just went right on pissing and looking down at it. I turned away in embarrassment and stared at a trail of blowing snow that had come racing off of a distant mountain peak. I wish I had the guts to piss that way, without fear of arrest, when I had to go, I thought. I always thought Christians didn't do things like that, but I decided, after watching Albert, it was because they were probably cowards like me. Of course, the thought had occurred to me, that Albert might just be drunk.

Suddenly I had to squeeze my legs together to keep from going in my pants. I took a sip of beer for courage. And just as Albert stepped on the gas and began moving towards the highway, I said. "Can you wait a moment Mr. Standing Tree while I go too?"

"Sure," he responded as he threw me a puzzled expression.

I climbed over the beer and ran to the edge of the abyss that hung suspended and empty beneath me. The stream of water just floated, then marched off into the gray-blue haze that surrounded me. No cars had come while I did it, but I kind of wished that a woman had driven by.

A short time later back in the warm Buick, the snow started to fall in earnest, and the Standing Tree brothers turned their attention to getting through it.

We followed the two tail lights for many miles, up through the steep mountains and around hairpin curves where our speed was reduced to a crawl. Sometimes the rear end of the big Buick would slide a bit toward the abyss that I knew existed not far away, and I just hoped that the person driving the car in front of us was drinking milk or soda water and not beer!

"We've got on good snow tires," Russell volunteered once when he had a chance to look back and notice the anxiety that must have been written all over my face.

Finally, after what seemed to be hours of following the old snow covered car in front of us up hill, it suddenly started pulling ahead moving down hill. And not long after that the clouds had lifted and the snowfall stopped. The highway again turned black with the wet, white snow standing beside it. A mountain peak suddenly loomed in front of us, while distant showers hung like white sheets turned gray by dirty wash water as they moved across the wild landscape.

A gust of wind shook our car as Albert sped up so he could pass the old car. It turned out to be an old green falcon with an old black man driving it.

"We don't need that slowpoke anymore," Albert said, ungratefully.

"Wow," Russell exclaimed when he saw the driver of the old car. "That old man has got a lot of nerve going across north Idaho alone like that! I wonder where he is from and where he is going. It is bad enough for us Indians moving across North Idaho!"

"Yeah," Albert said, as he sighed and leaned back in his seat. "We have all got our burdens to bear."

"Boy, I could sure use another Bud," he continued as he threw a friendly grin back at me. I gave him one and opened another for myself, this time without any invitation.

We advanced, slowly, methodically through the miles that took us first into Coeur d'Alene and then into Spokane.

Albert and Russell had become quiet and both of them started to concentrate on the highway in front of us. Albert bent over, his head just above the steering wheel, becoming business like, so he could stare at the white lines racing towards us on the black highway.

I became fascinated as I watched him. Finally I started watching them too, pretending that I was the driver. But I soon realized that if I were driving, we would all be dead because no matter how desperately I tried to focus on the white lines, I would end up going head on into the path of the oncoming cars. Finally exhausted from the effort, I fell asleep.

I awoke in Spokane when we stopped in front of a small café, and above it a neon sign flashed "The Chicken Roost."

"Don't worry, Bobby," Russell said as he flashed a smile at me. "We'll treat you to dinner, we know what it is like to be down and out. After all we are Native Americans, you know."

"Thank you," I said in genuine relief. I had a terrible fear of using up my money.

I followed them into the warm steamy kitchen. We sat near a window where I looked out to see that the snow was piled high on the sidewalk. Behind the counter, a cute girl with rosy cheeks was lining up plates of hot food. Her flaming cheeks made her look healthy. Watching her made me feel good while I ate my chicken fried steak.

Later at a motel, they gave me a cot to sleep on, and I fell asleep while watching *Gunsmoke* on an old black and white TV.

Spokane was cold and gray above the dirty snow the next morning, and the land outside of it was also gray but windy and empty, stretching on for miles and miles; its emptiness and loneliness never changing as it went along beside us.

Albert was quite cheerful as we crossed the empty land that rolled on forever. The toasty warmth of the Buick made me feel good too, especially with a full stomach. Albert paid for my breakfast. Russell, however, had been taciturn and quiet. He just stared out the side window at the rapidly passing grayness of the stretched out land.

"Well, Bobby," Albert began, breaking off a tune he had been humming and flashing a cheerful smile back over his shoulder. "What are you going to do in Seattle? Do you have friends or relatives there?"

"No," I replied, then I added, quickly, as the thought had occurred to me, "I'm catching a ride down to California."

"At least the weather should be warmer down there," Albert said. But he said it like he wanted to say something else.

"Do us a favor, Bobby," Albert began again, after a long awkward moment of silence. I suddenly realized he was watching me in the rear view mirror. So I looked back at him in the mirror and waited silently. "Come to the revival meeting with us," his voice popped out his mouth like an escaping gust of wind. "I'm sure it will be a wonderful experience for you, and you will be under no obligation to stay any longer than you wish."

Russell suddenly stopped staring at the gray distance and came to life! He reached for the floor board to pull out a brand new bottle of Jack Daniel whiskey from a twisted brown sack. He broke the seal, twisted off the cap and took a long swig, then burped contentedly. He then turned on me with purpose burning out of his intense dark eyes. "How about it, Bobby?" A beatific smile began to play with his lips as he licked the whiskey off them.

"I don't mind if I do," I said, nonchalantly, after letting the two staring sets of eyes wait in suspense for a few moments.

"Praise the Lord!" cried Russell in a victorious voice as he swallowed another gulp of whiskey.

"Praise the Lord!" Albert shouted into the rear view mirror. "That calls for a beer, how about popping one for me, Bobby?"

"God will bless you, Bobby McGee," Russell said with sincerity.

Beyond the rear view mirror, I detected the faded outline of a distant mountain peak. It was climbing up into the gray-blue haze of a now clearing sky. The highway clipped rapidly beneath the tires as we creeped slowly toward it. Then the mountain stood out alone. It was monolithic and humpbacked, like an old man with no head. Yet it was majestic as it appeared through the cold haze with its white crown.

"That's Mt. Rainier," Russell said when he saw my eyes glued on it.

# THE EVANGELIST

Seattle was cold, cloudy and damp. It always appeared as though it was about ready to rain. Sometimes it really rained, other times something would fall, but it wasn't rain, just dampness that you could feel but couldn't see.

When we arrived in Seattle, the Standing Tree brothers promised me a warm bed for another night if I would first attend a night at the revival with them. I was tired but was assured that the revival would do just that, revive and rejuvenate the lot of us.

We had dinner at a Kentucky Fried Chicken joint then had driven off along the wet streets beneath street lights until we came to a road that led us into a damp darkness that even our headlamps had a hard time shining through. After a short drive into this darkness, we rounded a bend to find five sets of tail lights moving slowly along ahead of us. Soon a large floodlight came into view and beneath it were rows and rows of parked cars. The cars ahead of us turned into this parking lot, and we followed.

"This is it!" I could detect the thrill of anticipation in Russell's voice as he parked by the side of the car that had led us in.

Russell had driven from the Kentucky Fried Chicken joint because he knew Seattle better than Albert. He had been there before.

I made out the big tent, standing, dark and foreboding back behind the floodlight.

Albert leaped from his side of the car and shouted, "praise the Lord!" then slammed the car door behind him.

"Praise the Lord!" it was a deep rasping croak that sounded like a talking tuba, and it was the voice of a figure that was climbing out of the car that parked beside us.

"Praise the Lord!" trilled a second voice. It came from the other side of the car that tuba voice had come from, but it was feminine, and I couldn't decide whether it came from an angel or a sexy girl.

"Hallelujah!" Russell shouted as he got out of the car and looked up into the dark at the falling dampness.

Then all the voices joined in, including tuba voice and the voice of the sexy angel to shout such things as "bless us Jesus", "hallelujah to the most high God," but when tuba voice said it everyone stopped to look and listen, as though they couldn't believe their ears.

And while they were all a shouting, they were shaking hands with each other. I, on the other hand, remained silent and kept my hands to myself. But I could feel the look of pity the sexy angel voice threw at me through the darkness. I dropped a little behind and followed them all toward the big tent as I wondered why she had looked at me that way.

Inside it was warm and dry, and it was quite pleasant. There were lights shining all over the place. One of them shone right on angel-voice as she entered the tent, and I was thrilled by the suddenness of her beauty, but before I could get a second look at her, I saw the evangelist. He was shaking everybody's hand, and he shook mine before I could take evasive action.

"I'm Reverend William Baker of Gatlinburg, Tennessee," he tried to make the Reverend part sound important by the inflexion of his voice. I had not been able to get a good look at him while he was hovering over me because he was so tall and skinny. When I looked up at him, all I could see was his bobbing Adam's apple, but from my seat, I watched him. He was tall and skinny and his neck popped out into an Adam's apple which rolled up and down like a marble in his throat when he talked. Most of his head was bald, but here and there little tufts would creep out of his shiny skin, and on the back of his head, there were strings of it hanging like the loose strings of an old rope. It almost looked like the hair on the head of a dead man that was about ready to fall out. I thought maybe he was trying to look like a hippie, but decided it was just too late for that. His two front teeth looked like the two front teeth on Bugs Bunny. But when he smiled, they were too yellow for that. And his shoulders were humped as though his big bald head was too heavy for them. At this point, I decided that I didn't like him.

I was sitting beside the Standing Tree brothers; they were both involved in a lively conversation with Tuba voice and his daughter. At least I assumed she was his daughter. No one as beautiful as she could possibly be married to someone with a voice like tuba had, and besides he had white hair that made him look as old as Moses. I tried to get a better look at her while I listened to the thrilling treble of her voice, but she was sitting on the other side of her tuba father, and I could only see the tip of her nose unless I leaned forward, and I didn't want to do that.

"Please pray for her brother Jumping Tree," it was the growl of tuba voice, and it interrupted my pleasant thoughts. I didn't know what he was talking about because I had not heard the rest of it, but I almost laughed out loud when he said Jumping Tree.

"It's Standing Tree," corrected Albert gently.

"Er….Standing Tree….sorry," he growled in a voice that tried to whine

"Names aren't important," Russell said in a business-like voice. Russell then looked up at the expansive canvas roof that hung over us.

"Dear Jesus," he bawled in a dramatically pious voice, "touch Angelica's heart that she might be receptive to your saving grace."

"You must have faith, brother," he said as he turned a pious smile upon tuba voice. "God is able to touch her, and I believe he will touch her," his voice had risen as though he was trying to make sure God heard him too. "Furthermore brother, you should ask for Reverend Baker's prayers. When he speaks, God listens."

"Praise the Lord!" rasped tuba voice.

"Amen," purred the sexy angel voice beside him.

So then I decided they weren't talking about her, though Angelica sounded like a good name for her. I couldn't resist anymore. I leaned forward so I could get a better look of her red lips, and then my eyes began to follow the curves of her body as they flowed in the right proportions all the way down to the tennis shoes on her feet. I decided, though as I sighed to myself, that she would probably be no fun. Her "amen" sounded too sacred. Besides I suddenly noticed that the Reverend skinny Baker was making his way to the front of the tent where the wooden platform stood.

Silence reigned.

"Praise the Lord, brothers and sisters, welcome to His revival."

I knew then why the crowds came. His voice reverberated off the canvass walls like rich, smooth silk and even hit me like an electrical thrill. It was like an electrical shock that felt good!

"Fuck you," I uttered in a desperate whisper, trying to go on feeling normal. But the thrill just kept on growing stronger with the constancy of the leaping marble in his skinny throat.

"Praaaaaaise you blessed Jeeeesus," he roared in a mellow rich bass. "You are descending on our little tent tonight to heeeeeal the sick, to heal those with broken hearts that cry in agoooony for relief, to fill those who are empty of your life, the life that you have given us with your holy ghost! You are here in the spirit precious God!" he continued with a cry that moved the very air like an electrical current zigzagging through the atmosphere. And its mellow deepness seemed to shake the ground beneath my feet.

"You are coming tonight with such overwhelming power that the Devil himself shall flee before You in self remorse that he has rejected you for all eternity."

"My Gooooooood, my Gooooooood," he cried, his voice rising with such feeling that the crowd was falling prostrate at his feet, their voices in a unified scream that sounded like electrified silence. His upturned face was pulsating with the Holy Spirit as it glowed up at the gray ceiling of the tent.

As the words, like silk, continued to roll off his tongue, the electric thrills started racing from soul to soul, and suddenly the intense silence became a rising murmur, and everyone began to twist in ecstasy. The thrill hit me like a wave from off the sea. I jumped up and grabbed the seat back in front of me and held on to keep from twisting. As the scream of the crowd rose and ebbed as a sea of sound, I could no longer even hear what Baker was saying but just watching him say it was sending electrical thrills through my body.

Suddenly Albert kicked me, but I instantly knew it wasn't his fault. He was twisting from the power of the Holy Ghost, and it had gotten a hold on his foot.

Then it began as an eerie whisper, it came out of the twisting crowd, to become a chant, "God is the light, God is the light, God is the light, God is the light," it climbed in crescendo until it became like a ghostly wave sweeping sanity and silence before it. I was inundated by the power of the chant, and my resolve collapsed. I began to twist and make unintelligible noises, like something stupid inside me was trying to talk. I looked up at Baker, his forehead was pulsating red and the marble in his throat was jumping so fast that it almost made me dizzy. But I thought, maybe, it was because I was twisting.

Behind me an old lady screamed into my ear, and this broke the rhythm of the chant, but at the same time, sent out tornadic shock waves which got a hold on certain bodies and began to twist them violently, almost obscenely. A crippled lady started running up and down the aisle on one leg, shouting and hopping with one hand in the air and the other held out to balance herself. Gradually chaos had taken over. All had become a cacophonic scream of lifted voices climbing towards the gray canvass roof top. The currents of power that hit me then were unpredictable. I sat down and clung tightly to the arms of my chair and clenched my teeth together in preparation for I knew not what.

The head on skinny Baker suddenly dropped. No one saw it but me. It was now his tufted baldness that was pulsating. And then I noticed that there was a small red light pulsating from the canvass tent top, and that it wasn't his head that was pulsating after all!

"Sing praises to the almighty God, hallelujah blessed Jesus." It was Albert beside me. He leaped to his feet, his voice wild with excitement.

Then, from the corner of my eye I caught sight of Baker's long skinny arms jumping toward heaven again.

"Now, dear precious Savior," his voice rose in mellow clarity, like the church bells in a dale somewhere. His voice pierced the cacophony and brought it to silence. He even shut Albert up. "Touch the hearts of your people gathered here," he continued. "Teach them that generosity here on earth will earn them rich rewards in Heaven. Speak to their hearts dear Jesus."

His voice had suddenly become the epitome of helplessness and innocence. "Bring gently to the forefront of their awareness, the urgent need You have of their financial support in spreading Your good news." His voice reeked in mellow sorrow and divine pity. I, myself, had started to wish that I had enough to give something to his needy God.

But just as his voice had taken a nose dive into the divine sorrow of a country song, it suddenly started climbing turning sorrow into the joy of victory until his voice had began to sound like the voice of God himself.

"Hallelujah," he roared, like a lion standing above his kill. His lips were puckered against the microphone, "do I have volunteers," he hesitated, then in a voice, breathless and oiled with certainty, he screamed like a wild hyena, " to bear the offering plate of Christ the Savior?"

One could almost see a holy drop of olive oil fall on his shiny bald head. But I figured it had to be a drop of sweat and that it had been there all along.

There was a mad rush of many feet. You could hear them trampling the earth beneath the tent as seemingly all the men made their way toward the podium. I figured it was because they wanted to collect the money so they wouldn't have to give it. The women all stood and hollered in ecstasy because they figured they had enough money to keep God in the business of pouring out his Holy Spirit, and that Baker would have enough to feed his skinny frame.

When an old woman behind me shouted "hallelujah", I turned to look. She enthusiastically pulled her purse from her bag, but when she looked inside she grew silent. But when she saw me looking, she started shouting some more, but she turned sideways so I couldn't see how much she pulled out.

As the offering plates made their rounds, a fat lady played an organ while an old man with a crackling voice sang sweet and sticky songs and looked like he was about to cry.

Baker stood at the podium, his eyes flashing fire as they greedily roved from one plate to another, and his oily voice kept shouting above the music, "bless them Lord, bless them Lord."

In the crowd, you could tell where the offering plate had been because the shouts of glory faded after it had passed.

When the plate came to me, it was piled high with green money, and there was a twenty dollar bill lying right on top of it all. As I took the plate and jabbed it into Albert's ribs, a miracle happened. A little puff of wind came along and picked up the twenty dollar bill, and it just floated off the pile, going down between my legs and landing on the floor. I couldn't believe my eyes, and I looked quickly about to see if anyone else had seen it. I looked up at Baker, his eyes were flashing at some other offering plate. The man in the suit who had handed me the plate was talking in a whisper with the old lady behind me, and Albert, beside me, was staring up at Baker his eyes full of worship.

So I got to thinking real hard about it. Maybe it was God's breath that blew it off because he really didn't need as much as they were collecting, and he was giving it to me. But then I decided that probably wasn't it since I really didn't believe in Him anyway. So I got to thinking even harder about it, and it came to me that God was probably not going to get the money anyway. Baker would probably keep it all, and I figured I needed it worse than Baker did. And besides, it wasn't like that I stole it. It had come floating over to me of its own free will. That made me feel real good. I reached down, picked it up and put it in my pocket.

Finally the men with the money plates went to the back of the tent somewhere so they could count it in secret, and the power of the Holy Ghost quickly returned and went racing through the crowd again, like someone went and plugged it back in.

Baker threw his head back so that his red face would begin to pulsate again. He looked like a skinny angel with his arms spread and lifted into the air, except that he was a man and not a woman. Then his legs began to dance, and the fat fingers of the lady at the organ went into a frenzy. The power that swept through the crowd turned it rampant. Many began to dance in the aisle, imitating Baker. Some danced alone, some danced in pairs, but the Holy Ghost had a hold on them all. In the aisle across from me, I noticed two girls kissing passionately, and I couldn't help but wonder if that was really the Holy Ghost doing it.

Suddenly my heart leaped wildly. Angel voice had gotten up and was dancing in the aisle beside me. Her jeans were so tight that she almost looked naked. When I saw her, the current racing through the crowd hit me, and I jumped to my feet under the power of the Holy Ghost and raced into the aisle and began dancing beside her. I felt the power of God bouncing off her twisting curves. I closed my eyes and imagined that I was dancing on the streets of gold, and the angel of God was dancing beside me. But I peeked to see how close she was getting to me, and so that I could watch her gyrating curves.

"Praise the Lord," I screamed as one of her boobs collapsed against me.

"Praise you Jesus!" her trilling voice climbing high into ecstasy. She clasped her arms tightly around me, her eyes closed with both of her boobs collapsing against me.

"Save him Jesus!" she cried, "Save him from the gates of hell!"

"Amen," I said as I grabbed her around the waist making her feet leave the floor. I then danced for the both of us under the power of the Holy Ghost. As I continued to shout praises to Almighty God, I was suddenly aware that my arms were wrapped around bare skin. Her boobs had come out from beneath her bra! And her lips were right in front of mine, and they were whispering about how much she loved God. Her breath smelled real good, like she had taken a breath mint before she came, and I couldn't resist them. Our lips met so that we kissed and our tongues started getting twisted around each other. But then I dropped her, and my arms slid up to catch her by the armpits.

"Raise your arms to Jesus," I whispered to her soft red lips which appeared somewhat petulant in their surrender, "He loves you."

She raised them high like a dreaming somnambulant. And then I saw them standing free and firmly naked. The sight left me in speechless disbelief and a bit embarrassed. I then grabbed her, pulling her against my chest to hide them in case anyone else should come to and see what I was looking at.

But then Baker blew it. The Holy Ghost evaporated. He did it with a boom with his melodious voice through the microphone.

"It is time for healing," he cried in an authoritative voice.

The crowd stopped dancing and turned toward him. Before I could release the girl, she had come to her senses in my arms, she was staring down at her naked boobs then up and into my eyes. Embarrassed, I turned and fled, but not before I saw the prickly skin around her nipples.

After that I sat in the back beside an old lady that kept blowing her nose. She didn't have a cold. It was just that she couldn't keep from crying at everything Baker said.

Baker began to heal people right and left as he touched them with his powerful hands. They would rear back, some would fall to the ground as though electrocuted, but then they would leap up again to testify, most in an unknown language so that no one knew what they were saying, but it was a gift of the Holy Ghost. The brave ones would start shouting in English. One old lady held up a lump that she claimed had fallen off when God's anointed had touched her. "It was a cancer," she said, "now I'm healed, praise the Lord!"

But I just couldn't believe it. From where I sat, it looked like something that had fallen off because it was rotten.

It was then I noticed a man in a wheelchair trying to maneuver his way through the crowd. Baker had also noticed him struggling.

"Make way for that man!" he bellowed like a singing bull.

The crowd had fallen back on either side. A pathway suddenly appeared between the cripple and Baker. Baker stretched his arm in a sympathetic welcome. The wheelchair rolled forward with the fervor of one who has reached the promise land. Baker fell on him like a vulture, whispering in his ear. The cripple whispered back in reply.

Suddenly Baker leapt to be skinny and straight like an arrow that has been drawn and is ready to be shot.

"This man is a paraplegic," he cried, "but Jesus is going to heal him tonight!"

A murmur of awe raced distinctly through the crowd, and you could hear an ever present "praise the Lord" and "hallelujah" here and there.

Skinny Baker grabbed the paraplegic's head roughly. His own head went back, taut, pulsating with the power of God. The paraplegic stiffened like a dead man in his chair.

"Come out of him Satan!" screamed a voice that seemed to have a profound and distant source. It came through Baker's lips distorting them grotesquely.

Could this be God talking, I wondered? I glued my eyes on the distorted lips with growing fascination. Excitement began to climb out of my stomach as I waited and watched to see what was going to happen next.

"I said come out of him Satan!" the power of the voice was overwhelming. It inundated noise and silence alike, sweeping everything before it like a gust of sacred wind.

I leapt to my feet and stood shaking and thrilled to the bone. The old lady beside me was standing and bawling uncontrollably. People all around me stood to shake silently. It made you feel like you were in a divine eggbeater.

Baker just continued to stand there and twist. His mouth was wide open, and his tongue protruded as he tried to shake Satan out of the vibrating stiff in the wheelchair.

Suddenly the paraplegic screamed. It was a bloodcurdling scream, and it sent a chill through the charged atmosphere. My body stopped shaking, and I sat down, weak in the legs.

"That's the Devil," shouted Baker, "and he is a fleeing."

Then the crowd started singing loudly, "we shall overcome" to overcome the chill of the Devil's voice.

Quicker than the eye could see, the paraplegic seemed to leap into Baker's arms. Baker held him tightly around the waist, and they danced around the stage. They began to leap like spawning salmon. Baker was trying to hold him up and help him lift his arms at the same time, so that he might sing praises to the most high God.

When the crowd saw the paraplegic leap, it went berserk. The noise became a holy scream, so intense that my head began to throb, and I couldn't tell whether I was screaming or not. The old lady beside me was grabbed like a puppet and yanked by an invisible hand out into the aisle where it looked like somebody had cut the string, and she fell sobbing to the ground.

I watched then, as in a dream of superimposed silence, as skinny Baker kicked the wheelchair from the stage. It fell, then collapsed onto the dry earth. As one, Baker and the paraplegic continued to dance in a silence that transcended supernatural noise. My own body began to lift itself and to float in ecstatic communion with the multitude. The noise had become physical, fluid, sweeping all before it.

It was then that out of the blue, a fearful thought struck me. What if I couldn't find the Standing Tree brothers for my ride back to the warm bed that they had promised. The thought sent me reeling, and I collapsed to the floor hitting my chin on the back of the chair in front of me. I rubbed my sore chin and listened to the pain. I must go find them I decided. Angel voice wouldn't dare tell on me. After all it was as much her fault as mine. But then a more terrible thought hit me, what if she was tuba's wife and not his daughter at all? The thought of confronting her father was bad enough, but her husband....? That was too terrible to contemplate. I decided to just sit there where I was and watch for the Standing Tree brothers as they walked by me. I would follow them at a distance and wait for them to part with tuba voice and his wife.

But then a real silence suddenly hit me, and it came from the stage. The paraplegic had fallen to the floor.

"Hold the faith! Hold the faith!" Baker's scream had turned weak, and the crowd suddenly just gawked. "God cannot heal without faith. You must believe! Oh, dear Jesus," he screamed, in a begging voice. He lifted his face to let it pulsate but it just pulsated with gray desperation. His face turned long and haggard. "Let this man walk again!" he demanded into the microphone with a hoarse whisper. "Oh, let him have faith even half the size of mustard seed."

The man didn't get up. He just sat there on the wooden stage, his face lifted, pulsating in pain. Baker's cries didn't do any good. God had withdrawn his power for the evening. Baker then started talking in an ordinary voice. He told the man to be sure and come back tomorrow night and to work on his faith in the mean time. "It won't happen unless you believe it will," Baker said with finality.

"But I do believe," cried the poor fellow as his devoted eyes looked up at Baker as though he were God, himself.

"Belief is like muscles," shouted Baker so that everyone could hear. "You have to build their strength before you can use them."

The poor guy started to talk again. Baker must of liked what he was saying because he squatted and stuck the microphone to his lips.

"I believe that God has healed me!" he shouted out of his white face. "It is just up to me to believe He actually did it so strongly that I can't doubt it. Tonight I let myself doubt it. All I need now . . ." he tried to make his voice climb an octave higher, but it cracked and his white face twitched in pain, "is to accept God's healing and to walk out of here."

It was then I noticed several men in black suits putting the man's wheelchair back together. They then rolled it back up beside him on the stage. Then two of them picked him up and sat him in it. He again motioned for the microphone.

"Tomorrow night I will walk out of here," he said, in an attempt at enthusiasm.

"Amen, hallelujah, praise His Holy Name," shouted Baker, trying to get the spirit moving again. He grabbed the microphone from the paraplegic's trembling hand and lifted it to the lips at the top of his skinny frame. His words were starting to turn oily and zestful again. His eyes began to search the crowd as though looking for someone else to heal, maybe someone who was easier.

But it was not to be. The crowd had started to grow restless and to mill about. Then several brave souls made a beeline for the exit. A mad rush started to ensue. Everyone wanted to be the first out to avoid the traffic jam.

I could hear Baker's voice yelling above the trampling sounds of many feet, "don't forget tomorrow night, God will bless you, God will heal . . ."

Suddenly I remembered to watch for Russell and Albert, but people were rushing by me on both sides, and all of them seemed to go by at the same time. Shortly there were only stragglers and none of these were the Standing Tree brothers. In my disappointment I began to realize that I had missed them and would be left behind. I continued to wait anyway, in hopes that they might come back looking for me.

As I sat there my mind wondered about the poor man in the wheelchair and how he had fared in the mad rush for the exit. Then as the last of the stragglers began to disappear, I saw him. He was alone at one of the exits sticking his hand out to see if it was raining or not. He then slipped out into the darkness of the night.

After he was gone, I began to wonder what I was going to do. I had given up on the Standing Tree brothers, and I never saw them again. And now there was no one else left to catch a ride with. I wrapped my coat more tightly around me against the increasing chill of the empty tent. I sat in apathy with the hope beginning to lurk in my brain that I might sleep in a dark corner of the tent through the night.

It seemed like I started to doze as I sat there in my seat, and Angel voice was there again beside me in her tight jeans. Her boobs were naked and firm with the goose bumps around her nipples. I wondered if she had known it when her boobs had popped out and just pretended that she didn't, maybe it was just a trick to get me saved. Then I wondered if God got a thrill out of seeing her naked boobs like I did. He must have, I decided, since he made them that way. Then I wondered if God had ever fucked the female angels. I remembered that he was supposed to have fucked the virgin Mary and that was how Jesus got here. But I did feel kind of guilty for thinking about this because I knew that you didn't call it "fuck" when God did it. But I just couldn't remember what it was that you called it.

But then I wondered about the poor paraplegic again. He had looked like a puppet on a string, yanked around by a mean puppeteer. I could see Baker again, grinning like God himself, watching his puppet wallow in anguish on the floor, while he told him he needed to be stronger. Even my dad said once that God was there to help the weak folks that couldn't help themselves. Baker was an asshole, I decided.

"You have to leave now."

It startled me when I felt the hand that went with the voice on my shoulder.

Then I saw the quiet people with bent postures, ducking, like ducks on a pond as they dragged big plastic bags through the dimly lit aftermath.

"Ok," I said, as I got up and moved slowly toward the exit, then through it into the eerie silence beneath the floodlights and falling dampness.

There was a scattering of automobiles still parked here and there. I figured they belonged to the cleanup crew that were dragging the big plastic bags. A pair of disappearing tail lights reminded me of my predicament. I had no idea how I was going to find a place to sleep. It must be miles to the nearest motel, I thought.

I glanced back at the wall of canvass that stood behind me and for nothing better to do, started to walk along its circumference. I had hoped, half heartedly, that someplace cozy would present itself.

As I moved around the large tent, a big long trailer house came into view. A light glowed brightly from the rear window. I stopped and stared at it, longingly. The window was steamed over. I knew that it was warm inside. I sighed, then chided myself for wasting time. Obviously it was occupied, probably by Baker himself. But this thought roused my curiosity, and I decided to move toward the steamed over square of light.

As I got closer, I noticed that little streams of water were running in rivulets down the glass. It must be awfully warm in there, I thought, and shivered from the dark damp cold around me. I then found myself standing beneath it, straining my ears to see if I could hear Baker talking. It was then that I distinctly heard a woman's voice.

"Please Reverend Baker," the feminine voice begged, "don't make me do those things." The voice was soft and urgent, and it came right through the walls of the trailer.

"I told you, honey, not to call me that. You can call me Billy." It was the oily voice of skinny Baker, sure enough. The pious voice sounded like it was being persecuted. It sounded like it was trying to have the infinite patience of God.

"Please, Billy," the voice of the girl rose this time in an urgency that bordered on despair. "Please don't touch me. Please don't force me to fuck you. Can't you please just look and let me go?" Her voice ended in a gasp, and I figured he was sticking it in. But no!

"Why you little hussy!" I heard him pant. But then the next time he spoke, it was with a patient voice. "You should consider it an honor, young lady, to give of yourself to God's anointed. Consider the virgin Mary, she has been remembered throughout history for her sacrifice." Yet there was still a hint of frustration in its oiliness.

"But not this way," I heard her plead gently, "I have always worshipped you as a man of God. How could you do this to me?"

"Ha," his voice turned cruel and mean again, and he sounded like he was panting with the potency for even more anger.

"What do you think I am, God or something, that I can look at you like a piece of art and let you go! I'm human too." He was beginning to shout.

"I do my duty and devote all of my time to God's work, and all I ask from you is a little relaxation and appreciation. If you would only give of yourself freely, God would bless you freely."

"But you promised me Billy that you just needed someone to talk to."

"Ok, bitch," he hissed, "I won't make you fuck me. You probably have taken nothing for birth control anyway. We'll do it this way."

"Please," I heard her gasp.

"Forgive them, dear Jesus, their selfishness," Baker's voice again turned oily and patient. "Forgive their lack of vision. If it were not for your infinite mercy, dear Jesus, there would be no females in heaven."

"Now, you little bitch," he said, his voice sinking low and mean so that I had to strain to hear it, "open your mouth and pretend it is nectar from heaven."

"Noooooo," the pained gasp ended in silence, but I could hear skinny Baker panting as though he were working real hard at it.

From then on all I could hear from the girl was a pitiful whimper now and then. I knew then, like I had never known before, what had really happened to Charlotte.

As I thought about it, I began to get angry. It came out of my stomach like a burning flame, and I knew that I had to get my hands on this bully. I felt as though it were my chance to get even with Studs Gatlin for what he had done to Charlotte. I found myself beating on the thin walls of the trailer.

"Get off her you mother fucking bully, you Pentecostal rapist, you skinny marble throated bastard! I hope the Devil rapes your white bony ass in Hell!" My voice was hysterical, and it just kept on coming out, and

I couldn't believe it when I heard what I was saying. But I continued to beat violently on the side of the trailer.

Suddenly the door on the other end flew open, and skinny Baker stuck the bald part of his head out. It wasn't pulsating anymore, and I ran toward him like one possessed.

"I'll kill you!" I screamed.

"Security guard!" screeched Baker as he looked frantically toward the big tent.

I grabbed the door as he belatedly tried to close it.

He was naked except for a dirty pair of shorts with the front wide open so that I could see his long sticky dick hanging inside.

"Security guard!" Baker screamed again, alarm ringing like a bell in his voice. He tried to kick me away with his long slender foot. I grabbed the long white hairy leg as it came at me and with a yank of super human strength, I pulled him from his lodgment. We both fell to the ground, he, butt forward, on top of me. His foot was in my face, and I noticed his toenails, dirty and full of cracks, sticking unevenly over the ends of his toes. I didn't have much time for observation, however, for my next realization was the feeling of Baker's long sinewy fingers finding, then clutching tightly the windpipe in my throat. I began to panic and twist violently to no avail. I could not break his hold.

"Security guard, security guard!" he continued to scream, his voice, like a siren stuck on the high note.

His dirty shorts inched closer, and I watched in horror as his sticky dick had fallen from the opening and hung above me. It was a long thing that swayed like a pendulum, and I wished that I could just puke once before I had to die. But he had me in a death grip that cut off the blood flow and nothing could come out of my stomach. Like a fish I gasped for air, but each time I jerked and fought for it, it only left me weaker. The long thing continued to sway above me. Finally it blurred and became insignificant, but the shriveled balls behind it became vivid, and I grasped for them in a desperate effort to save my life. I managed to get a hold on them and squeeze with all the power I had left in my body.

Baker howled in pain. He threw back his head and howled at the moon which had just broken through the clouds to be large and full. I gulped in mouthfuls of cold damp air as he released the death hold on my neck. At the same time I yanked violently and he fell backwards to twist and moan in agony.

"Why don't you pray," I rasped through my sore windpipe. I got to my feet and began to kick him while continuing to hold on tightly. "Pray," I ordered again in a rasping gasp.

"Dear Jesus," he whined.

I twisted his balls harder, and for a moment, I thought I was going to kill him and eliminate his ugliness once and for all, but the soft voice of the girl penetrated my frenzy.

"Don't kill him," the voice said softly, "he's a man of God."

It was a pretty face that I turned to look at, as it faced the moonlit shadows of the night. Her gentle sensuality was accentuated by the soft glow of the lamp behind her. Her legs were naked and the towel that she had wrapped around them barely hid what was between them.

The sight of her standing there softened the hard murder in my heart. But I turned back on the man of God and shouted, "I ought to kill you, you mother fucking rapist!"

I continued to hold on a while longer and watch him twist and whimper, "dear Jesus," into the mud.

Suddenly, with repulsion, I became aware of what I was holding onto. I withdrew my hand in disgust, letting the preacher go free.

It was then that I heard the sounds of running feet coming from behind me. I figured it was the security guard and turned to run, but it was too late. A pair of powerful arms grabbed me and held me tightly.

"What did he do sir?"

"What did he do?! What did he do?!" Baker was trying to stand now, but he was bent double. "If you had been here where you were supposed to be, you incompetent jackass, you would have seen what he did, in fact you would have been able to prevent it." His voice was weak, but nevertheless expressed piety and a squeaky outrage.

"But sir," the guard responded in a contrite voice, "you told us not to hang around here, but to watch the cleaning crew to be sure that they not carry off anything valuable!"

"But you still should have heard me yelling!" reproached Baker.

"Roberta, honey," Baker said as he tried to turn so he could face the half-naked woman framed in the soft lamp glow. "Call the police." His voice was boldly self assured even in its weakness.

"Ok," she responded softly, "but when they come I'm going to tell them what really happened and what you did to me."

"Do you think they would take your word against mine? I, the famous evangelist, Billy Baker, loved by everyone, divine healer . . ." he couldn't stand straight yet, but he still stared boldly up at Roberta.

"Maybe not," Roberta answered quietly, "but it would still create a scandal when I described in detail what you did."

"Why are you doing this to me, honey?" His voice was beginning to turn oily again, only it was trying to sound shocked and disbelieving.

"I'll be a witness," I said loudly. My voice was returning.

"I'll kill you, punk!" His voice suddenly turned mean and evil again as it turned into a hiss. "No one gets away with what you did, punk!"

"What is going on here Reverend Baker?" the guard asked, cutting into the conversation. At the same time, he released his hold on me. I looked back at him, but he was looking at Baker's dirty shorts and the sticky dick that was still hanging out the hole in them.

"You just do your job, you derelict, and get a hold on that punk before he gets away!" He tried again to stand straight but couldn't. The guard halfheartedly got a hold on the front of my shirt.

"The punk started beating on the side of the trailer while Roberta and I were having a cup of tea."

"A cup of tea!" Roberta gasped.

The guard looked at Baker, bent double, half-naked and muddy, and then at Roberta framed by the soft light, wrapped in a towel. He snickered softly as though trying to hide it from Baker. His arm dropped, releasing me again.

"Are you alright, mam?" asked the guard.

"Of course she is alright!" hissed Baker as he stared threateningly at the guard. "And you had better mind your own business if you want to keep your job."

"No, I'm not really alright," Roberta said as she looked down at Baker. "But I'm willing to forget all that has happened tonight if Reverend Baker will let me leave now."

"What do you mean, let you leave? What are you trying to do to me woman? Nobody is keeping you here! You see what I get God, for trying to save souls and heal the sick?" He tried to stand again so that he could look up at the black heaven, but he couldn't. The moon started to sink deeper and deeper behind the laden winter clouds.

"Good," Roberta said, "I'm leaving." She then disappeared back into the trailer.

Baker stared at me then, sending hatred through the darkness that sent a chill up my spine. I'd never want to be caught alone with this man, I thought.

The guard stood fidgeting, moving his weight from one leg to the other while he picked at his nose in silence.

Roberta reappeared, her image boldly framed. She had on a dress now, with a fur coat over it. She hesitated for a moment and threw a long glance at Baker. He started to wobble toward the trailer, but stopped when Roberta reappeared. He hung his head and stared at the ground. She walked past him then, like he didn't exist. Baker's skinny humped frame began to pivot and pivoted 180 degrees as she walked past him. His hatred followed her, then he tried again to scare me with his hatred through the darkness, but I just stared back at him and tried to out hate him.

"You are going to be sorry for this, you fucking whore!" His voice came as a hissing squeak through the damp darkness.

"Fuck you," I said, half bravely. I quickly shoved the finger at him, violently. The air between us became charged, and for a moment, I thought he was going to come at me. But he thought better of it and just stood and watched us.

"Come on, let's get out of here," Roberta said.

"You better hope we never meet again, punk!" He let it out with a screeching whisper.

"If we do, I'll kill you with a baseball bat," I shouted back at him.

"Come on," Roberta said again and began to tug at my arm. I turned and followed her. As I did, I noticed the guard still standing and picking his nose while he stared intently at Baker.

"What are you staring at asshole." I overheard Baker saying as the parking lot came into view again.

"My car is over there," Roberta said as we made our way across it. We were soon moving up the dark road.

"What is your name?" she asked. A wan smile seemed to be playing with her pouting lips. Her lipstick was smeared down onto her set and angry looking little jaw, but her face was still beautiful, I thought, even though I could not see it distinctly as she sat in the dark on the seat beside me.

"My name is Bobby McGee," I said.

"I think you know my name," she said and smiled, showing her white teeth through the darkness. "I want to thank you, Bobby, for saving me back there." She was silent then as we drove along the dark road.

"Aren't you going to tell the police?" I finally asked her.

"No, Bobby." Silence reasserted itself and the dark road continued. "He's a man of God," her voice startled me, especially what she said. "Maybe he is right, and I'm wrong. I just don't know."

"Where do you live, Bobby?"

The streetlights of the city had returned to the roadside.

"Just take me to an inexpensive hotel," I said.

"I'm sorry, I wish I could offer you a place to stay, but my studio is too small."

"That's alright," I responded.

It was on a backstreet near downtown Seattle where she stopped.

"Thanks again, Bobby," her smile was warm and she bent over and kissed me on the forehead.

"Goodbye, Roberta," I said and then got out and watched her tail lights disappear around a corner up the street.

As I made my way toward the half lit lobby, a light cold rain began to fall. Just as I was about to open the door, I noticed a half dead neon light across the street. It was flashing sickly, like a tired ghost. "Repent," it said, "Jesus is coming soon."

# PART 3

PART 3

# THE ROAD TO
# SAN FRANCISCO

I BECAME VAGUELY aware of my surroundings, and I felt the dampness creeping in. The first thought that came to my mind was my money. I remembered that I had put it in my shoe. But when I tried to sit and feel for it, the pain went through my head like a river. So I fell back into the dampness and began to fade back into the sleep from which I came.

But then I heard a voice that said, "Are you awake son?" I nodded and felt the damp earth beneath my head. I tried to remember how I got there, but it only made the pain worse.

I looked up then to see a figure standing over me, but I couldn't see much except the big hat he had on his head. I wondered where I was and who he was, but the pain made me want to go back to sleep again and I did.

The next thing I remembered was a siren wailing over me and a soft pillow beneath my sore head. And then I saw him sitting beside my bed watching me. I remembered my money again, and I remembered the man who had tried to rob me. Panic seized me as I wondered if he had taken it. I couldn't remember. I gently turned my head toward the man sitting there so I could ask him to check, but it started the pain to flowing again so bad that I decided to forget it.

But he had seen me turn toward him. "Are you ok, son?" he asked.

"My money," I said, "will you check to see if I have my money?"

"Where is it you want me to look, son?"

"It is in my shoe." I said.

"You had no shoes on when we found you, son, someone had taken them."

When he said that it made me so tired that I simply fell back asleep again.

The next time I awoke it was dark and silent. There was a tall object standing beside my bed, and I quickly noted that there was a needle stuck in my arm with tape wrapped around it. As I lay there in the darkness, everything started coming back to me. I decided that I must be in the hospital and that the ambulance had taken me there. But I also remembered the face of the man who demanded my money. He had picked me up when I was hitch hiking on the road at the edge of Eugene, Oregon. I remembered the bad feeling I had as soon as I got into his car.

"How far are you going?" he had asked.

I had told him, "San Francisco, California."

But after this, my memory began to fade again. I did remember that he had been sort of quiet and didn't say very much. I also remembered how he kept looking over and staring at me and how he made me think of the man who had picked me up in Indiana.

Suddenly I remembered that my money was gone, and it nearly took my breath away. Somehow he had found it in my shoe, but I couldn't remember how.

And I slept again.

When I awoke again the lights were on, and people were talking. And when I opened my eyes, a tall cop was standing beside my bed, looking down at me. When he saw my eyes had opened, he smiled and said, "welcome back."

After this he started asking me questions about what had happened. When I started talking about it, it all started coming back to me. I remembered how he had asked me where I was coming from and how I had started telling him too much about myself, even though I didn't feel I should trust him.

I told him how I had spent the last two years as a security guard in Portland, Oregon. I told him how I had walked the grounds of an apartment complex filled with yuppies. It seemed they were always coming and going in a rush. Some of them, sometimes, would drag a kid or dog behind them, but when they passed me, they would look down at me as though I were a necessary evil. I had always been in their way. But at least they had been people. The night watch had been so boring that I would spend it dreaming about the time I could quit, but I had been determined to save enough money so that when I got to San Francisco, I would have enough to go to school, maybe part time at first . . .

"But son," the cop interrupted in a gentle voice, "can you tell me what this man did to you? Did he pull a gun on you?"

"Yes!" I suddenly remembered, "he pulled a gun from under his seat and pointed it at me, after I told him I didn't have any money except for the twenty dollars I had pulled out of one of my pockets. After he pulled the gun, I was terrified and told him everything about the money I had in my shoes. I had two thousand dollars in my shoes!"

"Son, I'm very sorry about that." The cop continued in his gentle voice. "Can you remember what this guy looked like?"

"Yes," I responded, "he had a butch haircut, and his eyes always looked like he was guilty of something. He was always staring at me, but wouldn't look me in the eye. He was always looking down towards my legs or my feet."

"See if you can identify him in one of these pictures," the cop said as he spread them out on a table in front of me.

When I saw them, I recognized the guy immediately and said, "That's him," and pointed.

"Ok, son, we've got him, but unfortunately, he only had forty dollars on him. You can probably have that, but we are going to need you to testify at his trial."

"Ok," I said, "but when can I have the forty dollars?"

"I'll see what I can do." the cop said then left.

Left alone again, I was really sinking into despair. Forty dollars was nothing. Two miserable and boring years had been wasted, I thought.

I simply was not going back to the job as a security guard in Portland though. Besides, I couldn't, not after the way I had quit. And I could not bring myself to face the owner of the apartment building who had given me the job.

He had been a nice guy who had picked me up on a wet road where I had been standing in the rain outside Seattle nearly two years before. On our ride south, he had offered me the job and had even given me a cheap place to stay as long as I worked for him.

But I simply could not stand it, the methodical walk on the beat. Nothing ever happened, not that I wanted it to, but my boredom had finally been more then I could take.

One day I walked along my beat, a beat that I had so memorized that I could have walked it blindfolded, I was walking like a somnambulant, deep in daydream so complex, that I was hardly even aware of where I was when a loud and rude voice had suddenly penetrated my consciousness.

"So do I have to repeat myself, guard, I'm late for a board meeting." The voice was haughty and demanding.

I didn't even know what he was talking about so I had just ignored him. It seemed that I was somehow blocking his way. Our shoulders had collided as he, in his perfect suit, whisked past me, smelling of deodorant. I was knocked off balance and fell from the force of the collision. But as I fell, I had reached forward and tripped the bastard in the suit. I had gotten up and simply walked away from the job forever. Over my shoulder, I could see his bloody knee and the red face that looked like a wrinkled apple staring at it.

The next day the cop came back, gave me forty dollars and asked if I was going to stay for the trial. I told him that I had no place to stay. He told me that he would see what he could do about it. But that night, I got up and walked out of the hospital. I found my way to the bus station by asking people as I went. I bought a ticket to San Francisco. I had five dollars and thirty six cents left when I got on the bus at one thirty in the morning.

On the bus, I sat beside a man who had his face glued to the window and who stared out into the dark night all the way to Red Bluff, California. When we stopped at the bus station in Red Bluff, the man sighed and stood up and waited for me to get out of his way. I stood and let him out.

When we again pulled out into the dark night leaving the city lights behind, I decided to take the man's seat by the window so I could stare out and think about what I was going to do when I got to San Francisco. When I bought the ticket, I simply refused to think about it because it caused my head to ache. I had just known that I wasn't going to hitchhike no more, and that I wasn't going to stay in Oregon.

But when I sat down in the man's seat, I felt a bump under my butt and reached under to pull it out. To my shock and surprise, it was a wallet. I began to shake in my excitement and quickly opened the money section. There were five bills in it. But in the dark I couldn't see what they were, and I didn't want to turn on my overhead light for fear of attracting the attention of someone else. I finally decided to go to the restroom and look at them. There I looked at them and began to shake all over again in my shock and disbelief. They were five one hundred dollar bills! This is a miracle, I thought, only God could do something like this, and I started to believe in Him again.

When I got back to my seat, I hesitated and started to thinking. What if this guy caught up with the bus, somehow, and came in looking for his money? If I was sitting here, I would have to give it back. So I decided to sit somewhere else, but first I stuck the wallet in the holder behind the seat where he had been sitting after taking the money from it. I then found me another seat where I sat wide awake and hoped he didn't return because I would feel really guilty and sorry for the guy and might just decide to give it back to him anyway. From then on I sat and held my breath at every stop, desperately hoping that I would never see the man again.

It was with a feeling of great relief when our bus pulled into the huge bus station in downtown San Francisco.

# BUBBA

"Now, LOOKY HERE," Bubba said, his voice penetrating my consciousness like a kick in the ribs.

Bubba was not a hobo like Joey. Bubba was just a bum.

"Now, looky here Bud," he repeated. "It's not a crime to be down and out."

He was feeling sorry for me and his pity cut into me like a knife, twisted into my gut, seppuku-style. How dare he show me pity, I thought. He was a degenerate. I didn't want to hurt the old bum's feelings though, so I just tried to sink further down into my sleeping bag so I wouldn't have to hear his ramblings. He ignored my silent hostility, and I just had to go on hearing it.

"I've been living on the streets now, for nigh on three years, and I must say that I've done some pretty low down things to survive. First you've got to get rid of all your ego and pride, and secondly you can't have no respect for the filthy rich. 'Course them are the ones that snub their noses at you anyway. Besides kid," he continued then hesitated.

I could feel his vacant stare, trying to penetrate my shapeless form buried in the sleeping bag. I peaked out. The street lamp had faded, obliterated by a slithering finger of fog that stealthily creeped in from the sea. "You are lucky to have a sleeping bag," he finished.

"Looky here, Bud," again a moment of hesitation followed. "Don't take it so hard," he finally said, with a whine that petered off into a whimper.

After that he gave up, and I could hear him trying to get warm beneath an old blanket that was too short and full of holes. Besides the old blanket, he just had an old overcoat and the hard sidewalk on which to lie. I heard him twist and sigh for awhile then he was silent.

In the silence, terror struck again and pulsated through my brain with each thump of my wildly beating heart. It was the realization of my predicament that was pulsating through me. I could hear the growl of my empty stomach but felt no desire for food. "I am a bum," I pronounced the words slowly to myself then shivered violently. I tried to eradicate the words, but it was too late. I wished for Bubba's voice to drowned them out, but Bubba remained silent.

Gradually the gray-black fog obliterated the storefronts across the street. The streetlights above me came and went. Suddenly a breath of the obliterating soup-like darkness overwhelmed me with its nothingness and its meaninglessness. I was alone between the empty space above me and the cold hard sidewalk below. For a July night, I thought, it's cold like winter. I shivered and waited for the light of day, which in my misery seemed so far away. Slowly my memory began to march before me like an invading army.

I had only been in San Francisco for a month. Things had gone so wrong so fast. I had thought that five hundred dollars was plenty of money to hold me over until I got a job. I had been thrilled upon my arrival in San Francisco with all that money in my pocket, miraculously coming to me out of the blue. And I soon decided I wanted to live there. Of course, there had been the uneasy feeling when I had to fork over three hundred dollars for a month's rent for an apartment, but I assured myself that a month was plenty of time to get a job. Surely, if nothing else, I could be a security guard again, I reasoned. But my remaining money dwindled rapidly in spite of my efforts to conserve it.

My first day job hunting, I filled out six applications, carefully and truthfully and had been so certain of acceptance that I agonized that evening over which job to take if all of them accepted me. The next day I sat by the phone and waited on the call that would give me the good news. But it didn't come, and as the chill wind brought the darkness in off the sea, it brought with it a fear, an uneasiness which left me sleepless into the next morning.

After that, each day became a repetition of the last. I roamed the streets of San Francisco, my newspaper under my arm, on the bus or on foot, filling out applications, one after the other. At the end of the day, I would not even remember how many I had filled out. I grew ever more desperate as fear began to pervade and to motivate my every movement.

It had just been a week before, in terror of destitution, I had rushed in off the street into a big office building which had a sign in front that said, "security guards needed, inquire in Rm. 203". I rushed up a flight of stairs, and then as I was gasping for breath, I inquired about the job.

"Have a seat," she said without even looking up, "he's with another applicant right now."

As I sat there waiting in the stuffy old office, my confidence was somewhat reinforced, after all, I had experience, two years of it, and there shouldn't be too much competition for such a humiliating job.

Suddenly a door opened and a big guy with healthy red skin and blond hair walked out. He walked right past me and out the door.

"You can go in, now," the non-descript woman said, without looking up. I could not help wondering what she was doing that could be so important, I remembered thinking as I had walked past her and through the open door.

A sweating fat man sat behind a desk, and he told me to sit and waved a fat hand toward a chair in front of his desk. I sat while his eyes looked down at my application and read it real fast.

"If you can pass the simple high school test that we give, you can have the job," he suddenly said, looking out of his smug face with bored eyes.

Terror swept over me then, like a ghost wind, bringing with it the realization why no one had hired me. I had truthfully stated on all my applications that I had only completed the eleventh grade. I cursed my father beneath my breath. If he would have only let me get my high school diploma.. I felt like one reeling out of control through space, but I forced myself to look at the blurred fat man and say, "sure, when can I take it?" I tried to make my face look like a mask to hide the terror.

"Right now," came the bored reply. The dull brown eyes threw a distracted glance at the window. Below a blowing horn sat at a red light while above it the gray fog moved up Geary Boulevard.

I took the test in a side room with a window overlooking an alley where tramps sat on rotten benches and drank whiskey out of brown sacks. I went right through the English part and felt real good about it. But in the math part, I got bogged down and had to skip most of it just so I could get to the next part. I worked feverishly.

"Time is up," croaked the fat man as he poked his head in to pollute the room with his boredom.

My terror began to rise again like out of a bottomless pit. I had not finished the third part and there were four parts! I would fail, I decreed, pronouncing it in my brain like a judge decreeing a death sentence.

"Go sit out there," the fat man said, pointing to the waiting room where the nondescript woman sat waiting. As I had passed, I tried to see over her desk to see what she was always looking down at, but I couldn't see.

I sat by the window and watched the traffic on the street below. It would appear then disappear, enveloped then released by racing billows of fog. I finally just got up and left. I didn't want to see the fat man's face when he said that he was sorry.

Down on the street, I felt the bitterness of defeat. I felt destitution closing in as I slowly walked the long distance to my apartment. But I relished for the moment the self-oblivion of being lost among the blowing horns and indistinct people that moved around me.

Back in my apartment, my lethargy deepened. I would sit and do nothing for hours on end. I just waited for the knock that finally came.

The three big cops were standing there in spotless blue. I couldn't even hate them, and I didn't listen to what they said. I just gathered my few belongings and went down the steps and out into the street. The three big cops followed me, but I didn't look back at them.

I shivered again and peaked out at the surrounding black dampness. It must be morning, I decided, but I'm not sure how I decided it. Maybe the black fog didn't look so black anymore. I squirmed down into my sleeping bag for more warmth but couldn't find it.

Where had I left off? Had I gotten to the part where I ran into Bubba? Had I fallen asleep or had I reminisced right through them? I must have slept, otherwise I would remember. I wanted the night to stretch out a little longer so I began to remember Bubba.

The first time I saw Bubba, he had been ragged and dirty, sitting on an old milk crate in the shadows of a backstreet in the tenderloin.

"Looky here boy," he said as I was passing him by. I saw him with my side vision and walked faster. I tried to ignore him, but I heard his fast approach as he came up behind me. "Looky here, boy," he had startled me with his close proximity. I turned to face him and could not help but wince at the sight of him. "Don't suppose you could spare a little something, could you?"

"No," I had replied. "I guess I'm broke too."

"Well I'll be doggoned, I'd a never have guessed it." He had shaken his gray and grizzled face as though to shake away a veil that was clouding his vision.

I glanced over at Bubba, sleeping on the cold hard sidewalk. He looked like a faded black lump, silent and still, like an insignificant bump on the sidewalk, in the damp fog. He must be really cold, I thought. I remembered all the holes in his blanket. I felt another chill creep up my spine, a chill that did not have its source in the damp fog. What if that faded black lump over there had frozen to death during the night. I turned my gaze away, afraid to look any longer. The hum of an invisible automobile motor gave some relief, at least I was not alone with that black thing, so silent, over there in the dense fog.

More invisible motors had passed. Suddenly, my ear, against the hard sidewalk, detected the hard rapid approach of something that went, clip, clip, clip. I decided quickly that it must be a woman with high heels approaching on the concrete. I sat bolt upright and climbed out of my sleeping bag into the clammy San Francisco dawn. I then stood shivering and faced toward it as it got louder and closer, turning into a clip clop, clip clop, clip clop, sounding like a proud horse a coming marching up the street. I became defiant as I began to imagine her snobbish features.

"Looky here, kid," the voice was whiney and came at me from behind. It infuriated me that he had chosen this moment to speak. I decided to ignore him until the high heels passed. I didn't want a rich snob to know that I was an acquaintance of this bum!

The form loomed and came forward, business-like, through the gloom. It was at this moment that I became suddenly aware of my forgotten sleeping bag, spread out across the sidewalk in her path. I frantically grabbed at it and dropped my flaming features to let them stare at the gutter.

"Looky here, Bobby boy," the voice was clear, distinct and very much alive. I could have killed it, held a sack over its head until it stopped breathing, just to keep it quiet! The high heels hesitated, breaking their stride. My vision creeped upward, outward through my shriveled metamorphic, wormlike skin.

"Looky here, Bobby," Bubba repeated more gently, "if you's a getting out of your sleepin' bag, maybe you won't mind if I borrow it to warm up in, huh, boy?"

The face that was walking along on the high heels, stared in disgust. "You look awfully young," she mumbled, staring at my wormlike skin.

I just turned and stared at what I couldn't see in the fog.

"And you," she said, turning on Bubba, "are a bad example!"

"Fuck you, bitch," Bubba screamed, his voice winding out like a high pitched shiver. "If you got anything to give us, fork it over, if not, just keep your highfalutin trap shut!"

The high heels moved away quickly, grinding into the sidewalk their fear and hatred.

I threw my sleeping bag over at Bubba.

"I appreciate it," he said, through teeth that began to rattle. He got into it and zipped it up tightly. I could see his body shaking for awhile, before it got warm. I just sat, squatted, on the sidewalk with his dirty old blanket wrapped around my shoulders and waited for him to wake up.

"Looky here, Bobby," he said after awhile, when I had thought he was sleeping, "After a bit, we can mosey on down to Saint Anthony's and wait around for them to serve something to eat."

"Ok," I said and continued to stare out at the invisible motors that were increasing and becoming more noisy. My pride had been stomped into the concrete by that high heeled woman!

Soon, people were walking by on a regular basis, one after the other, some of them were men, some of them women. But Bubba just kept on lying there in my sleeping bag.

"What time is it, Mr.?" Bubba's voice popped out of my sleeping bag, startling me.

I stood up. The passing person stopped and looked at me instead of Bubba. I turned my head away, to face the approach of the next passing person. She was a female, but I wouldn't look to see if she were cute or not. It didn't matter anymore. But then the idiot, the one Bubba had asked the time of, was trying to see my face! He acted as though he were trying to recognize me! I turned my back on him and slouched while I raged at the uncouth bastard.

"Eight-thirty," he said, I felt him throw me another piercing stare before he moved on.

"The audacity!" I shouted, in my silence, between clenched teeth.

"I have to go to the bathroom, now." I finally said as I turned, to bravely face Bubba. He was stretching and yawning and looked like he was warm. Besides it was my sleeping bag, and I was tired of waiting on him.

"Alright," he said and sighed, "you can do it at St. Anthony's when we go for breakfast."

The street suddenly appeared again and the motors had become cars. Everybody could see us now, and Bubba reluctantly got out of my sleeping bag, and we began to walk.

"Looky here, kid," Bubba began again as we trudged up hills and down them again, "if you want to hitch up with me, I can show you some of the ropes."

"No thanks," I said, in disgust, "just show me where St. Anthony's is."

"Suit yourself," he responded in a hurt voice.

After that we walked in silence. Damp new fog was racing passed us, trying desperately to replace the old, but the sun seemed to be gobbling it all up, old and new alike.

When I walked behind Bubba, I could smell him in the damp fog. He smelled like mold in an old garbage can. His smell kept me from feeling how hungry I was. All the people we met on the street would stare at Bubba, with his unkempt beard and clothes that looked like they had been stolen off a coal miner.

Out by St. Anthony's, the sun had burnt all the fog away, and it started to feel kind of warm when you got out of the wind.

"That's St. Anthony's," Bubba said as he slowed down and pointed across the street.

We crossed the street and walked into a crowd of mostly old men with beards and dirty clothes who were holding paper plates and eating scrambled eggs and sausage out of them. I went to the table where the food was and got me a paper plate and filled it with eggs, sausage and two slices of bread. I didn't see any toaster. I then ate the food standing up beside Bubba. I quickly left, followed by Bubba. The smell of everyone had drowned out the smell of the food.

Out on the street Bubba said, "Looky here," but then he didn't say anything else and started to stare at me in silence.

When he just kept on staring at me, I finally and begrudgingly said, "What?" The intensity of his stare made me feel that I was being stripped, exposing my dirty skin.

"I know a place where we can soak up some of this sunshine out of the wind." I looked at his watery eyes, then, and they were glittering and hopeful. He was acting like that he wanted to be good to me. A wave of guilt swept over me.

"Ok," I said and followed him. We climbed up an old fire escape, up into the chilly wind that rushed in from the sea. We climbed right up to the roof of the building. The roof had a five foot wall around it which kept the wind out. Bubba threw me a triumphant grin then fell fast asleep in a warm corner beneath the sun.

When I awoke, I found myself in swirling heaps of gray fog. Jumping to my feet, I looked about in wild disorientation. Then my eyes fastened on Bubba, who lay with his mouth open snoring loudly. It all came back to me, then, and I didn't hate Bubba so much. I woke him up so that we could go to St. Anthony's.

I heaped my plate with all the food it would hold and tried not to look at the people around me. But even then once I had eaten, I felt dirty. I thought about how Bubba smelled and felt that way too. I'd rather be a hobo and steal my food, I thought. At least a hobo could be proud and independent. A bum just hung his head and begged so that the proud preachers could give him something and say that God had done it and then shout "praise the Lord" about it, while they breathed their minted breath in your face. I felt ashamed then, that I had run off and left Joey the way I did, back in Montana. My punishment was to be a bum on the streets of San Francisco, I decided.

"The chairs, over there," Bubba said, as he pointed where old men were sitting, "is for the old folks, those who are too tired to stand up anymore."

During the next few days, I followed Bubba around San Francisco in a torpid state, nearly oblivious to what he said or did. I finally got so I didn't much care about the stares from anonymous faces around me, either. I would just stare back with my vacant anonymity.

"We all go through this stage," Bubba had said once, "it's the shock of it," he had added.

Bubba had become like a permanent fixture, after awhile, like a distant relative that was always talking, or like a dirty father, hated but necessary for support. Each day we would make our way back to St. Anthony's for breakfast and again for dinner. Why we even left the place was beyond me, but I simply followed Bubba around, never letting him out of my sight. He seldom interrupted my lethargic oblivion, though occasionally I would hear his "looky here son . .," but I would usually ignore what followed, and he stopped repeating himself.

Then one day beneath a warm sun, I awoke in a sweat to find myself following Bubba down Geary Boulevard. It was out near the security agency where I had applied for a job. The people around me had suddenly become painfully real again and were throwing sparks of recognition at me as they stared. I hurried to narrow the distance between Bubba and I.

"Bubba," I said, raising my voice slightly.

Bubba stopped, turned and watched me as I hurried toward him.

"Looky here, kid," he said as I slowed and shuffled to within a few feet of his dirty beard. "Let's go down this way." He pointed down Twenty Fifth Avenue, "Baker's Beach is not far from here, and this is a good day for a little sun."

I followed Bubba as I had followed him everywhere else, but I was apprehensive. I didn't want the girls in skimpy bathing suits to see me dirty like a this.

Long lines of cars were parked everywhere as we approached the beach, and the people were scattered here and there as they walked toward the sea. I noticed a group of girls walking along in tiny bikinis, carrying beach chairs and their pocketbooks. I refused to look at their faces for fear they might be looking at mine. Instead I just looked at the soft skin on their long skinny legs and the red and blue polka dots that covered what was between them.

At the beach, I looked out at the distant water to avoid the mass stares that came from the sea of bathing suits scattered on the sand at my feet. A distant ship emerged from the glaring haze to slowly, but distinctly, make its way across San Francisco Bay. In the other direction, the big red Golden Gate bridge spanned the bay boldly, climbing high above it, to reach out and connect with the point of land that jutted out from the hills of Marin County. Cars moved slowly, like playthings across it.

"Let's go this way," I said and turned toward the Golden Gate. I scanned the skimpy bright patches of color from which brown skin leaped seductively, and I longed to plant myself among it, but didn't dare. "It's too crowded here," I said.

"Can't go far, though," Bubba said. He focused a hard stare down toward the end of the beach. He threw a glance at me. Red color had suddenly leaped out from behind his beard and into his cheeks. "There are naked people down there," he said in a voice that seemed to rise in shock. "They are all over the place. I've never seen such wickedness. We can walk down a ways though."

I followed Bubba, my feet bare in the hot sand. My eyes were focused on the heat waves that were bouncing off distant forms that I now knew were naked bodies. I had never heard of such a thing. I decided that I just had to see it before we left!

"Up here, Boy," Bubba said, pointing to a sandy ledge on the cliff that rose above us, "is a secluded spot where we can get a little sun without anyone seeing us."

Bubba was soon snoring on his blanket beneath the warm sun. But I sat, restless, staring down the beach toward where the naked people were. I wondered if it was just men or whether the women went naked too. Finally, unable to contain my curiosity any longer, I started walking on the sand toward the forbidden sights of the distant beach. Then, suddenly, I was able to see them, and my heart started to thump against my ribcage violently. Down by the surf, a group of naked people were playing volleyball! My jaw dropped open in disbelief as I watched their naked curves swaying gracefully. The surf was throwing fingers of foam around their ankles. My heart simply thrilled at the sight of it. But I looked down at my dirty clothes and felt my dirty skin beneath them, and my courage failed me. They would laugh me off the beach, I thought. Besides, I had not been sure that I had the courage to go naked in public yet, even clean naked.

I turned and walked down toward the sea. I let its icy foam chill my bare feet then shuffled along through the cold damp sand back toward Bubba.

I started to climb the cliff up to where Bubba was when I was suddenly overwhelmed by an aversion. I didn't need him anymore, I thought boldly, and with that thrilling resolution, I turned and walked down the beach toward the parking lot.

It was like a breath of fresh air, the freedom I felt, and it grew with each step I took away from Bubba. I would steal me some good clothes and start looking for a job again. I also knew that I would go back to the naked beach and lie with my body free on the hot sand, and that thought sent my blood racing with exhilaration. I walked along briskly with newfound purpose as I climbed over the hills to Geary Boulevard.

Gradually, though, as the trickles of sweat began to roll down along the crevices of my dirty skin, my pace slowed. My optimism began to fade, punctuated with uncertainty. What if I got caught stealing? The memory of them dragging Joey away kept racing through my mind. Maybe being a bum was the only way after all. After awhile, I became exhausted as I walked up Geary and sat down on a street bench. I sat there, I don't know how long, as returning lethargy began to pull me back into bondage.

# STEPHANIE

A CHILL AWAKENED me as it came racing on a puff of wind down Geary Boulevard. And it was in that instant that I saw her. The burnished gold in her red hair glistened, touched by the westerly sun, as it twisted wildly in the chill of the rising wind. Her slightly freckled cheekbones stood out boldly, beautiful, like two wild red roses. Yet it was a boldness that hinted of worldly wisdom, a boldness that flowed in graceful concentricity around a determined little nose that was slightly snubbed and connected to an upper lip that was pulled up sharply by two little ridges that tried to look obstinate. Yet, her upper lip rested lightly on her modest lower lip as though her obstinacy were in reprieve. Suddenly, she reached with white teeth to bite the upper lip which gave a petulant twist to the small rounded nose, dotted lightly with freckles. This led me to her puckered brow which stood out as a sharp outline to the clear blue eyes that were spitting sparks of fire.

She was carrying a heavy red can. She would run with it for a few paces, set it down to look about her as though looking for someone. She ran out of gas somewhere, I thought, with growing interest.

Her appearance was unkempt. She had on an old pair of faded blue jeans, threadbare at the knees. With each of her running steps, a white knee would protrude, to glisten in the late afternoon sun. The shape of her boobs were hidden by an oversized shirt that appeared to have been thrown on as an afterthought. Over the shirt, she had on a denim jacket that was too small. It hung open and seemed to have nothing to do with the chill in the air, but rather, appeared to be there just to hide the shirt. Which it failed miserably to do.

She stopped again and the heavy red can was sitting on the pavement. She then went right out into the street to face the traffic. She was trying to get a ride! The realization hit me with disappointment. I can't let her do that, I found myself thinking, but I continued to sit and watch fascinated with her beauty and moves.

A car slowed as it passed her and then came to a stop, with a jerk, just down the street. A gangly man with large bones unwound himself and climbed out. He raced back toward her with an awkward gait as though he were afraid that she would get away. She watched him without making any attempt at moving or picking up her can.

"No thank you," I heard her say as the gangly being hovered over her and tried to get a grip on her gas can.

"It is too heavy for you," I heard him beg. His voice was distorted as it floated over to me on the chill wind.

"I'm alright, really!" I heard her voice, now more shrilly say. "I'm just fine, I assure you."

The gangly being hesitated. His hard brown eyes found me and they stared angrily. I stared back as hard as I could to let him know that I was watching. I guess it worked because he turned and walked away with lopsided steps back toward his car.

I then looked back at the red headed girl. She was standing, her bold cheeks aflame as she watched his retreat. Her lips were slightly parted as though amused. Black smoke poured from the gangly man's car as he raced away. The girl then turned and went back to her red gas can. She picked it up and raced with exhausting little steps back to the sidewalk. She dropped it with a k-thud on the concrete. She glanced at me without seeing, then picked up her burden again, with a sigh, to run another few yards.

I watched her mesmerizing figure without moving until I noticed her tightly fitting threadbare butt. I could have sworn that the threadbare strings were pinching white skin, though it was too far away to be sure, but I came to life anyway. I felt the passion begin to rise in me as I watched it and watched her bend over to drop her load again. She turned and glanced at me again with the bold flush in her cheeks. I knew then that I had to meet her at all cost.

When she picked up her red can, I followed with quick long steps. When I caught up with her, I felt my face begin to turn hot even with the chill wind against it. I could hear my heart thumping violently against my ribcage. "I must not blow this," I told my feverish brain. At that moment, she again dropped the heavy red can on the concrete sidewalk.

My words exploded from me in a gasp, "Why don't you let me carry that?" I heard them say. I then felt much better and added, "I'm going this way anyway, and it looks like you are having a pretty rough time of it."

She turned her bold flushed cheeks upon me in what appeared to be sincere surprise. Her perfect little lips fell apart to expose a neat row of pearl white teeth. She moistened her upper lip with a flippant touch from her tongue, and her blue eyes began to dance with amusement.

"No thank you," she responded demurely, letting her blue eyes fall upon her heavy red gas can but not before they quickly went over me in detail. I stood proudly and smiled for her as though posing for a picture. "No thank you," she repeated. Her voice becoming soft, like a purring kitten. She then threw a shy glance at me with her deep blue eyes and then let them fall slowly to my feet. I thought I detected a little sigh as she attempted to lift the heavy red can.

"I'm sorry," I said, in a soft but disappointed voice as I blurted out the first things that came to my mind. I was behind her then. "I didn't mean to waste your time, I know that you are in a hurry, but that can looked awfully heavy, and they say, you know, that it is not good for a young women to carry things that are too heavy for them."

She hesitated, then, dropping the heavy red can that she just managed to pick up.

"Who says that?" She turned on me, her cheeks and voice defiant, but her lips spread widely into a smile.

"Uh...uh....uh I'm not sure," I blurted out, "I just figured that someone must have said it." I looked bravely back into the blue eyes that began to penetrate me.

"Ok, ok," she said in a shrill voice, but she let her smile turn into a mischievous grin. "Just remember, you got yourself into this one so don't blame me if you're exhausted before you reach my car. She cocked her blazing gold head to one side, twisting her lips into a victory grin and sparks of mischief beginning to dance in her blue eyes.

"Where is your car?" I asked, as I tried to control my voice to keep it from turning into a shout of joy! I picked up her red can quickly before she could change her mind.

"Oh, about a mile from here," she said casually. Her victory smile widened and the penetrating blue of her eyes was tearing at my heartstrings. "Just kidding," she said quickly as she chuckled softly, "it is just several blocks from here." I was disappointed as I had hoped it was a mile!

"My fucking gas gauge is broken," she volunteered. "This is the second time that goddamned old Cadillac has ran out of gas on me. I guess it only gets about seven or eight miles to the gallon but Jude…" she broke off and hesitated for a moment before continuing. "A mechanic told me that it should get twelve or thirteen. The first time I thought that I had just miscalculated, but this time I know I didn't, and it really pisses me off, the motherfucker!"

"Excuse the language," she said suddenly, turning her flaming cheeks upon me. "I don't know why I talk like that in front of strange men, but that fucking car pisses me off."

"It's alright," I said, but she was silent then, as we walked along side by side.

Sweat started to pour from my armpits in spite of the chill wind, and I could smell it, and I was worried that she could too.

"What is your name?" I asked. My voice sounded shy and afraid, and I hated the sound of it.

"Stephanie," she responded in a voice that also sounded shy, but she was staring straight ahead at the hill we had to climb.

She didn't ask me my name so I volunteered it, "My name is Bobby," I said, then adding more volume to my voice, I said, "Bobby McGee."

"It is not far from here, now," she said, ignoring my name.

As we were climbing the last hill, I was suddenly seized with the fear of what would happen once I poured the gas into her tank, and I started desperately thinking about what I could do or say to prevent us from having to part. Stephanie clammed up and walked on ahead of me after I asked her for her name. With a sinking feeling, I began to feel that it was probably hopeless, and I would probably just have to go back to being homeless.

Then out of the corner of my eye, to my shock, I saw Bubba coming up a side street. I ducked, nearly dropping the heavy red can and turned my head, hoping desperately that he had not recognized me.

"Looky here, Bobby," I heard him yell. But I just kept on walking, trying to ignore him. I simply couldn't let Stephanie find out that I knew someone like Bubba. "Looky here Bud," his voice was getting closer from behind, like he was running or something.

Up ahead Stephanie stopped and looked back at me, then over my shoulder at Bubba.

"Didn't you say your name was Bobby?"

"Yes," I responded, meekly.

"I think that guy behind you is yelling at you."

I stopped, putting the can down, and watched as Bubba came at a fast pace towards us. I glanced back at Stephanie, and she met my glance with puzzled blue eyes. I felt myself sinking into despair. She was going to find out that I was a bum.

"I know him," I said meekly.

"What does he want?" She asked sympathetically.

"I don't know," I answered.

Bubba's fast gait turned into a shuffle when he noticed that I was with Stephanie.

"Looky here boy," he stuck his dirty beard into my face so that he could speak in a low, whiney voice. "I'm heading for St. Anthony's, are you a coming?" He then threw an offended glance toward Stephanie.

"No, not now," I responded in a fierce whisper.

"Looky here, are you sure you can find it by yourself? You have been sort of out of it the last few days, like you were lost or something."

"Sure, Bubba," my voice trailed off in my embarrassment and despair. I wanted to kill him! He was blowing any chance I might have had with Stephanie, the bastard!

"Suit yourself," he said and threw a hard and offended look back at Stephanie, then turned his watery eyes, full of fake concern back on me. "Suit yourself," he repeated as he turned again to make his way methodically back toward St. Anthony's.

Stephanie turned in silence to continue walking on up the hill. I followed as the last of my hope evaporated. I wasn't sure I could find St. Anthony's, but I didn't want to see Bubba again anyway.

"Where do you live, Bobby?" her voice became more gentle, and I felt her gaze piercing me.

But I remained silent, pretending that I didn't hear her.

I looked up to see that she was standing there watching my approach. I stopped to rest and turned my gaze upon the neat row of Victorian homes beside the street. I felt her soft blue eyes continuing to penetrate right through me, and they were breaking my resistance. What the hell, I thought, I might as well tell her the truth. I had nothing more to lose anyway. We now topped the last hill. Her old Cadillac was down there somewhere.

"I guess right now I don't live anywhere," I said.

"There's the old junker down there," she said, pointing at an old army green Cadillac at the bottom of the hill. It was parked at an angle, its long heavy rear end sticking out into the street.

"I hope I didn't get a ticket, I left a note for the pigs," she added.

My pace slowed as we started down the hill, my brain working at a feverish pitch. "What could I do," I asked myself. What could be said at this late moment? But my brain seemed empty of solutions. We were walking side by side in silence when I felt her soft blue eyes resting on me again.

"Bobby," she asked, "are you getting tired? I can carry that the rest of the way, it is not far."

"Oh no, oh no," I said.

"You have been slowing down, that's why I was wondering."

"Bobby," she said, then hesitated. I felt her soft blue eyes going through me and seeing everything. "What did you mean by saying that you don't live anywhere?"

"Well," I said, taking a deep breath. I set the can down beside the big Cadillac and looked up the next hill. A gray Victorian stood boldly, dark against the late afternoon sun. I shivered from the chill of the wind and then looked into her soft blue eyes. They nearly took my breath away as well as some of the fear. Her flaming red cheeks stood out wildly, making my heart throb loudly.

"I came here from Oregon," I said, "but couldn't find any work so I ran out of money. I finally got kicked out of my apartment." I added in a voice that had fell almost to a whisper. But I continued to look back boldly and with defiance into the soft depths of her blue eyes. However, my heart was sinking.

I would pour the gas into her tank and she would say, "thank you Bobby," and then drive off. She might not even say Bobby, but just "thank you."

"Bobby," I heard her say. Her lips parted mischievously, her cheeks were turning to fire.

I was standing beside the gas tank, afraid to pour it in as I watched her lips, waiting for the fatal message.

"We ain't going no place," she said, "if you don't put that gas in the car." My eyes exploded with the sight of her. She was standing with her small hands on her hips, her elbows turned out with authority. She dropped her hands impatiently, then reached for the gas can.

"No," I said, "I'll put it in for you." I then tore my eyes from her and focused them on the old red can.

"Well, thank you," she said, in a voice shrill and impatient yet mixed with genuine appreciation and a dash of mischievous humor.

"I think I know a place where you can stay for a while," she suddenly said in a matter of fact voice.

The gas was gurgling, taken in with big gulps by the Cadillac's gas tank. I nearly dropped it, the gas splattered out and rolled over the army green paint. I gripped it tightly in an effort to control my excitement.

"Do you have a house, Stephanie?" I asked in a cool, civil voice. I was concentrating on the gurgle that was flowing from the spout.

"Yes," she said, with a chuckle, "but that is not what I meant. My family has a beach house out in Thunder Bay. No one is there now. You could stay there for a short time, maybe until you can get a job."

She turned the big Cadillac around right in the middle of the street while cars honked and waited. She just said "fuck you," to them all.

After turning around, she went back to Nineteenth Avenue and took it north. On the Golden Gate, one could see a finger of fog slipping into the bay from off the sea. The Marin headlands jutted out of it, exposed to the damp, chilly wind. Soon we were on a narrow, winding mountain road. The big Cadillac appeared too wide for the narrow lane, but Stephanie handled it like a pro.

"So you are from Oregon," she said, after a bit of time while she had maneuvered the big car around the streets of San Francisco. She flashed me a smile full of white teeth.

"No, not really," I began and then went on to tell her almost everything about myself. I even told her about the dark night when my family, Agnes Everbe, and the rest of them waited for the flying saucers that never came. Stephanie had a hearty laugh over that.

"I've never heard of anything like that before. It is so unusually funny. Your Dad must be quite a character!" She again laughed and turned the sparkle of her blue eyes upon me.

"Now it's your turn, Stephanie, to tell me about you," I said, smiling at her, hopefully.

"Ohhhhhh," she said, throwing me a little knowing grin as though relishing a secret. "There is not much to tell. Nothing strange has ever happened to me, and I have never taken any trips, except to Tahoe. I've lived a pretty ordinary life." She threw me a cheerful smile as though that was that.

"Where do you live?" I asked boldly.

She threw me a shy glance, her eyes meeting mine only for a moment before they fell. The flames seemed to leap into her cheeks as her lips parted so that she could touch the upper lip lightly with her tongue. "San Martin," she said, her voice a bit shrill. "Do you know where that is, Bobby?" She chuckled and looked at a sharp curve in the road ahead.

"I'm not sure," I responded. "Is it somewhere around San Francisco?"

"Of course," she said, laughing, "I don't live somewhere far from San Francisco!"

I just grinned in my embarrassment and looked at her delicate little earlobe, with a gold earring, that hung seductively from her right ear.

She immediately turned her chatter to other topics, giving me a distinct feeling that she didn't want to talk about herself anymore. The feeling left me with an intense curiosity and a determination to find out more.

Then as we rounded a curve, the panorama of the vast Pacific Ocean was stretched out far below us. The precipice beside us and the infinite blue distance nearly took my breath away.

"That's Thunder Bay down there," Stephanie said, pointing to a distant settlement that seemed to cling to the cliffs hanging above the sea. "Our house is not on the beach, though, it is up the hill a ways."

"Oh," she said, as though just remembering something. She touched my shoulder and pointed down a steep cliff that fell beside us to the sea. "There's a nudist beach down there." Her eyes fell again as she flashed me a shy smile.

"Do you ever go to it?" I asked, gazing intently at her flaming cheeks.

"Welllll, not really," she chuckled softly, her soft blue eyes falling shyly, but I caught them resting, momentarily on my crotch.

"I was at Baker Beach," I volunteered.

"To the nudist part?" Her eyes were on the little narrow road that was dropping down into Thunder Bay.

"Almost," I started to say, but Stephanie interrupted me.

"Oh... they are everywhere around here," Stephanie said in her matter of fact voice.

In Thunder Bay, we climbed from the sea along a tree-lined street, and then she turned into a sandy drive.

"This is it," she said with a smile, "let's go in."

Inside she showed me around quickly and told me to help myself to the contents of the refrigerator.

"I have to hurry back, now, Bobby." Her voice was gentle when she touched my arm. "I'll see you in the morning about ten," she said as she threw me another bright smile, then she was gone.

From the window, I watched the big Cadillac as it roared away to disappear down the otherwise quiet street.

The shower was hot and felt so good after so long without one. And as I took it, I wondered how Stephanie could have stood the smell that I must have made as I rode in the car beside her. And I ate the hot dogs cold, wrapped in buns right out of the refrigerator. I turned on the TV, but didn't hear it as I had sat and marveled at my good fortune. I could hardly believe it, especially Stephanie. She was so much more beautiful than Robin had been. I went to sleep trying to guess what she would be wearing the next day when she came roaring back in her big Cadillac.

Only she didn't come in the big Cadillac. She came roaring into the drive in a Jeep Comanche with no top on it. Her long red hair glistened in the late morning sun that had just broken free from the mountain that stood high above us. The shorts she had on had nearly made me cream my pants as I watched her approach from the small window.

"Anybody, here," she hollered, laughing joyfully, "are you up, Bobby?"

"These are my old jogging shorts," she said lightly, then laughed, when she saw my eyes glued to them. "I wear them when everything else is dirty, and I'm in a hurry."

"Are you ready to go, Bobby?"

"Sure," I said, in the flat voice of a hypnotic.

I followed Stephanie around that day like a somnambulant in a trance.. We went through a used clothing store where she bought me some clothes, several pairs of jeans and a couple of shirts, I think. She picked them out when I couldn't make up my mind because I couldn't take my eyes off her. I listened to her cheerful laughter and constant chatter and was jealous when she insisted on putting her own gas in at the filling station. Bent over, her soft white butt was the object of stares from behind the station window.

"Go get into these," she said, throwing me a pair of jeans and a shirt from the back of the Comanche, before sticking the nozzle into the gas tank.

She finally took me to a big tall building in downtown San Francisco. The words West Coast Telephone stood out in big gold letters above the entrance. I looked at Stephanie for a clue as to what was next on the agenda.

"You are going to go in there, Bobby," she ordered, firmly, "and fill out an application for a job, I think they are hiring now. And, oh yes, don't forget to say that you have a high school education."

She was grinning at me mischievously as I gazed into her intense blue eyes. "Ok?" she asked, cocking her red head coquettishly.

"Ok," I responded, doubtfully.

Her smile turned gentle and her blue eyes soft, but the fire in her cheeks was almost violent in its wildness.

"What are you waiting for?" She demanded when I had continued to sit and stare.

"Uh.." I stuttered, off guard, "let's go then."

"You have to go in by yourself," she purred softly.

"Why?" I asked, in a breathless gasp.

"I can't go in like this, now, can I?" as she asked this she glanced down at her skimpy little shorts that appeared even more skimpy when she was sitting.

"I guess not," I said as I tore my gaze away from her.

"Wake up kid, get your wits about you," she suddenly said in a brisk business-like voice. You're going to go in there and ask for an application to fill out for telephone operator position. You will have to take a test, but you shouldn't have any trouble with it. I didn't and if I can pass it, anyone should be able to," she said, laughing modestly.

"Are you a telephone operator, Stephanie," I asked, giving her a quick glance.

"Nope," she said, "but I once was. I pour drinks now in a little bar down in Redwood Bay. But that 's beside the point right now, it's time for you to get a move on, Bobby McGee."

I walked toward the large swinging doors, but without Stephanie there for support, my heart began to sink. What's the use, I thought.

No matter what I told them, the truth was I didn't have a high school diploma..

Beneath a sign that said job applications, I asked for an application form and was given one. I filled it out and where it said, "education," I boldly wrote high school and beneath the word "where," I wrote Woodlake, Florida. I just hope, I worried, that they didn't ask to see my diploma!

As it turned out, I didn't have to take the test that day, and I walked out of the building with a newfound self-confidence. My steps were solid and determined. Maybe I could pass the exam after all.

Stephanie left me, again, at the end of the day, back at the little house in Thunder Bay.

"I'll loan you the money for the first month's rent on an apartment," she said in her matter of fact tone of voice, "as soon as you get a job."

Her voice became soft and purring when she had said goodbye. "You be a good boy, Bobby McGee, and I'll see you tomorrow."

She cocked her red head and flashed me a red angelic smile, then she was gone. She left me with her image, like a fairy in a child's dream, and her image was all colored with red and gold, her lips were apart, spread in a teasing smile of promise. I heard her Comanche engine fade into the distance.

Things went well for me the next few days as Stephanie continued to captivate me and step by step bring me back to respectability.

Back at the telephone office, I entered feeling light like a butterfly, but suspended without wings, waiting to glide back to earth and reality. I passed the test and was overwhelmed by my joy and relief. The answers flowed out so smoothly and so quickly.

"What the heck, we'll just hire you on the spot," the lady said after first telling me that "we'll give you a call."

I exited the building into a damp and heavy summer fog that rested on the concrete street and muffled the noise of the city. I thought I detected the black canvass of Stephanie's Comanche through the soupy gray half light, but couldn't be sure. I started toward it but suddenly, Stephanie appeared in front of me, looming like an apparition of a fiery little fairy god.

"Well," she said, cocking her red head slightly, her cheeks undaunted by the chill. Her lips fell apart expectantly, then they smiled and waited.

"I passed and was hired," I said, trying not to shout.

She ran to me without a word and kissed me. Our moist lips clung tightly for a moment, leaving a sweet taste upon my tongue, but then I awoke to find my arms around her. She became aware of it at the same time and pushed free.

"We have things to do now," she said. "When do you start?"

# JUDE

THREE MONTHS LATER, I sat by the window in my new office along the coast of Redwood Bay, punching out telephone numbers. I was a telephone operator now, and my new office was just across the highway from the sea. I already had a favorite sitting spot, over by the window where I could watch the raw power of the Pacific as it displayed its different moods. I especially enjoyed my view on a day like this when it would turn wild and frothy and bite hungrily at the dwindling seashore. I would hold my breath as the climbing waves would throw themselves with a vengeance at the highway that was between them and me. And above and behind the splitting boom, boom, boom, came the harsh cry of the seagull upon the raw wind.

My mood had turned somewhat dour to match the scene that was framed by the cold wet window.

Of course the "elp, elp, elp" of incoming calls was always present. An aged shrill voice would scream, " I just got cut off operator, while I was talking to Sadie Hookwither!"

"Sorry ma'am," I would console, then reconnect her, so that she might chatter her last few years away.

Then it would come, "Collect from Peter Bushwinkle," in a cool, crisp clear voice of a scorpion, to interrupt my gaze at a mountain of water that was making a last ditch effort to hit the coast highway.

It would climb to be walls of foam-capped water, climbing so high as to hide the ominous clouds that banked in the west. Then the angry gray walls connected to the sky with sheets of falling rain which came at my window like the tail of a thick gray rope to beat it with damp winter gloom.

"Operator, bill to 321-2232." The squeaky voice wavered, a mere flutter to disturb the airwaves.

"Area code first, please," I would say, heavily with a hint of my dourness. The breath of silence followed, nothing but the empty distance between us. Then click and "elp, elp," the world continued. You learned to live with it, responding to "elps" that weren't even there, "May I help you?" to the dead and "elpless" board.

My mind was on Stephanie. I missed her, sitting there alone, but what disturbed me most was her sweet charming way of always keeping me at arm's length. Even once when she let her guard down, she treated it as a mistake. At times my anger at the little knowing smile that hid her secret would nearly overwhelm me. I would see her nearly every day because the little bar where she worked was just down the highway from the telephone office. Lately, it seemed she had stopped coming to see me except to pick me up and take me to work.

During the first evening in my new apartment, she had been there with her vibrant red cheeks and joyful chatter. She seemed more thrilled with my new place than I had been.

"See," she cried from my bedroom, "you can see the ocean from here, just like you wanted it! I think you are going to like it here, Bobby!"

"Yes, I know I will," I said as I walked up behind her and tried to rest my hand on the slender white nape of her neck. She moved out from under my hand to let it fall and to move back into the living room. I just followed her, a sigh escaping me as I watched the twist of her firm little butt, outlined sharply by her tight and faded jeans.

"I'll show you the beach," she said, turning to flash me a bright smile, "get your coat."

We walked in silence to the wooden steps that fell down the cliffside to the sea. I stood near her on the sand and watched her, as she watched the distant sea come closer to leap and twist as exhausted froth, wet upon the sand. I wanted desperately to touch her so that I might feel the softness of her skin.

"Wow," she exclaimed, "that wind is chilly. Look out there, Bobby," she said while pointing. I looked at her pointing finger, then, out at the huge cloudbank that billowed above the sea. "That's a fogbank," she said, "and it is coming towards us."

"What about you?" I asked, trying to change the subject.

"What do you mean by that?" her voice was shrill as she turned her inscrutable soft blue eyes upon me.

"I don't know......or rather I don't know how to say it."

Her soft eyes continued to penetrate me, thoughtfully while the name Jude kept revolving around like marbles in my brain. She had mentioned it only once, on the day we met. It had been as though she had been carefully trying to retract the name Jude by changing it to mechanic.

"Stephanie," I finally said, accumulating all the reserve courage that I could muster.

"What?" Her voice was shrill as she twisted her red head to expose flaming cheeks, in an attempt to be coquettish.

"Why don't you invite me over to your house for dinner sometime?"

She laughed softly to conceal the secret in her heart, then lowered her gaze to the damp sand beneath her feet.

"Who is Jude?" I suddenly blurted out unable to maintain my silence as my passion began to escape like steam from a volcano. I held my breath and stared at the rising fogbank. I felt her silent eyes upon me. "Is he your boyfriend?" The words escaped me, feeling hot upon my tongue.

"How did you know about him?" she finally asked in a weak voice.

"You mentioned his name once the day we first met."

Again she was silent, to turn her gaze back at the fogbank that hung above the sea.

"No," she said, startling me with her abruptness, "he was once my husband."

"You're divorced?"

"Yes."

"Then why are you keeping me away from your house?"

"Because," she responded softly, hardly above a whisper, "Jude still hangs around a lot."

"But why?"

"Because I think he still loves me and thinks he is going to get me back. Furthermore he is very jealous."

"Then you can come and live with me!" I couldn't help myself. It was coming out like water from a faucet.

"No," she said firmly, "I don't know if I want to live with you or not, and besides Jude would just come looking for me." I looked into her troubled blue eyes, but she veiled them more completely.

"Then will you at least have dinner with me in my apartment more often, Stephanie?"

"Yes, Bobby McGee," she said, squeezing her tightly closed lips into a smile.

She kept her promise and started eating more frequently at my place, and sometimes we would go together down the coast to the A&W boardwalk that trailed out above the sea. But she became more self-conscious and ill at ease. She would slip like a delicate butterfly from beneath my touch. She would throw me charming smiles from a distance, leaving me unfulfilled like a panting dog, frustrated and puzzled.

Then on a hot day in October, she came over in her jogging shorts, the ones that had driven me wild that day, when she had dragged me, like a somnambulant, around San Francisco. She was in my apartment waiting on me when I had returned from the store with three 6 packs of Guinness Stout.

"Hi, Bobby," she chirped cheerfully, like a robin in springtime. She had been standing at the window and turned again to stare down at the parking lot. "Looks like you are planning on having a party with all that beer," she said, throwing a mischievous little grin over her shoulder.

"You are irresistible from behind, Stephanie," I said, then waited for her reaction, and it wasn't long in coming. Blood was rushing violently to the already flushed cheeks that she turned upon me. "Your front side is also irresistible," I continued quickly, trying to sound casual. I was putting the beer in the refrigerator.

"Ha…ha…. ha, whatever you are trying, it isn't going to work." she said as she quickly turned her flaming face to stare back down at the empty street. I joined her and looked at it with her.

"Come," I finally said, taking her moist hand. She let me lead her to the couch.

We sat side by side, drinking Guinness Stout. She crossed her white legs tightly and drank silently. Shortly I became aware of her intense blue eyes upon me. I looked into them as they searched me with the depths of a woman. She began to talk, then we finished the first beer.

"You see this?" she asked softly as she pulled her loose jogging shorts up high around her hip to expose an ugly dark bruise. "Guess who did it," she said in a matter of fact voice. She didn't bother to cover it back up. Rather she uncrossed her legs and slid down on the couch as the deep blue of her eyes continued to gaze up at me. A ray of autumn sun touched her bruise as I stroked it gently.

"Who?" I asked sharply. I felt my anger surging as though throbbing with my blood flow.

"Will you promise me to keep cool, Bobby, and not go off half cocked if I tell you?" Her legs fell apart then, one of them soft against mine.

"Ok," I promised, "who was it?" I promised her, even though I knew who the culprit was.

"Jude," she said, "he kicked me, but it wasn't all his fault," she quickly added. "I called him a mother fucking jackass and some other choice expletives. I also told him he was dimwitted." She grinned at me. "So you see, I'm not such an angel myself."

"I wish you would just leave the bastard and come live with me." I said hopefully. "Then he wouldn't be able to hurt you anymore." I let my hand slip down to the warm leg skin near her crotch.

"I know, Bobby McGee," she said in a soft sympathetic voice that hinted of teasing humor. She became aware of my bold hand that began to feel its way beneath the loose crotch of her shorts. She grabbed it and pushed it away. "You men are all alike," she said laughing.

After that we were silent again as we continued to drink our beer. Suddenly Stephanie sighed and put her feet upon the couch, her legs standing widely apart above them. Her hand had fallen lightly against mine.

"He's a car salesman," she began.

"Who is?" I had asked.

"Jude is. He works across the bay for a Pontiac dealer. He was really angry at me for being a bartender." Her lips spread slightly in a mischievous grin. "It started out as a joke. I kidded him once that I was going to be one, and he threw such a fit about it that I started considering it seriously. I thought I could do a lot better with tips and all than being a telephone operator. So I went to a bartending school in secret, and when I finished the course I got a job down at the Seafroth without telling Jude, and he didn't find out about it for nearly two months.

"Then one night, just by accident I guess, Jude walked in while I was working. When he saw me behind the bar, he just stared, silent-like, in disbelief at first," she chuckled softly to herself and then was silent for a moment. "Boy did all hell break loose after the initial shock! He tore that place apart. He tried to get a hold of me, but I managed to get away from him. Then the police came and took him away and threw him in jail for the night. I was afraid of him after that and stayed out at Thunder Beach for a few days. When I finally got up the courage to go home, I found all my personal belongings out on the front lawn. So I went back out to Thunder Beach and sued for divorce. It went through pretty quick because he didn't fight it. Then after all that, he started being nice to me again and began spending his evenings down at the Seafroth begging me to come home. Gullible sucker that I am, I moved back in with him."

As the afternoon passed, Stephanie's chatter had gradually risen in voluminous abandonment. As she tipped the bottles of beer to her seductive lips, my fingers had began to probe again, over her soft white skin and finally, unopposed, beneath her skimpy little jogging shorts. They sought hungrily for the well-formed lips that marked the gateway to her passion. But just as my finger was at the point of entrance, she leaped suddenly from the couch.

I followed her, like a horny and feisty little schnauzer, to the bathroom. As I watched her pee, my blood raced like fire through my veins. She looked at me, almost benignly as she wiped herself. When she started to stand, I grabbed her, pulling her away from the seat almost violently. I held her leg high, so that I might feast my hungry eyes on the wild pink vaginal folds which climbed boldly, in their naked beauty to the little knot of red and gold which protruded as though in an attempt at modesty, then blended with the head of red hair above it. I fell on her with passionate abandonment and felt the fire flow through my tongue as it penetrated.

"Get out of there," she was yelling, "what do you think you are doing, Bobby McGee?"

The next afternoon she picked me up to take me to work. We were working nearly the same hours.

"I'm going to have to stop drinking," she said, speaking with lips that were somber and parted slightly on her long face.

"Why?" I asked, "we had fun yesterday."

"Maybe," Stephanie replied, "but the problem is I can't remember it." She then turned a searching gaze upon me. "Who knows what I might have done!" I looked away then to avoid her gaze and felt the blood rushing toward my cheeks. I looked back at her to see her face growing longer, but her lips were beginning to twist in a mock solemnity that turned into a grin. Her face relaxed then, and she smiled at me and in relief, I returned her smile.

A sudden gust of wind was dumping rain by the bucketfull against the window and a mighty wave, capped with froth, climbed…. climbed up the deserted sand beach to roll with the split of thunder, throwing its froth, with a victorious sigh, out upon the highway. My reverie had suddenly been jarred into the present moment of the rising storm. But what was passing was just a portent of what was to come.

For a time, the rain, driven by the wind, blotted all else out with its intensity against the window, but the deadly surf continued to climb, ever higher with each reverberating boom. Then there was a lull in the wind, the rain fell straight, in voluminous, drenching gray curtains that hung from the sky. Suddenly, like a surreal moment in eternity, a bloody red sun setting in the west broke free, sending showers of fire out over the deep to turn the gray twilight purple black. Eerie shadows played over the water mountains as they would hide then reveal the setting bloody ball of fire as it continued to sink deeper into the wild and frothy sea.

At first it was simply surreal, a distorted play shadow, but then it had quickly blotted out what was left of the glow in the western sky. It just kept climbing, climbing, the gray shadow mountain, superimposing itself on the gray shadows around it. The shadow world around it was soon to be snuffed out, becoming part of the shadow mountain itself as it swallowed them up eating them like a hungry monster.

It's real! The realization suddenly hit me, leaving me breathless with terror. The shadow mountain continued its silent march toward me ever climbing to be bigger. The rain stopped as though to watch with us mortals in awe. I continued to sit, frozen to my seat for what seemed like an eternity while the shadow mountain crossed the sand beach, obliterating it. I opened my mouth to scream, but it just fell open to utter gasps of silence. I could not take my eyes off the oncoming monster. But then I knew that I had to sound a warning and a gurgling scream escaped my lips as I pointed in terror out the window.

"Oh my god," screamed Sheri Lupenstein, a manager that no one liked.

"Get away from windows!" cried Hedi Hebron, the boss.

I heard the chaotic rush of bodies fleeing, but like a paralytic, I just sat there, unable to move. I just had to see that thing through to the end! I was feverishly fascinated with my own terror. As I watched, my eyes fixated, it seemed to trip slightly at the highway, but no, it recovered and kept coming, silently, fatefully! But just as the gray monster began its march across the short remaining span, it suddenly tripped and collapsed upon its own weight shaking the ground beneath it like an earthquake sending its pool of water out like an inland sea. The water lapped hungrily at the window sill and salty foam ran in rivulets down the cold window pane.

"Back to your positions," ordered Hedi Hebron, the boss.

I began to shake violently as I peered fearfully into the gathering darkness, imagining that I saw other monsters coming out of the deep.

"Evacuate the building!" It was Hedi Hebron again, not five minutes after she had ordered us back to our positions. I leaped to my feet, startled, as I threw another piercing glance toward the sea, but could not see anything. "Hurry," chided Hedi Hebron, "the water is rising!" I soon saw what she meant, the water was creeping in under the door and when they opened it the water rushed in, rising to our ankles and higher.

Outside, again the rain fell and hung like a dark wind blown blanket out of the dark sky. As I stood looking at it, wondering if the bus would go by on the highway, I noticed a girl named Annie Sidleborn standing beside me. Her face was screwed up in a frown and her mouth hung open as though in disbelief.

"What am I supposed to do?" she asked, throwing her voice at the watery world in front of her.

"Where is your car?" I asked, hoping for a ride home.

"Up the hill on the street," she said, sighing then shivering as though searching for courage.

"Good," I responded, "no one is going to get out of the parking lot tonight." I knew that it would be under water.

"Come on Annie," I finally urged, "I'll help you to your car." But she continued to hesitate and look at me with pleading eyes.

"We'll get soaked," she squeaked, her face crumbling in despair.

"Just pretend that it is a nice hot shower," I said, trying to cheer her up. I then pulled her with a quick jerk out into the rain, but at the same moment, she opened her mouth to let out a derisive laugh but ended up with a mouthful of water and nearly choked.

Soaked was not the word for it. We were bone chilling drenched by the time we reached Annie's car. And the street, it was a river down which the water flowed toward the sea.

The deluge let up shortly after we got into the car, but the damage had already been done. The coast highway had been inundated and served as nothing more than a riverbed. Annie's car sputtered and died. Getting out into the night, we could hear the roar of the invading sea nearby, so we waded quickly back through the deep water to the office, holding our soaked shoes above our heads.

We spent the rest of the night in the office, sitting on couches and chairs, trying to hold our feet up out the water until it gradually receded. There were others there besides me and Annie, and we all just sat around and dozed or stared at each other as we shared our misery.

The next morning, I was sitting in my apartment as near the heat as I could get when Stephanie walked in without knocking. I just finished the ride, on a slow bus, up the highway buried in sand and strewn with logs thrown in by the violence of the sea. I was sitting with a towel wrapped loosely around me, letting my body toast in the warm heat. She threw me a cheerful smile with a fleeting glance.

"Good morning," she said, trying to sound formal. She walked straight to the window and stared down at the street. "Just stopping by to see how you fared through the storm, I knew you were working."

"It is a good thing you didn't work," I said, "or you would have been stuck alone with your booze all night."

"Funny, funny," she said as she continued to stare down at the street.

"The water flooded the telephone office, and I couldn't get home until this morning."

"I figured as much, once I saw the highway this morning."

She turned around and her eyes riveted on my nakedness. I put my feet on the couch to get them warm and slid out to let my balls hang freely. I knew what she was looking at so my cock started getting hard as well and began to jump out toward her.

"I thought one big wave was going to go right over the building!" I said.

"Wow!" Stephanie exclaimed, but she still continued to stare down between my legs, so I wasn't sure what was exciting her, the big wave or what she was looking at. She began moving toward me, her eyes fixated, her cheeks, red like sugar beets.

"Bobby," she asked, in a voice that had become throaty and hoarse, "did you get wet?"

"I got soaked, soaked to the bone," I said.

"Poor boy, poor Bobby McGee," she said, her voice husky, distant, preoccupied. Suddenly her eyes flashed upward and into mine. "You know, your cock is in plain sight!" she said in a voice that sounded breathless. "It is becoming obscenely hard," she added, gasped, almost shyly.

"It is excited by your red cheeks," I said bravely. I made no effort to cover it, even though I could feel it continue to plunge toward her.

She quickly and silently turned to stare back down at the street. "Don't be silly," she finally said in a husky whisper.

I got up, letting my towel slip to the floor, and walked toward her, my naked body tingling with intense passion. The nape of her neck was aflame with the spreading color from her cheeks. I touched it softly with my hand. She was silent, but non resistant. I wrapped my arms around her bosom to feel her boobs collapse from the gentle pressure. I rammed my cock against her tight, faded, threadbare jeans into the crack of her ass.

"Just don't make me fuck you yet, Bobby," I heard her say softly, barely above a whisper.

"Don't worry, Baby," I responded, thrilling at the sound of the word baby as I uttered it.

"So get your clothes on," she said, turning to give me a push. She had control of her voice again. It was strong and earthy.

"By the way, Bobby, you never told me whether you passed your high school equivalency test or not." Her blazing cheeks and soft blue eyes were turned wildly upon me again.

"I passed," I said, "but you were standing at the window staring down at the street when I told you, and you probably didn't hear me."

"Shoo." she hissed, waving the back of her hand at me, "go get some clothes on."

"That's great that you passed your high school exam!" she shouted from the living room as I was reluctantly putting my clothes on.

"Do you know what, Bobby?" She said as I joined her again, "I would like to enroll in a Philosophy class next semester. They say the professor who teaches this class is a wild and popular lecturer. His classes are supposed to be always packed. I thought maybe…that since you have passed your high school equivalency exam that you might like to enroll with me."

"Sure," I nearly shouted, "I would love it!" I grabbed her and brought her lips next to mine. She was pliant, and our lips locked softly for a moment.

"You don't have to be so demonstrative about it," she said, teasing me with a soft little chuckle.

Boy was I glad, I thought to myself, as I looked longingly at her ruddy cheeks that I had went to the trouble of taking the high school exam.

"I gotta go now," she said then, flashing her white teeth in a promising smile. "There are things I have to do." She was gone after a quick kiss.

I watched her little Comanche burn rubber as it turned into the street, to blend with the other cars then fade into the hazy salt air. I sighed and just continued to stare absently from my window.

She would never tell me what it was that she had to do, it was just "things.' I had to find out where she lived, I decided. I had to get a look at this Jude fellow. I would buy a car. I had enough money saved up for an old one, I figured.


It was 4 p.m. and I was waiting for Stephanie on the corner beneath my apartment for a ride to work when I saw the topless Comanche coming down the street. She was poking along behind a slow moving old Buick. But then, after I had made a few impatient struts around the stop sign, she was there beside me. I climbed in quickly, and she continued the slow pace on down the coast highway.

She just said hi and stared directly ahead down the road as though it demanded all of her attention.

"I wonder if they have cleaned the office up yet," I said, hoping to get a conversation started.

"I wouldn't know," she said in a voice that was slightly offensive and shrill.

I tried to see into her face and leaned over toward her, but she turned her head and looked out the side window.

"Is something wrong, Stephanie?" I asked, almost timidly

"No," she responded flippantly, in her shrill voice. She continued to look through the side window.

"Something is wrong!" I asserted, alarm escaping in my voice.

"If there is," she responded, her voice turning harsh, "it is none of your business." She looked at me then, her normally smooth white forehead creased in a frown. But what I saw was the dark purple skin around her left eye.

"He did that, Jude did that, didn't he?" I almost shouted.

"What if he did? Like I said, it is none of your business!" Her voice was harsh and cut through me like a knife.

"I am going to find out where you live, Stephanie," I warned, my voice rising in anger, "and I'm going to teach that motherfucker a lesson."

"I'm sorry Bobby," the harshness fled her voice, but it had left it taut and shrill, almost as if it were laced with fear. "I had no right to be angry with you. Yes, it was Jude that did it, but it was mostly my fault. I called him a mother fucking wimp," she said softly.

"It can't be always your fault, and besides that is still no excuse, even if it was your fault. I don't know why you keep hanging around with him, Stephanie, so that he can continue to beat you."

"Just be patient, Bobby McGee," her voice turned soft and coaxing, "please don't do anything rash, I'll be alright." She showed her white teeth to me in a forced smile. Then as an afterthought, she stuck her little pink tongue out at me. It was soft, like a lone cherry hanging enticingly from a tree in early summer, and my anger melted like snow before a Chinook wind beneath the mountains of Montana. "Ok, Bobby?" Her lips fell apart and seductively puckered like a kiss.

"Okay," I responded with a sigh, hopelessly spellbound by her presence.

Suddenly we were in front of my office. Stephanie leaned over to give me a big wet kiss on the cheek then one on the lips before I climbed out to watch her turn around and drive back down the highway toward the Seafroth.

On my first break, Walter Whitenfield, a fellow operator had come up to me, "You are Bobby McGee, aren't you?"

"Yes," I responded, "you're Walter Whitenfield?"

"Yes….you don't have a car, do you Bobby?"

"No," I said, wondering how he knew.

"Come," he said, "I want to show you something." I followed him out into the parking lot. It was still covered with sand from the flood. I followed him over to an old, but shiny, Dodge. It looked real nice.

"This car wasn't here when the flood hit, was it?" I asked, at first dubious.

"Thank God, no," he said.

The motor started like a charm, and it ran softly and smoothly. "I'll take it," I said, forgetting to ask him the price.

"I only want $500 for it.'

"I'll bring the money tomorrow."

"That is fine." he said. His voice was cheerful and he threw out his hand to be shook.

Stephanie was all chatter that night after work as we met the oncoming beams from the headlamps along the coast highway. I was mostly silent, thrilling over my secret new car.

"Did Walter Whitenfield show you the car he has for sale?"

"N..o..I mean yes, I..I told him I would think about it," I stammered, startled out of my silence.

"He was at the Seafroth the other night and was asking me if I knew of anyone who needed a car. So I mentioned you." After a moment of silence, she continued her chatter.

# THE SPY

THE ROAD WOUND sharply and steeply up the hillside. It wound among the houses that clung precariously to the mountain's green slopes watered by the perpetual fog that hovered around them. At the top, one could turn and view the sliver of land at the bottom that was backed up against the mountain. This was Redwood Bay. Wisps of fog floating along its coasts gave it a stoic gloom as it faced the cold gray sea. The small coastal town began where the road began its descent down off the cliff top, falling abruptly to the sea and ended where the sea began.

In my new car, I climbed the steep hill without looking back. Rather I directed my gaze to the distant shore of San Francisco Bay to the east. The bay was also gray beneath clouds that looked to tired to rain.

Scenic Drive ran along the ridge top, and I followed it south to where it intersected with San Martin Avenue. San Martin fell sharply as it wound down towards the east and the Bay. On this day, it took me down in a rush of wind to St. Martin town.

My new Dodge fell rapidly with the avenue as my spirit soared with anticipation above it. It was not without trepidation, however, my stomach quivered with the butterflies of the unknown. I was on a quest to find out more about Stephanie. I had no idea where she lived, except that it was down near the highway by the Bay somewhere. But that was alright, I was thrilled at my newfound freedom.

I wound off San Martin Avenue almost by accident on to Santa Barbara Street, and before I knew it, I was in downtown San Martin. Then, suddenly, my heart was throbbing wildly in my throat like it was going to gag me. I spotted Stephanie's topless Comanche. It was parked on the street just ahead of me. As I drove past it slowly, my throbbing heart climbed higher, and I was gasping for air. In my rearview mirror, I saw her red hair and tight faded blue jeans crossing the street. I stopped in my tracks right in the middle of the street. And simply watched as she climbed into her Comanche and spun around in a u-turn to go back the way that I had just come from.

My body and mind were galvanized into synchronicity, I had to follow at all cost. A horn was blowing loudly to my rear. In front of me, the cars, piloted by narcissistic drivers, kept coming towards me. I was not going to budge until I could turn around! The horns behind me became a chorus of angry idiots. The honking car immediately behind me bumped the rear of my new Dodge, so I swerved into the path of one of the sociopathic bastards that was coming toward me. His rubber screamed and his horn blew bloody murder, but he stopped. I turned around, nearly backing into the impatient jerk that was trying to get around from behind me.

By the time I turned around, Stephanie's jeep was nowhere to be seen. I had to catch her, I thought, this might be my only chance of finding out where she lived. Then far ahead of me at an intersection where the light was red, I saw the silver bars that stood above her black jeep glaring in the sunlight. I raced toward them, but by the time I had got there, the light was red again, and she was gone. I was furious and fearful that I had lost her. I crossed the intersection and drove slowly as I kept my eyes on the side streets, looking for the telltale silver bars of her little Comanche. Luck was with me. With a leap from my heart and the flutter of butterflies in my stomach, I saw the silver bars. It was parked half way down a long and narrow street.

I could hear the exhausting throb of my heartbeat as I turned and parked at the end of the street. "There is nothing to worry about you coward, Bobby McGee," I whispered angrily to myself. "She doesn't even know you have a car," but my heart kept right on throbbing anyway.

I slowly edged the old Dodge out into the street and let it creep toward the bright silver blotch in my vision. I felt like a flimsy, disintegrating box, torn apart by the wild throb of my heartbeat. With a sigh of resolution, I stepped on the gas so as not to attract attention. Out of nowhere, a huge St. Bernard tripped out into the street in front of me. I smelled the rubber from my screaming tires as I came to a stop right in front of her house. I waited, my eyes straight ahead, for the old dog to cross the street. But in my side vision I detected movement in her yard and couldn't resist a quick glance. It was Stephanie and our eyes met as if by an act of destiny.

At first her mouth fell open, and her blue eyes stared at me in surprise. However, she quickly got her wits about her, and her forehead creased into a frown. Her lips began to move rapidly and violently as I just sat there helplessly and stared. She started to wave her hands and to point down another little side street. I got the message and came to life. I must get away from there, she was telling me. I turned back and looked for the big dog, but it was gone, so I turned the way she was pointing. I would have just left in my dejection, but in my rearview mirror I saw her running down the street behind me. I parked and waited while the butterflies in my stomach leaped around wildly.

"What the fuck are you doing in that car, and what the hell are you doing snooping around my place?!" Her frown was deep and her voice harsh.

"I just bought it, how do you like it?" I said meekly as I tried to flash a smile that would appease her. I was partly successful. Her frown lost some of its potency.

"That doesn't explain why you are here!" her voice lost some of its harshness in spite of herself.

"Oh," I said, putting everything I had into a charming smile. "I was just driving around and happened by here by accident."

"Uh….hu,.. I bet," she said, but her frown disappeared and her lips spread slightly into a knowing grin. But then in an afterthought, the frown reappeared, but her voice turned gentle. "Bobby," she said, "this is serious business, you just can't come around here like this. Jude is extremely jealous. If he caught us seeing each other, or even suspected it, he would beat the shit out of me, and you don't want that do you?"

"If he did, I would kill him," I said intensely.

"No, he's big," she said with a harsh laugh, "he would just beat you up too." She put her hand on my shoulder and looked gently at me with pleading soft blue eyes.

"Okay," I said in resignation. "Is Jude back there now?"

"No, thank goodness, but he has a way of popping up when least expected. You must go now Bobby McGee, please…be a good boy. I'll be over later this afternoon.." she added, cocking her head and letting her lips part in a teasing little smile, "I promise to be good to you then."

Those words were like a key to my ignition. I would do anything it seemed for a soft word and a promise.

"Would you like to have me fix you some dinner?" I asked as I started up the old Dodge.

"I don't think I will be very hungry, Bobby, don't fix anything for me." She penetrated me with charm from her soft blue eyes as she bent over and kissed me softly on the lips. Then, her butt was twisting, beneath the tight jeans as she ran back up the street.

I drove back over the mountain and down the winding road into the chill wind that blew as it carried a dismal gray fogbank in off the sea.

# THE PASSIONATE AFFAIR

IN THE EVENING, the dusk gathered, the street lights began to glow, and the headlamps paraded by, one by one. Each was heading on down the coast somewhere, probably to a cozy home with dimly lit windows, hazed over by sea salt that came on the spray that rolled inland and hovered like fog. Boom…boom went the distant surf to break the silence. I could not hear the cars behind the headlamps as they passed below.

Finally my patience could bare the headlamps no longer, they had become an irritant. They distorted and finally hid the looming dark shadows that followed behind them.

With the shadows gone, each pair of headlamps were potentially Stephanie's, but my impatience had turned them into a blurred parade of broken promises. I was angry. Stephanie had promised to come over later in the afternoon. I had watched from my window as the salt air had thickened and turned the fading light into a gray mist. The beat of the distant surf had grown louder, it seemed, with the approach of darkness, a darkness which left nothing but the slow advance of headlamps.

I fixed a meatloaf to eat in case she were hungry. In my own restlessness, I ate half of it, and now the other half was growing cold in the oven.

Finally, just as I started another round of pacing back and forth in front of the window, I noticed it. A little yellow bulb was blinking toward the right as it came toward me below with the slow advance of headlamps. My heart leaped hopefully. Could that be Stephanie? Was that her jeep? I strained my eyes to get a glimpse of the dark shadow as it came closer. "Yes"! I nearly shouted. She turned into the parking lot beneath the glare of the streetlamp. I ran from the apartment, still half angry, to greet her at the bottom of the steps.

"Hi," she said, with a cheerful lack of concern as she advanced toward me, adding a smile to her friendly greeting.

The little anger I had left was beginning to melt in spite of myself. "Stephanie," I tried to say, sternly, "it is so late, and I have waited so long for you that I had almost decided that you weren't coming!"

"I'm sorry," she said, softly, her smile spreading wide to charm me, "but Jude came home after you left, and I couldn't get away until he was gone. I did get a treat for us though," she added as she dropped her eyes mysteriously.

"What is it?" I asked as I stared at her wild red cheeks.

"Just you hold your horses. And will you please invite me in out of this chilly damp and salty air?"

Inside I closed the curtain to put the parading headlamps from my mind. The world seemed so much smaller then, as though there were only two people in it.

Stephanie was over at the table, wiping a small mirror with a napkin.

"Are you hungry, Stephanie," I asked, "there is some meatloaf in the oven if you are."

"Not really," she responded as she took something from her purse. It looked like a simple piece of paper, folded neatly. It had a rubber band around it. She turned to me then, her lips spread in a victorious grin. Her eyes were a bright and innocent blue, yet hinted of mischief, like those of a naughty child.

"It's a couple of grams," she said, holding the little package out to me. "Jude brought it home and hid it, but I was watching and when he left I stole it. Ha….ha."

"Grams of what?" I asked as I reached out to take it from her.

"No!" she said, withdrawing it quickly, "this is precious stuff, about $200 worth."

"For that!" I exclaimed.

"Sure," she said, flashing me an angelic smile. "It's coke, and really why I had to wait on Jude to leave. But I'll probably get a beating for it later."

The thrill of the unknown began to race through my veins again. I only had a vague idea of what *this kind of coke* was, but I did know that it was illegal like marijuana was and that in itself added spice to my anticipation. I remembered Jorje Carlyle and the pleasant afternoon we had spent together smoking joints. This was going to be even more fun, doing it with Stephanie!

A new surge of confidence began to race through me as I continued to stare into her deep blue eyes that still sparkled with mischief. I went closer so that I could look more deeply into her soul, but the sparkling stopped, and they threw up a shield to block my view. She put the little package of coke on top of the mirror and turned back to face me. I knew then that she would fuck me. I began to unbutton her shirt.

"What are you doing!" she asked, in a meek, half-pleading voice.

"I'm going to fuck you," I said breathlessly as my shaky hand yanked her shirt off and began to fumble with her bra. She just stood there, silent, her face beet red with passion. I continued to fumble with her bra, and the longer I fumbled, the shakier my hand became. Suddenly, she reached back over her shoulder and deftly unfastened it. The bra fell to the floor, her boobs stood out, soft, firm, white and unashamed. I let my hands run over their freedom gently. I then held them tightly against my own bare chest.

Then, with a thrill, I felt her soft moist lips as they searched for mine. Our lips met in a fit of passion as I fought with the buttons just below her navel that held the crotch of her tight jeans together. Finally, on my knees, I pulled, almost violently with my shaky hands until they came crumbling down around her ankles. There before me were her little bikini panties, covered with petite little pink flowers. Standing, I picked her up and took her to the bed where I finished my handiwork.

She lay there completely naked, white and vulnerable. Her soft skin was everywhere and seemed to beg for my touch. "Oh, Stephanie," I murmured as I fell on her, letting my skin tingle wildly from the thrill of her touch.

With chaotic humping motions, I began my search over her soft skin and then into her warm crotch. Finding its mark, my hard penis sank deeply into her with rhythmic strokes of passion. Stephanie's arms wrapped themselves tightly around my neck and her legs climbed high to rest upon my back.

At first she clung to me quietly, letting my passion spend itself, but then I detected the rhythm of her movement, faintly at first, but then with all the robust vigor that she possessed. As our mutual rhythmic motions climaxed, I took the nape of her neck in my palms and brought her lips to mine. Clasping, our lips clung, the taste sweet, until the rhythm faded, and I lie exhausted on her soft damp skin.

"Come, come," she finally said, "what do I look like, a featherbed?" She laughed softly and pushed at me.

I rose to my knees, my cock hanging, long, sticky and wet with spent passion. She slid quickly from under me and ran to the table. She sat on the chair, wildly naked, propping her feet on the seat of it. Her pink vaginal lips were spread wide open, sticky with passion. They glistened like erotic honey.

"I hope this is good stuff," she said as she took a razor and chopped the white powder more finely. She made long lines of it, then took a straw and inhaled a line. She held her breath and looked at me, her cheeks like wild roses.

"Try it, Bobby," she said, "it will set your adrenalin to pumping."

Her feet fell to the floor and her white legs began to sway with a seductive rhythm, flashing her pink lips at me like a flashing pink neon on a summer night.

After that we just sat together, naked, snorting lines of intense pleasure, chatting about different things. Once Stephanie started talking about Jude and called him a fucking bully. I went to her then, picked her up and sat her on my lap. I pulled her close so I could feel the firmness of her soft boobs against my chest.

"I love you, Stephanie," I whispered, then sighed as I put my arms more tightly around her. She drew back to look at me with the deep, gentle blue of her eyes. But then she fell back against me, her head on my shoulder, to continue the soft chatter about different things.


On Christmas day that year, I sat alone at my console in the telephone office. I was depressed. Stephanie was having dinner with Jude's family, and I knew that Jude would be there.

"Elp," the console would say and I would respond, "may I help you?" The "elps" had come with boring regularity, and as the day progressed, my mind had begun to wander. I was sitting alone by the window, staring out at the choppy dark blue sea. Frothy whitecaps crowned the dark blue waves as they fled before the stiff northwest wind. At times the wind would clip a whitecap with its gusty violence and foamy froth would come flying ahead to race up the beach like clean, white unused toilet paper. Above the frothy crowns, white fair-weather cumulus clouds skipped lightly across a bright blue sky.

I pouted when Stephanie told me about the dinner the week before. I pouted because there was not much else that I could do. I had just been scheduled to work Christmas day and had rushed to the highway to wait for Stephanie and my ride home. I was hoping that Stephanie would be scheduled to work too, but it was not to be.

"The Seafroth is going to be closed Christmas." she said, "and Jude's mom wants me to come over for dinner, and since I don't have any family, I guess I'll go, Bobby, besides," she said, after noting my long face, "you are working."

I just rode along in silence after that.

"Cheer up, Bobby McGee," she finally said, trying to flash me a bright smile. "We'll do something together later."

"What?" I asked in a sulking voice.

"Wellllll.." she said, throwing me a knowing little smirk as only she could do. Then she turned and looked out towards the vast and distant sea that leaped and flickered in the twilight. "We will discuss it later at your place," she finally said.

"Okay," I said, meekly, turning and trying to smile at her, knowing that I was being unfair. We both remained silent after that. And our silence continued as we climbed the steps and entered my apartment.

I went to the window and stared down at the parading headlamps, heading south along the coast highway. I remained quiet as I waited for her to speak. However she went and turned the TV on to watch in silence. With that, resentment again began to form a knot in my stomach, and in my restlessness, I turned to confront her. But then I noticed a mischievous little grin beginning to play around her lips. She pretended to be grinning at the TV, but I knew she was enjoying my discomfiture.

"Bobby McGee," she said, suddenly, startling me, "why are you so quiet? Are you feeling ill or something?" And she continued to stare at the TV set.

"No," I responded somewhat roughly.

"Are you angry at me?" She then turned a penetrating blue gaze upon me.

"No," I said, more softly, caught off guard by her directness. I began to feel not only selfish but stupid in my self pity. "I have just been thinking about my own family," I said, lying

"Does your mom know where you are?" she asked, concern suddenly rising in her voice.

"I don't think so."

"Then you must write her a letter, Bobby McGee! She must be very worried about you. When was the last time you wrote her?"

"In Oregon," I responded.

"Did she write you back?"

"I don't know," I answered. "I left Oregon right after I wrote her."

"Then you must write her as soon as possible and let her know where you are, Bobby! I never had a mom, Jude's family raised me."

"Okay, I will," I said, deciding not to tell her about my fear of my Dad, that he might come looking for me and attempt to force me to go home.

"So tell me, what was on your mind, Stephanie?"

"Oh, that," she said. The mischievous grin came back and widened into a smile. She turned her blue eyes toward the window before touching me delicately with a fleeting glance. Then she quickly fastened her gaze back upon the tube. "Well," she said as though her mind were somewhere else, "we don't have to talk about that now if you don't feel up to it."

"God dam it, Stephanie, quit teasing me and rubbing it in. What is it you had planned for us?"

"Okay, okay, already!" she said as though she were taking her attention away from the tube with great sacrifice. "I had just thought that maybe, since you have a new car, that we might take a trip somewhere."

"You mean just the two of us?" I asked, my voice rising in excitement.

"Unless you would like for Jude to come along," she cracked, her eyes flashing with mischief.

"No thank you and don't be such a wise ass! And where do you want to go, Miss Funny lady?" I was trying to bring the excitement in my voice under control.

"Oooooh," she said as she yawned widely, "I thought maybe we'd like to go to Tahoe and see the snow and maybe win some money at the slot machines, who knows?"

"That is a wonderful idea, Stephanie!" I lost all control of my excitement, and my voice began to climb. I pulled her off the couch and into my arms and our lips met. Hers tasted sweet and moist as my tongue tried to penetrate them.

"Here, here, Bobby McGee," she said, laughing and pushing me away. "Enough's enough, I gotta go now, I have things to do."

"At this hour?"

"Sure," she said, grinning.

So now the marching "elps" that make up time were completing their journey, with the fading light of a Christmas day. I left the office light of heart, basking in the promise of the 'morrow.

Up the coast highway, one could see the distant undulating hills of water, their white crowns now touched by pink, the leftover color from a setting sun that had just slipped below the sea.

At home, I suddenly remembered the letter that I had promised Stephanie that I would write to my mother. The letter, and the fear I had of writing it, began to rotate through my mind. It would be nice to hear from Mother, I thought, but what would Daddy do? Would he come looking for me? I finally decided to write it and take the chance, otherwise what could I tell Stephanie? I could lie, but then she would be constantly asking if I had heard from her yet. And so I wrote:

Dear Mother,

How are you? I'm fine and happy. I'm living near San Francisco, California now. I have met a beautiful girl who I'm close friends with.

How is Charlotte, Eddie and Jonathan?

Tell Daddy, I'm sorry I left, but that I was just sick of waiting on the second coming. Tell him that I'm still a good Christian and to please let me be and I will be fine. Someday I will come back to see you all when I get a little older.

Love, Bobby.

The next day when Stephanie came over, I showed her my letter after I had it in an envelope and sealed it. We then took it to the post office, put a stamp on it and mailed it.

A light rain was falling. You could hear its soft touch on the roof of the car when you didn't talk. We had driven up through San Francisco beneath a gray laden sky that had followed us with dripping rain right on east across the Bay and up through the hills that bordered the Delta country to the south.

"It's probably snowing in the mountains," Stephanie said, breaking the silence that surrounded the monotonous hum of the motor. "Why don't you turn on the radio for a weather report, Bobby?"

Sure enough, the broadcaster warned us that snow was falling heavy in the Sierra and that chains were required on Highway 50, from Pollock Pines on east.

Uneasiness began to invade my security and to dampen my thrilling anticipation. In the first place, I didn't have any chains, and even if I could get some, I had never driven in snow before. What if there was ice on the road, and my car started sliding around? The thought sent chills of fear up my spine, and a sense of foreboding came over me as we crossed the wet miles toward Sacramento.

In fact my driving experience was very limited. I had never been allowed to drive at home. My first experience had been in Portland, Oregon. Partly out of boredom from my empty life among the yuppies, there, I had bought an old car, an old lemon as it turned out. But it had run long enough for me to teach myself how to drive and to get my driver's license. It then conked out and never ran again. I had not driven again until I bought my old Dodge that I was driving as we made our way towards the unknown in the mountains.

"Bet you don't have any chains, do you Bobby McGee?" Stephanie questioned, lightly, as though feeling out my silence. I felt her eyes as they rested softly upon me.

"No," I said in a half hearted voice, letting my concern escape, in spite of myself.

"That is okay, Bobby boy," she bent over and touched my cheek lightly with a kiss. "We can get'em in Sacramento."

"Good," I said, trying to sound relieved. Anyone should be able to drive with ease on ice and snow if they had chains on, I thought in an effort to reassure myself. So I buried my uneasiness and finished the drive into Sacramento, where we had to take Highway 50 into the mountains.

"We can probably buy some at a gas station," Stephanie speculated, but when we pulled into one and tried, they didn't have any.

"You have to get them at a parts store," the attendant informed us and then pointed in several different directions as he told us where to find one.

"Shall I put them on now?" I asked Stephanie after we had finally found the store and bought some.

"No," she said, giving me a quizzical look, "not until we have too, you have to drive real slow with chains, and they make too much noise on the road."

So we put them in the trunk and headed up Highway 50, which soon started climbing into the mountains. Soon the sense of foreboding returned and became a burden to my mind. It became heavier and more oppressive as we climbed into the foothills and the rain became more intense. I stared into the cold rain, my eyes fixed and my body tense, already becoming fearful of the heavy rain beating on my windshield.

"Aren't you hungry, Bobby?" Stephanie's voice relieved the silence and broke my concentrated effort to see the highway through my rain swept windshield.

A sign just went by that said Placerville, and I was hungry and I suddenly knew it. Stephanie's question turned it on like the flip of a light switch. A rush of relief came over me at the prospect of food and a rest from the challenge of the highway.

"Yes, I am starved," I responded, "let's eat in this town."

We ate sandwiches in a cozy little café by the side of the wet road. Stephanie ate several long hot dogs with mustard on them, and I ate two big hamburgers with plenty of ketchup.

Stephanie was wiping her lips with a napkin when she said, "You haven't been very talkative, Bobby McGee." Her voice was probing and inquisitive.

"No," I said simply, "it takes all my concentration just to see the highway through this heavy rain."

"I think you should let me drive for a while, Bobby, so you can take a rest."

"No, Stephanie, it's too dangerous out there."

"What do you mean, 'too dangerous'?" Her voice was beginning to rise in irritation. "I've driven in the rain many times and I'm a good driver." Her lips turned petulant, "Besides you're tired," she finished with finality. She put her hands on her hips, cocked her head and set her chin with stubborn determination.

"But we are soon going to be in the ice and snow, and I bet you haven't driven in that kind of weather."

"Nooooo…" she said, "but at least I can drive until we get to the snow."

My heart had sank at this and my foreboding had returned with a surge of disappointment. For a moment, I had hoped she would say, "what do you mean, Bobby McGee, I've driven in ice and snow many times."

Stephanie drove up through Pollock Pines. Her unconcerned and cheerful chatter gave me some relief. I began to feel that maybe things were not so bad after all, and that I was just making much ado about nothing.

"Do you see that, Bobby?" Stephanie asked as she pointed out into the storm. I looked and saw them, they were mixing with the rain that blew into the windshield.

At Pollock Pines, the rain was gone, replaced by big white snowflakes that fell thick and fast. They melted when they hit the windshield but started to turn the road ahead of us white.

Then out in the dim light ahead of us, a cop stood in the road directing traffic to the side of the highway.

"Chains are required from here on, young lady," he said, "do you have some?"

"Yes," Stephanie answered, "in the trunk."

"Hurry, put'em on," he said in an urgent voice, "they may have to close the highway, soon, if this gets any heavier."

I was all thumbs with the chains. The cops words added a chill that was not from the cold to my foreboding. The more I tried to hurry, the more useless my effort seemed. Finally with Stephanie's help, we succeeded.

I got behind the wheel then with Stephanie's consent and surprisingly, my confidence gradually returned. The snow continued to melt on the warm windshield, and the chains were plowing right through the snow. But then suddenly, the four lane highway ended. The cars and especially the big trucks seemed to come at me head on through the thick falling snow. The road grew increasingly narrow and the mountain curves grew sharper. Suddenly I felt my tires slipping on ice in spite of my chains. My newfound confidence collapsed, but I had no choice but to swallow my terror and plow on. I felt Stephanie's watchful eyes upon me, but the road ahead of me demanded all of my concentration, and I could not return her gentle gaze.

"Do you have your seatbelt on, Stephanie?" I asked once, not taking my eyes off the snow that was racing toward me.

"No," she said, in unconcerned cheerfulness.

"Put it on," I ordered harshly, "this road is dangerous." I heard the click so I knew she had done it.

"You don't have yours on," she said with a hurt voice.

"I'm sorry, Stephanie, Honey, I didn't mean to shout at you. But this road is getting on my nerves." But she was not to be so easily appeased.

"Why don't you put it on, then, if it is so bad?" I could tell she was still nursing the wound to her feelings.

"I can't do it and drive at the same time." I said. "I'll try to find a place to pull over, but it's hard to see far enough ahead in this snow."

After that I'm not sure what happened.

"Watch out! Watch out! Watch out!" I remember distinctly that she screamed it three times.

I remember a big dark object coming at us, head on through the falling snow. I also remember, though indistinctly, frantically turning to miss it. It all happened so fast. The last thing I remember hearing before the crash was Stephanie's plaintive cry, "We are going to die, Bobby McGee!"

The crash that followed was kind of like the last big bang, consciousness was snuffed out by a world exploding into eternity.

At first I was only dimly aware of the eerie wail that was coming out of the darkness. In the dreamtime, I thought it was small cuddly pup that someone was beating. But then it hovered more distinctly above me in the dim light. It seemed to come and go, then became the death howl of a wild wolf wantonly being slaughtered. My awareness steadied, became more focused, suddenly it was the siren of an ambulance that I heard wailing above me. It seemed to hang suspended, riding along above me. But then it faded and drifted as I rocked gently, beneath its howl.

Stephanie! Her memory shot through my drifting brain like a bolt of lightning. I grasped desperately for my failing consciousness. Where was Stephanie? It burned like molten lead through my drifting brain. My eyes popped open like the eyes of superman, and they saw a figure outlined in the dim light above me. My mouth popped open to speak, but in the silence, there was only a gasp. The figure bent over and tears fell gently and salty to my cheek. Stephanie! My brain shouted as my mouth opened to utter another gasp. With a soft napkin, she brushed the tears that had fallen on my cheek, and the touch swept over me like a dream slumber that was somewhere warm and tropical. I gasped again, but there were no words. She saw my effort and smiled.

"Don't talk, Bobby, you need the rest," she said.

"Do you love me, Stephanie?" What I heard was a cracked whisper that came out of a gasp.

"Do I have any choice but to love you, Bobby McGee?" She buried her face in my blanket and sobbed softly.

The siren then faded back into the dreamtime.

The next time I awoke, the light was bright, and I soon realized that it was sunshine coming through my window. I felt rested in spite of an intense headache.

"Good Morning, Bobby McGee!" Stephanie's voice startled me. Somehow, in my dreaming, I thought that she had left me, "I have things to do," she had said. But here she was, her flushed cheeks spread widely in a smile.

"Can I kiss you?" I asked weakly.

"Ohhhhh, I guess so," she said, bending over to touch me with her lips as she flashed a mischievous smile.

"How do you feel?" she asked but before I could answer, she continued, "the doctor says that you are going to be fine. You just had a mild concussion besides that awful gash on your forehead. But its improving rapidly and according to the doctor, you can leave the hospital this afternoon."

I touched my forehead to feel the big bandage.

"What about you, Stephanie, weren't you hurt?"

"Not really, they took an X-ray and couldn't find anything wrong, I feel like that I have went through the wringer of an old washing machine though. I got shook up a lot. I'm the one who had the seat belt on, remember?" She grinned sheepishly and cheeks flushed more deeply red.

"Where are we?" I suddenly wondered and asked.

"At the hospital in Placerville."

"Where's my car?"

"It went over the cliff," she said, "we must have fallen twenty-five feet before we stopped. Your car was totaled, but it wasn't your fault, Bobby. The trucker who caused the accident was real good about it though. He stopped by the hospital this morning to say that his insurance company would handle everything."

"What happened?" I asked then.

"The truck driver said that his trailer jackknifed on the ice."

That night we slept in a motel in Placerville. My head hurt into my sleep.

I lie awake in my apartment, the lights were on bright. I always had them on bright when Stephanie and I were naked together. It lent intensity to my vision of her and lent wildness to her thrilling presence. My headache was gone, but I was still a little wobbly on my feet, so I was resting while I waited for her.

We returned from Placerville the day before, and I had not seen her since, but she called me at midmorning to assure herself that I was okay.

"You get some rest today, Bobby boy," she said, "and I'll see ya this evening. I'll get some stuff and fix dinner. Maybe we can even spend the night together," she added, her voice trailing off into potent seductiveness. "You be a good boy, I've got things to do now," she concluded then was gone. I held the receiver to my ear until the dial tone returned.

In the warm heat that had radiated from the furnace, I had fallen asleep.

Now, suddenly, in the gathering darkness, I was awake again, and when I remembered, I jumped out of bed to turn the lights on. I was nearly breathless with anticipation as I heard the key turn in the latch and the kick of her little foot against the door. She came in with a breath of fresh damp air. Her cheeks were blazing, and she was breathing heavily as she crossed the room and dropped her bag of groceries on the table. Then she turned toward me and placed her hands on her hips in a pose of authority.

"Well, I see that you've recovered enough to turn all the lights on," she said, throwing me a wry little grin. "So how do you feel, Bobby?" she asked then, in a more gentle voice as she bent over to look at me more closely.

"I'm fine," I said, trying to smile as charmingly as I could. "All I need now is to be with you Stephanie, in your birthday suit."

"You just hold your horses, Mr. McGee, until I empty the grocery sack and get dinner started." She, then, took out two large steaks and dropped them on the table. She turned back to me and smiled. "Okay," she said, "you just wait there." She grabbed her purse and went to the bathroom. I heard the door lock behind her.

My curiosity was roused. What could she be up to? I went to the door and listened. I tried the door knob.

"I know you are out there, Bobby McGee, curiosity killed a cat, you know!" Embarrassed, I silently went back to the couch where I sat and squirmed while I impatiently waited.

Suddenly the bathroom door opened, and she walked in naked and stood before me, spreading her arms, palms upward as though posing for a photo. Her beauty was vivid, and the striking nearness of her body nearly took my breath away. As usual, her cheeks were aflame with the heat of her passion. And her lips . . . .yes, it appeared that she had touched them with the pale pink of a rose petal. They were parted and spread slightly in an anticipatory smile, waiting for my reaction. And her eyes . . . yes the blue was deeper and wilder! They sparkled with passion, drawing me into her to hold me like a magnet of fire. But something was different. Something was enhancing, drawing attention to the beautiful blue entrance to her soul. Then I saw it. She was flashing them at me. Her eyelashes were longer, and now black and wild!

My cock started to climb getting hard in the dry warmth.

"Stephanie!" I whispered hoarsely, "your eyelashes are so sexy!"

She, silently began to move toward me as I took in her slender neck, aflame with the overflow of passion from her cheeks, her boobs, modest protuberances crowned with puckered little nipples. I followed her graceful lines down to her navel, centered on flat white skin, then finally, to her crowning glory, the head of gold fire that hovered protectively over her vaginal lips, intricately woven, boldly pink, yet innocent like the pink stroke from the artist brush, suspended like a miracle before me. Then it all wavered, distorted by the heat waves that danced in the passion that existed between us.

Stephanie came to me, eliminating the distance between us, and our passion became one. She stood over my hard cock that was climbing freely towards heaven. She squatted and wrapped her hand tightly around it. She took it, inserted it and rapidly massaged it with the to and fro rhythm of her naked body.

Pumping, my magma of passion grew hotter, climbed higher, until it finally exploded as it sought to climb to infinite heights within this woman I loved.

Tired, she fell on me, her legs apart, to let her damp pussy drip spent passion upon my navel. Her moist pink lips found mine, and I inhaled her sweetness.

"Enough," she said, then, lifting her body above me to stand on hands and knees. "I bet you are starved, Bobby McGee!"

She went and washed her hands in the sink and turned the broiler on.

We ate our steaks in the nude with mountains of French fries boiled in oil. For dessert, we had cherry pie that Stephanie had baked in San Martin.

She surprised me then, with two pre-rolled joints of hash. We inhaled deeply of their contentment, then fucked again under the power of their sweet smoke. We finally slept, wrapped in each other's arms until the street traffic disturbed the silence of dawn.

# PROFESSOR
# STUTTGARDT IN
# OVERALLS
# AND
# THE DEATH OF GOD

THE DAMP GRAY fog clung precariously to the San Francisco seacoast. It then moved inland several blocks and set up its defense with a wind that chilled the sunshine bouncing off the white Victorians that stood on the hills to the east.

Stephanie and I entered the damp gray mist as we made our way into San Francisco to attend our first Philosophy class. Stephanie drove her Comanche slowly along the residential streets, inundated by the twisting, wind driven fog. At times, all before us was obliterated, but then it would lift a little to give us a peek at the chilly dark gray street.

"There," I said, and pointed to two red coals which suddenly appeared, suspended, in the soup-like dampness, tail lights backing out into the street.

"Good," Stephanie said, sighing with relief, "I was beginning to think that we were going to be late for class. It's a fucking pain in the ass, trying to find parking around here." She stopped and watched as the ghost of an automobile twisted and squeezed its way out of a tight parking spot.

We walked at a rapid pace, at times it nearly turned into a trot as we rushed across campus toward the classroom. I was lost, racing between non distinct shapes of buildings that loomed surrealistically in the gloom. Stephanie, however, had attended classes before and knew her way around campus.

"This is it," Stephanie said breathlessly as she glanced at her watch. "We are right on time." The gray stone building was monolithic and colorless behind the fog.

I gasped for air at the top of a long flight of steps, but Stephanie was moving on and I followed.

"The classroom is 135," she said. "I think it is around this way." We went down a long corridor and there it was before us, 135.

My heart was pumping as I glanced into the nearly full classroom, and it wasn't just from over exertion either. I was about to enter my first college classroom! Inside I looked around with embarrassment for a place to sit. Stephanie saw an empty seat and took it. I just stood by fidgeting, not sure what to do. I couldn't see another empty seat nearby, but was not looking very hard in my search for one either. I didn't want to meet the stares, I felt were upon me.

"If you want to sit together just move one of the other desks," he said, in a booming but melodious voice which seemed to have the unique power of putting one at ease.

Relaxing a little, I found a chair and settled into it beside Stephanie before I looked for the source of the voice.

He was a little man, short, slim, hardly more than five feet tall and probably weighing no more than 120 pounds. He looked to be somewhere in his middle fifties, but his head was a shock of black hair, untouched by gray as far as I could tell. It was unruly, trying to stand where it was supposed to lie, defiant of the oppressive comb. When the professor turned his back to you, the back of his head resembled the proud plumage of a turkey gobbler's rear. His face was small boned and slightly wrinkled. He was a plain sort of little man. However his eyes were brown coals of intense heat that burned his message into your brain.

He had on old white overalls that day, overalls that people usually wear when they are painting houses, the bib hung too low and was held up by suspenders and legs so long that he walked on them with what appeared to be dirty old tennis shoes that peeked out from beneath them.

"Good morning, class," he said in a booming voice, so disproportionate to his size that one couldn't help but look around to see if it were actually coming from somewhere else. But then a scowl touched his forehead, lending authority to the melodious bass and confirming that it was indeed him that spoke. "My name is Rudi Stuttgardt, Professor of Philosophy. I received my PHD at Sorbonne University a number of years ago and have been teaching here in San Francisco for the past ten years. Are there any questions about my credentials?"

One could have heard a pin drop, until a 747 broke the silence in the twisting fog outside.

"In this class," he boomed, drowning the roar of the jet outside, "I do not teach in the traditional method. By that I mean I do not regurgitate the worn out theories, themes and interpretations of other philosophers. That is not to say that philosophical traditions have no value. It's just that I choose to leave the explication of these traditions to lesser minds. What I have to say is more urgent. My message deals with the present and is a warning to clean up our act so that we might have a future, not only for us but for our children. We must break with tradition and move ahead with the urgency of our self-preservation."

"Now none of you need feel cheated, there are plenty of competent professors in this department who teach the many philosophical traditions, and I urge you to enroll in their classes."

"Now for the nature of my message," the booming voice hesitated and fell silent. His intense eyes seemed to go from student to student, boring into them, exposing their inner beings like an x-ray machine. When he came to me, I stared back boldly. A hint of a smile played about his lips and his scowl was gone. "The nature of my message," he repeated, "is to expose the emotional and intellectual garbage in the social fabric of our world which obstructs reason. That is to say: obstructs our ability to think clearly, distracting us from the most basic issue of our present day existence. This basic issue is none other than our continued survival as a human species and the preservation of our planet."

"What do I mean by emotional and intellectual garbage? I mean all the clutter in our human world which has no basis in scientific fact nor in reason, superstitious clutter that makes no sense in human language. I mean, for example, the excremental dogma that leaps boldly, regurgitated, from the mouths of theologians. Dogma which has no foundation in reason nor logic in language. What I mean is," his voice leaped, turning into a shout that reverberated off the walls of the classroom.

He was suddenly silent and stared, seemingly in deep thought, at a gust of fog racing by the window. You could have heard a pin drop until someone cleared their throat as though trying to get up the courage for a comment or a question.

"What I mean by garbage is," his voice was deliberate, taut with emotion. The air was charged. I could feel anger escaping from someone, and it was touching the back of my neck, "is the dogma of religion which has no grounds in reason nor logic in language. The king of this garbage heap is God," he fell silent so that all might hear the gasps of disbelief that floated about the room.

The anger on the back of my neck felt hot, like a puff of wind moving in from the silence of the desert. I turned to see if I could find the source. What I saw was an angry red pockmarked face which appeared sexless and hovered, with no regard for symmetry, above an obese and flabby body. I looked into the dull and pulsating eyes and knew that I found the source of my discomfort.

"So," continued the professor, "we must not only show why ideas must conform to logical struture to have any meaning, we must also show that even ideas which conform to logical structure and are given meaning do not in themselves create existential beings. For example, the idea of a unicorn is a meaningful idea, but this meaningfulness does not create an actual unicorn. In fact there is probably no such creature. So what we have here is two ideas or concepts, the idea of a unicorn and the idea of existence. We understand what a unicorn is, now we need to understand what existence means when used in conjunction with a meaningful noun. For, if we do not know or understand the meaning of existence then we cannot rationally affirm or deny the actual existence of anything. You notice I said CANNOT" the professor said raising his voice and turning toward the blackboard to scribble it wildly and underline it. "If you do not know WHAT it means to exist, then you are rationally incapable of determining whether or not something actually does or does not exist, even though it might be standing right in front of your eyes! So we see that logical structure enables us to give meaning to our ideas, and meaningful ideas, such as the idea of existence, enable us to not only affirm or deny the actual existence of something, but also to understand why we can know that something standing right in front of us actually exists."

"Yes ma'am," the professor suddenly said as he pointed at someone in the back of the room. I turned to see a cute oriental girl lowering her hand and begin to speak in a sexy voice. I quickly noticed that she wore a very short mini-skirt, and her legs were rapidly swaying in a clutch and release motion as though there were something between them that was exciting her.

"Who determines the correct logical structure?" she asked.

"Yeah!" It came with another gust of hot air and hit the back of my neck.

But I couldn't take my eyes off the girl and her swaying legs. I was wishing that I could stand where the professor stood so that I could look between them when they spread.

"Logical structure is developed by simply observing how we actually think and communicate. For example, if A then NOT not A." He turned and scribbled it on the board. "This is to say that A, what ever A is, cannot both exist and not exist in the same time or same place. This is intuitively self-evident and is a basic rule of logic. The product of violating this rule is an absurdity. If one were to try and argue that this and other rules of logic were arbitrary and not essential to the nature of reality itself, they would be in essence arguing that there is no universal order in the universe, and thus there is no universal meaning by which we can understand the universe and subsequently undermining the validity of their own argument. These rules are apriori only in the sense that they are the intuitive beginnings of our thought process and are the product of the universe in which we live. These rules are discovered through self-observation as we relate the self to the external world. So, as I said, when one violates this rule, we immediately and intuitively detect an absurdity, a meaningless statement. We, of course, are free to either take note of the intuitive warning or ignore it. Theologians and religious believers simply ignore it."

"Now as you can see I have come directly to the point. I want to move ahead now and show how when we use the term God in conjunction with the term existence, we will end up in an absurdity, a meaningless statement. I then want to show the relationship of logical meaning to the reality of intuitive meaning and discuss whether it is possible for a logical absurdity to have intuitive meaning as something beyond what can be known. Furthermore, under the topic of intuitions, I would like to discuss organic nature and how it fits into the scheme of things and finally the relationship of reason to the organism. Then," said the professor, grinning as he looked about the room at the blank faces, "we shall apply our knowledge of reality to solving or at least finding possible solutions to the real problems of survival for each of us as individuals and for our planet which gives us our sustenance."

"Are there any questions concerning the nature of this course?"

The silence was heavy. I could feel it like the anger. I looked at Stephanie. She flashed a big smile back at me. I turned and looked quickly at the pockmarked face behind me. It was furiously red and looked old and fat. I still couldn't tell if it belonged to a male or female. Suddenly the mouth on it popped open with a guttural explosion. It sputtered like a big Mac Truck coming to life.

"Yes," said the professor, encouragingly as he pointed at Pockmark. All eyes turned upon the sullen, red face.

"Nuttin," the voice mumbled. The eyes dropped to stare sheepishly down at its big shoes.

I decided he must be a man. No women had feet that big.

"Well we will get right down to business then," the professor said, briskly.

"First we might ask, where did the idea of God come from? Is it derived from a combination of direct intuitions, including the self intuition of man himself or would it have to be derived from God himself as some would say? Let us investigate the latter scenario. It is true that most of the ideas we have are derived directly from external reality. They are, as it were, a rational reflection on things coming to us through our senses of seeing, hearing, touching, tasting and smelling. This is why that most of our ideas come to us with intuitive certainty, they are the direct results of sensation. Once, as children, when we have mastered the language of our birth, we are given the tools to understand the meaning of snowcapped mountains, for example, and when told to look from our window to view the beautiful snowcapped mountains, we can look with our EYES," the professor turned and violently hit the blackboard with his chalk breaking the chalk stick, half of it falling to the floor and scribbled it, EYES, in capitol letters, "and intuitively know whether they are actually there or not," he continued. "We know the meaning of snowcapped mountains and intuitively know whether they actually exist without any need of rationally understanding the meaning of exist. But I would further suggest that all of our ideas come to us, intuitively, through sensation, and it is this naïve intuition that allows such terms as God, soul, and spiritual beings to invade our thoughts and be rationally accepted as real in the same way that we intuitively accept the beautiful snowcapped mountains as being real. A blind woman could look from her window and 'believe' that the beautiful mountains were there whether they were or not. But only if she had HEARD from a human voice a visual description of mountains and then believed the audible words of the one who told her they were there. In the same way when we are told that God exists, especially as a child, even though there is no direct intuitive manifestation of His presence, we believe because we have been given a HUMAN DESCRIPTION of a wonderful being" again his chalk stick crumbled as he wrote it.

"All ideas, then, come from sense data, even the idea of existence. However, ideas in their immediacy are intuitive and not subject to rational or logical structure. They are, in fact, as I just stated, the source of logical structure. Rational thought is not something foreign to direct intuitions. It is an evolutionary product of the same direct intuitions that sustain the lives of dogs and cats. When we see the tree with its green leaves standing beside the river, we intuitively know that it is real in the same way a cat or dog does. Logic and rational meaning simply give us the tools to confirm it. We as humans, dogs, cats and roaches instinctively accept the existence of the world around us. Only when it is logically conceptualized and given rational meaning, does it become uniquely human. Intuitive belief in existence is found in the phenomenal images we have in our brains when we look from our window to view the snow capped mountains, and if what we see does not correspond to the image we have of them we intuitively know that the mountains do not exist. The blind person, lacking the sense of sight, is dependent upon the sense of hearing or touch if reading with braille. She is forced to accept the immediacy of sound or touch to compensate for the lack of sight and to believe in that which cannot be seen. However, the blind person lacks the ability to intuitively confirm that the mountains exist, but he could intuitively believe by simply accepting the affirmative word of another."

Suddenly, out of the corner of my eye, I saw a hairy arm stand high, and the professor said, "Yes sir." I looked at the face, and it had a scrubby gray beard on it, and he had gray hair that hung to his shoulders. It was tangled as though he had lost his comb. I decided that he was probably a retired hippy or someone who was trying to look authentic.

"But even though the blind person can only intuitively believe and is not able to intuitively confirm that the mountain exists," rumbled the hippie, "those who can intuitively confirm that they do exists, can know that they exist, and not just intuitively, and I think this is the reason that the blind person takes their word for it."

"Yeah," the hot air hit my neck almost like a shout, and I even thought I felt a little spit coming with it. The professor turned and looked at it, and I decided to turn and look too. Stephanie turned and a bunch of other people turned also. The face looked violent and was so red that it almost looked like a beet that someone had just dug out of the ground. But when it saw that everyone was looking the face fell and looked at its feet.

"Let me explain again, the distinction between the intuitive idea of existence and the rational idea of existence," the professor continued in a voice now being pervaded by what sounded like patronizing patience as he turned and directed his gentle, but condescending, eyes back upon the hippie. "The intuitive idea is really nothing more than the instinctive acceptance of our senses as a reliable source of information. We trust the immediacy of the data presented to our eyes and ears as existing phenomena. We believe it because we see it or hear it. But then I might ask you, how do you KNOW that you are not delusional? How do you know that the mountains are external to your brain? You believe that they exist because you see them, but seeing something doesn't prove that they exist for anyone other than yourself. And remember even the blind man believes they exist because he trusts the sound of your voice or his touch. How does he know that what he is hearing is not delusional? Most of the animal kingdom is not bothered by such questions. They simply accept without question, as does most of mankind a lot of the time. The problem is that mankind has evolved to the point where he can reason and give rational meaning to the intuitive data that is presented to us through sensation. So we trust our senses not to lie to us, much of the data that we receive is self evident, such as seeing the snowcapped mountains. Their existence is intuitively confirmed in the act of seeing. However, we as humans are capable of receiving sense data, such as the written word, which points beyond itself and requires more than direct sense data to be understood. This is where human reason and logic comes in. To understand the written word, we need to have logical structure that allows all humans to think essentially in the same way, and we need a linguistic structure which allows us to communicate with others of our species. Lacking these essentials items, we would have no idea how anyone else thinks or what they were talking about. And even though these essential elements are available to all, and at least partially present in all thinking and communication, the uneducated and misinformed constantly violate the rules of thinking and communication. These violations of the human thought process have created major flaws, especially in the nature of religious thought. So though we intuitively grasp the nature of existence through our direct contact with our world through sensation without a rational understanding of what it 'means' to exist, we become vulnerable to a whole range of rational and logical absurdities by declaring that they exist simply because we choose to believe the WORD or the hearsay we hear in the sounds of another's voice, pointing beyond themselves. Knowing the rational meaning of existence requires that first of all we understand that meaning must have universal application. If it has been demonstrated that to have meaning, an existing entity must have existential continuity through time and be in a particular place at any given moment in time, then any claim to existence that violates this rule would simply be void of meaning. And this must, of necessity, have universal application. Now this is not to say that such rational definitions are absolute. What it does say is that any claim to existence that violates the definition would be required to show how the definition of existence has been broadened or extended to give meaning to the subject in question. In other words, it would be required to fall within the logical structure that allows for all meaning." At this point, the professor stood quietly as he looked around the room, a slight smile playing around his lips.

"I know that I have said a lot," he began again. "There is a lot here to digest. But remember this is just our first class, and we will have more time to discuss these things in more detail later on. So now let me press on and complete my thesis by elaborating upon how definitions are formed. And of course, our example today is existence. Let's look again at the direct intuitions that come to us through sensation. We usually accept this sense data as confirming with certainty the existence of these objects that we have seen, heard, touched, etc. Then we might rationally observe the conditions which are always present and in common with the object of this intuitive certainty."

Suddenly a hand shot up, and it startled me because it was the hand of the girl sitting right in front of me.

"Yes," the professor said, with a slight hint of impatience in his voice.

"Sorry, professor," a timid voice said, "this may be a stupid question, but what exactly do you mean by 'meaning'?"

"No, young lady," the professor said. "A sincere question is never a stupid question. Meaning is found in the definition we give a term, such as existence. It delimits it so that it is only true when something falls within the definition. We can define a human being, for example, as a living organism, a mammal whose brain activity includes self-consciousness. Also, being human means that we exist through time and are always in a particular place at any given moment in time, and to exist in time, we must have a beginning in time. And this is not some arbitrary definition. It comes from the fact that all humans ever observed have fallen within this definition. If someone discovers a human that does not fall within this definition then this discovery would change the definition. For example, if a 'spiritual being' were to be ever OBSERVED, then this would change the definition of humans, but of course a 'spiritual being' or soul has never been observed."

"And with that, we have our clue as to how we are to define the meaning of existence. We gave a partial definition of what it means for a human to exist. But most would assert that all living things exist, and in fact, most would go on to assert that all things such as rocks and planets exist. So the question we must ask is, what are the common elements we find to be true for all things, that we are aware of that are phenomenally present within the universe? And remember that the existence of these things are only intuitively believed in one way or another until we have given them rational meaning by subjecting them to the structure of logical reason. Once we have done this, then it becomes communicable knowledge that can be confirmed or proven false by anyone willing to subject their beliefs to the rules of logic, the structure of communicable meaning."

"So what are the common elements that we observe applicable to all things that we have discovered that are present in the universe?" He turned to the blackboard with a brand new piece of chalk that he found somewhere beneath his podium, and he wrote as he spoke, "1) all things move, a. through space and the movement through space requires b. time. Or vice versa as they move through time, at any given moment they are in a particular place in space. Most movement in the universe is involuntary, only movement motivated by an animate brain is voluntary. Among us, the life of a mammal is essentially nothing more than the involuntary movement of a beating heart. The voluntary movements represented by the complexities of human life, including this discussion are <u>ABSOLUTELY</u> dependent on the involuntary movement of the heart. This heart throbs rhythmically in a particular place as it travels around the sun on an earth that wobbles as it twists in a rapid circular movement. We use these movements to measure the time it takes to go from <u>PLACE TO PLACE</u> and to measure the aging process of the beating heart."

"And what is the essence of this moving universe?" he cried as his voice suddenly grew tense as though talking to himself and looking squarely at the blackboard. "Quantum physics has shown us that when these moving phenomena are dissected into their smallest parts, they are nothing more than movement itself as it travels, motivated by the attraction of opposite charges, through empty space. There is really <u>NOTHING</u> there" he shouted, his voice rising several octaves as he turned a victorious glance back upon the class. "Is it possible that nothingness is the essence of all things in the universe? But I have diverged somewhat in my excitement" he suddenly said, lowering his voice with a short laugh.

"However, more importantly, I think I have demonstrated to you the <u>meaning</u> of existence for all things that are phenomenally present within the universe. And I guess I might anticipate the next question as being: is it possible for something to exist in the universe that would violate this definition? And my answer would be, of course, anything is possible, but don't forget what we are talking about here. We are talking about rational meaning, meaning that provides logical confirmation for our direct intuitions. As I pointed out, we can get along without rational meaning, with our direct intuition that come directly to us through sensation. The rest of the animal world gets along fine without rational meaning. They simply intuitively accept the world that is presented to them through sensation. However, humans are a whole different animal. We want to <u>UNDERSTAND</u> the world we live in. And it is rational meaning that gives us understanding and the ability to communicate among ourselves. So if there is something that exists in our universe that violates the rational meaning of existence, then it would require a different definition. And if one were not provided, the idea of this existence would have no meaning and consequently have no value. It would be an empty idea that reflects or points to nothing that we are aware of in our universe."

"So now that our class time is a flying, and we must all soon move off to different places, let's apply what I have presented to you to the possible existence of God. If God exists in our universe and is to have any rational meaning, He either could not violate the definition that applies to all other known entities that exist in our universe or He would have to fall under some other meaningful definition that would still NOT violate the definition that all other beings fall under. Remember a meaningful statement requires that something either exist or not exist, but not both. And we can only determine if this rule has been violated by knowing what is meant by exist. To state either A or NOT A tells us nothing in particular until we know what A is. Since we have defined what we mean by existence in our universe, we must ask: does God fall under this definition or does His existence violate it? If His existence violates it, and we continue to insist that He exists, then we are asserting an absurdity, arguing that he both exists and does not exist. Why is this so? Because we would be admitting that He does not exist according to the definition, but that He exists anyway. So unless we can provide another definition that does NOT violate the definition of existence within this universe that we have or refrain from calling it existence at all, then His existence would simply have no meaning and of what value would a meaningless idea of existence have for us?"

"So let us see what the theologians would have to say about this. First, most of them would deny that their Christian God exists under the definition of all other beings or phenomena within our universe. They would deny that He exists in, or through time, nor that he could have a beginning in time. They would deny that he exists in particular place in space. Thus from a logical point of view, they would simply be arguing that God does NOT exist. But they would go on to deny this and assert that He does exist. So how are they to avoid the logical absurdity of asserting that God both does and does not exist. Well they would try to avoid this absurdity by asserting that 'existence,' when used in conjunction with God, has a different meaning. They would argue that God does not exist through time therefore has no beginning in time nor does he exist in any particular place in space. But this would simply be telling us what 'exist' when used in conjunction with 'God' does not mean. It would have no more force than to further affirm that He does not exist at all. This does not give us a new meaning! This is merely rejecting the ONLY MEANING WE HAVE for existence." He turned on the blackboard with a vengeance with his voice climbing in victory.

"But let us give them another chance to provide for us meaning for the term 'exist' when it is used in conjunction with 'God'. They might argue that God is a 'spiritual being' rather than a 'phenomenal' being and has a spiritual existence. So now do we have a new meaning for the term 'exist'? To give rational meaning to 'spiritual existence,' we would have to logically define it just as we did 'phenomenal existence'. But you remember, intuitive knowledge or belief does not require rational meaning in order to believe. The blind man can intuitively accept the belief that the snowcapped mountains exist without being able to intuitively confirm his belief by looking out the window or even if he has never witnessed snow or mountains. He can do this by basing his belief on a creative imagination and accepting the HEARD word of others. His idea of the mountains might be very rich with meaning, but it would need to be private because he would be unable to share the intuitive beliefs with others who have witnessed directly through sight of the beautiful snowcapped mountains."

"As you might suspect, those who assert the 'existence' of 'spiritual beings' have so far been unable to provide for us logical meaning for 'spiritual'. Does this mean, categorically, that they do not exist? No, it means that their existence simply has no meaning. It would be like arguing over whether Hipperty exists or not. The gut reaction of most would be 'what the hell is Hipperty?' So why is this not the case with 'spiritual beings' and 'God'? The answer is very simple: we are told through the HEARD and the SEEN written word that God exists, and then we are told that He cannot be seen nor can it be intuitively confirmed that He exists. So, essentially, we are told that we are BLIND and must accept the WORD as it is told or written, and we must intuitively believe because we must trust the messenger. If the term Hipperty were substituted for the term God in a child's upbringing, then he would believe just as certainly in Hipperty as he does God."

"So asserting that God is a spiritual being without giving a rational meaning for the term spiritual, does nothing to correct the logical absurdity because they have not given us a new meaning. They have merely given us a new word whose only meaning is to deny what it means to exist in accordance with the only definition we have. Though they would argue that God does not exist through time nor have a beginning in time. They would at the same time argue that He is HERE WITH US in time. They would argue that while He does not exist at any particular place in space, He is EVERYWHERE IN SPACE AT THE SAME TIME. This is all logically meaningless. They are simply stating that God both exists and does NOT exist through the same time and in the same space which rationally CANNOT be understood, thus cannot be believed. To accept this, you simply must defy the absurdity, as the Christian existentialist philosopher Soren Kierkegaard did, or ignore it. Their WORD tells them that the wisdom of man is foolishness with God. Maybe so. But the ideas of God's existence that have no rational meaning are foolishness for men as well. I guess this might be best expressed by the meaningless babble one sometimes hears at a Pentecostal revival. And to further pursue their exercise into absurdity, there are those who would claim they have the 'gift' of being able to translate this babble into English."

"So in conclusion, while a divinity may exist, no divinity has ever been discovered by mankind. The divinities that we have in different religions are simply manmade gods invented by the creative imaginations of men and women whose thinking is based upon the assumption that they are BLIND and must accept the word intuitively upon faith. Unfortunately, the WORD points to nothing beyond itself, if what it points to has no logical definition or meaning."

"So, what have we successfully concluded here? Have we proven that God does not exist? Yes and no. We have shown that God cannot exist for us rationally. God's EXISTENCE can have no meaning for us. But we have not proven that there is no divinity beyond our rational capability to understand. Have we proven that the term God has no rational meaning? No, far from it. The term God probably has more meaning attached to it than any other word in any language. Whole dogmatic religions are built around 'God'. Then what is it that we have proven? Actually 'proven' is the wrong word for what we have concluded. Rather we have DEMONSTRATED that the term existence, when used in conjunction with the term God, has no meaning. In fact it is an absurdity. So where does that leave us? It tells us that no matter how much meaning we attribute to our God, His existence has no rational meaning. We can't know whether the god we worship actually exists because the term 'exist' is a rational term, the meaning of which, we subject the data that comes to us through sensation to, in order to confirm or deny their actual existence. And God does not meet the rational criteria necessary in order for us to confirm His existence."

"So, you ask, who or what is the God that volumes have been written about, that men for thousands of years have supposedly quoted and worshipped? We have no choice but to conclude that He is nothing more than a rational construct of human origin. How or why or where did the idea of God come from? That is a whole different topic that we might touch upon later."

At this point a jarring, clanging bell rang loudly above the sound of the professor's voice. And it brought an end to the professor's lecture.

"Have a good day," he shouted as students streamed from the room and others streamed in.

Stephanie and I remained sitting for a moment, her blue eyes throwing sparks of humor at me.

"That is a lot to swallow in one lecture," she said. She turned her eyes and let them fall, staring absently down at the tight jeans that hid her nakedness from me. She laughed softly, the embarrassed laugh of uncertainty. "I was raised a Catholic, you know." She lifted her blue eyes again to meet mine.

"I didn't know that, you never told me," I said. I searched her, trying to see more deeply into her blue depths.

"I don't know if I am one anymore." Her voice had become preoccupied and her blue eyes fell again only this time she appeared to be staring at the jeans that held my nakedness. "Not a good one anyway," she continued. "I think the Pope is losing touch with reality, or maybe, as the professor would say, has never been in touch with it. His stands on abortion and birth control are irrational and make no sense in our hungry and over-populated world."

Her eyes met mine again as we found each other's hand and walked from the classroom and then across campus to the Comanche.

# EROTIC CHILDREN AND STEPHANIE'S PAIN

MY PENIS HUNG limp, sticky damp, its passion spent. But it was there, to recover with thrilling anticipation of another future moment when it, again, would erupt to shoot from its depths the organic fire of life into the abyss of she, the enigmatic female.

"Bobby McGee," she said it softly from behind me. I halted my approach to the bathroom and turned to face her. She wore a coquettish little smile that played teasingly with her lips. She lay on the floor, naked, a throw rug beneath her soft white skin. Her legs were standing up and rocked gently back and forth. Her folding pussy lips were sticky as though glazed by honey that oozed from her, coaxed out by the gentle rock of her firm white legs.

"What, Stephanie?" I asked.

"Are you still angry at me?" she twisted her flaming red cheeks around to face me. The motion lifted her butt slightly from off the floor to make her look seductive and vulnerable.

"How am I to stay angry at you?" I asked, nearly breathless from the sight of her.

Her smile widened in an expression of victory, and she pulled a flaming lock of her gold hair down over the sparkle of her mysterious blue eyes. The arch of her muscular, pearl white legs also widened as they increased the pace of their clutching and releasing motion.

We had argued earlier when she went to put her diaphragm in.

"Please, Stephanie," I had said lightly, hardly above a whisper, "let's stop using that thing."

"Are you out of your mind?" she had squealed in a shrill voice.

"What is wrong with wanting a baby?" I had continued bravely, off handedly but with a sigh.

"For you and I, now, everything," she had retorted sharply as she stood in front of the full length mirror, inserting it.

But then she walked over and proceeded to take the wind from me with a full, rich kiss on my lips. I continued to remain quiet and somewhat piqued by her stubbornness. Now she was teasing me with the seductive sway of her feminine bipeds and then wanting to know if I was still angry!

I went to her and fell between her legs, my knees up against her soft butt. I brushed away the red-gold lock of hair and looked into her deep blue eyes as they met mine. I tried to fathom infinitely into their depths, but at a certain depth, they became mysterious, leaving me restless in my longing to see more.

"Bobby," she said softly, as she ran her little finger down the bridge of my nose, "I want your baby passionately, and I dream of it each time your hard thing climbs inside of me, but you know as well as I do, if you will rationally think about it, that there can't be any babies now. So stop fretting and enjoy what there can be. Okay?"

She then grabbed me around the neck and pulled my lips to hers. She wrapped her soft legs tightly around my waist so that her damp pussy was warm against my skin.

"Now," she said firmly as she released me, "let's talk about Professor Stuttgardt's lecture." She stood then, lifting her arms to stretch her naked body in the lamplight. She went to her purse to rummage through it. Finding a comb, she ran it through the fiery gold of her hair. Again she rummaged until she found the little packet of cocaine. "Do you think the Professor is right, Bobby, about there being no God in the universe or soul in humans?" She was chopping the white powder rapidly with the single edged razor.

"It makes sense to me," I responded but my mind was on more important things at the moment. I was watching the nipples on her firm boobs quiver.

But as she chopped, the image and intensity of Professor Stuttgardt's eyes suddenly flashed before me. I remembered how, in his second lecture, he beat the blackboard and summarily eliminated as meaningless the existence of the human soul. He said that the existence of a spiritual being held no more logical meaning in conjunction with phenomenal human existence than it did with God. He had said it was a THEO-logical attempt to escape the logic of the phenomenal world. And when he said it, he had written it on the board, boldly breaking his chalk. And in the next lecture, he had talked about science and about the difference between the meaning of ignorance in the Newtonian world view, and the new meaning of ignorance that came with the discoveries and development of quantum physics. But most of this stuff simply went over my head.........but then the image of the pockmarked fellow suddenly wavered in my brain. He always seemed to end up sitting behind me, breathing hot hate on the back of my neck. What was his problem anyway?!

"Some people claim that they have contact with dead people. If that is so, they must have souls," Stephanie said and then bent over to snort a long line of coke that she had neatly prepared for herself. She then pushed the mirror toward me so that I could snort my line.

"Yes," I said hotly, "just like they claim to have contact with God. But to communicate, it takes a body with a larynx, a tongue, throat and lungs. Talking is a mechanical act. So tell me, will you, how these bodiless beings are supposed to talk!" I was proud of myself for being so logical as I moved along, inhaling deeply from the white line on the mirror. The moment of pleasure was intense.

"Boy, aren't we animated!" Stephanie was grinning broadly. "Anyway," she said and sighed as she looked off into space as though seeing something that wasn't there, "I guess it is best that way. If there were a soul, then there would probably be a hell, and I would probably end up in it."

"Don't be silly," I responded, "if there is a hell then it is right here on earth, and the same could be said for heaven."

"You can say that again," she said with a cynical chuckle, "at least about hell anyway. Christianity was probably invented by someone looking for a way out of hell on earth. But if it is all a lie, why waste your time with it." The coke was rapidly climbing into her straw as she guided it across the surface of the mirror.

She looked up at me her cheeks aflame, with the deep blue of her eyes fastened poignantly upon me. The heels of her little feet stood precariously on the edge of the chair and her arms were wrapped lightly around the white legs that climbed above them while her naked boobs collapsed softly upon them.

"But Baby!" I said as I tried to fathom her two moist circles of blue, "there can be heaven on earth too, you know." But she remained silent, her blue eyes unblinking, as though defying me to prove it.

"What is it Stephanie? Why are you looking at me that way?" I asked, as softly as possible.

"Oh, it is nothing," she said, trying to sound casual. She lowered her eyes modestly, to stare thoughtfully at her pink toenails, spread out beyond the edge of the chair.

"Something has happened that you haven't told me about. What is it Stephanie? I'm your friend you know."

"Well," she said as she bit her upper lip and pulled it down coquettishly and continued to stare at her toes. "It happened when I was thirteen." She said, then stopped and threw me a fleeting glance. She started to pick at her toenail as though forgetting that she started to say something.

"What happened?" I prodded gently.

"I was raped," she said, in a matter of fact voice. "It happened down on the beach in Santa Cruz." Her feet had fallen to the floor so that she could inhale another line of cocaine. "I have never told anyone except Jude and an old friend Susie and now you, Bobby McGee." she said after exhaling the breath that she held for a long moment.

"Who was it, Baby?" I asked, as I felt restless anger begin to stir within me.

"I don't know," she responded, her voice rising slightly as though in frustration. "I was just walking on the dark beach, all alone and feeling sorry for myself."

"What were you doing on a dark beach down in Santa Cruz all alone, Stephanie?"

"Oh," she said, grinning sheepishly then biting her upper lip again to pull it down sharply with her teeth. "My mother had grounded me for two weeks for saying 'fuck'. She had been listening outside my bedroom door while my friend Susie and I had been chatting. I was really pissed and decided to run away. Susie had agreed to run away with me, but at the last minute she chickened out so I went alone. I didn't have any trouble catching rides to Santa Cruz, but when I got there I didn't have any place to stay and I had no money."

"I must admit I was really frightened on the dark beach all alone. I was walking along wondering what I was going to do next. The night was getting cold, and I was starting to shiver beneath my old coat. I thought I heard someone behind me, and I nearly froze in my tracks. I started to turn around, but he didn't give me a chance. He had a big rough hand, and he covered my eyes with it. I was too terrified to even scream."

"'It is best you don't see me,' his voice was harsh and terrifying, 'because if you do I'll have to kill you, so you better keep your eyes closed tight. Besides', he said and then laughed, it was a harsh laugh like his talk, 'if you don't see me, maybe you won't hate me fucking you so much, you might even enjoy it. And by the way' he said after that, 'if you scream I'll stab you in the heart with this knife I have.' I was afraid to even breathe, and I was holding my eyes shut so tight that they were hurting."

"You mean you just let him do it?" I felt my voice rising in spite of myself.

"What was I supposed to do? I begged him in a whisper to spare me. I told him I was just a kid, thirteen, and had never done it before."

"But he just laughed and said 'sorry baby, but there is a first time for everything.' He forced me to take off my jeans and panties and threw them toward the incoming surf. He took my coat and threw it up the beach. I can't even remember him doing it. I guess I just shut it out."

"After he left me, I was even more terrified of being naked and alone to freeze on the beach. There was no way that I could have run naked for help back into town, for all to stare at. Lucky for me, I found my jeans and my coat although they were soaked with salt water. Half dazed, I walked back up the beach through the dark and into town. I went to a payphone and asked the operator for the police."

"I just told the pigs that I was lost and that a big wave had hit me. The police called my parents and they came down and got me. And guess what Bobby!" Her blue eyes had lighted with mischief.

"What?" I asked.

"I wasn't grounded anymore!"

Stephanie snorted another line of the fine white powder then turned the little mirror around to me.

"Why didn't you tell your parents?" I asked after having inhaled my line.

"Didn't dare, not after what I had done."

"But what if you had of gotten pregnant?"

"I didn't!" she said, "why deal in hypotheticals?"

"A bully named Studs Gatlin raped my little sister Charlotte once," I volunteered.

"It happens all the time," Stephanie said, in her matter of fact tone of voice. "And usually the law is more interested in protecting the rapist than avenging the victim."

I got up from the table, went to the fridge, and got two bottles of Kirin beer. We both took a long swig, and Stephanie licked the foam from her lips.

"Anyway," Stephanie continued, then sighed. "The rape forebode of worse things yet to come."

"You mean something worse than rape was about to happen?"

"Yep," she said.

Her firm naked legs fell to the floor. "I have to piss," she said.

So I watched her butt, red, from sitting on the hard wood chair, disappear around the corner as she made her way to the bathroom. I heard her water flowing into the stool, and then her voice trying to talk above it.

"It was about a year or so after I was raped," she was saying, almost shouting, to make sure that I heard her.

I went to the bathroom door so I could watch her while I listened. Her cheeks were flushed, and she flashed a smile full of white teeth at me.

"We lived in Oakland back then," she said lowering her voice. "My parents used to go most every weekend to our house over in Thunder Beach. I would go occasionally, but more often than not, I would beg to stay behind so I could spend the weekend at Susie's house."

Stephanie spread her legs and wiped herself with toilet paper, then came and took my hand, leading me back to the table.

"Then one Saturday, my parents had left as usual for Thunder Beach, after dropping me off at Susie's house. During the afternoon, Susie's parents left for awhile. Susie and I had stolen a six-pack from the fridge and were proceeding to get drunk when we heard a knock on the door. We went out where we could peek from the front window to see who was there. We saw two guys in blue uniforms that looked like cops. Susie was afraid to answer the door. 'you never know what a pig is going to do,' she said. But I told her she had to. But when she still wouldn't answer it, I went and did it for her. The first thing they did was ask for Stephanie Jones. How they knew that I was at Susie's house, I'll never know."

"It was almost as if they struck me dead, and I was having an after death nightmare. They just came out and told me that both my parents had been killed in a car accident over on the road to Thunder Beach. They said it so fast that I couldn't even cry."

"How did it happen?" I asked for lack of anything better to say.

"Oh, I guess they had a head on collision or something and both cars went over the cliff."

She swigged more beer and licked the foam from her lips with her tongue again. She flashed a fleeting glance at me from her flushed face as she tossed her golden red hair impatiently. She twisted, and leaned to one side so that she could scratch the red spot on her soft bottom.

"So what happened to you after that, Stephanie?"

"Oh.....I got put into a kids' home for a while, but I kept running away. Neither of my parents had any living family left so I didn't either. Sometimes I would hide out at Susie's house. When I was sixteen, I met Jude and moved in with him."

"Jude was already in his twentys, and he beat me into behaving myself most of the time. I guess I needed someone like him back then to keep me under control."

"Bullshit!" I exclaimed in disgust. But Stephanie remained silent. She just sat, her chin resting on a knee and sipped her beer. I got up and went to her then and kissed the damp skin on her forehead and stroked my fingers through her fiery red hair.

"But that doesn't mean that I still need the beatings," she suddenly muttered as though only at that moment had it occurred to her. A tear slowly emerged and made its way down her flushed cheek, and she reached over and got a hold on my dick as though for support. I scooped her up then, wrapping my arms around the small of her back and the softness of her legs and butt. I sat with her on my lap, her buttocks spreading to engulf the hardness of my cock. Stephanie turned, her hot breath upon me. Our noses touched and I pulled her closer.

In the night a siren wailed, awakening me. Stephanie her back against me, snuggled closer. But then we slept until dawn.

# PROFESSOR STUTTGARDT IN FORMAL ATTIRE AND THE NUDE BEACH

THE SUN SHONE brightly on the ridges of green water below us as we made our way along the bluffs that climbed out of the deep. Distant white sails glistened in a row, each following the other out to sea. The leader danced then faded at the point where water and sky met. There was no wind and it was already warm on this day in early February.

"Are you going to look for another car, Bobby?" Stephanie yelled, above the roar of the noisy engine.

"I suppose," I responded halfheartedly.

"What?" she yelled more loudly.

"I say, I suppose!" I screamed loudly back at her. I had received some insurance money for my old car the day before. But I had reservations about buying another one. I guess I enjoyed hitching a ride with Stephanie too much.

"I bet you anything," Stephanie suddenly said, changing the subject, "that the Professor will pull his surprise on the class today." She turned and threw me a mischievous grin.

"What are you talking about?" I shouted above the engine as I tried to read the sparkle in her eye.

"Oh, you will just have to wait and see!" she said teasingly, as she looked forward to a curve in the road ahead. When she looked back at me, her grin had broadened into a knowing smile.

"Shit," I said, "how do you know about it?"

"Oh, somebody told me about his class once. That is one reason we are taking it." She chuckled softly. But I bit my tongue to hide my curiosity.

We had arrived early on campus and found parking almost immediately so were taking our leisurely time making our way to class.

"Stephanie," I said, glancing at her as we walked. "Do you have any idea what the Professor was talking about when he lectured on the difference between Newtonian ignorance and Quantum ignorance?"

"Welllll," she said hesitantly, "I think he was saying that with Newtonian ignorance, it was thought to be a weakness in man's ability to know the future. Remember he said that with Newtonian ignorance, the future was knowable. God, for example, could know it. Humans couldn't know it because we had imperfect minds. But with the science of quantum physics, they discovered that the future was unknowable even by God himself."

"I remember," I interrupted, "he said that if God had created the universe, then he was gambler, and this is because of the principle of uncertainty that is inherent in the way it was created."

"Yeah, something like that," she said, "If it was actually created."

In the classroom, the Professor wore a light blue suit, including what looked like a tailored jacket and flowing from his small Adam's apple was a wide white tie covered profusely with the blossoms of wild red roses. Beneath the tie was a light pink shirt. His shoes were white. He looked like a preacher standing in a pulpit on Easter Sunday. It seemed he always dressed to startle you when you first walked into the room. One time he even wore a bikini bathing suit beneath a long shirt that hung to his knees that said CABO on it.

After overcoming the initial shock of it, I decided his dress might have something to do with the surprise Stephanie mentioned. But then I heard Stephanie mutter "I guess I was mistaken," in a breathless whisper beside me.

"About what?" I asked, returning her whisper. I looked to see her eyes bugging in disbelief at the Professors formal attire.

The Professor was standing, his hands behind his back, waiting politely for the class to come to order.

"Never, you mind," Stephanie said, throwing me a confused glance.

"Good morning class," the little man's voice boomed heartedly.

"Good morning," mimicked a scattering of voices, including my own and Stephanie's. Stephanie's voice had stood out among the voices and her cheeks suddenly flushed red with embarrassment. She returned my look with one of defiance.

The Professor was adjusting his notes on the podium and seemed to ignore the half hearted response to his greeting.

"Today," said the Professor, looking up at the class, "I was going to discuss body morality, the morality of pleasure that we left behind when we created the god morality and in our conceit became self-sanctified. Body morality is the morality of environmental attunement, the morality of love and happiness. But further elaboration upon in this topic must wait for another day because the warm sun outside calls me."

"I guessed right after all," Stephanie whispered excitedly beside me.

"Right about what?" I whispered back fiercely. Stephanie just smiled knowingly without even looking back.

"On this piece of coastline, you have got to grab opportunity when it presents itself," the Professor began. "So today all of us, who have the moral courage to do so, are going over to Baker Beach to absorb the warm sun, and we are going to do it in the buff."

The announcement was greeted with silence.

"Is there anyone here," continued the Professor, "who needs a ride or doesn't know where Baker Beach is?"

This was also greeted with silence and not one hand was raised.

"Good," said the Professor, then, "Yes," and he pointed over my head.

"I don't have my bathing suit," said a sweet but frantic voice.

I quickly turned to let my eyes rove, in search of its source.

"You won't need a bathing suit where we are going," the Professor responded innocently

"But I just couldn't go naked in public," she said pleadingly.

I found her then. She was a stunningly beautiful black girl. Watching her pink lips move had nearly taken my breath away. Even her expression of alarm was stunning, and I could only imagine her being naked in the sand. Suddenly she glanced at me, shyly, fleetingly but then she turned her gaze back upon the Professor.

"What is your name?" he asked.

"Susan Hale," she said with a voice that seemed to be regaining its equilibrium.

"Susan," the Professor said in a gentle voice. "There is a reason for taking this excursion without prior warning. I don't want anyone wearing bathing suits. If I had of warned you, half of you would be there in a bathing suit, and this would defeat the purpose of the outing."

"I was hoping that a few of you that have the moral courage can look at this as a human encounter session. On the other hand, those of you who cannot find the courage to participate will not be penalized in anyway except, of course, that you will miss a new experience in communication the natural way, and you will also miss the warm sand beneath a sunlit sky."

"You see my dear class, bathing suits are nothing more than a compromise to the religious shame and fear of pleasure. To go naked is an expression of our moral freedom. And moral freedom is a terrifying condemnation of the dogmatic slavery of religion. Clothing is for one of two purposes, either it is for warmth or it is something to hide behind. Moral freedom is to have nothing to hide."

"But I will further add that to join us, nakedness is not absolutely mandatory. If there are some of you determined to be there with clothes on, then so be it. Indeed some of you may need them to shield your white asses from the hot sun, but I do not think that includes you Susan Hale," he concluded gently as he gave Susan a broad smile.

I could not resist another quick look back at Susan. Her dark cheeks were flushed and her body was twisting. She threw me another glance, less shy than before, and directed her gaze out into the hallway as though in an attempt to further gather her composure.

"We'll go now," said the Professor, "we'll meet in the parking lot at Baker Beach."

At this moment, the pocked marked fellow walked in. I think it was the first time that I hd noticed him being late. "We are going to Baker Beach," I said as I walked past him. He simply turned like a robot and began to follow me.

"Why did you tell him?" Stephanie asked, her face beaming with a broad grin. "You know he ain't going to like it."

"I just wanted to see his reaction," I said, grinning back at her. "But I guess he just doesn't know what is out at Baker Beach." Stephanie laughed and playfully slapped me on the shoulder.

"So this is the surprise you were talking about?" I turned to watch her red hair blowing in the wind.

"Yep," she said. "It is a good thing I have a lot of sun tan lotion for my sensitive skin."

"Don't worry," I said, trying to sound innocent, "I'll put plenty of it on for you."

"I bet you will," she said as she turned a wry grin upon me. "You better not get too carried away, Bobby McGee, I don't want you making a spectacle of it!"

"Don't worry, Stephanie, my nymph, I won't embarrass you."

"I ain't no nymph!" she said defiantly.

Up Nineteenth Avenue, the deep shade tree jungle of Golden Gate Park went off in either direction as the traffic on the avenue raced from one part of the city to the other. The cool shade was inviting as we raced along with the traffic, but where we were going was more exciting.

We went west on Geary Boulevard until we came to Twenty Fifth Street. We took it down to the bay. Soon we grabbed a parking spot at Baker Beach.

There, lo and behold, waiting on us was Pockmark! I stared in disbelief. What was his hurry? I grinned to myself when I speculated as to how he would react when he discovered the nature of our outing to the beach.

When Stephanie and I walked up, he ignored us, then Stephanie left me to walk down towards the water's edge. I felt awkward with Pockmark standing silently beside me. So I concentrated on observing Stephanie's figure as it twisted sensually in her tight jeans, as she made her way over the hot sand. She had stopped at the water's edge and stared out over a tranquil San Francisco Bay. I thrilled in the anticipation of seeing her naked body stretched out beneath the hot sun. Glancing off to my right, I could see the big long bridge brilliantly red in the bright sunshine. Its bold outline nearly took my breath away!

Pockmark caught my attention again as he fidgeted nearby. What the hell, I thought to myself, I might as well find out what his real name was.

"My name is Bobby McGee," I said, trying to sound congenial.

Pockmark stared absently at me for a long moment while he continued to fidget. Then he hesitantly proffered his hand in silence.

"And what is your name?" I asked as I shook his limp, flabby paw.

"Alfred Nummy," he whined.

"Pardon me!" I said quickly, leaning forward to hear better. It had sounded like he said "dummy" with a clogged nasal passage!

"Alfred Nummy!" he repeated, his voice rising angrily, and he yanked his limp paw violently from my grip. No wonder he had an inferiority complex, I thought, with a name like that!

"Couldn't ask for a nicer day," the voice said from behind us. I instantly recognized it as the Professor's voice. I turned to see him standing there in a pair of jogging shorts.

"I see you two have met," he said. "I know your name, Bobby McGee, but I don't believe I have heard yours," he said as he turned towards Alfred Nummy.

"Alfred Nummy," he said with a loud voice that sounded defensive. The Professor was silent. He turned his face toward the parking lot just in time to see some of the other students coming.

I turned to excitedly see a group of girls, and the first one to my surprise was Susan Hale. Right behind her was the beautiful Chinese chick, Natalie Wong. I figured Natalie would take her clothes off. She only had on a cute pair of short shorts anyway. They were so short that you could see the ridges of her bottom popping out. I wondered though about Susan Hale after what she said in the classroom. She had on a tight pair of jeans that made her figure twist almost like Stephanie's. Would she take them off or not? That was the question that I posed for myself.

Shortly, I recognized Albert Seidweiler as he came bouncing over a sand dune and into the parking lot. His hair hung loose, down to his shoulder, and his unkempt beard made him look like a hippie straight out of the sixties.

Then I became aware of Stephanie beside me again. She had gotten close enough to touch elbows. So the seven of us continued to wait while the Professor made small talk.

While the others followed the Professor's finger as it pointed toward a distant container ship that appeared coming around the point, my eyes were busy roving around the parking lot to see who else might show up for our adventure. Suddenly, with growing excitement, I noticed two beautiful young women coming toward us. One was strutting forward boldly, the other was hanging, shyly, behind. The one that was hanging behind was white with fair skin and blond hair. She was tall and probably a little thinner than Stephanie. I was staring at her when

I felt the gentle pressure of Stephanie leaning against my shoulder. I glanced quickly at the other girl. She was deeply tanned with dark olive skin. It looked soft and well cared for. They both had on tight jeans. Sure enough they walked right up to where we were waiting.

"I don't think I have met you girls," said the Professor as he turned to meet the new arrivals.

"I am Laura Jacobi," said the dark one boldly, "and this is my friend Jeanie Whitfield." Jeanie, the tall fair one blushed violently and her blue eyes fell fleetingly upon the Professor's shorts.

"We'll wait another fifteen minutes," said the Professor, looking at his watch, "then we will move up the beach."

Shortly, a big guy with a huge stomach and a crew cut walked up. He introduced himself as Peter Humpster. Then before we knew it, we were all walking up the beach on the hot sand. We walked, mostly in silence, as we threw timid but inquisitive glances at each other. It was probably the first time for most of us, I thought, but I wondered though about Stephanie, she never said.

Suddenly there were naked people all around us. The first one I noticed was an old lady so fat that her belly hung down between her legs. She might as well have her clothes on, I thought! Another man was lying on a blanket, his red legs spread, to let his penis and lobster red balls hang freely. Then Alfred Nummy saw him!

"What in God's name is going on around here?" he whined. There seemed to be a little color creeping into his sickly pale cheeks, and he stopped in his tracks.

"What is the problem, Mr. Nummy?" The professor's eyes were sparkling with amusement as Alfred's mouth fell open, speechless, and he just pointed in disgust at the naked red balls. "Don't you have a pair of those yourself, Mr. Nummy?"

"Huh . . ." said Alfred.

"I thought I made it quite clear before we left the classroom, Mr. Nummy, that we were coming to this part of Baker Beach. Weren't you listening?"

Alfred remained speechless, ignoring the Professor, so we moved on and Alfred continued to stumble along behind us, his mouth agape.

Soon there were nude people everywhere, and I found myself gawking at first one then another in near disbelief at what I saw. Jeanie Whitfield seemed to be gasping for air and looking straight ahead.

Suddenly the Professor stopped and yanked his shorts off to stand naked before us! His dick was long and limp for such a short little man and his balls clung to it. We all turned to stare at the brazened act.

"Huh," mumbled Alfred Nummy, and then he began to breath heavily and fidget as he picked at his nose. As though in disbelief, he turned and looked up at the bluff behind the beach, and I followed his gaze to see a pair of binoculars looking back at us.

It was Laura Jacobi who broke the group paralysis by starting a struggle with her tight jeans. As she pushed them down, her panties came off with them. Her pussy was hidden by a profuse head of black hair. She fell on her brown butt and continued to struggle with them. Albert Seidweiler, coming to his senses, rushed to her assistance. As her legs flew high, he freed them with one violent yank. It was at this moment that I got a glimpse of a glistening pink pussy touched by a glancing blow from slanting rays of sunlight. It was beautiful as it leaped from the dark shadows that surrounded it! In an instant Albert himself had stripped. His body was so black with hair that one could hardly see the penis that hung out of it. He was soon sitting beside Laura on her towel.

I was soon distracted from this activity, however, when I caught Stephanie's glance of resolution and noticed her starting to struggle with her jeans. They fell, exposing her body in detail. I glanced about in a sudden surge of jealousy to notice Peter Humpster staring at her. So I asked her to sit so that I could pull them off for her.

I was soon sitting beside her, both of us naked, and I felt my penis begin to get hard and climb through the open air in an arc. Stephanie put sun tan lotion on it to calm it, but it didn't seem to help. So she then told me to lie on my stomach for a while. When I did this I soon had control of it and was in the process of putting lotion on Stephanie's pale skin when my eyes suddenly riveted upon the naked body of Natalie Wong.

My heart leaped violently at the sight of Natalie's wild femininity which had appeared to throb like a pulsating heart between her legs. It was beautiful, a mix between purple and pink, and it protruded boldly. There was only a tuft of fuzz above it, stuck on as though an afterthought. It was there as if to say, "in case you go north, young lady, from this garden of Eden!" it hovered there at eye level, from my perspective, seducing like a fuck magnet as she twisted in an effort to put her suntan lotion on the soft skin that leaped when it was touched.

"Bobby McGee," Stephanie whispered fiercely. "at the pace you're putting that suntan lotion on, I will be roast turkey before it does me any good!"

"Sorry," I responded, and, taking my eyes off Natalie with a sigh, I began to apply lotion to her body with vigorous strokes.

"I bet you are," Stephanie said, throwing a knowing little grin over her shoulder.

But I couldn't resist another quick glance towards Natalie, but it was not Natalie that caught my eye, however, for beyond her, lying on a blanket, was Jeanie Whitfield looking back at me. Her boobs were modestly protuberant like Stephanie's, but their modesty made them look even more naked.

"My God," I gasped in ecstasy as my pulse rate shifted into high gear. I almost immediately was distracted from Jeanie's naked body to Laura's! Her boobs were protruding like big, soft, ripe cantaloupes. They would quiver seductively with each movement as she hovered over Jeanie, massaging oil into her fair skin.

Albert Seidweiler turned around on his blanket so he could watch Laura's nakedness from behind. Laura was on her knees which were planted firmly on either side of Jeanie's body and her brown ass swayed hypnotically as she rubbed the oil into Jeanie's skin.

I followed Jeanie's curves down to and between Laura's legs and only then did I become aware that she was only naked from the waist up. I noticed her blue eyes were flashing and flickering with apprehension.

Suddenly I became aware again of Stephanie's restlessness. "Don't you think you have put enough oil on my back?" She said throwing another knowing grin back over her shoulder at me.

"Okay," I said, attempting a matter of fact voice. "I'll do your butt and legs now."

"Sure," she said, "but keep your hands away from you know where!" Her white bottom was soft and pliant as I began to massage oil into it.

But then out of the corner of my eye, I suddenly became aware of Susan Hale. She was still fully dressed and nervously going from one foot to another on the hot sand. Perspiration stood in droplets on her forehead. Her damp boobs were bulging against her shirt, soaking it wet. The outline of her nipples punctuated the damp cloth. She seemed to be busy watching everyone else get naked. I followed her gaze to Albert, who now took the liberty to apply oil to Laura's swaying brown ass.

Then Laura stood up on her knees to let Jeanie roll over. And Albert stopped what he was doing. Jeanie lifted her long legs with a sigh, and I watched breathlessly as Laura tugged on her jeans which slid quickly from beneath her white ass and up her legs.

Albert jumped up, his organ swaying, to get a hold on the jeans to assist. And as her legs were yanked skyward, she blushed violently and wildly. Her blue eyes were flashing, embarrassed beauty at me. Then I saw her long slender fingers slip quickly down between her legs in a desperate attempt to hide her intimacy. She was too late. For one exhilarating moment, I had seen it, her wild nakedness outlined in bold pink above the hot sand.

"If you are so good at that," it was Susan Hale! And she was saying it in voice, deceptively coy, "then maybe you can help me get mine off also."

I gasped for air, almost breathless with anticipation. But I continued to methodically apply pressure as I massaged the oil into Stephanie's legs. I moved slowly, my eyes on Susan, as my massage descended towards her feet. I wanted to keep Stephanie's back toward me, at least until Susan got naked. But it was not to be. Stephanie suddenly rolled over.

"It is your turn Bobby!" she said with a victorious grin. I complied, with one last disappointed glance in Susan's direction. All I could see from my new position was Albert's penis swaying.

When I finally had the opportunity to look again, Susan was naked, black and beautiful. There seemed to be no end to the seductivity of her big black boobs. They were larger than Laura's. I had never seen anything that seemed so naked and free before! Albert had lay down beside her and was trying to make small talk. Natalie Wong sat on her blanket cross legged watching the Professor expectantly.

Then catching movement from the corner of my eye, I turned to see that Peter Humpster was undressing. He did it quickly while he stared at his feet. He threw his clothes to one side and lie down quickly on his big stomach. As he did so, I caught a glimpse of his penis. It looked like a shriveled pea pod. With this, I was reminded of Alfred Nummy. I found him sitting fully clothed, his back toward us. He was still picking his nose and staring up at the cliffs above us. The binoculars above were still staring back at him.

"Well, let's see," said the Professor after he cleared his throat. He was sitting cross legged, now, like Natalie, and all you could see of his penis was where it joined the rest of his body.

"There are forty five students in this class," he continued, "and nine of you have had the courage to show up for this excursion. I have had better semesters and there have been worse." He sighed and glanced down at the heat waves which seemed to dance as they climbed from off the hot sand.

"Mr. Nummy," the Professor said loudly, "why don't you turn around and join us."

All of us turned to stare at the back of Alfred Nummy's head and most of us followed his gaze up the cliffside to the binoculars that were staring back. I heard Jeanie Whitfield gasp, and I watched her cover her boobs with her slender fingers. She turned, still holding them to look questioningly at the Professor.

"Don't worry," he said, glancing up at the offending gazer. "That is someone who wallows in the fear of the pleasure that they so desperately long for. They envy our freedom to enjoy it. The poor body is to be pitied."

Jeanie, reassured, let her boobs stand free again.

The Professor then turned back to Mr. Nummy, "Are you angry about something, Mr. Nummy? If so why don't you get it off your chest? You have come of your own free will. I made it clear back in the classroom that lack of participation would not be penalized."

Alfred Nummy then stood and turned violently. He shoved the flabby finger in our direction as though to say "fuck you all."

"That is uncalled for, Mr. Nummy!"

"Fuck you all!" growled Alfred, out loud. He stared with a horrid scowl at the hot sand. The heat must have been penetrating the heels of his shoes because he was shuffling his weight from one foot to the other.

"I was not told we were going to do this!" he hissed in a high-strung whine that sounded like a radiator about to burst.

"Pardon me!" said the Professor.

Alfred made no effort to respond. He threw me a dull, angry glance, then stared out at the waves that were climbing the beach. A droplet of sweat fell from a pockmark on his nose. Then, it started as a shuffle, slowly at first, but he was moving off down the beach.

"I can't figure what makes him tick," the Professor said as his eyes followed Alfred's retreat. "I wonder why he even keeps coming to class."

When I turned back, Natalie had freed her legs to let them sway hypnotically, like Stephanie did when she was horny.

"Anyway," said the Professor, "I must congratulate the rest of you for your courage in coming out to boldly make this experiment in body freedom." His dark intense eyes were racing among us, looking for contact. I let them meet mine for a moment, but their message was too powerful so I turned and looked back at Stephanie. Stephanie bit and pulled her upper lip, thoughtfully.

"Are there any of you who have been to a nude beach before?" the Professor asked as he continued to let his intense gaze alight on each of us.

First Laura Jacobi raised her hand, then Natalie Wong raised hers. Stephanie was fidgeting restlessly beside me, she gave me a long glance then raised her hand.

"That is great," said the Professor.

"What is your name," he asked, pointing at Stephanie.

"Stephanie," she replied, in her abnormally loud voice.

"Do you go to the nude beach often, Stephanie?"

"No," she replied loudly, "I only went once before, out near Thunder Beach."

"How about you, Laura and Natalie?"

After throwing a glance at Laura, Natalie said that she "came occasionally here to Baker Beach," and Laura said that she "came all the time."

I should have known it, I thought, as brown as Laura was, even her soft butt was as dark and as brown as the rest of her!

"Why don't all of us give a short introduction to ourselves and our background," the Professor said. "Why don't we begin with you Peter?"

Peter Humpster still lay on his stomach. No one had put any oil on his butt and it was already turning red. Laura Jacobi had suddenly noticed this and had deftly leaped to her feet, her supple boobs quivering, yet standing out firmly. Laura squatted, exposing the deep pink of her pussy lip that again leaped from the dark shadows. She began to rub oil into Peter's butt. Peter Humpster blushed and gripped his blanket.

His eyelids momentarily drooped to stare at the sand particles that lie in heaps around him.

"Well," said Peter, his voice sounding shy and disbelieving. He glanced up at our waiting faces and squirmed slightly from the pressure being applied to his butt. "There is not much to tell," he said, falling silent again. He glanced back up at us and noted that all the facing were still waiting so he continued. Laura, on her knees, started to move up his back with the oil and firm pressure.

"I was born on a grape vineyard down near Selma, California. As far back as I can remember, my father had me out in the hot sun of late August picking grapes and laying them out on mats to dry into raisins."

Laura, on her knees, was straddled, hovering over his back like a dark sex goddess.

"My Mother died when I was fourteen and my Father died when I was eighteen. I have two brothers who are running the vineyard while I go to school.....and bake nude in the sun." He looked up again and chuckled softly and shyly. We all laughed at that.

Laura stood, her pussy lip glistening damp in the hot sun. then, sitting beside Albert again, she began to massage oil into his back.

Susan was twisting and turning restlessly on her blanket while she threw envious glances at Laura.

"What about you Natalie?" the Professor asked, as he turned his intense brown eyes upon her.

"I was born and raised in Hawaii," she said. "My father is Professor Wong. He teaches physics here in the Science department. We only moved here three years ago. My father spent most of his career teaching at the University of Hawaii."

"You don't say!" exclaimed the Professor. "I know Professor Wong well. I have worked with him several times in my effort to get a better understanding of quantum mechanics."

"I like it better here though," Natalie continued. "There is more freedom here for things like this."

"I can believe that," the Professor said. "What about you Albert?"

"I'm from Winnipeg, Manitoba," Albert said in a proud, bold voice as he glanced at Laura, beside him as if for support. He irritated me. He probably needed all that hair if he went naked up there in Canada, I thought.

It was then that I saw her, there, across the sand. I gasped for a gulp of hot air, and the thrill that raced through me nearly caused my heart to stop in its tracks. She was sitting directly across the sand in front of me, facing me, just down the beach behind the Professor. How long she had been there, I didn't know, but when my eyes found her they bore into her with the tenacity of a corkscrew.

Her skin was gold beneath the California sun. stringy beach blond hair fell over her forehead, creating a shadow for her soft, tanned face, a face that was bowed in innocent preoccupation. Her legs stood boldly, widely apart to let her arms fall between them. They were gold and smooth above the sand. Her boobs stood out proudly, displaying their crowning pink nipples and her belly button was but a sliver in her flat brown stomach. Her dexterous and slender fingers were busy dipping a small brush into, what looked like a tiny bottle of red paint. Yes, it was a bottle of red paint, she was painting her toenails red and letting the hot sun dry them. In the background, her purple-brown pussy lips were twisted intricately, tanned and damp with the soft touch of coconut oil.

Suddenly she looked up from the seductive shadows and our eyes met. My heart-pulse surged violently as she shook her wild stringy hair to the rising breeze and it stood out towards the Golden Gate that majestically crossed the bay behind her. She smiled sweetly, flashing her small white teeth that were arranged neatly in a row like small white seashells by the sea. She adjusted her perch upon her bare little ass and started to paint another toenail red.

"Bobby McGee!" the Professor was waving his hand at me to get my attention. At the same time, I felt Stephanie's sharp fingernail pinch deeply into my bare leg.

"Wake up, Bobby," she was whispering fiercely.

"Er...oh....uh....I was born in Florida," I stammered as I threw another longing glance back at the naked fairy perched on her blanket up the beach.

"My father was a preacher," I said with a sigh, "who was always trying to determine with biblical chronology the date of the second coming."

"How interesting!" the Professor said softly, almost as if to himself. "Did he ever set a date that passed without the fulfillment of his prophecy?"

"Yes," I said, "that is why I left home. I started not to believe in it anymore, and it became impossible for me to live at home."

"Have you ever been back?"

"No, never!" I responded, harshly, almost as much to myself as to the group of eyes that were upon me. "When I left home, he thought I was a lost soul, I guess."

"So what brought you to California?"

Fuck, I thought to myself. Becoming restless, why can't he end this interview and move on to someone else? I glanced back to where the golden haired girl had been but she was gone. My heart surged with disappointment, but I turned dutifully back to the Professor.

"I don't know," I said. "I think a better question would be what stopped me here in California and the answer would be, the Pacific Ocean." Everyone laughed at that and the Professor finally turned and looked at Susan Hale.

I then frantically turned and looked again to search for the golden girl. And I had finally found her down by the sea. She was bending over to pick up seashell and her bottom was facing me as it rose to directly to face the rays from the goddess of light, the sun. It was then that I awoke to the gentle pressure of Stephanie's body beside me and felt the surge of my love for her. I put my arm over her naked leg that rested against me. She spread her legs further apart then, to expose her intimacy to the throbbing heat of the sun goddess. It was then that I became aware of the strong but gentle voice of Susan Hale.

"I was raised by a Baptist minister in a little segregated Mississippi town. It was not segregated by law, but it was in fact. Virtually all the White folks lived on one side of town and the Black folks on the other. My dad's church was up near the dividing line in an area where the more well-to-do Black folks lived. Now I must say there were quite a few Whites that came to my dad's church in support of racial equality. But this earned the ire of the militant KKK kooks. I remember when I was only four that a bunch of these kooks gathered in our front yard late one night, hurling racial slurs at our house. My dad had quickly turned off the lights, but we continued to watch from the front window. Then suddenly they lit a fire, and we could see a makeshift cross that the flames were rising from. I remember my mother saying, 'oh no' and picking me up and running into the dark bedroom. My father was a peaceful man, but he went out to confront them. He had asked them 'in the name of Jesus' to leave us in peace. But they had taunted him, forcing him to retreat back into the house. If it hadn't been for the good White folks that came to our church, I would have ended up hating them."

"As a teenager, I remember the KKK marching through our neighborhood. My mother had warned me to stay away from them because they were dangerous, but I was always sort of a precocious kid with a will of my own and joined a group of Black kids with a couple of good White kids among us and started a counter demonstration, and we began throwing rocks at the kooks. They were wearing long white robes that covered their faces, but I threw a rock that, to my surprise and shock, hit the bastard right where his forehead was supposed to be. He let out a roar of rage and stumbled as though about to fall. But another white robe ran to his rescue. One of them, which appeared to be the leader started shouting at us, telling us that they 'would come back after dark and string us all up!'"

"By this time I was so worked up that I ran out into the street screaming 'fuck you, asshole!' And do know what that dip shit did?!" Her healthy black boobs were dancing now, in their anger. Perspiration trickled down them to drop from her quivering nipples. Her dark eyes flashed fire at me. "He spit on me!" she nearly shouted in indignation. "And do you know what I did? I kicked him in the shin. I could hear him over my shoulder roaring in rage, but I didn't stay around after that. I got out of there as fast as I could."

"Good for you, Susan," the Professor said, excitedly.

But Susan wasn't finished yet. She began again. "Now I understand," she said, "that the black man's slavery didn't end with the emancipation. The White man made sure of this by forcing their religion on him while he was yet their physical slaves. So now he continues to be a slave to the White man's religion."

"That is a very good observation, Susan! I have never thought of it that way."

"Turn over Peter, your butt is on fire!" the Professor had suddenly said as he glanced in his direction. Peter winced as he sat on his tender butt and gave everyone a chance to see what was between his legs.

"My butt and legs are burning," Stephanie complained as we made our way down the coast highway, and these tight jeans aren't making things any better."

"Why not take them off," I said. She pulled to the side of the road and swung her legs around towards me.

"Okay, start pulling," she said as she grinned across at me. I then yanked them from her for a second time that day. From then on she drove naked, from the waist down to my apartment. She wrapped a beach towel around her to get up to the cold shower.

# DEATH, AT THE HANDS OF A BAPTIST

Two DAYS LATER when Stephanie and I walked into Professor Stuttgardt's classroom, the first face I saw was Susan Hale's. She was flashing a smile at me. Though I felt Stephanie's glance, I smiled back anyway. And it had all come back to me, with Susan on her beach towel!

After everyone had introduced themselves, we had all relaxed and chatted among ourselves until a chill breeze coming across the bay hit us in the late afternoon. Then as everyone started getting dressed, Susan had twisted around to sit firmly on her butt, and for an instant had flashed pink fire at me from open purple lips, but then she had leaped up to stand on supple, perspiration streaked legs and it had all disappeared within her matt of curly dark hair. With that my day on the beach had been complete. It was as though she had intentionally given me a chance to see!

Susan was sitting behind us after I followed Stephanie to our chairs.

The professor, who stood by the podium in old gray jogging shorts had began to talk. At first, for me, his voice was just noise that rattled calmly through a distant classroom silence. My mind was absent, in another world, where images of naked women marched through shimmering heat waves to the beat of drums, drums that throbbed like the pulsating blood in my brain. I was staring, absently, out through the rain streaked window at a patch of gray sky, from which the cold rain fell.

But then, the booming passion in his voice invaded my privacy. I shook my head to bring it into focus, on the little man's roar. He was shouting and beating the blackboard with his chalk stick. Chalk powder was climbing into the stale gloom of winter which was filtering into the room. A woman sneezed three times then covered her face with a hanky.

"A criteria for a just morality does not come from any sacred book nor does it come from the fake profundity of a Baptist preacher!" He was shouting at the blackboard as though he were condemning it to hell. "Rather," he continued, "a just morality is determined by a THINKING ORGANISM'S ATTUNEMENT with its environment." He had written this in large letters across the blackboard. "It is not some absolute morality predetermined by some conceited divinity to test our commitment to him for his own edification, but rather a morality which changes as our awareness evolves and our environment changes, an environment from which we draw our only sustenance."

A gust of rain came out of the gray to pound the cold window.

From the corner of my eye I saw him then, hunkered, sullen, standing on his feet. It was Alfred Nummy, and he had started to move, slowly, like a zombie, toward the Professor. All eyes had turned upon him. Only the Professor seemed not to have noticed, or maybe he was ignoring him as he turned and jabbed his chalk at a student to make a point.

About half way to the podium, Alfred stopped, but the Professor continued to ignore him. At this point no one was listening to what the Professor was saying. All eyes were riveted upon the pockmarked face of Alfred Nummy.

"Stop it!" He suddenly hissed. The hiss was deadly and his pockmarked face had turned white like a sheet washed in dirty water.

"I beg your pardon!" It was the Professor, and he sounded surprised as he turned to face Nummy.

"I won't allow you to talk that way about the Baptist!" His voice was a gasping hiss of hate.

"Why?" asked the Professor, "are you a Baptist?"

"Yes," replied Alfred Nummy in a voice that continued to spit it out like a cat hissing. "It is my duty," he continued, his voice rising hysterically. "I must defend Christ's word and the Baptist faith, even if it costs me my life...." He waved his arm melodramatically through the stale classroom air as though to emphasize his persecution complex.

"You are making it easy for me Mr. Nummy, you are providing me with a perfect example of the basic insanity of a true believer."

(as an accent) "Shet up!" Nummy screamed.

"However, I must ask you to leave the classroom now, this disruption has gone far enough." The Professor started to move toward Nummy.

"Stop, stay back!" his hiss began to sound more like the hiss of an adder than that of a cat. Then out of nowhere, there was a gun in Alfred's hand, and it was pointed at the Professor.

I could hear the violent, rushing gasps of air around me. I looked, to see mouths agape, twisting nostrils and eyes that bugged in horror.

It was then that I began to feel it, rising out of my gut, like volcanic magma, to climb and become fury when it reached my heart. Like an incredulous observer, I watched myself leap to my feet. I felt the grip of Stephanie's sharp fingernails trying to hold me back to no avail. My voice came out of me as though from a seething cauldron.

"You are the one who had better stop it, Alfred Nummy! Put that gun away before I have to come over there and take it from you and proceed to take you apart piece by piece without the benefit of an anesthetic!" My voice was shouting, and I was stunned at what it was saying.

But then it happened, all so fast. He turned the barrel of the gun on me and shot. I didn't feel it and the noise from it seemed harmless enough, but the student behind me screamed. Students everywhere were diving for the floor. Stephanie was dragging me down on top of her. I guess I fell just in time for I heard another shot and something whizzing just above my falling head. Over the bodies of students, between the legs of empty chairs, I watched in horror as the Professor's legs ran at Alfred Nummy only to stagger from the impact of the bastard's bullet. I watched him fall and heard his head hit the floor.

I leaped to my feet overcome by rage and despair and began to walk with deadly determination toward the gun that was pointed at me.

Faintly, like in an empty vacuum, I heard her cry, "please my Bobby McGee...don't do this Bobby McGee! He will kill you! The maniac will kill you!"

I knew it and I was deathly afraid, but I couldn't stop my feet from walking. I saw him point, but I didn't feel anything so I kept on walking. I watched as he aimed the deadly piece of steel at me again.

Then I heard it! "Nummy," screamed a voice from the back of the room. "Every shot you take is a bullet to the heart of the Baptist faith for if it creates monsters such as you, it should be held accountable and outlawed from human society!"

Nummy wavered, his eyes searching for the source of his tormenter, but the voice was coming from a hiding place on the floor. It was at that moment that I rushed Nummy. He turned about to run for a better shot at me, but it was too late. Like a cat I was on him, throwing my foot in front of him so that he tripped and fell to the floor. I stomped viciously on the outstretched hand that held the gun. Whining in pain, he released it. Violently I kicked the gun toward the door and then turned my violence upon his pockmarked face. Blood squirted from his twisted nose as he tried to grab my foot and failed. He tried to lift himself, but I pounced upon his back and sat on him. Then I took him by the hair of the head and began to beat the whole thing into the classroom floor. It seemed that I was almost delirious and was overcome by a flashback where I was confusing this piece of human trash with the one where I was twisting the balls of the evangelist.

"Stop it! Stop it, Mr. McGee!" I became suddenly aware of the chorus of voices around me. "You are killing him, Mr. McGee!" someone said and I felt strong arms grab me around the chest. They pulled me off of Alfred Nummy. But someone else put their foot on him to keep him from moving.

I remembered the Professor then and was allowed to run to his side. A pool of blood was all around him. It was running out of his back. Natalie Wong was bent over him. The Professor looked at me and smiled, but his face was so white that it made me wheezy and want to puke. I turned repulsively away and shouted, "someone get a doctor!"

"It's taken care of," I heard Natalie say softly. I met her almond eyes and saw the tears that were flowing gently down her cheeks.

I looked back at the sheet white face of Professor Stuttgardt. "Will you be alright?" I asked him, lamely.

"No," he said calmly, "but I have lived a good life," he continued, turning a wan smile upon me. "I have touched the moment in flight, something that few are privileged to do. And I can only hope," he said his voice dropping to a gasping and distant whisper, "that I have succeeded in communicating this joy to someone else."

Susan Hale was standing there then, and she started to sob, softly. Natalie turned her beautiful eyes toward Susan as though in an effort to comfort her, but they were also red now, from her own tears. I felt a sob grab me in the gut, and I felt Stephanie's hand grab mine for support.

"Don't be …..so……sad," the Professor said, but what was left of his wan smile faded and his open eyes seemed to quit seeing us. A jerk ran through his body, and his head fell to onside.

"He is dead," said Natalie softly

But I continued to stand and watch him lying there, for I don't know how long, as the blood began to dry and turn cold. I remember thinking that he had died just like they do in the movies.

I then became aware of Stephanie gently tugging at my arm. "Let's go Bobby McGee, it's all over," she said.

I turned around just in time to see the cops enter, and they were coming towards us. One of them grabbed Alfred Nummy and put handcuffs on him.

"Let's get out of here!" Stephanie whispered urgently in my ear, "before the pigs want to question us."

We moved slowly, among the babble of excited curiosity seekers, toward the door. No one stopped us, and we soon left it all behind. Side by side, we walked across campus in the cold rain, oblivious to its soaking fury.

# THE END OF TIME

I AWAKENED IN the wee hours of a fogbound dawn in a cold sweat. It was a nightmare, I quickly determined, in which I had relived the Professor's death. And the nightmares repeated themselves over and over again in the nights that followed the classroom tragedy. And during the days, I would sit while the stern accusing words pounded through my brain with a chaotic pulsating beat: "if only you would have remained seated, Bobby McGee, the Professor would have handled it and no one would have gotten killed. There was no rhyme to it, just pain. Why couldn't you have kept your fucking mouth shut?"

The cops had come to see me the day after, and they hadn't helped matters any. One big one, who looked like a preacher with sunglasses on, even though my room was dark and the fog slithered about outside my window, had reprimanded me for my involvement.

"You jeopardized the lives of all the students in that classroom," he had said. He then took off his dark glasses to impress me with the authority he thought I would see in his cold, steel gray eyes.

"Don't leave town," he added. "We may need your testimony."

But I had shoved my "fuck" finger at his dark blue rear as he had walked out of my apartment.

When I would remember the cop, my pain would turn to anger, but then my memory would usually encompass Stephanie, and my anger would be pierced by stabs of pain. If only she could be with me, I would think, in self pity, she would distract me from this horrible truth. But as it was, I had to face the pain of my grief and guilt alone. Stephanie called me at the telephone office the day after the Professor's death.

"Jude has rolled the Comanche," she said. "We got into a fight because I didn't want him to borrow it. He took it anyway after hitting and knocking me down. And now he is here at the hospital in critical condition. I feel guilty, Bobby…" the silence that followed was broken only by the hum on the telephone line. "I won't be seeing you for awhile, Bobby McGee, at least until Jude gets better. He might even die, Bobby…."

"Stephanie…!" I cried.

"Be a good boy, Bobby McGee!" she said and then she was gone.

The days without Stephanie had been boring, especially at work, where the "elps" of the incoming calls of helpless customers would lead me on a forced march through time. But then at night when the day's work was finished, I started going down to the Sea Froth, where Stephanie worked. I would sit and drink and wait into the wee hours of the morning.

"Where is Stephanie?" I asked, the first night, of a dried up little old man behind the bar.

"She took a leave of absence," he mumbled, after removing the drooping cigarette from his lips.

Night after night I would sit there alone, taking in the gloom of the quaint little bar that was perched on a cliff above the sea, and nurse the hope that Stephanie might suddenly appear. On quiet nights, the little old man would stand behind the bar and blow smoke rings into the gloom and watch me, while in the distance, one could hear the roar of the sea as it beat against the rocky outcrops on the beach below.

At times I would gulp beer and be angry, first at Stephanie because she would not call nor answer my calls to her, and then I would curse the assassin Nummy, with a constant stream of vulgarity. The mother fucking jerk had destroyed the new world of thought that had just began to open up for me. I even started blaming Nummy for Jude's accident and started looking forward to the day when I could condemn him to death upon the witness stand.

Then, suddenly, one day it was April and the seemingly constant rain and wind of late March came to an end. I found myself looking through the office window at bright warm sunshine. The "elps" of incoming voices seemed to surround me like a swarm of mosquitoes as I sat alone and tried to watch the bold march of breakers climbing out of the sun swept sea. On the beach, they would collapse, sending their froth skipping across the sand toward the highway.

"What is the area code for Geary Boulevard?" an aged, and crackling voice demanded.

"Four one five is the area code for all of San Francisco," I answered with methodical patience.

Click-clack, the old lady had made a noisy exit.

"Yes, may I help you?"

"Collect from Moneybag!"

"Alright, sure, if you say so." And so the day ended on a cheerful note.

And now I walked along the highway beneath the stars that glittered. I saw a falling star that streaked across the sky above the black sea and remembered the one that everyone had thought was a flying saucer, except for Mr. Barnes, of course. I was walking down to the Sea Froth for another evening of beer and solitude at the corner table.

Earlier at home, I had been shocked by a letter I had received from my Mother. My hands had been shaking as I opened it and began to read the words that had left me breathless by what they said.

"Dear Bobby" it began "I cried tears of joy when I received your letter and was so relieved that you were alright. But Bobby I have some terrible news for you. Your Father has died...." upon reading this I dropped the letter and rushed to my window in disbelief. I was so shocked that I didn't know if I was sad or happy. After catching my breath I went back and continued to read the letter. "He went into his closet to pray for enlightenment as to the correct date of the second coming. He had spent the whole afternoon in there, but that really wasn't unusual for him. Then it was supper time. I called him, but he didn't come out. Finally I went and opened the door. He was sitting there, his hands folded as though in prayer. His head was lifted towards heaven and his lips were twisted in a smile. But he didn't look right. I said 'Daddy, it is supper time,' but then my heart nearly stopped because I reached out and touched him and knew that he was dead. You know how I am, Bobby, I'm a crybaby and I fell sobbing to the floor. The boys helped me get to bed and called for help. If only I had of known how to contact you I would have, so that you could have come home for the funeral. He looked so peaceful in his casket."

"But you know what really bothered me, Bobby, is why God let him die without getting to witness His second coming. It seems that

God owed him that much after he had prayed so hard for it. The only thing I can think of is that maybe the second coming happens to each of us when we die and that maybe God answered his prayer after all."

"I am so happy that you have a girlfriend now. I hope she is a godly girl and that you both have found a good church to go to……….. and oh yes! Your sister Charlotte is dating your old friend Reggie Smithers. I have tried to tell her she is too young for that, but without your Dad around, I don't have much control anymore. And you also might be interested to know that Studs Gatlin was killed in a car accident. His mother is in an insane asylum and poor Agnes Everbe is in the room next to hers. And I don't hear from the Barneses anymore…………."

At the entrance to the Sea Froth, I yanked at the heavy wooden door and entered. I looked for the old man, the wisp of human flesh that seemed to always hover in silence behind the bar, but no one was there. That is strange, I thought. But then, suddenly, her flaming beauty popped up before me like an angelic apparition.

"Stephanie!" I cried, stunned, all the way down to my toes.

"I hear you been around a lot, Bobby McGee," she said, in her matter of fact voice

Sitting at the bar I watched her work. It was a busy night, while in my gut I longed for her.

"How's Jude?" I asked calmly when she brought me a drink.

"He is getting well fast," she said. "In fact he is so well now that he tried to beat me up in the hospital just before he went home. And this time it was his fault. I told him 'never again'. I'm leaving him, Bobby, and am never going back."

I looked into the enigmatic blue of her eyes and decided that it was better not to comment. I just waited in silence to see what else she had to say.

"The last month has been very depressing for both of us." I heard her say

I looked again into her eyes and the enigma seemed to have faded. Encouraged, I looked more deeply into them and found the hurt that was in me begin to melt like butter.

"I have been thinking, Bobby McGee."

"Oh…oh…..disaster is about to strike!" I kidded.

"Shut up!" she ordered, her face blushing with the sweet passion that I remembered.

"I think we ought to do something to cheer ourselves up," she said, throwing me a shy glance.

"And what shall we do?" I asked with growing excitement.

"I know of a nudist beach down near Santa Cruz..."


In front of us, the rock formations were worn smooth as they climbed, stoically, like pinnacles from another age, to stand sentinel before the empty expanse of the westward sea. They also bore the brunt of the wrath thrown against them by the frothy water cliffs that were whipped up and driven by the wind. There were two of them, separated by a low rocky outcrop which caught the belligerent surf and tamed it, as it made its last effort to rendezvous with land.

Behind us, the cliff was rounded and precipitous, creating the cove for the white sand beach far below.

It was a restful place, especially in the springtime when the sand would bake and the fog would rest on the surface of the far out sea, while the constant, methodical beat of water-thunder against the outcropped rocks would lull one into a warm naked sleep.

We were feeling the joy of heathens, Stephanie and I, lying naked side by side on a blanket baked warm by the sand. Like sybarites, we inhaled deeply from the clean blue air so that we might feel the elements as we did each other.

In the late afternoon, we found ourselves alone, touched by a stiff chill breeze which had sent my cock climbing in delight.

Stephanie sat up and reached toward the blue empty heavens to stretch and yawn. Spying my climbing cock, she squealed in delight and bent forward to meet it with a soft kiss on the head. She then turned to me with her soft blue eyes, their infinite depths exposed.

"I love you, Bobby McGee," she said in a passionate whisper, "let's make a baby." Her soft words thrilled me. But I couldn't help but wonder, had they come from her or had they blown in on the wind from off the sea?

Her eyes flashed again at my full blown head with impish delight, her face flushed with passion. She brushed it with a soft tickle from her fingernails then fell on it, to be impaled by its pleasure. She gasped from the power of the moment, and our lips turned kisses into probing tongues of fire, seeking for an instant to be one, a single eternal moment captured by two lives, becoming one, representing the single heartbeat of eternity.

But from the cliffs above, we were mere stick figures, entwined and twisting like euphoric children, as we played in a sandbox on the distant planet Mars.

Made in the USA
Coppell, TX
12 February 2025

45852358R00204